Lucy F~~ ~~~~
By Stephen Amos

Dedicated to Gracie and Ieuan.
Until you came along, I didn't know what life was.

Acknowledgements

The first person I must thank is my wife, Afua. When writing this book, I would sometimes disappear in to this fictitious village called Trehenri and not come up for air until the kids were in bed and the house was quiet. If it wasn't for Afua, I would never have had the time to have a cuppa with Tal, watched a film with Jimmy, or ever met Catryn and Morgan.

Thanks sweetheart.

I also need to thank Delme Thompson who gave me permission to use his fantastic photograph of the cross that overlooks Penygraig and Tonypandy. It was this picture that formed the basis of the cover of this book. I've not yet met Delme, but I know he is a gentleman.

Finally, to the guys at Film89.co.uk. For Skye, Haydn and Neil for giving me the push a few years ago to join them in the wonderful world of movies. Up until then I barely had the confidence to post anything I had written. Guys, I doff my hat to you and all the other friends I've made along the way.

If you want to read reviews and listen to podcasts by myself and the gang, pop over to the website and check them out.

Tuesday and Wednesday

Prologue

He lifted the baby's legs with one hand and slipped the nappy beneath her. She gurgled softly, obviously relaxed despite the power of his large, rough and callused hands. He gently dropped her down and pulled the nappy straps each side. The child smiled as he lightly tickled her soft, vulnerable belly. As he did so, he hummed softly. It was a tune as old as time, the lyrics lost from his memory,

He gently lifted his charge and held her close to him; her bare skin, her soft baby fat. Her helplessness seemed incongruous in these enormous, life and death toughened, hands. Yet he held her delicately and with practised efficiency.

He moved from the table, ensuring it was clean and tidy, crossed over to the settee and sat, holding her close, rocking her softly to sleep. His voice was low, and she could feel the vibrations through his chest. It was just what she needed, he thought watching her as her eyelids grew heavy and she succumb to sleep. She looked tranquil, secure in the assurance that no harm could befall her.

He sat with her for a while, enjoying the closeness. His role, he saw it, was of protector. His strength was for her, to keep her safe; this defenceless child had a defender, and defend her he would. He wanted no harm to come to this meagre frame or the soul that resided within.

After a while, he stood and reached to turn off the small lamp that had provided them with their only illumination. The room was dark, but darkness was his friend. Besides, even with his eyes closed, he knew it all well enough to navigate. Every chair was where it always was; the table to his left, the small cabinet with the lamp and a vase to his right. There was a rug beneath his feet, and long, heavy curtains over the windows and the ornate light fixtures on the wall. They all spoke of familiarity and security. But mostly, it was the child in his arms. This small bundle of life, of hope and of the future.

He picked up the soiled nappy and crossed the room to the kitchen. The room was illuminated solely by the glow of the full moon, the silver light shining through the windows. He stood on the lever at the foot of the bin and dropped the nappy inside.

The child adjusted herself slightly, moving in his muscular arm. Her skin was pallid in this light and it glowed spectrally.

He waited for her to settle once more before returning to the living room. He looked around, careful not to disturb her further, then he crossed the room, slowly and delicately opening the door and stepped out into the hallway. He stopped momentarily listening for any sounds of disturbance.

There was a creek; nothing much, just a very slight rasp from the floorboards. The man froze for a moment, warily listening for something else. Was there someone there? or was it just the settling of the house?

He waited but all he could hear was his own breathing. Presently, he began to climb the stairs, the child in one arm, the other using the bannister for guidance. It was time for the child to go to bed. He was almost to the top when he heard the voice:

'Who the hell are you?'

The voice was accompanied by the light, turned on by a man who had just stepped out of the bedroom and was now standing at the top of the stairs.

He was of average height, weight and appearance. A nobody. He wore a tee-shirt and large baggy shorts; his thin legs and his feet were bare.

The big man just sneered, staring at this opponent. His malevolence oozing from every pore.

'Get out of my house now or I'm calling the pol-' The small man stopped mid-sentence as he noticed the baby cradled in the muscular arms.

'Lucy...?' he whispered hesitantly.

The big man looked down at the baby. He had wondered

what her name was but had been content to merely call her 'the baby'. Now he knew.

'Lucy' he whispered only to her. He knew then why he was here, and he smiled with the understanding. It was good.

A door opened, and a woman appeared squinting in the light. She wore a small nightie and the big man was drawn to her; to her legs, to her rounded breasts that were prominent beneath it, to the slender neck. He could see the curvature of her hips and the slight hint of yellow panties. He took a deep breath. He wasn't here for the woman despite the movement he felt in his loins. All that mattered was the child.

The small man stepped in front of the woman, shielding her. His eyes were both panicked and feral. He was obviously not a worthy contender although his protection instinct was admirable, as it should be for a father.

'What are you are doing with my daughter?' the man hissed, his voice laced with panic. He was becoming frantic, a shrill tone was creeping in. He spread his arms wide and held his palms flat, trying to give an impression of calm.

'Put her down, please.'

The woman wiped her eyes. 'What's going on, Paul?

The man was amused at this question. Were the lights so bright to her unadjusted eyes that she could not see the truth as it stood before her? Was she really so stupid?

It didn't last long. As awareness dawned on her, as her eyes adjusted to the light, she began to scream. At first, it was a howl, a screeching wail that seemed to put her whole body into convulsions. Then slowly a word emerged in spasms:

'LUCY, LUCY, LUCY'

The bellowing caused the child to stir in his arms. He looked down as she started to cry, joining her mother in an incoherent moan. He felt anger roiling in his guts. How dare they make this child cry! How dare they cause these tears, this sorrow in his Lucy!

'Please,' the father was saying. 'Put my daughter down, just go. We won't tell anyone; we won't call the police. Just leave'.

The man looked <u>back and fore between</u> the crying child and her father. His heart ached to see her like this. He felt hat<u>red</u> for this small weak man who couldn't really protect his own child, but he also realised there was nothing he could do right now. He had no other choice. He felt a tide of impotence collide with resentment <u>and enmity,</u> which he had to fight to control. The agitation was palpable, but his self-control was great.

He bent down slowly, putting the child delicately onto the floor, away from the danger of the stairs.

Then he turned to the two frantic parents and sneered. He said nothing but the rancour he felt for them burned in his eyes. Yet, as he turned one last time to look at the child, those same eyes shone with tenderness and warmth.

He backed slowly away from the child, one step at a time, cautiously receding into the darkness below. The woman pushed passed her husband and rushed to take charge of her daughter. She picked Lucy up quickly and took the baby into her arms, holding her tightly. She backed herself into the bedroom, her eyes not leaving his as he disappeared into the shadows.

***

Paul stepped tentatively forward, his eyes searching the dark shadows. He saw nothing, heard nothing. There was no sound of doors opening or closing, no sound of footsteps. All he could hear were Lucy's cries.

Is he still here? he wondered.

Angela pushed passed him again as she took Lucy into their bedroom, but he didn't see her. He stood there staring, waiting for some sign that it might not yet be all over.

Finally, he made up his mind and backed up into the bedroom. He quickly crossed the room and reached for the phone on the nightstand. He didn't take his eyes off the door, expecting the devilish beast to return at any moment.

Angela sat at the edge of the bed, rocking Lucy, trying to get her to calm down. The child's cries had lessened, replaced by convulsive sobs.

Paul glanced down quickly and pressed the call button. Then, with his heart pounding loudly in his ears, he dialled 999.

***

'What happened then?' DCI Mann looked tired. His suit was rumpled as if he had been sleeping in it for a few days. He was in his mid to late 30s with dark eyes and a dirty grey beard which covered half his face. Yet, Paul noticed, his tie was immaculate. It seemed odd, out of place. It should have been loose and rumpled as the suit, but it was perfectly clean, pressed and knotted.

'Nothing,' Paul replied. He also felt tired, the weight of the night pressing down on him. He thought he knew tension and stress at work, but tonight he realised he didn't have a clue. 'I stayed on the phone with the operator until I heard the door-bell. The operator confirmed it was the two officers, so I went downstairs to let them in.'

Mann wrote this in his notebook. Paul could see the sprawling, unruly penmanship which seemed to mirror the man's shirt, but he couldn't make out what it said.

'You didn't hear the intruder leave?'

'No, although Lucy was still crying so we couldn't hear much.'

The DCI nodded, then slumped back on to the settee. He seemed to hum to himself for a few seconds, a tune that Paul felt he recognised yet could not place.

'Well we've checked the house and it is secure. No win-dows broken, no doors unlocked, and everything locked from the inside.'

'So how did the bastard get in, then!'

Paul threw up his arms in frustration. He could feel the panic rising again and hated the thought of not being in control. His life was ordered, it had reason and purpose. He didn't like surprises at the best of times, and this certainly wasn't one of those.

Mann leaned forward again and held out his hands in a placating manner. His nails had obviously been bitten and he wore a large wedding band on his muscular, rough hands.

'Have you noticed anything unusual recently? Anything out of place? Anything that just didn't sit right?

'No,' Paul sighed heavily, his shoulders slumping. 'No, I dunno, like what? What type....' He stopped, and his eyes widen as the realisation and the panic hit him like a wave. 'What are you saying? That he has been here before?'

Mann shifted uncomfortably in his seat. 'We're just trying to think of all possibilities...'

Paul stood up and started pacing.

'He's been here before? In this house, while we were sleeping...?' His voice was starting to become frantic and his breathing more erratic.

Mann stood up. 'Mr Downs, please...'

'I will not calm down,' Paul shouted. 'How can I calm down? This fucking stranger was in my house.' He crossed over to the window and stared out. 'Oh shit,' he whispered. 'Oh shit, shit, shit.'

Mann reached for him just as his legs gave way. Another officer, watching for the doorway, ran across to help. They led him to the sofa and slowly helped him down. Paul whispered under his breath, but they couldn't make out what was being said.

'Get some water.' Mann said to the officer. 'Paul?'

Paul looked up at him, his face was a picture of dread and horror.

'The nappies,' he whispered gruffly.

Mann crouched down in front of Paul. He tilted his head so he could look at this broken man in the eyes.

'What about the nappies?' he asked.

The officer returned with a glass of cold water. Mann took

it off him and held it in front of Paul, who took it off the detective, his hands trembling.

'What about the nappies, Paul?' Mann repeated.

Paul breathed deeply.

'We were only talking a few days ago that Lucy never needs changing at night. Every morning she is completely dry. She's only four months old, this shouldn't happen, should it? Surely a four-month-old child would pee at night? Are you a father?' he asked Mann.

The DCI shook his head.

'Go on.'

Paul took another deep breath; tears fell from his eyes.

'A few times we have noticed nappies in the bin when we thought we had emptied it. I assumed that Angela had done it without telling me, and she assumed I did the same. We've even argued about it.' He sniffed a laugh, 'She said I was getting old if I couldn't remember changing my own baby. What else could it be? Why would we think otherwise?'

His body shook as he spoke, and new tears started to fall down his cheek.

'You don't think...?' he asked the DCI.

Mann looked up to the officer.

'Check the bin,' he said. 'If you find anything - bag it.'

'Yes, sir.' The officer left the room leaving the two men alone.

'I'm going to post a couple of officers here tonight. They'll be in a car out front and will do regular checks. In the meantime, we'll catch this bastard. You have my word. OK?'

Paul closed his eyes. 'You make sure you do,' he grunted.

***

Hours later, as the nightmare spilt over into another night, Paul finished putting a sheet on the baby's mattress. He had moved the cot into their bedroom, so it was next to their bed. Angela held onto Lucy. She had not put her down all day, fearful of letting her daughter go for even a moment. Paul lay the little quilt in the cot, then he stretched his back trying to get the long day's knots out of his muscles.

With heavy legs, he crossed to his wife and sat down next to her. Putting his arm around her shoulder he said, 'Let me hold her for a while, go have a shower.'

'I'll be ok,' she said; her grip on Lucy tightened.

'No,' he persisted. 'She'll be ok. I'll hold her. You need to clean the crap of today off you. You'll feel much better.'

Angela sighed heavily. 'I suppose you are right but...'

'No buts,' Paul reached over and carefully pried Lucy from his wife's hands. She slowly relinquished the child, her eyes fixed on this tiny, precious jewel.

Go,' Paul said. 'You'll feel better.'

***

The bathroom door was open, and steam hung in the air. He could hear the shower and the movement of the woman as she bathed. He stepped out of the shadow and moved closer to the door. He could see her behind a steam misted window. The outline of her naked body, her round breasts. He smiled as he watched her and could feel himself getting aroused. She was washing her legs and although he couldn't see anything behind the misted glass, he could imagine. He closed his eyes and could smell the soap and the shampoo. It filled his nostrils and he held his breath momentarily so he could taste it on his tongue.

He wanted to go in there, to open the shower door and grab hold of her. To hold her breasts, to kiss those lips, to pierce her and to rid himself of this lust. He could do it, he knew. It would be silent, although he wasn't sure he could control his passion. He could feel the pulse of blood in his groin, a beat that extended to his temples.

He stepped back suddenly, back into the shadow. This was not why he was here, he had to remind himself; it was for the girl, not his own ecstasy. She was all that mattered.

'Paul?' Angela called.

'Yes, sweetheart?' Paul called back from the bedroom across the hall.

'Everything ok?'

'Everything's fine, don't worry and enjoy your shower.'

Had she heard him? Had he dropped his guard too much? Let his passion and lust control him? He stayed in the shadow and though he could see her get out of the shower, he closed his eyes. He was safe here; the shadow was his patron; it gave him comfort and protection. Everything that he wanted to give to the child, the darkness gave him. It allowed him to move without fear of being seen, to enter and exit swiftly. Time and distance had no hold on him. He was the Spirit of Darkness, the Father of Despair and the Lord of Grief. As he had breathed in the shampoo, he now imbibed the dark and he felt something greater than passion.

He felt power

He opened his eyes once more, knowing what mattered. The child. He needed the child, an innocence to corrupt so his master's power could flourish. He needed to cultivate the righteousness of virtue and feed on its annihilation. This child had been chosen and he was the bringer of her soul.

Tonight.

The woman passed him, oblivious to his presence. He knew he was safe and he knew what he had to do.

***

Angela looked down on Lucy who slept peacefully in the cot. Her brow was knotted in that way that only happened when she was under a lot of stress. Paul hadn't seen it often, thankfully, but he recognised it when he saw it. It caused the knot he felt at the pit of his stomach to tighten further. He loved that woman and even though he had not been the best of husbands, he knew he would always stick by her.

He felt his face flush red with shame and guilt as he

thought of Megan, the woman he had had an affair with for about six months. It was over now, cut short not by Paul but by Megan herself. She had found someone who would commit to her fully, not just on the occasional Friday night when he told Angela he was out with the boys from work. He had resented her, told her she was a bitch for dumping him like that, ignoring the irony of the situation.

Angela never found out, he was confident of that. She had been pregnant at the time and loving it. A natural mother, a natural wife and naturally trusting. And he loved her for it, even though he had looked elsewhere for something she couldn't give him. She was quite sexually conservative, liked to keep it simple. He wanted someone to excite him, to take charge, to seduce him. Angela would even get embarrassed at the suggestion, but Megan was exactly what he wanted and did it all to please him.

'You ok?' Angela asked him. He had been staring at her without really seeing her. He nodded slowly.

She smiled, crossed over to him and put her arm around his shoulder. She sighed deeply and rested her head on him. She didn't say anything and didn't need to. He knew she loved him.

The guilt welled up in him again, this time attached to it was another, more terrifying thought. *What if it was my fault?*

It was so powerful an accusation he could feel his heart beat harder. What if this was because of what he had done? What if this whole episode, the confrontation with that beast of a man, was punishment for his sins?

He believed in God and knew that this wasn't how sin and punishment worked. As a Christian, he knew, in theory, that his sins were forgiven. However, doubt occasionally plagued him, gorging on his humanity. This was a natural way to feel, he knew that. Believer or not, doubt was a constant in many people's lives, but today the sting was so acute he felt it in the marrow of his bones, as relentless and unforgiving as cancer.

Angela sighed deeply, he put his arms around her, closed

his eyes and silently prayed for this nightmare to be over.

***

Paul's eyes felt very heavy. The day had been catching up on him for a while now. He sat up in bed, Angela lay beside him finally succumb to a light sleep. Lucy was in the cot next to their bed; they had moved the chest of drawers in front of the door for extra protection. There was a police car parked out front and he had checked a couple of times to make sure they were still there.

They had decided to try to rest and had taken comfort from their precautions. As they got into bed Paul had reached over and kissed his wife passionately. She had received it and returned it. She had not complained as he held her breast and squeezed it intensely. Yet, when he had reached below the bedclothes and tried to pull down her panties, she had resisted him.

'Not tonight, I can't' she said, almost dreamily.

He tried to kiss her, to show her how much he needed it, but she pulled away.

'Tomorrow, I promise. I'm too tired and stressed tonight. I would have thought you were too.'

He felt a slight flush of anger, then that guilt again. He sighed deeply, knowing that she was right, so he pulled away from her and forced a smile.

'Go to sleep,' she whispered. 'Let's just get through tonight first.'

He nodded and lay on is back facing the ceiling.

'OK,' he said finally. She manoeuvred herself until she leaned on his chest and kissed him on the cheek.

'I love you,' she said.

He lay there for a while until she was asleep. He thought of Megan, what she would have done and felt a momentary resentment towards his wife. He had needs too and at times like this it may be a good thing; it could relieve the tension, to get closer and forget, however briefly, the horrors they were going through.

He sighed heavily, the pendulum swung back again to guilt and he started to feel selfish and careless. This is not who he should be. Angela needed him as much as Lucy did.

So, he just lay there, occasionally looking over to the two women in his life. As he watched Lucy sleep, he thought of that beast again. Was he a man? A demon? Death itself? He shivered as he thought of those huge, monstrous hands holding his baby. She was defenceless, and he remembered how helpless he had felt when he had confronted the man who he knew would haunt his thoughts for the remainder of his life. He looked over to the chest of drawers, happy that they would be safe that night.

Eventually, he lost the fight and slowly drifted into sleep.

***

The man stepped out of the shadow and looked at the sleeping figures before him. He glanced back to the chest of drawers and snorted in derision. Who did they think they were dealing with? Did they not understand?

Silently, he crossed the room and looked out the window to the street outside. A policeman leaned on the car looking up and down the street. He looked like he was talking to someone, probably his partner who was still in the car.

Another snort.

He returned to the bed and the cot. The child was so beautiful, so innocent, so perfect. He loved her completely and knew she would give to him so much more than her parents could expect. The cot was pulled up next to the bed where the mother slept. He leaned over the woman and smelled her hair, the freshness of the shampoo, her skin cream. He wanted her again, to hold that smooth skin and take her. He wanted to make the husband watch as his weakness was exposed. He would be dealt a lesson about the fragility of his role and the vulnerability of all he thought was his. This puny man would be punished for allowing his family to suffer as they were.

The woman grunted in her sleep and seemed to say a few words, but he could not make out what they were. He could have reached into her dreams and turned them to nightmares, but it would serve no purpose.

Standing full height again, he walked to the side of the cot and reached down and lightly touched the baby's cheek. Lucy smiled, as did he. She made him very happy, and he would love her and protect her. She would feel special, a princess, right up to the moment he would crush her innocence and his master would feed on her destruction.

He felt good, the eternity was his.

Silently he reached down and deftly lifted the child into his arms. She gurgled slightly and he pulled her closer. The parents did not move. The pathetic mortals. They thought they could provide all this child needed yet they slept as their child was taken. He wanted to destroy them as they slept but knew the worse he could do to them was to leave them live with the guilt of their folly.

With Lucy snuggled in his huge arms, he walked into the shadows and was gone.

***

The next morning Paul awoke to his wife's screams.

Friday

CHAPTER 1

The feeling didn't really hit Catryn until she crossed the bridge. It was an obvious place for it to hit her, she supposed. In fact, she probably expected it deep down. It was the border after all. It was the moment she left England and the life she had lived for the last 15 years, and crossed back into her old life, the one she left behind.

She could see the distant hills and thought of home. She knew it was a cliché, the hills and mountains of Wales, not exactly Switzerland but legendary in their own way – at least to the Welsh. To others, they were something to sneer at. From her first day at University in London all those years ago, she had been teased.

'Oh, you're Welsh, I could tell by your accent.' They'd say, followed inevitably with 'How are the valleys then, boyo?'

It wouldn't have mattered if she was from the Valleys, according to everyone in London the whole population of Wales lived in 'the Valleys'. It had also surprised her that hardly anyone had ever thought of calling her 'girlo'. It was always 'boyo'.

But she hadn't minded. Many of the clichés they spouted were the very things she had wanted to escape from. She had hated the accent; the supposedly sing-song quality just reminded her of backwardness. It was the accent of people on benefits, of uneducated Neanderthals; of White Lightning, poppers and roiders, and gropes down the alleyway behind the Hot Zone nightclub.

She had wanted out in her teens; she was better than it all and as soon as she got her A levels she was gone. Wales was mostly a memory and an occasional trip to see her parents. But even those trips had become few and far between. Why travel 180 miles when you could Skype? She soon lost track of her friends and knew she had been slowly losing track of her parents.

But that didn't matter. She had a good job as a Forensic Accountant with PWC investigating business fraud and had recently had a key role in a big case with the Met involving organised crime. That had been so much fun. She had worked ten hours a day, six and occasionally, seven days a week. The pressure had been heavy as she poured over receipts, journals, balance sheets, tax returns and financial statements. She knew most people would have been baffled by the detail and probably bored out of their minds, but she had loved it. The accounts, the mass of paperwork had, with hard work and dedication, changed from a mass of impregnable data into a living organism, one that could be understood, predicted and spoken to. As the organism had evolved, she felt as if she could speak to it and it would speak back to her.

She couldn't explain this passion to anyone; who would believe her when even a partial explanation would send them to sleep. People believed accounting was math and math, as everyone knew, was boring.

After nine months of intense work she had been relieved it was over and sorry she couldn't continue. It resulted in a promotion, a pay rise and the conviction of nine men on money laundering charges. She had been assured that there would be more in the future.

Everything had seemed perfect, it was what she loved, and she knew her reputation would ensure more involvement with future cases.

After the case had been solved and she had appeared in court explaining what the numbers meant, her boss – Mark Greenward – had singled her out with a few others for their exemplary work. Greenward was very old school, a tough, no-nonsense boss who liked to give out broad instructions to his staff and leave them to fall or fly on their own talents. Some people didn't like this, afraid they might follow the wrong lead and end up humiliating themselves. Catryn didn't mind at all. She knew that if she listened to the numbers, they would speak to her and tell her where to go. It was like an inverted pyramid, start with everything until the data starts to narrow and the organism revealed itself.

She called it biological accounting and had, when she was alone and there was no one there to laugh at her ideas, intended to write about it sometime, to see if she could put her thoughts into an academic paper.

Not that anyone would read it. Still, it was a fun idea.

Outside work things had started perfectly. She had met and married Joe Gibson, an advertising executive. They lived in a nice house not far from the city, with beige walls and leather furniture, and a home office with a large ornate oak desk. There was a cat called Buddy, a light grey British Shorthair that seemed to reflect the contentment she felt. She had money and happiness and a future.

But then, of course, as such stories are apt to do, it all went wrong.

***

The dirty white struts of the suspension bridge zoomed passed as Catryn maintained her sixty miles per hour. The intermittent changes of air pressure created a rhythmic beat which she found quite relaxing. The sign at the side of the road as she left the bridge, however, caused her anxiety to grab hold of her belly once more. 'Welcome to Wales, Croeso I Gymru' read the tall white letters on the brown background. Above them a small red dragon resting in a white square. The Welsh certainly did love their dragons. When on holiday as a child, her father always pointed out the sign and exclaim proudly that they were now home, even though they still had over an hour's drive to go. As the years had passed this pride had started to grate her. The dragon represented, not the pride of a nation, but the shadowy prison bars of small-minded nationalism. The significance of crossing the bridge and passing the sign eventually evaporated, her eyes would roll and she would just accept there was still some way to go.

Today though, she felt something different. There was some joy in passing the sign. Certainly not hiraeth – that romanticized longing for home - but it wasn't unpleasant. Her father's words – 'not far to go now kids' - only fed the butterflies. Time was different to a thirty-seven-year-old woman than it was to a nine-year-old. Distances were shorter, an hour quicker. It really wouldn't be long before she saw the old valley again, before she turned up her parents' street and knocked the door.

***

An hour later, she stood outside her father's house, with its white door, frosted windows and a black knocker. There was never any doorbell as the school kids always smashed them. Catryn had been concerned that her father, whose hearing wasn't exactly the greatest, wouldn't be able to hear someone at the door, but it never seemed to bother him. 'If it's important then they'll come back,' he would say with finality.

The drive up the valley, on old roads that were crowded with memories, hadn't been as difficult as she thought. She had walked these streets as a child and the buildings had seemed colossal. She had relied on the comfort of her mother's hand to guide her. As she got older, the streets became smaller and less impressive; alleyways had become familiar, somewhere Catryn and her friends could run without worry of cars or adults. Now, as an adult, they seemed both massively familiar yet small and ordinary. The tight overcrowded streets of London with their array of foreign accents, sounds, and smells were forgotten, replaced with something that had never gone away. Her anxiety had been multilayered but, confronted with the familiarity of the streets, the first layers of worry were slightly, and thankfully-, assuaged.

There was the 'In Cod We Trust', the chip shop that had been run by Leanne Jones' family. She would go in with her friends, Sarah King, Dani Williams, Menai Price and, of course, Leanne, and ask for scraps – those little pieces of chips and batter that no one wanted. They would dowse them with ketchup and walk up to the park where they would sit on the benches and gossip. She couldn't remember what it was that they spoke about anymore – boys, probably; there was always lots of boys talk.

It was on these benches and on these streets, that her socialisation had taken place. More so, she thought, than at home and in school. Yes, school prepared her for the future but to stay sane and get to that future, she had to navigate her teens. It had been her friends who had helped her on this journey. They had kept her grounded whilst encouraging her to fly. They had accepted her seriousness and her drive, protecting her from the ridicule of others, whilst ensuring a fair dose of ridicule from each other.

Opposite the chip shop, were the steps where Dani fell and broke her arm. They were narrow and very steep, with brambles growing each side. The water from the hill often spilling onto the steps causing a fine layer of very slippery moss to grow. It was one of the perils of living in such a steep valley, where a road could be higher than the rooftops of the parallel street. She could never work out how people could live in those houses, knowing that someone could look directly down on you. Into your bedroom, or possibly see your shape through the frosted glass of the bathroom. And downstairs was worse. Windows that should have opened onto gardens only opened to brick walls, casting the back of the houses into a perpetual darkness.

But, at the same time, she knew she missed it. London was great, historic, busy, but these narrow streets, the houses built at improbable angles on the sides of hills, the clash between the pre-1900 buildings and the 60s nondescript social housing that dominated the so-called new estates, warmed her somehow. She smiled at that phrase – 'new estates'; there were estates dotted around the valleys with buildings almost fifty years old, yet they were still referred to as 'new' estates.

The last mile up to her father's house was perhaps the strangest. A new bypass had been built sometime in the last few years which meant the last stretch of her journey was completely changed. It was also a painful reminder of how long ago it had been since she had been home – almost 6 years since the death of her mother.

Her face flushed with shame and anger.

It was those feelings that tried to overwhelm her as she stood in front of her father's house. She could feel her heart pounding through her breastplate and could even feel the pulse in her eye sockets. But she was here for a reason. Her father knew all about what had happened in London and had called her, leaving a beautiful message on her answer machine. He told her that he loved her, that he didn't understand but wanted to and, no matter what the explanation was, he was there for her.

She hadn't returned his phone call, yet here she was – a hundred and sixty miles away from a life that was forever gone.

She knocked the door.

CHAPTER 2

As the bells rang out, Morgan Williams did his ritual raising of hands and voice, trying one last time to grab the attention of the kids in his class. It always seemed to him that, if the kids learned anything in school it was the power of the end-of-the-school-day bell. It was like some operant conditioning response to the sound. Without thinking they would automatically close their books, start putting away their files and stationary, and start getting up to leave. It was usually in one continuous movement.

Then they would start talking; not about the class, not about school or even learning, but about all those other things that a crammed into a fourteen-year-old's mind. As the bell stopped, the voices would take over. It didn't matter if Morgan was in the middle of a sentence or if they were in the middle of a test, when that bell rang out, so the pupils rose.

So, he had developed a way to fight against the conditioning, at least long enough to get the last word. He would raise his hands, manoeuvre himself in front of the door and raise his voice.

'OK, calm down...' (like that would happen!) 'Remember, your essays on the Kristallnacht are due on Monday morning. I know a lot of you haven't even started it yet, don't deny it, I know you all too well by now! Remember, the focus is on how the world reported it and how accurate it was when compared to the actual experiences of the Jewish population....'

He could have gone on but a queue was forming in front

of him and the agitation in the pupil's eyes at this unwanted delay was obvious. That was ok, he had said his piece and, deep down, he knew the majority of them would hand something in on time.

He stepped to the side and the jostling began. The weekend was here, at least for the kids. For Morgan, there was marking, meetings and a few drinks – his usual weekend.

'Marcus, I'm talking to you too,' knowing that if there was one kid who could write a perfectly good essay but probably wouldn't hand one in, it was Marcus.

The boy averted his eyes and pushed his way out of the class quickly.

Morgan sighed heavily. He was tired and a little worn down, but it was Friday afternoon. His weekend may be busy, or as quiet and as lonely as a solitary cell in a maximum-security prison, but at least he didn't have to be here.

***

Morgan lived in a two bedroom terraced house on Bevan Street, just off the Main Road. It was a small house, a traditional two up, two down. He lived alone and hoped he would get used to it soon. He didn't like the quiet and would put on the radio as soon as he got in. A few years ago, he had invested in a Wi-Fi radio, one that could pick up channels from all over the world. As a blues lover there wasn't a lot of choice in this part of Wales, a few clubs and pubs he knew regularly put on live performances but there is little, if anything, on mainstream channels. But thanks to the wonders of wireless technology he was able to listen to internet stations like KCOR. Ok, the quality of presenters wasn't always up to scratch, but he loved the music and that was all that mattered.

He put his bag on the small breakfast bar as normal and turned on the radio which was located on a shelf in the kitchen. In the living room, he could play the same channel through the TV, but he still preferred the sound of the radio.

Even in these days of crystal-clear sounds, he still preferred the smallness of a radio, it felt more intimate. Now, there was the pulsing piano of late great Professor Longhair performing Big Chief. Morgan smiled and started tapping to the rhythm. He was starting to relax, and the stresses of the day were starting to loosen. He would still have to revisit Marcus Vaughan and his classmates for a few hours as there was homework to mark, but that was later, that would be on the sofa, legs curled up and glass of red wine at hand, and the bottle within easy reach.

And that was exactly what he wanted now. He opened the fridge and looked inside, trying to decide exactly what tempted him. He ended up with a glass of beer which he opened quickly and then took a long, cold and very satisfying mouthful.

He took out his lunch box from his briefcase, opened it and dropped it into the sink. He didn't feel like washing it just yet and that was fine. There was no one to argue with, no one to upset and no one to chastise him. If he wanted to be lazy, he could. As Billie Holiday once sang: 'Ain't Nobody's Business If I do'.

This was his life. It was the quiet life of a divorced secondary school history teacher. Sedate, relaxed, free but also lonely at times. He didn't have to go out for an hour and wasn't hungry yet; besides Friday was takeaway night, a Chinese from The Golden Dragon. He would walk through the door at about quarter past eight this evening and his Singapore Chow Mein and Salt & Pepper Chicken would be waiting for him. He had been going there for, how many years? Probably too many but, most of the time, he ate well, kept relatively fit and didn't think karma would begrudge him a weekly Chinese.

He took off his shoes and went upstairs to have a shower. He left the bathroom door open as he stood naked in front of the mirror because that is something single people could do. There was never anyone to walk in on him, no one to catch him all soapy, no need to worry that the kids would walk into the bedroom at night to discover he had gone to bed commando style, and no need to turn the computer's volume down if the occasional need to relieve his sexual urges overcame him.

Once out of the shower he crossed to the spare room, which acted as a walk-in closet, naked because that was another thing he could do. There were only a few benefits from living alone and, he supposed, nakedness was a small one.

Of course, when he and Chantel had gotten married, nakedness hadn't been a problem then either. In fact, they had both enjoyed it. One night he had even chased her from the bedroom, down the stairs and into the kitchen only to realise that the kitchen blinds were open and the neighbours were in their garden. Chantel had shrieked, and he chased her back up the stairs and back into the bedroom where they had made love, more ferociously, more passionately and with fewer inhibitions, probably spurred on by the near miss in the kitchen. It had been fun, or at least for a while. When the kids came along, this freedom had occurred less and less and, as the kids grew old and streetwise enough to notice these things, it was replaced with locked doors and snatches of privacy. But now he was divorced and hey, if it meant he could exercise his free will by occasionally freeing Willy, then exercise it he would.

He selected a grey t-shirt with the iconic picture of King Kong roaring from the top of the Empire State Building, some jeans and a dull green hoodie with a zip down the front. It was still early spring and although it was dry, the evenings could get very cold sometimes. By the time he was dressed it was just gone 6pm, leaving him just twenty minutes to get to the hall where his bi-weekly historical society meeting was taking place. He picked up his old battered briefcase and replaced the marking he had brought home with the notes for his presentation. As he left, he felt the light flutter of butterflies as he always did before he gave a talk. You would have thought that standing in front of a room full of kids for thirteen years would have prepared him for this kind of thing, after all, he basically doing what he did at work, but no, this was different. This lecture was to be made in front of people he liked, mature people, and people who were actively interested in the subject he was talking about. Not like school kids whose attention had to be grabbed, and learning had to be sometimes hammered into their young, delicate brains.

But he knew the butterflies would still pass, as soon as he stood in front of the small crowd and took a deep breath, he knew the words would come. They always did.

***

The hall was cold, but then again, it always was. It was situated in an old church which had since briefly been revived as a night club, a community class and now a Boys & Girls club. From Monday to Thursday it was home of mini football, brownies and guides classes for the kids, along with a Zumba class for the older clientele, but, every other Friday it became home of the Historical Society, an enthusiastic group of amateur historians of Trehenri, the Rhondda and the wider Valleys area.

They were mostly a little older, mostly male and entirely white. Not entirely Welsh though. There was one Englishman – Sean Bedford – a retired teacher whose late wife, Helen, had been born and brought up in the town. Trehenri wasn't like the clichéd small town where you were always a stranger until you had twenty odd years under your belt, Sean always said he had found the town suited him perfectly, although even after almost forty years, he still got jibed about his accent. It had to be said though that he was probably stricter about the pronunciation of some of the local place names than the locals were. To Sean, the town had a local feel he hadn't experienced growing up in his native Leeds, perhaps because Helen seemed to know just about everyone. They couldn't walk down the street without bumping into this person or that. If he wanted a private life, he soon realized, he had come to the wrong place. Luckily, he maintained, it was just what he was looking for, and now Leeds was a memory rarely conjured up.

Sean always sat next to Mike Williams, another retiree who had spent his working life in JP Evans Printworks, a local printer who had opened up shop in 1946 when John Price Evans, recently back from fighting the Italians in North Africa, found out that his factory job at the steelworks was no longer available. He had started his own company printing timetables for British Rail and posters selling the virtues of rationing. Mike had started as an apprentice in 1952 and had worked there for fifty-one years. He was probably the oldest of the group but sometimes he was also one of the spriest. A tall, elegant man, Mike always wore an immaculate suit and sported a beautifully carved walking stick. The Historical Society had been the brainchild of Sean and Mike and now could attract as many as 20-25 attendees.

Morgan and Mike had known each for most of Morgan's life. As a child, he had lived a few doors away from the old man in Davies Street. Morgan had moved many years ago, but Mike was still there, in the same house with his wife, Glynis, who was slowly succumbing to dementia.

Mike and Sean took their seats in the front row as usual. Next to them was Fran McCarthy and Eddie Evans, who lived next door to Mike and gave him a lift to the meetings.

Each meeting began with the hum of conversation interrupted by the occasional laughter. Although each person there had an interest in local history, the society was, first and foremost, a social occasion. There was always gossip, chit chat and, more than occasionally, rumour.

Eventually, they would settle down to listen to the presentation, then, later when it was over, the hum would be back, this time interrupted by the occasional 'thanks' and 'That was really interesting, I didn't know that' to whomever the speaker was. Sometimes there would be a guest speaker but, more often than not, it was Morgan, mainly because he was free of charge (guests would at the very least expect to get their transport paid and occasionally expect a little more for their time and trouble).

Tonight though, there was a little more conversation. News had started to spread about the little girl who had gone missing. It was news that couldn't go undiscussed.

It was different to the usual gossip, It was more urgent, closer to home. Someone had targeted a family here in Trehenri, someone had broken into their home and had abducted their child.

No one had any real information, there was just rumour and concern but that was probably enough, at least for now. The rumours were exchanged, fodder for later conversations back home and over the garden fence with neighbours.

Morgan sighed heavily. There was always that meeting when the individuals in the group were more interested in the world outside the walls than the history inside them. He understood this and understood the need for it. Many of the members there didn't get out of their houses a lot, so this was a social night. Most people there had known each other for many years and rarely saw each other throughout the week. It was their way of holding on to their present as well as their past.

He waited for a few moments, checking the laptop that the Society owned, to make sure the PowerPoint presentation he had prepared was working ok, careful not to get sucked into a conversation that could distract him. Finally, he stood in front of the group, full screened the first slide and waited. He didn't have to hush them, he wasn't in school, he just smiled until the murmur died down and all eyes were on him.

'Good evening everyone, thanks for coming out again. I think that considering the news we've had today, it would be nice to talk about something a little lighter, so without further ado,' he pressed a button on the computer and a picture appeared on the screen behind him. It was of a man and woman in Victorian dress, they stared out of the painting with stern, unsmiling faces. He stood behind her with his hand on her shoulder, she sat with a bouquet in her hands.

'We all know Sir Charles Henry, the man who gave his name to our fair town, Trehenri. Well in 1836 he embarked on a steamy affair with Mrs Mary Smithfield, wife of Sir Charles Smithfield who had been sent to Wales to oversee the Taxation of the booming Industrial Revolution. This picture was supposedly taken from Henry House, just up the road from here. Not sure if anyone here has ever been up there? No, perhaps we can arrange a field trip some time. The picture was painted a few years later, after Mrs Smithfield had separated from her husband – or booted out and publicly disgraced – the affair was indeed very steamy...'

There was a ripple of laughter and Morgan began to relax.

CHAPTER 3

Catryn took a sip of her tea and leaned back in the chair. The room was getting dark but neither she or her dad made any move to put the lights on. There was a silence in which Catryn felt comfortable. The TV was on but the sound was low, her father had got into the habit of leaving it on to fill the spaces, he said.

The room was familiar yet different. The decoration was the same although there was now a slight layer of dust that her mother would never have allowed. The chairs were in exactly the same places as the last time Catryn had visited, the TV was newer – a larger flat screen HD TV - but it occupied the same spot as the old one. On the mantelpiece, the pictures were the same, a pictorial history of Catyn's childhood and her successes, although nothing to celebrate her marriage, she was happy to note.

Next to the photographs, there was a small collection of pigs – some wearing clothes walking upright, a few in amusing poses and the occasional anatomically correct version, eating from a trough or just standing, staring out towards the window. These had been Catryn's, a long time ago. She had gone through a short phase collecting these little toys and ornaments, and her father had taken a lot of pride displaying them. He would often move them around and pretend they had done so on their own volition. Of course, Catryn had known what he was doing but always played along, humouring him because it had given him so much pleasure.

They didn't look like they had been moved in a long time.

Even the wallpaper, a pale, floral design that was several

decades out of date and starting to peel in the corners close to the ceiling, was the same.

It was all there but there was that one thing missing – the busyness, the bustle and the constant presence of her mother.

Catryn sipped her tea again and looked at her father. He sat staring at the tv, watching some cookery programme although, she knew, he hadn't turned the channel over for a few hours. It was obvious that this was his routine: turn the TV on and watch whatever it was that was on at the time; occasionally getting up to go to the toilet, make a meal or a cup of tea. And that was mostly it.

When he had opened the front door to see her, there had been a moment when he just stared at her, the shock of seeing her momentarily paralyzing him. Then he had shaken his head and a broad smile broke out on his face.

'Dad,' she had whispered.

He hadn't said anything; he had just lifted his arms and pulled her close to him. A tear built up in his eye and she could feel his body shaking,

'Cariad,' he said eventually. It was the Welsh word for 'love' and she hadn't heard it for a long, long time. She almost lost control there and then.

They had gone into the house and he sat her down. He had busied himself tidying the room quickly, almost in embarrassment.

Catryn had been struck by how old he was; she hadn't seen him for over six years, and she was taken aback by the hesitancy in his step and the hunch in his back. This man, who had carried her on his shoulders, who had cwtched (another Welsh word which meant 'to hug', that seemed appropriate here) her to sleep when she was ill, who had chased her through autumn leaves in Thomas Park, was no more. Instead, there was only this OAP living alone, sustained by a natural instinct to carry on and by the memories that were slowly deserting him. Her parents had been in their forties when she had arrived; a very happy and surprising accident, they said. She had never really noticed their age before, a child accepts without condition, but now it was obvious.

Catryn felt a wave of emotion sweep over her, she was aware of a single tear fall down her cheek. She felt sadness that the vibrant man of her youth was gone, and she felt embarrassed that her absence for such a long time was part of the problem.

They had made small talk, catching up with general health and minor illnesses, neither one mentioning the big issues: her mother or her husband.

Now, several hours later, they sat and watched TV. Catryn had moved her things into the spare bedroom, a dusty box room which smelled stale and slightly damp. But she didn't care, she would sort it out tomorrow. Right now, she was home.

***

'Catryn? You ok?'

She looked at her father and smiled.

'Of course, I'm fine.'

'You look, I dunno, far away.'

Catryn smiled and nodded.

'Lots of memories,' she said. 'As I drove through town a load of memories came back. A lot has changed.'

'Not really,' he said. He shifted in his seat and leaned towards her. 'Any changes that do take place tend to happen slowly, in increments, so people hardly notice. You might see things with fresh eyes, you might notice things but you'll soon realise that nothing much has changed.'

'I suppose you are right. The Bypass is fairly new.'

He nodded.

'They were just starting it when you were last here. Not the digging but the preparation. The old church up in Merthyr Road was first to go.'

'They tore down the church?'

'No, the church is still there but they tore up the graveyard.

Had to dig up the graves and relocate them. Most of them had been there for hundreds of years so no permissions were needed. Remember that large statue of Mary holding the baby Jesus?'

Catryn nodded.

'Well, I reckon that's where the traffic light is now.'

'I didn't notice.'

'No, you came up the road from Cardiff. You'd have to turn up to Ton Road by the square.'

Catryn nodded again. She remembered the churchyard, how the kids had squeezed through the fence on their lunch breaks from school and sat on the tombstones eating their chip baps and drinking their cokes. There had never been any fear, it had just been a convenient place to sit down and eat, just a five-minute walk from In Cod We Trust. There never seemed to be anyone there, no adult to shout at them or chase them off, no mad parishioners to wave their cane and accuse them of sacrilege. They had made up stories about the dead rising up and stealing Sarah's battered sausage or pinching Leanne's backside, but that was all. She couldn't help by smile at the memory. It was funny what was scary to a child and what wasn't. Today, there would be no way she would think about doing it, not because she thought these things were scary, but she certainly would have found it distasteful.

Catryn came to a decision. The night was still young and twilight had started its creep, but the fresh air would do her good.

'I think I'll take a short walk, Dad.' She said.

'You sure? It's getting dark.'

'I won't be long, I might just walk up the hill and take a look at the valley, see what is what.'

Glyn nodded and smiled. Catryn got up and reached for her jacket. As she put it on her father stood and crossed to the m-antelpiece. From a small, colourful saucer he took a key.

'I'll lock the door after you leave so you'll have to leave yourself in.' He handed the key to his daughter. 'And be careful.

A baby was taken from a house up in Heol Aberfan a few nights ago.'

'A baby? What happened?'

'Dunno, it seems strange. Police outside the house because an intruder had broken in the night before, the bedroom was barricaded apparently, and the baby was next to her parent's bed. They woke up in the middle of the night and the child was gone.'

'Wow, how do you know all this?'

'I went down the club the other night, Marty Willis told me the details. His daughter lives a few houses down the street, in the new houses down by the river.'

Despite the subject, Catryn couldn't help but smile. That was how news travelled in the valleys. A friend tells a neighbour, tells someone on the bus who tells their husband.

'I'll be careful,' she said.

She moved towards him and kissed him on the cheek. There was a pause as he held her, she could feel his arms tense slightly around her. Then he pulled away smiling.

'Don't stay out too late,' he said.

Catryn smiled and put her jacket on.

'I'll be no more than an hour,' she said. 'Probably a lot less than that.'

***

The night was cool, a wind had picked up and the sky to the south had turned dark with clouds. Twilight hung on the valley like a teenager's mood but, at least for a short while, above Trehenri the sky was still clear and Venus was shining brightly and clearly.

Catryn had always been fascinated by the stars and the planets. Not to study them but to marvel at their distance, and the sheer size of the space between her and them. She often tried to translate that fascination, to try and feel some mighty awe at her smallness in the universe but this never really happened. The numbers were huge, far too large to truly imagine but that was ok by her. Her imagination had never extended into the infinite. Just the thought of them, of massive balls of fire floating in space, was enough to satisfy her. Besides, here in Trehenri, without the light pollution of the city, they looked truly beautiful.

She walked away from her father's house and headed towards the adjacent street. This would take her up the hill to the entrance of the local farm. She knew there would be a track which would via off to the right and, after a small rise, there would be a clearing. From there she would be able to look down on town. Hopefully, there would be enough light to pick out the streets and, possibly, some houses.

She became aware of the smell; there was a freshness in the air that was missing in London. She had grown accustomed to the slight taste of constant pollution. It was something she just wasn't aware of until it was gone, and it made her feel good. Lighter, almost.

At the end of the street, just before the turn to the farm, was the corner shop. Catryn wondered if it was still owned by the same Indian family who had been there all those years ago. Mr Patel was a fiery man with a quick temper. Although he was always very nice to the adults and knew just about everybody in the village by their first names, he always seemed to shout at the local children. He followed them around the shop, watching them like a hawk in case one of them was a little light-fingered. As far as he was concerned, if there was a possibility that one could steal, then there was a probability that all would. Mrs Patel was completely different. She would sit behind the counter, sharing her philosophy of life with anyone who would listen. She always had a phrase to share as she handed over the change. The local children would make fun of her but they all loved her because, it seemed, sometimes her optimism was contagious.

Catryn couldn't help but smile as she remembered those sayings: 'Always do right, it's the gift everyone will enjoy even if they don't know it', 'Today's struggle is tomorrow's strength, 'A broken crayon still colours the paper.'

Of course, the kids didn't really understand the meaning of most of these, they went completely over their heads, but there was one saying that Mrs Patel used to say regularly that Catryn took with her and used throughout her life – If you fail to prepare, you prepare to fail.

Outside the shop, a group of young men stood, base-ball caps on backwards, tracksuits and cigarettes. As Catryn walked past them she could hear their laughter and their appallingly bad language. She knew it was hypocritical of her, but she felt ashamed and saddened by this. These boys trying to reassert their masculinity in the most stupid way possible. It was a phenomenon that seemed to be attached to small shops, wherever you were in the world. She had seen them in London, in the suburbs of Paris and Rome. She supposed that there was a version of them in just about every town or city in the western world.

She continued past them and shut out the noise. It didn't seem to fit with her mood.

She followed the road as it snaked up the hill until she arrived at the farm. The track was still there, larger than she remembered, although not as overgrown as it was when she was a child. The evening's shadows were getting longer, but she could still see clearly as she started up the slight rise. She hoped there were no kids up there, as there would have been twenty years ago when she and her friends used to meet.

Her brow was starting to sweat as she reached the top of the rise. She was certainly out of shape, the last few months had really taken its toll on her. The stress, the worry, the sleepless nights. She had enjoyed jogging for many years – she'd put on an audiobook and off she would go – but recently she had stopped completely. She knew people who, when faced with the kind of thing she had been faced with, would push themselves harder, faster. But not Catryn. She had retreated into her apartment, curled up on the sofa and stared blankly at the TV each night.

The path was quiet and inwardly she breathed a sigh of relief. She quickened her step until she came to the edge of the hill and could see Trehenri below her. The sky above her was getting darker and streetlights were beginning to come on. It was at this time that you could appreciate the beauty of the valley. Maybe absence does make your heart grow fonder, she thought.

Was she happy to be back? The question popped into her head seemingly from nowhere. She certainly felt more relaxed tonight than she had for a long time but whether that was because she had returned home – whatever that meant – or merely because of the change in surroundings, she didn't know. That was probably it, she decided. It was just a change. It wasn't the familiarity as much as it just wasn't London anymore. If she had gone to Sydney, Australia, she may have felt the same.

Did this mean she was just running from her problems? Possibly; she was willing to accept that but was there anything wrong with that? She couldn't have stayed in London, but there was nothing to keep her there and she had to go somewhere.

Had she made the right choice? What was it that brought her back here? She could have visited her father for a week or so then gone somewhere else, but she knew she was here to stay. This was her 'new' home now. How was that for ironic?

With the shadows getting longer, Catryn suddenly felt a chill run through her. There wasn't any breeze that she could determine, just a coldness. Why was this? Was it anything to do with her decision? With her new future back here in the old town?

No, she thought. She could feel the hairs on the back of her neck stand to attention and a wave of goose pimples move down her arms. She glanced to her left. The clearing extended about twenty meters before ending at an overgrown area full of brambles and bushes.

Was there something there?

The chill ran through her again with this thought. She could see nothing. The sun had gone down behind the hills and the shadows were reclaiming the landscape. She could make out no detail in the mess of branches, thorns and leaves but, for some reason, it gave her a chill. She forced herself to turn away and look at the village she had grown up in, but no memories surfaced. Instead, the creeping fear, this irrational uneasiness, prevailed.

Was she being watched?

She couldn't help it, she had to turn back to the bushes. Had they moved? she thought.

A sniffed laugh escaped her. How the hell was she going to determine that? she thought. She couldn't really see anything. There could be a giant bear hiding there and she wouldn't know.

The thought that there could really be something there, even something as ludicrous as a giant bear, suddenly gripped her imagination. She turned and faced the bush, squarely, as if challenging it to move. A breeze blew up the hill and the branches did move. She knew it was a breeze, she had felt it on her face, her clothes had moved with it, but this rationale didn't seem to make any difference. The fact is the bush had moved, and her brain told her it was moved by something, or someone, who was watching her intently.

She took an involuntary step backwards.

Shit girl, she thought. What's got into you?

A hush had fallen on the clearing and she listened intently for any sound. There was complete silence for a moment, she couldn't even hear the cars on the bypass down below her.

Then...

Was that a breath?

Catryn was aware that her own breathing had stopped. Or had it? Was it her breath that she could hear? Surely it couldn't be anything else. If it has been an animal – a fox maybe, or more probably a cat – there would be no way she would hear any breath.

41

She tried to think rationally. It was a cat out for its evening hunt. Nothing more than that.

But she knew this wasn't the truth. There was something there, just on the other side of the branches, on the other side of the shadows, watching her. It was big and she could feel its threat, it's desire to do her harm. To reach out and grab her, to rip her body apart limb from bloody limb.

Of course, this wasn't true – it couldn't be.

Yet, she felt it was true.

She began to step backwards, slowly edging towards the rise. The bushes seemed to stare at her. The thing on the other side watched her intently. Another movement, just a shadow but Catryn knew it was real. In her mind she could see the creature, rising up from behind the bush, stepping through the shadows towards her.

She turned quickly on her heel and began to run out of the clearing and down the slope, back to the street. With each step, she could feel the beast following her. Its fangs dripping with blood, its claws churning up the ground, its red piercing eyes baring down of the back of her neck.

She stepped out into a streetlight. At the bottom of the hill she could hear the boys outside the corner shop. A car passed her, turning up Park Street, lighting up the surroundings. It was all very normal. She turned slowly towards the farm entrance but there was no one there. No movement, no beast following her. No sound of footsteps in pursuit.

She breathed heavily, admitting for the first time just how frightened she had been. Yes, it was her imagination, but it had seemed too real.

She focused on her breathing, concentrating on each intake and controlling each exhale. She counted each one until she felt she was in total control, then turned and continued back to her father's house. This place, with its memories of friendship and making out with boys, was spoiled for now and she was determined never to go back there again.

CHAPTER 4

Jimmy Bevan always liked to compare himself to the film director, Martin Scorsese. An ardent film-lover when he was growing up, Scorsese famously was on the path to join the priesthood before switching one hundred and eighty degrees and ended up pursuing a career in the movies themselves, making some of Jimmy's favourite films. In all honesty though, despite occasionally standing in front of a mirror and pretending to be Travis Bickle in Taxi Driver ('You talkin' to me?'), Jimmy was a sedate, comfortable man. He hadn't gone into the movies, but he had become a Minister of Religion. Perhaps he was everything that Scorsese would have been if he had not picked up a camera.

Probably not though. In fact, Jimmy didn't have a creative bone in his body. He liked his small, valley's life too much. He was relaxed, happy and content – none of the attributes of someone born to bring life to flickering images on the silver screen.

Tonight, he sat with his wife, Carys, his daughter Jenny and her husband Gareth. There was a warm glow in the room that spoke of satisfaction with life. A bubble that protected them from the outside world. But now the world had breached this bubble. The news that a child had been kidnapped from inside the parent's bedroom, had invaded. It didn't threaten to pop this bubble, Jimmy was much too comfortable and the news still seemed too unbelievable for that to happen, but it still cast a cloud over their little get together.

Jimmy had popped to the kitchen then returned to the living room, handed Gareth a beer and sat down opposite him.

The room was warm, spacious and comfortable.

'I have to say, Gareth. You look beat.'

Gareth Mann took a swig of his beer and sighed heavily.

'I am,' he said. 'It's not been the easiest of weeks.'

Jenny Mann took her husband's hand in her's. She didn't say anything, but Jimmy was aware of the reassurance his daughter was giving his son-in-law. He hoped Gareth was aware of it too. He hoped that the trauma and the stress that Gareth was facing at work right now was not too great as to eclipse the relationship these two had. He didn't think so when faced with such stress, but it was a possibility. He knew because of experience – he had seen it before; seen the signs and seen the consequences.

'Are you allowed to talk about it?' Jimmy probed. Careful not to push too hard.

'James Bevan, don't you pry where you shouldn't,' Carys said. Her voice was light, but Jimmy knew that she too wanted to know. She also wanted to keep as far away from it as possible.

'I was only asking if – if – he was allowed. He doesn't have to tell us if he doesn't want to,' Jimmy protested.

Gareth smiled and took Jenny's hand in his. Inwardly, Jimmy smiled too.

'That's OK,' Gareth said. He shifted on his chair as if to get comfortable. 'Actually, there's not much to tell. It's all on the news. There's nothing much more than that.'

'I can't understand how he could get out without anyone seeing him, and the doors were all locked from inside. Isn't that right?' Jimmy asked.

'How he got in was a mystery too, don't forget,' Carys said.

'I know,' Jimmy replied. 'But if he was one man, he could have been watching the police, waited for the opportune moment and got in.... however unlikely,' he said before Carys could object.

'But coming out,' Jimmy continued. 'First, he had to wait until the parents were asleep, then creep into the room...'

'A chest of drawers was pushed against the door from the inside' Gareth added.

'Really?' Carys asked. 'And what do you make of that, smarty pants?' She asked her husband.

Jimmy shrugged.

'Look, I don't know,' he conceded. 'All I'm saying is that getting in, he was alone. Getting out, he had a baby in his arms. Even if the baby slept through the whole thing, which seemed likely yes?'

Gareth nodded the affirmative.

'Even if the baby slept, getting out he still had the use of only one arm instead of two. One to hold the baby, the other to handle the doors, the chest of drawers -'

He gestured to Gareth who nodded again.

'Plus,' Jimmy shifted his weight as if putting it all behind his point. 'He couldn't see the police from inside the house. How would he know if they were distracted? Unless he had an accomplice.'

Jenny laughed. 'Dad, I think you missed your calling,' she said.

Jimmy joined her laugh. It was good to add some levity to the conversation.

'I'm pretty happy with my calling, thank you very much, little miss. However, I think I could have made a pretty good detective, eh Gareth?'

Gareth just smiled and Jimmy saw the tiredness in his eyes. It wasn't just his body that was exhausted, he noticed.

'I think you could,' Gareth said as amiably as he could muster. 'Sam Spade eh?'

This was Jimmy's favourite subject – the movies. He affected his best Humphrey Bogart and said: 'It's the, uh, stuff that dreams are made of.'

Carys and Jenny both rolled their eyes.

'Dad,' Jenny said. 'I've been listening to you do that for decades and it's still bad.'

Everyone laughed, except Jimmy who pretended to be

offended, although he understood how bad an impressionist he really was.

'Have you ever seen The Maltese Falcon, Gareth?' he asked.

Gareth shook his head. 'No, I don't think so.'

'Well,' Jimmy said, leaning forward. 'It's a true classic. Detectives, bad guys, cops, guns and treasure. Once all this is over, you'll have to come over one evening and watch it with me. I have it on Blu-ray. Perfect picture. You'll love it.'

'It's in black and white,' Jenny said.

'Oi!' Jimmy exclaimed, wagging his finger at her. 'None of that bigotry in this house, my dear. Monochrome is beautiful.'

Gareth nodded.

'I'll do that,' he said. 'As soon as this is over.'

'And are you close to catching him?' Carys asked.

The mood in the room changed again as everyone settled back into their seats.

'Not yet,' Gareth said. 'Not yet.'

'The poor parents,' Jenny said. 'I can't imagine what they are going through.'

Jimmy closed his eyes as he leaned his head back. Silently he said a little prayer, for the child, for the family, and for Gareth and his colleagues whose job it was to solve the mystery and crack open the case.

***

The evening was almost gone, although wisps of light still managed to hold back the full darkness of night. There was a coolness that was just on the wrong side of refreshing and a breeze was beginning to build from the south.

Jimmy stepped out onto the porch and took in a deep breath. He loved this time of night and sometimes wished he had a dog so he could go for long walks. Of course, there was never any time for these walks, always something to do with the church, visits, writings, and meetings. But he was home a lot, he supposed. Maybe she should talk to Carys about getting one. It wasn't like they ever went on long holidays abroad; when they did have a break, it was usually made up of day trips here and there. Nothing that would lead them to neglect the dog.

Inwardly, Jimmy smiled. Just maybe he thought.

He saw a puff of cigarette smoke rising into the air and he shook off his reverie. He turned to see Gareth sitting on the steps a few yards away. This is why he came out in the first place, prompted (or pushed?) by the women of his life to come out and make sure everything was ok with his son-in-law. This was his job, after all, to speak to those in trouble, to make sure they were fine, to make sure the balance of the force was maintained.

He smiled. I'm a priest, not a bloody Jedi, he thought. Being a huge fan of the Star Wars saga (and, yes, that included the hated prequels), he had often dreamed of having the powers of a Jedi. Wouldn't that be so cool? Wouldn't it make life so much easier? Truth be told though, he suspected that, despite his good intentions, it would probably make him lazier. Why go to the kitchen for a drink when you could will it to come to you? Why spend so much time convincing people he was correct when he could just use the power of suggestion?

He sighed heavily, aware of the childishness of his fantasy and shoved it to the back of his mind for later.

Gareth turned to him having heard the sigh.

'Hope you don't mind?' he said indicating the cigarette.

'I thought you had quit?' Jimmy said.

'I have.' Gareth snorted. 'I'm very good at quitting, I do it fairly regularly.'

Jimmy nodded in understanding. 'We all have our vices.'

'Even you?' Gareth asked, obviously not believing a word his father-in-law was saying.

'Even me.'

'Yeah, Like what?'

Jimmy thought for a moment then said: 'Films.'

'Films? I doubt they qualify as a vice.'

'You'd be surprised.' Jimmy said. 'You've seen my collection? I have over four hundred Blu-ray and almost a thousand DVDs. And they are not the cheap ones. I just have to have the ones with all the extras – the makings of, the commentaries, the histories. It's an expensive and time-consuming habit.'

'Do you watch them?'

'Oh yes,' Jimmy answered. 'I can go in there now, pop one on but not watch the film, I'll listen to the commentary track instead. Carys thinks I'm nuts, the film is on but people are talking over it, but I'm in hog heaven.'

'Life is easier in the movies,' Gareth took a deep drag of his cigarette and pushed what remained into the stone step.

'No, not easier. More fantastic, more outrageous, maybe. The good thing about the movies, of course, is that no matter how seemingly insurmountable a problem is, the heroes usually find a way.'

'I suppose,' Gareth leaned back and looked up into the night's sky. A few stars could be seen between the incoming clouds.

'Ok, if this was a movie,' he asked, 'how would that man get into the bedroom? Into the house?'

Jimmy thought for a moment, a smile playing on his lips.

'Well, vampires are known to turn into mist. They could easily get underneath a door and rematerialise the other side. Ghosts can just walk through doors.'

'That's the difference between the movies and real life then. Vampires and ghosts don't exist.'

The silence hung in the air between them for a moment. It was heavy, pressing down on them like a lead weight.

'The way I see it, ' Jimmy said finally. 'There are only two possibilities. Firstly, there was more than one person involved.'

'No, that would have been harder for them to hide and they still would have had to get into the bedroom, passed the chest of drawers without waking the parents; then, having left the room, put the drawers back against the door inside of the room. Impossible.'

'True. But that only leaves a much worse possibility. The parents are involved somehow.'

Gareth didn't say anything, just continued to stare at the sky. Jimmy knew that the police had thought of this. Whenever a child was abducted the immediate family were suspected, however briefly. This was always the case and had been proven many terrible times in the past. Even when there was little evidence, the suspicion would remain.

'The only problem I have with that theory,' Jimmy said finally, 'is why they would go to such extremes with their story. If you are going to hurt your own child and try to cover it up, why push the drawers in front of the door. Why go to such lengths to tell the world that the only people who could possibly get to the child was you? Surely, it would make more sense to allow some way for which the abductor to get to the child? For some story to be concocted.

'Of course, I don't know the family, I'm just saying it doesn't make much sense to me, that's all.'

Gareth stood up slowly, stretching his legs. Again, Jimmy could see the weight he carried on his shoulders.

'We'd better go,' Gareth said. 'I've got an early start tomorrow.'

He passed Jimmy on the steps and patted his father-in-law's shoulder, then entered the house leaving Jimmy alone with his thoughts. The priest waited for a few moments, taking in the night, wondering if there was someone out there so terrible as to rip a child from its parents; or if it was the Downs themselves who were the ones with evil in their hearts.

It struck him that, even though he had read about evil many times - watched films about it, studied it in the Bible - this was the closest it had ever come to him. Here he was, discussing evil - not the banality of it but the realness of it - on his own front porch. He had already written his sermon for Sunday, but now he decided to make a few changes.

He got up too quickly and had to fight the dizziness that accompanied it. He then stretched his legs and went into the house.

CHAPTER 5

Morgan inhaled as deep as he could and waited for his head to clear. It was his own fault after all. Instead of walking up the streets, he had decided to take the steps. There were stages of this so-called shortcut which must have been 45 degrees straight up. It wasn't far but he wasn't fit. If he had followed the road which slowly zigzagged up the hill at a reasonable incline, he would have been alright; instead, like the idiot he was, he decided that was too easy.

There were a lot of paths like this in these parts, narrow lanes crowded by overgrown trees and brambles each side. Steps rising up, up and further up. The water would drain off the hills and gardens each side and soak the stones, covering the steps with greasy, slippery moss. The steps could be treacherous, especially descending but they still served as popular shortcuts for the locals.

Of course, it helped if you were fit. It helped if your lungs had the capacity to take on this exertion. Morgan was starting to realise that he wasn't as fit as he wanted to be.

Admittedly, fitness had never been a priority. It was ok when her was a teenager and was always running around and riding bikes with his friends, but when and where this slipped away, he couldn't really remember. It had just happened, slowly and oh so very surely.

What made this route more difficult was that the steps weren't uniform. They were haphazard, some small, others steep and difficult. He knew this beforehand yet took this route anyway. It was his own bloody fault.

He stopped briefly, aware that he was getting a little lightheaded, and took a few deep breaths.

The evening had gone as well as expected. He enjoyed meeting the others, enjoyed researching and sharing the history of Trehenri and the surrounding valleys. There was plenty of history out there, plenty of tragedy, poverty and politics. The home of the industrial revolution when it was said, coal was king. This was true to some extent but not the whole story. Money was king. Money brought the industrialists to Wales, bought the equipment and the men to dig up the hillsides and spew out the black dust. And from this dust came more money. Morgan was a believer in the idea that this history had left indelible scars on the psyche of the valleys. The scars that potted the landscape also marked the people still. They had bought the lie that their history was a glorious one, that the people should still feel privileged all these centuries later, when in fact, the poor had been exploited as the poor have always been vulnerable.

Yet, every two weeks he would meet up with others and discuss the myth, without a sense of irony. He tried to lace his presentations with the truth but, in the end, people preferred the myth.

He resumed his walk and thought of that line from an old western – when the legend becomes fact, print the legend – but he couldn't for the life of him remember which film it came from. Something with John Wayne, he was sure, although that certainly didn't narrow it down. As he got to the top of the steps, he put it to the back of his mind. He would have to ask Jimmy Bevan, he thought; he would know. The man may be a priest but he probably knew more about movies than he did the Bible. He would probably see him over the next couple of days, he would ask him then.

There was no pavement at the top of the steps, they just ended on the road and a car was parked in his way. He shuffled around the rear of the car pushing through some brambles which caught his jacket and scraped his hand.

Some people were so selfish, he thought. Why park there?

Surely there were better places, less inconvenient places. He looked at the car, a spotlessly clean Ford KA, and snorted at it in derision, as if that made any difference.

He crossed the street and was thankful for the gentle incline for the rest of his journey up Henry Hill.

***

He didn't knock the door, he just opened it and went straight in, as he knew it would be unlocked. It always was, as many of them were around here. People would unlock them in the morning, and they would stay like that until nighttime. It seemed that it was mostly the older people who did that, the very ones who seemed afraid of every youth on a street corner, who were afraid of immigrants raiding their houses, and who wouldn't go to Cardiff in case there was a terrorist attack.

Inside was a small hallway, just enough to turn and close the door before entering the living room. He wiped his feet on the doormat and entered.

'Evening Donna,' he said.

The woman looked up and smiled. She had a tiredness in her eyes, a look of resignation which he recognised immediately.

'Hiya, Mogs,' she replied. She stood up, reached toward him and gave him a kiss on the cheek. 'Didn't expect to see you tonight.'

'Just finished at the hall so I thought I would pop up and see how he is, I'm going shopping tomorrow morning, thought I would see if there's anything I can get you.'

Donna smiled, and it almost reached her eyes but seemed to be pushed back by the bags that sagged beneath them. She had once been a smart looking woman who, a long time ago, could have boasted being one of the most attractive girls in the village. But now her black hair lay heavy and without shape, and her skin's smoothness had been replaced with deep lines and wrinkles.

On the chair next to her sat an old man, his legs covered with a blanket, his head drooping to one side.

'Tal!' She said, her voice raised slightly. 'Tal!'

Morgan passed her, leaned down and touched the man's legs. He came awake, slightly disorientated before really seeing Morgan standing in front of him.

'Morgan? What are you doing here? As someone died?'

Morgan looked to Donna who rolled her eyes. 'I'll make you a cup of tea,' she said.

'That's ok,' Morgan replied. 'I can't stay. I'm starving and I'm sure Chan is wondering where I am this evening.'

'Well, grumps will want one,' she smiled ruefully and crossed the room to the kitchen.

'What did she say?' Tal asked, a little too loudly.

Morgan pulled a chair from under the nearby table and sat down. 'She's going to make a cup of tea.'

Tal snorted. 'She probably won't make me one. She'll make herself one, sit in the kitchen with a packet of Rich Tea and keep them all for herself. The bitch.'

Morgan sighed heavily.

'She'll make you one, don't worry, although why she would, I have to wonder sometimes.'

Tal raised his hand dismissing the conversation. 'So, what are you here for?'

'Your amiable and erudite conversation.'

'Have you done your bit for the *historical society*?' Tal almost spat out the last two words.

'I have. We discussed the affair between Charles Henry and Mary Smithfield.'

'Ha!' Tal exclaimed. 'The bitch and the bastard. You know this very street was named after that fucker. Her husband was an accountant, making sure the robber barons weren't robbing the treasury! You could say that all Henry did was fuck the wife of the man who was supposed to prevent him from fucking the country. Ha!'

Morgan smiled. This snarly old man in front of him, a

man who was as abrasive as sandpaper, probably knew more history than any other person alive. Although he knew that Taliesin Jones was only seventy-eight, you would think that he had lived through it all as he knew so much.

'That's basically what I said this evening, although probably not as succinctly as you.' Morgan said.

'I should write a book about those two. The Bitch and the Bastard. Good title, yes?'

'I think you should.'

'I will, not yet, I got too much to do. We watched a marathon of Diagnosis Murder today. That bitch in the kitchen loves that crap. I just sit here and hope I die.'

Morgan laughed lightly; he had heard this all before.

'There will be a lot of people who will be sad to see you go,' he said.

'Ha!' Tal snorted. 'Most people would be surprised I'm still alive!'

The kitchen door opened, and Donna returned with two cups, she placed one down on a small folding table beside Tal's chair and sat down with the other on her chair.

'Are you sure I can't get you one?' she asked Morgan.

'No, I'm fine, I've got to be going in a minute.'

'Terrible about that baby being kidnapped, isn't it?' she asked. 'You don't hear things like that around here, do you?'

Morgan nodded.

'Lucy!' Tal exclaimed, loudly. 'That was her name, right?'

'I don't know,' Morgan shrugged.

'Yes, that's it,' Donna said. 'It was in the paper.'

'Lucy,' Tal repeated. He nodded to himself but didn't continue.

'What's the significance of that?' Morgan asked.

Tal was quiet for a moment, lost in thought.

'Ancient History,' he said finally. 'Ancient History.'

Morgan gestured for the old man to continue but there was only silence.

'Do you know what he's talking about?' Morgan asked

Donna.

'Nope,' she said, shaking her head.

'Well, on that strange note, I'll be off.'

Morgan stood and put the seat back to where he had found it. Donna stood with him.

"So, you need anything from the shops?'

'We're fine,' Donna said quietly. 'Don't you worry about us.'

'Nos da, Tal,' Morgan said, but the old man had closed his eyes again. He turned to Donna. 'You ok?'

Donna nodded. 'I'll put him to bed in an hour then I'll go home. We get a nurse up in the morning so I can get a couple of hours off.'

Morgan stared at her for a moment. Donna was the same age as he was and they had been in school together, but she looked a lot older, worn away by life and responsibility. She was Tal's niece and had taken care of him for the last eight years. Her husband, Barry – one of Morgan's friends from those school days - had died aged only thirty-two, taken by lung cancer even though neither of them had ever smoked. There were no children, nothing else to live for, so after Tal had suffered a terrible fall and broken his hip, she had taken over as his full-time carer. Her only respite was Sunday mornings in church and the occasional nurse who would sit with him for a few hours once or twice a week. She had to live with his insults, his bad language, his suspicions, but she had always done it without complaint. Morgan knew that, if there were such things as saints, Donna was one.

Morgan nodded. 'You look after yourself,' he said finally.

She reached over to him and kissed his cheek again.

As he stepped out into the cold night air, they said their 'good nights' and he began walking. He would take the steps again, he thought. He was absolutely starving, and he didn't want Chan at the Golden Dragon to think he had fallen into the arms of another Take-Away.

CHAPTER 6

When Catryn got back to her father's house he was, as promised, in bed. She unlocked the front door quietly and stepped into the hallway which was brightly lit as her father had left a light on for her. This was something her parents would always do for her as a teenager.

A warm sense of deja vu washed over her like a soft summer's breeze and, for a moment she leaned against the door and enjoyed it. She remembered those nights out with the girls, going down to the Hole for a few drinks, then onto the Hot Zone to dance the night away. Leanne, who lived at the end of the street, would call on her first then they would walk together down to March Street for Dani and Menai, and finally Brynmawr Crescent for Sarah. It wasn't far, a little over a mile, and if the weather was good, they would usually walk and catch a taxi back at the end of the night. If it was raining – and if there was one truism about Wales it was the rain - Leanne's father, who was a taxi driver, would take them out.

The Hole, a dump which had once been named the Watering Hole but had gone through several owners and names by the time the girls were able to enjoy its pleasures, was situated on the Main Road. It was a grand old building on the outside, dating back to the 1870s, but inside it was a different world, one dominated by sticky carpets, a jukebox that, when it worked, was far too loud, a pool table cramped in the corner making it impossible to play certain shots, and run by a gruff but lovable beard called Tony. There was no other way of describing him really, he had a massive mop of curly grey hair that seemed to bleed into his huge Grizzly Adams beard and continue onto the hairiest arms that you would ever see. He was a huge bloke, dominating his area behind the bar, but also the most lovable hulk. He always had a smile, always had a friendly word and a witty line.

The clientele, as Tony referred to the same bunch of reprobate locals that frequented the Hole, were mostly friends of Catryn and her gang, most of the youngsters had been in school with them. It was a motley crew of current and past relationships, friends and those who were not quite enemies. They had shared puberty together, discovered love and heartache together. Catryn's first long term boyfriend, Iestyn, who she had started seeing in school, had dumped her in the corner by the Juke Box. There was no way to sugar coat it, he had dumped her. Not because there was another girl (for they were certainly not yet women) that he had fallen for, but because she was too 'serious' for him. In retrospect, she knew that they were never destined to remain together and it wasn't because she was too serious – it was just that he wasn't serious enough. He had no ambition, no drive and probably not much of a future. She wanted to go places, he wanted to get pissed on a Friday and, sometimes on a Saturday night.

Alone in her father's hallway, she sighed heavily. Yes, she had gone places, earned good money and, for a while, lived a very good life, full of promise for the future.

A future which resulted in her standing alone in her father's hallway thinking about the past.

She made sure the door was locked then entered the living room. Her father had left a lamp on and the room had a quiet, lonely quality. She crossed over to the mantelpiece and looked at the photos.

She picked up the picture of her parents on the beach. She smiled, although her heart felt the reoccurring hint of sadness.

Her mother had been only 59 when she died, taken after a

severe stroke. It had come out of nowhere they said, with no warning, no hint that the life of this wonderfully colourful and loving mother was about to end.

Catryn touched the glass and traced her mother's outline with her finger. She hadn't been there when it happened as she had been living her life in London. Was that bad? Should she have been there?

No, there was no shame at a daughter leaving the nest, that was what parenthood was supposed to be about, preparing your children with the right skills and street sense to leave and to prosper. Yet, at the same time, knowing what was going to happen to her, that her life wasn't the bright light her mother had always hoped for, she felt a tinge of regret.

She put her picture back and picked up a pig. It was small and very light. The pig wore a smoking jacket and cravat, it sat on a chair reading a newspaper.

What a waste of time and money this lot of junk was, she thought smiling. It had taken her over a year to collect this rubbish, encouraged by her father who would buy her a new one whenever he saw one he knew she didn't have yet. Her interest had waned long before she had had the heart to tell him to stop buying them. And now they were on constant display on his mantelpiece. Maybe he was secretly buying them for himself, after all, she thought.

Her phone began to buzz in her pocket. The sound was turned off, but she could feel the vibration on her hip. She took it out of her pocket, wondering who was calling. There were still plenty of people who had her number as she still had lots of good and loyal friends, many of which she had not yet been able to tell that she had returned home to Trehenri.

But the number on the screen certainly didn't look familiar. She hesitated for a moment then pressed the 'accept' button. She put the phone to her ear and said 'hello' quietly, conscious of the fact that her father was in bed in the room above her.

'Hi, is this Catryn?'

The voice was unfamiliar. Considering it was now getting quite late, it was a very light voice; airy and a little over friendly.

'Who is this?' Catryn asked.

'Oh, hi Catryn. This is Robert Head. How are you?'

'Who are you?' Catryn asked. 'I don't recognise your name.'

'That's ok,' the name answered. 'We haven't met. At least not yet. I was just wondering if I could have a word with you.'

Catryn moved to the settee and sat down slowly. She could feel her guard rising, something she hadn't felt in the last few weeks, and had hoped would disappear the further away from London she got.

'About?' she asked.

'I just wanted to know if you are ok.' The voice changed slightly, becoming, it seemed, more intimate.

'Why? I don't know you. Who are you?'

'Well, I know what a strain the last year must have been. You've certainly been through a lot and I just wanted to know how you are? You know, how you are coping? What your plans for the future were?'

'Who are you?' She could feel her voice rising and she was becoming aware of a growing sense of panic. It tightened around her stomach like a tough guy crushing a beer can.

'Like I said, my name is Robert Head. Known to my friends and colleagues as Bob but I prefer Robert or just plain Rob. Bob Head just sounds, well I dunno, like one of those toys you see in cars. Don't know what my parents were thinking when they named me.'

He laughed lightly, although it seemed to Catryn that it was a line he said often; a tried and tested one-liner to break the ice when speaking to people. It wasn't going to work for her. She wanted the ice; she wanted a wall of it to enclose her and to keep the world at bay.

'I don't know you,' she repeated. She was beginning to suspect, however.

'Well, I'm a writer, and I've followed your courageous and compelling story, and I was wondering if you were ok. You know, how you are coping after your ordeal. You are a hero to many, and I think a few words from you could carry a long way. People really want to hear from you.'

'You're a reporter?' A tear escaped from her eye and cascaded down her cheek. She could feel its cold wetness burning through her skin.

'As I said, I'm a writer. So, how are you?'

'How did you get my number?'

'Don't worry, I didn't do anything illegal, you don't have to worry about it. And no one else will have it, I assure you. Everything is fine, there's nothing for you to worry about.'

Catryn didn't know what to say. Her tears had started to flow again. This couldn't be happening. She had escaped all this, she had run away, run into the arms of her father like a little girl who had fallen and scraped her knee. But this was much more than just a scrape, she knew. So much more.

She tried to speak but the words wouldn't come out. All she could think about was that dreadful night, of the blood, of the screams, of the police with their flashing lights. She remembered the police station and, for some reason that she could never explain, a large mug with the words 'World's Greatest Ass' above a picture of a donkey in a straw hat, which she had been given.

'Hello, Catryn?' Robert Head said on the other side of the line.

'I don't want to talk about it,' she said finally.

'Oh, I understand. After all, you've been through, I understand completely. But you must understand that you are now the inspiration to thousands of women out there. Women who...'

Catryn quickly pressed the 'end call' button, cutting him off.

She let the phone drop to her lap and buried her face in her hands. Her mind was a kaleidoscope of chaos, her thoughts colliding in a jumble of hurt, stress and pain.

The tears were flowing freely now, her sobs wracking her body. How could he have gotten her number? Had someone given it to him? Had she been hacked? There had been a big scandal a few years ago and she would have been naïve to think that wasn't still going on.

But, ultimately, it didn't matter. Running away hadn't worked. It didn't matter where she went, the past would follow her always. You can't outrun your memories, she thought.

In the living room of her father's house, with darkness surrounding her, with only one lamp doing battle against the night, Catryn sat in her father's chair and wept.

Saturday

CHAPTER 7

If you were to ask the people of Trehenri - or indeed anywhere in the valleys - if their community was a town or a village, you would probably get a number of different answers. People there do not think in those terms. They believe they live in an urban environment yet, anyone visiting from a large town or city would think the valleys were very rural. Places like this exist in a netherworld, trapped between various planes – not one thing or another, not modern, not traditional.

They are, however, communities. People know each other, they rely on each other; they marry and love and fight and compete with one another.

Within each community, there are sub-communities, which cater to quite distinct needs - the churches, the drugs, the school kids labelled by the colour of their uniform. Yet they are one – one group of people separated by age, by beliefs and success but tied by geography.

The communities can be quite strong. People want to be part of them, want to live in them and want to know them. Of course, there are many who live there because they feel they have little opportunity to live elsewhere: the young who yearn to spread their wings, the adults who can't afford to move, the wife torn between the desire to leave her abusive husband and the need for his love and acceptance. However, for the majority, this is their home and they want nothing more than to live their lives. Despite the rise in crime, the effects of alcohol and the dirty stain of drugs, people feel comfortable in these places. They are not afraid to go out at night, there are few 'no go' areas and many still leave their doors open in the daytime. This comfort can be deceiving, can give the sense that your walls are impregnable and that nothing can touch you.

Until it does.

Trehenri is no different. From the peak of Henry Hill to the Thomas Park and Trehenri High School at the base of the valley, the people always felt safe. It was a poor area; an area ignored by governments and the powerful, but a place where the people lived as a community.

A community is very much like a living entity. It is alive, organic and constantly breathing, and, even though Trehenri consisted of over fifteen hundred souls, it had a collective consciousness that is hard to define. The safety of the community comes from this collective. It fed off the individual souls and it, in turn, fed them back.

As the Friday slowly turned to Saturday, as the night held its vigil over the people, this collective was disturbed. People lay in bed wondering why they couldn't sleep, and for those who did manage to surf those slumber waves, their dreams were agitated and troubled. Men and women tossed and turned; their minds awash with worry. Some stared at the clock at hours they had not seen since they were teenagers, gripped by a tangible disquiet. They couldn't put their fingers on why, or what it was that was causing these feelings. Dreamers could not remember what it was that haunted them, only that darkness itself was bearing down on them.

Of course, people still went about their business. It was their livelihoods and vague feelings of restlessness and even foreboding, couldn't get in the way of responsibility. Yet, this uneasiness hung around them like a mist in a Hammer Horrors production.

Arthur Dando, 52, a milkman who started his round at 4am, dropped and smashed his first bottle since... well, he couldn't say when. He had been doing this job for over thirty years, a job that had once been common, but now only he and a few others were sufficient in number to cover the whole valley. It was a good job; he was his own boss and could listen to Classic FM without any complaints from any youngsters who didn't know their arses from their elbows. He had always loved the quiet of the night, the occasional car but little else for the first hour or so. Then the corner shops would start opening and the vans would appear with the day's newspapers or their loaves of bread. The early mornings didn't bother him and even on Sundays – his only day off each week – he would still get up before six.

Nevertheless, this morning he was tired. He could feel a weight on him that he didn't understand. It was as if something was going to happen, like the death of an old relative you had been expecting but didn't know when it would finally happen.

As the bottle dropped, he felt a sense of inevitability. It was as if it was destined to happen, as if he knew it was going to happen. As the glass shattered, crashing loudly in the cool silence of the early morning, his shoulders sagged, and he felt an overwhelming need to cry. He didn't know why; he wasn't a melancholy man - quite the opposite actually - but it was there. He stood over the remains of the bottle, watching the milk find a course down between the large slabs that made up the pavement and trickle away like a sailor after a night on the city. He lifted his leg and saw the white footprint left behind, proof of his crime.

Finally, he silently forced himself to pick up the large pieces of glass, dropped them into an empty container in the back of the van, and used a piece of cardboard to brush the remaining pieces into a nearby drain. Then, slowly, he got into his flatbed and drove away onto the next delivery. He didn't turn on the radio -he just drove on - the image of the milk streaming down the pavement caught in his mind.

***

Rachel Stanzy drove passed and saw Arthur leaning over,

scraping the floor with the cardboard. She didn't understand why but the sight made her want to sigh deeply. Her windows were down and the radio was on louder than she normally would have it at this time in the morning. She was desperately tired and needed to concentrate. She was on the way to Cardiff, only a forty-minute drive at this time in the morning, where she worked in a clothes shop. It was a sales day and the store was opening two hours earlier than normal.

The cold air was like the hands of a lover as it moved through her hair. However, she had no lover, just her husband Brian. He was good to her and she knew she loved him deeply, but tonight he felt a long way away from her. As she got out of bed, she saw his outline under the quilt, and it meant nothing to her. She watched him breathe and wondered what her life would have been like if they had never met. They didn't have any children – her fault biologically speaking, not his - yet this morning she resented him for it. It was irrational and wrong, and she knew it, but it gnawed at her bones like a dog with a hambone. The knot inside was tight, squeezing her very soul. It was stupid but it was there, and it stayed with her as she showered, ate her breakfast and got into her car.

She left Main Road, leaving the odd milkman alone, and turned left at the roundabout, leaving Trehenri behind her.

Although she would get to work safely, her mood stayed with her all day, as it would for the next few days. Her usually bubbly, effervescent personality was off, obvious to anyone who knew her. After a few days, her colleagues had decided that she had caught her husband cheating and had to throw the bastard out. Of course, this wasn't the truth, but if anyone had confronted her, she wouldn't have been able to explain why she felt like she did.

***

Danny Williams decided that sleep was overrated; so, at four-thirty, he put on his joggers and trainers and went for a run. He was fit and healthy, played Inside Centre for his school rugby team. He was also working with the Cardiff Blues Academy team and hoped that one day he could walk out in front of seventy-five thousand people at the Millennium Stadium, proudly wearing the Red jersey. He would hold his badge tightly as he sang the national anthem, belting out 'Gwlad, Gwlad, pleidiol wyf i'm gwlad' on top of his voice, shouting to the rafters!

This morning, however, he wanted to give up. He didn't know why, it just seemed pointless, all the work, all the effort, all for the remotest shot at glory. He crept downstairs not wanting to face his patents' questions. Outside he took a deep breath and started to run, not because he wanted the exercise, but because this is what he did, this is what he was programmed to do. He lived at the top of Heol Fawr which branched off at the foot of Henry Hill and climbed steeply to the Farm Road. Running down the hill was always a good way to start the day, but today his feet were leaden and his breathing erratic. He could find no rhythm whatsoever. He pounded onto Main Road, passed the hairdressers, the card shop and what used to be a butcher's until it became just another continually shuttered ex-shop. He struggled to control his breathing and could feel the beginnings of a stitch in his side. He thought of school, of the pointlessness of learning algebra, wondered why he was spending so much time reading Of Mice and Men, a book he found boring despite its reasonably short length. Outside the spar shop, he was reminded of his girlfriend who worked behind the counter on weekends. Ginny seemed like the perfect girl but why were they together? What did she see in him? These thoughts brought unexpected tears to his face which he wiped away with the back of his hand. What was the point? That was the question he was asking himself. Of Rugby, of school, of Ginny?

At the Oxfam charity shop, he slipped and fell heavily onto the pavement. He screamed in pain, his cries echoing off the tired old houses. No lights came on, no one peaked through curtains. It was as if the scream was expected.

He looked down at his ankle and immediately realised there was something wrong. Although there was no blood, the foot hung at an impossible angle. He lifted up the leg of his joggers and could see the obvious lump of a broken bone pushing at the skin. He felt lightheaded and had to fight to control his breathing. Finally, as he tried to get up, the pain hit him like a tornado hitting a lone cow on an Oklahoma farm. He threw up over the curb, over his joggers and over the protruding bone.

For a moment, he thought he heard a laugh; a chuckle from out of the darkness. He looked around, hopeful that someone was there, but he saw no one.

He waited an hour, sitting in his own vomit before someone drove down the street and noticed his attempts to flag them down. He would miss the rest of the season and there was considerable doubt if he would ever play topflight rugby.

***

In a bedroom of a terraced house at number 32 Garth Lane, 17-year-old Emma Bayfield held her baby in her arms and tried to rock it to sleep. This wasn't the life that she wanted or had ever dreamed of. When she had slept with Mark it had been a big adventure, he was both cool and very handsome. He said that he wasn't a virgin and had had a few lovers before, but she didn't think so. They had spent a few nights together, fumbling in her bed as her mother was passed out downstairs. A few weeks later the fun was over - Mark had dumped her and the screaming shit machine named Abby came along.

Babies were supposed to be fun; they were cute, they gargled and smiled, and all your friends would go 'ooo' and 'ahhh'. But the truth was so very different. They cried, they shat their nappies over and over again. Oh, Abby slept – in the daytime – but at night, when Emma had to fight the almighty just to keep her eyes open, the little shit screamed, and cried and moaned all fucking night.

Tonight, it felt like the world was lost to her. She sat up in bed, the baby in her arms finally falling to sleep. The room was an orange oppressive glow; the bulbs slowly dying, their light diminishing each time they were switched on.

She let the baby fall to her lap, her head bending backwards from the weight. Emma knew it was dangerous but right now she didn't care. She stared at Abby's chest, rising and falling and wished it would stop, for the pain and the tiredness to all go away. No one cared, Emma was on her own, with just the shadows to look after this child she was no longer certain she wanted. She glanced across the bed and saw her small pillow, the one with the Unicorn print that her father had bought her many years ago. He bought it at a car boot sale and gave it to her convinced that she liked Unicorns.

She didn't; she couldn't care less but she still treasured it as it was one of the only gifts her father ever bought her.

She reached over to it and felt the weight in her hands. This could be it; this could be the end. She could be free again, free to go out and meet her friends, free to drink, free to meet someone, free to have her life back one more time.

It was almost as if someone was speaking to her. She looked around the room but there was no one there, of course. Just her and the night.

Slowly she moved the pillow over Abby's face and let it drop over the child's mouth. She didn't press it, just let it balance on her child's face. Abby tried to move her head, but its weight was too much and she hadn't developed sufficient muscle strength in her neck yet.

Emma just watched for a moment. Was this the moment she regained what life she had? She thought of her life before Abby came around and hesitated. Had it been all that great? She no longer knew.

She thought of the tears of that family on TV whose child was taken. Their world was shaken, they were completely devastated.

Abby continued squirmed under the weight of the pillow and Emma lifted it up again. She was torn. She wanted that freedom; she wanted to feel the weight lift off her just as easily as she lifted the pillow off her daughter's face, to be able to sleep at night and not live continually on the cliff-edge of exhaustion. But she also wanted to give to that family the one thing that had been torn from them. Were they really a family anymore? she thought. Does it take children to make a family?

She thought of her drunken slutty mother, of her father who had left so long ago with a bimbo twice his weight and half his age, of Mark who wanted nothing to do with her or his daughter. They had never been there for her; they had let her down at every stage of her life. Did she want to do the same with her daughter?

'Her daughter': the words strangled her, yet, somewhere deep inside; she knew they felt good, even in the night's shadows.

She lifted Abby up and held her to her chest. The child moved in her arms, finding the comfortable sweet spot, and slept once more.

Emma closed her eyes but didn't sleep. The sting of her tears, the prick of her shame and the injury to her sense of motherhood haunted her and would continue to do so for the next few days.

***

Throughout Trehenri people stirred. And shadows controlled the night.

CHAPTER 8

Morgan sighed. It was as if the night itself was laying heavily on his chest. He had to fight to continue breathing. He knew there wasn't any problem with him, he may not have been as fit as he should have been, and he drank a little too much, but he as healthy as he cared to be at this stage in his life.

He hadn't been able to sleep. The oppressiveness was all around. He could feel it. Somehow, somewhere, he knew that it was external, that it wasn't him. He knew his own pain and this was different

He was sitting in his car, staring out of the window at the supermarket in front of him. The blazing white of the carpark's lights, which seemed far too intense for his current mood, lit the car park. He remembered how such lights used to be sulfur – they would give off a diffused yellow glow which seemed appropriate for stupid o'clock in the morning. When did that change? Who made the decision to change the colour of the streetlights? They were probably some environmentally friendly bulbs: brighter and cheaper with fewer carbon emissions. That was the way the world worked, now.

It was 3.13 am; a time of day that most people didn't usually know existed. It was a time that was usually only experienced by the young night clubbers, parents of very young children, and lorry drivers; yet here he was. And he wasn't the only one. The car park was busy. People of all ages walked back and forth to the supermarket, their feet shuffling as if they didn't have the energy to lift them completely off the ground. They were somnambulating zombies looking for a purpose in the dead of night so, of course, they would go shopping.

Friday had turned into Saturday, a new day slumbering into existence.

Morgan watched a young couple with two children. The youngest slept as her father carried her, cwtching her in his arms. The oldest was being pulled - no almost dragged - along by his mother. The parents' eyes looked lost yet determined to go and buy something; to do something normal.

They passed an old man who shuffled slowly, pulling one of those trolley bags that the elderly always seemed to use. On his feet, Morgan noticed, the old man wore slippers. A big woman wearing a tight onesie loaded bags of food into the back of her car. She leaned over to adjust something in the car boot, her big arse sticking up into the air. It wasn't attractive, he knew that, yet he suddenly wanted her. He felt so lonely right then, so isolated, that even an obese woman in a very unappealing onesie was enough to make him sigh with longing.

What was it was all coming down to? Shopping alone and perving over women who couldn't even be bothered to get dressed to go shopping? He licked his lips, suddenly wanting a drink. Something to jolt him awake or put him to sleep completely.

He hadn't intended to come here, of course. At home after his visit to Tal and Donna, he sat in front of the TV watching wildlife programs on some channel way down the listings, with a bottle of red wine slowly disappearing. He had drunk too much to drive but he knew he could handle it. He always did. It just didn't feel like enough at the moment.

He had gone to bed but couldn't sleep, gripped by a hint of terror that was just beyond his understanding. After a while, he had violently kicked the duvet to the floor and let out, what Walt Whitman had called, 'a barbaric yawp'! That's how he liked to think it was, but deep down he understood that screaming loudly into the dark was not a good sign.

Finally, he got up and decided to make a cup of tea only to discover he was all out of milk. Then, without thinking, he had picked up his keys and locked up the house. Now he was here.

***

He got out of the car and stood, leaning on the opened door. The night felt heavy around him, like a presence pushing down on the town. A killer holding his victim down forcibly whilst smothering them with a pillow. The car park seemed busier than Morgan thought it should in this ungodly hour. As he looked around, he noticed that over half the parking spaces were gone. No one looked at him, they were too enclosed in their own private cocoons.

Morgan didn't want to be there. He felt a terror which reached down his throat and tore at his intestines. His skin felt cold even though there was no wind that he was aware of. There was something else though. Something both beyond his comprehension and close to him, almost intimate.

He looked around, suddenly feeling he wasn't alone. But, of course, he wasn't. There were people everywhere. Men, women, children. Shoppers going about their ordinary lives doing those everyday things that people do. Fridays and Saturdays were probably a very busy time for supermarkets like this, it was the time that people shopped for the weekends, for their free times, for evening meals with friends. Others would do a weekly shop, a full trolley of goodies, cereals, potatoes, tins of beans, bottles of wine. This was a perfectly acceptable thing for these people to. This was probably completely ordinary, even at stupid o'clock in the morning.

So why did it feel so odd? Why was there this peculiar tingle in his spine? Why did he feel that the darkness itself was a blanket wrapped tightly around him, like a real, tangible, intimidating cloak?

He took a deep breath, determined to shake off this feeling. He was at a supermarket; one he had been to countless times in his life. This was no basement in which a beast lurked; no attic in which the ghost of the old maid who had died in the most mysterious and tragic accidents lived and now roamed in the shadows waiting to strike out at the living. Although it was all odd now, Morgan knew that inside, with the bright lights, colourfully packed shelves and that wonderful familiarity, the ordinary would win over and the darkness would loosen its grip.

And yet...

And yet...

Morgan turned towards the edge of the car park, behind his car.

The was a copse of tightly packed trees huddled together, providing the blackest of shadows. It was an area that he knew well having parked his car there many times. He usually tried to avoid it because the trees were often full of birds and where there were birds there tended to be an awful lot of bird shit. It was a bastard to try and get off, and he always had to be careful it didn't discolour the paint on his Fiesta.

But tonight, there would be no birds. Just a depressive corner where the light itself was defeated.

Morgan shook his head. What the hell was he thinking? he thought. Talk about melodramatic!

Yet he still stared.

It was as if there was someone there, a shade that did not belong to the trees. An alien form that existed just beyond his awareness.

He stole a glance around to see if he was the only one seemingly obsessed with this corner of the car park.

He wasn't. People stood still, gazing languidly in the same direction as him. It was as if they were all in a daze, hypnotized by some unseen conjurer.

Morgan looked back. Part of him wanted to go over there, to shake the branches and prove to his over-imaginative mind that there was nothing there. It was just a jumble of bushes, of leaves and frons. Yet he felt like the child who needed to reach over to the pile of clothes to prove to himself that the monster under the bed had not risen, was not there to terrorise him, to devour him.

Yet the irrational fear that he was now feeling told him to keep his distance. It warned him that the beast was indeed real.

And then it was gone.

A car drove past the trees, bathing the thicket in the bright lights of its headlamps. There was nothing there. Nothing that wasn't there in the daytime.

Isn't that what parents say to children? That the only things that are there in the night were the same mess they left there in the daytime? Isn't that what he used to say to Seren and David, his own two children? He would scold them for being messy, then chide them for being silly, before laughing with Chantel in the quiet of their own room?

He sighed heavily. Again. This seemed to be a night for sighing, he thought. He wondered what his children were up to now. David was only fourteen and probably sleeping deeply, but Seren was seventeen and could possibly be just getting home from a night out with her friends. She would argue with her mother that she was old enough to go out with her friends if she wanted to. Eventually, she would use her trump card and scream 'Dad would let me go!'

He wasn't sure he would, but he liked the idea that Seren was getting to an age where she could stand up to her mother. When she visited Morgan half the time was usually dedicated to telling him how unreasonable his ex-wife was. He would pretend to be on Chantel's side, telling his daughter that her mother only had her best interests at heart. Seren didn't really think he believed it and it would bring them closer together. He supposed he had it easier, he could agree with his daughter whenever they spoke, keeping his misgivings to himself. Chantel would have to deal with Seren herself. But that was the way she wanted.

As he walked towards the shop entrance, he saw an old man walking alongside him. The man nodded a greeting to Morgan who smiled back.

'Good Evening,' Morgan said politely.

The man looked to the sky pensively.

'A funny evening,' he said eventually.

Morgan nodded. You've got that right old man, he thought.

CHAPTER 9

Shadow watched the crowds and smiled. He could see their faces, their listless shuffles in and out of the super-market. He watched in disdain. The hatred seething in his intestines. These paltry, inconsequential humans, trying desperately to find the ordinary. They did not realise, they could not understand, who was amongst them. These puny individuals with only vague dreams and indefinable yearn-ings to keep them company at night. If they only knew the truth, that their lives were nothing but pustulant boils on God's arse.

They had confidence in a future that would never be theirs. They thought they knew how to live, to try to be good people, follow the laws of morality and decency.

He snorted. Yes, they really believed that God gave a rat's arse for their morality. They believed that when they shuffled off their mortal coil, God would be there to greet them with open arms, a benevolent father who would for-give their hatred and dismissal of him when they were alive.

But he knew better. He knew that when their bodies be-came homes for worms, their souls would be cast aside, no better than dog shit on a city street. They would belong to him and his diabolical and iniquitous kin. There would be a feast of human souls for eternity.

He stood in the shadows at the corner of the car park, aware that his presence would be felt. No one would see him unless he wanted them to, but they knew he was there. They were moths and he was the devilish light.

He saw the families dragging their children, the old man

shuffling in his slippers, the man staring in his direction whilst standing by the open car door. He licked his lips in anticipation. He could see in their eyes that the village was feeling something new. Something that they couldn't understand. It was something that gnawed at their innards, like a cancerous cell. Soon the world would know it too.

Then he saw the mother, father and young daughter get out of the car that had just parked in a family bay. The child seemed tired and disinterested, as did her parents. She also looked radiant. A child of sublime beauty and innocence. She was his. He knew it and soon, she would know it to. She was only four years old, but she understood more than her parents ever could. She wore a red coat, buttoned to her neck. Under her coat, he could see that she wore pyjamas. She carried a small doll under her arm – a yellow figure in blue jeans. It had one eye, and looked both endearing and dopey, as it bobbed up and down as she walked.

Both her parents seemed only marginally aware that she was even there, her mother holding her hand instinctively. The woman was about 30 years old, a little large with tight leggings and a light pink coat. His attention turned to her for a moment and he pictured her naked, her tits bouncing up and down as she walked. He imagined taking her here in the carpark, on the floor with her husband, the child and everyone else watching them. He would penetrate her deeply, filling her with his satiated seed, rupturing her insides and killing her with ecstasy. He would then grab the father, pull him down to the floor so he could watch his wife's last moments. She would reject her husband, exclaim his futility and declare her lust for the beast who was killing her by copulation.

He remembered the last mother, lathing herself in the shower and he felt incredibly good. He could feel his erection grow and said a quiet thanks to his master who had bestowed this corporeal body. He just needed to satisfy its demands now, to let the overpowering passions express themselves.

But not now. He had a job to do. The reason he was here.

But there was no reason why he couldn't have fun, was there?

He turned his attention away from the woman and back to the child.

He breathed in deeply as she turned to look at him. He revealed himself to her, ensuring that she could see him when no other could. He smiled at her and, from the distance, she smiled back. She recognised him, he was sure, and that was good.

He thought back to that night some time ago when they had first met. He had stepped out of the shadows and into her bedroom. It was a room fit for a beautiful girl. Her walls were pink, as was her bed. The duvet cover showed the cartoon character Doc McStuffins – her favourite he knew. He had been there in the room with her as the winter nights had drawn in. She was watching Doc treat another toy when her father had come in and turned the TV off. The child had cried and her father had tried to pacify her – the strong yet sensitive kind of father. Shadow stepped behind him and touched his shoulder with the slightest of contacts, a whisper of a breath. The father had shuddered and paused for a moment before relenting and turning the cartoon back on.

Tucked in bed with her were the girl's toys: a bear, a blue dragon from the show and a long-legged monkey.

Later, he had leaned down to her and blew into her ear. She started to fidget and woke up with a start. She was about to cry but then she saw him. He smiled at her and whispered to her in that most ancient of languages. She smiled back.

'No worries, little one,' he said softly. 'No harm will come to you.' He knew it wasn't what he said what mattered, it was the tone of his voice, the softness of his words and the calmness he projected.

'I am here to protect you, to watch over you and to prepare you until the time comes and the Master calls.'

***

Joseph Farhadi blinked as the bright white lights of the supermarket hit his retinas. He stopped walking for a moment waiting for his eyes to adjust to the change.

He felt tired, unbelievably so. He had been on his feet all day doing the stock check of the DIY store he managed. It had been entirely tedious, of course. It always was. Slowly ticking off item by item, Billy Bones rattling off story after inane story about his troubles with women, his troubles getting a loan at the bank and, of course, his favourite subject – Star Bloody Trek. It could pick up a brick and it would remind him of an episode of that damned TV show.

'Don't get me wrong, Joseph had told his wife,' Terry, that evening. 'He's a lovely kid but he just seemed obsessed. No wonder he was having girl trouble.'

Apparently, he had gone out for a date with Tracy in Garden Supplies. Why Joseph couldn't fathom. She was a sweet, young thing, only seventeen whereas Billy was twenty-three. She was soft spoken and still had that teenage shyness that would soon pass. She was also incredibly pretty and probably could have her pick of just about any of the young men (and older if that was her thing) who worked at the store. He had taken her for a meal in the Indian up on the high street, had been a complete gentleman – or so he claimed – and then they decided to take a walk downtown for a quiet drink. It was on this walk that she became irate and unreasonable and...

To be honest, Joseph had stopped listening and really didn't have a clue what had happened. He just nodded and agreed and sympathised. Later, however, if you were to ask him what he was nodding and agreeing and sympathising about, he wouldn't have been able to answer. It just seemed to be the right thing to do at the time.

By the time Joseph had got home, his nerves were fried, his feet were killing him and his brain had just shut down. After he had eaten, the dishes cleaned up, and Lucy was tucked up in bed early, he thought sleep would take him quickly and completely.

It didn't happen.

Neither he nor his wife could settle. The duvet had been kicked and adjusted, then turned over and finally thrown to the bottom of the bed. Each time Joseph thought that he was just about to succumb to sleep, his head would be filled with the most horrible images. Nothing he could put his finger on. Nothing tangible that he could describe to anyone later on, just a feeling of uneasiness as if he was expecting something to happen, something that may be quite terrifying.

Terry had felt the same; she had laid still for as long as she could, determined to go to sleep. It was just like her, Joseph knew. She had a stubborn practical streak running through her, and she believed that nature itself could bend if she willed it to hard enough. However, tonight, she had failed. After a while, the sighing started. She often did this, and Joseph had long believed it was a none-too-subtle way of getting his attention. *If I can't sleep, then neither can you*, the sighing indicated.

Eventually, they had retreated downstairs and given in to the urge to turn on every light. This had happened a lot recently as if the very sanctity of their home had been corrupted. Whereas before, they had been happy to wander around the house in the dark, in the dead of night, now they needed to turn on the light, even if it was just to take a midnight piss. The landing light would go on, then the bathroom and, as the lights were turned off again, Joseph had to fight the urge to jump under the covers and hide like a child.

And tonight was worse.

They had turned on the television and turned the volume up too loudly. They sat together, holding each other closely, not to romance but to seek protection from each other.

At one point, they had run upstairs to collect Lucy, convinced that some harm was about to befall her. She slept through it all, but it was a restless and fitful sleep. As they sat together tightly on the settee, Lucy had tossed and turned.

Even in her father's arms, a place where she would normally be at her most restful, she was unable to settle.

Eventually, Joseph had suggested they go for a ride somewhere. He didn't know where; he just knew he needed to listen to his instincts and get out of this house. Terry didn't need any convincing, she had just gathered a few shopping bags and declared it was time to do their weekly shop. At 2.30 on a Saturday morning.

***

Morgan gathered his trolley and entered through the big automatic doors. The light was brighter here and he appreciated it. After the shadows of the car park, the bright fluorescent lights of the store were welcoming. He didn't want to see shadows, he wanted everything to be bathed in an omnipresent illumination.

He had to pause for a second to remember what exactly he needed. His head felt cloudy from a lack of sleep and he yawned as he tried to concentrate. He had read once that the reason we yawn is to cool our brains down when they are working too hard. This why yawning was contagious. If one person saw another yawning their brain would interpret that to mean that the conditions were optimum for a fresh gulp of cool air.

His brain was certainly working hard now. It had to fight the urge to shut down completely, to allow Morgan to collapse in a heap in the doorway. Although he knew that this would be embarrassing, it also seemed quite enticing.

He pushed the trolley down the first aisle, glancing at the magazines and the last of yesterday's newspapers. The headlines seemed so remote, so disconnected from the rest of the world. Most were about politics, a few covered the latest pop star wannabe TV show scandal, and another celebrated the break-up of a footballer's marriage.

He glided passed them without interest. He paused briefly at the end of the aisle and picked up a copy of History Today.

Henry VIII glared out at him and Morgan put it back on the shelf. He knew from experience that his students cared little about the Kings and Queens of England, however important they had been to the history of Wales. In order to kindle excitement in history, you had to start local, give people a sense of the place they lived and had grown up in, then slowly extend outwards. Too many people felt that History had nothing to do with them; it was too remote and involved people, all dead, who felt unknowable. Or as the kids would put it – boooorrriiiinnngggg!

Even when teaching the Tudors or the Romans, Morgan would try to connect it with their present, so they could see the past all around them. It was the only way he knew how to teach.

He turned into the next aisle to and was surrounded by toys and games. He was just about to skip this altogether when he heard his name being called. He glanced up and saw Gareth Matthews, an ex-pupil of his, surrounded by open boxes of toys which he was placing on the shelves in time for the next day's rush.

He smiled warmly and pushed his trolley up the aisle.

'Hello Gareth,' he said. He found himself putting on his 'teacher voice'. Slightly lower in tone and more formal. He was aware of it and the absurdity of using it at such an ungodly hour with someone who was no longer in school.

'How are you, Mr Williams?'

'Knackered,' he smiled. 'Utterly shattered.'

'You and me both,' Gareth said. He was a tall boy with long gangly arms and unruly hair. Morgan had always found him likeable but wasn't really surprised to see him stacking shelves for a living. He silently chastised himself for being so uncharitable. A job was a job, and there were lots of good people who worked in supermarkets.

A man passed them carrying a basket. He seemed to stare blankly at the shelves as if looking for something but not knowing what it was he wanted.

'It's busy,' Morgan said as he watched the man.

'Yeah, it is tonight,' Gareth answered. 'Normally about now you would have a few people in the food sections getting a few supplies, like. You don't normally see people browsing for toys and shit.'

He realised his error and blushed. 'Sorry, Mr Williams,' he said. 'I didn't mean to swear.'

Morgan raised his hands. 'I'm not Mr Williams anymore Gareth. I stopped being that the day you left school. I'm just plain old Morgan now.'

'Aw, I dunno sir. That just doesn't sound right.'

'Well, it's who I am.'

'Yes,' he paused. 'Morgan.'

Morgan laughed, and for a brief moment the night's strain seemed to loosen.

'See, it wasn't that hard was it.' He took hold of his trolley again. 'Well, Gareth, I'll no doubt see you again if I happen to be looking for a toy or two in the future. He held out his hand and Gareth looked at it for a moment unsure what to do. Finally, he took it and gave Morgan a vigorous shake, his confidence obviously boosted by the conversation.

'Yes sir,' the young man said then: 'Yes Morgan.' His grin was wide, and Morgan could see what looked like pride on his face.

'See you later,' Morgan said, and continued pushing his trolley. The conversation had buoyed him, and he felt lighter because of it. He liked Gareth, always had. He had been the type of boy that always had a quick quip and a happy circle of friends. He often forgot his textbooks and had absolutely no interest in history, yet he always attended class with a smile.

At the end of the aisle, Morgan had a choice of where to go next. To his left were the birthday cards, straight in front of him was the start of the food section. He turned to his right towards the clothes when he saw the huge man standing there, not watching him yet seemingly on the lookout. Morgan's brief flirtation with humour vanished.

The man was big enough to be a bouncer at a nightclub. Probable bigger. He looked totally out of place standing between the children's bedclothes and boy's school jumpers. He was dressed entirely in black. Dirty black trousers, a tight black shirt with what looked like some sort of cravat around his neck, a long coat with buttons running down the front and huge workman's boots. He looked like some bizarre undertaker from a production of Oliver. His arms were massive as if he was a bodybuilder, but Morgan didn't feel the usual arrogance of roiders radiating off him. Instead, he felt a disdain for the world. It seemed to surround the man and Morgan felt a cold chill run down his back. There was only one word he could think of to describe how he felt about himself in the presence of this beast of a man – inadequate. He felt small, like a mouse caught in the giant hands of a malevolent and malicious adult. This man was sinister, corrupt.

He didn't look at Morgan at all, and for this the schoolteacher felt grateful. He looked down at the handle of the trolley and saw that he was gripping it so tightly his knuckles were white. He stole another fleeting glance that the man mountain and turned his trolley left towards the birthday cards, all the while trying to ignore the hairs on the back of his neck which were standing to attention.

***

Joseph stood back so Terry could lift a tee shirt off the rack. She held it away from her for a moment to scrutinize it. She always frowned when she did this, as she focused entirely on the job at hand. Then she turned to her daughter, holding the shirt up in front of her. It had a picture of a smurf on the front and the logo for the popular kid's film.

'What do you think sweetheart?'

Lucy studied the top, the same frown on her brow. Then she nodded vigorously.

'I like it,' she said.

Terry nodded agreement and put it into the trolley.

'Can we go now?' Lucy asked.

Joseph ruffled her hair. 'You think we came all this way to buy you one tee shirt, buddy?'

Lucy looked determinately at him then nodded. 'Yes,' she said.

'If you are tired why don't you sit in the trolley,' Terry asked her.

'Or I can carry you if you wish,' Joseph added.

'No, I'm fine,' Lucy answered. 'I'm not tired anymore, just bored.'

She said it so clearly with such confidence that Joseph could easily forget how young she really was.

'We're just going to get some food then we can go,' Terry said. 'Tell you what, we'll buy you some chocolate on the way round so you can eat it in the car on the way home.'

Lucy nodded again, this time more in defeat than determination.

Joseph knew that as a family they were incredibly lucky. When Terry had become pregnant, many of his friends who had small children teased him about it. They knew that he was an orderly person who usually didn't get along with children. They warned him of sleepless nights, of tantrums at bedtimes and meltdowns in the supermarket but so far, Lucy had been so easy. She settled into her sleep routine after only two months, and now, four years or so later, she still kept to it. She was very picky about her food and had gone through one period when she refused to eat anything but bix – her word for Weetabix – but when there was something she liked in front of her, she would lap it up. Her current favourite was noodles and curry sauce.

He hoped that this affability would last through puberty, although he was under no real allusions.

He took his daughter's hand as they left the tee shirts and turned towards the bedclothes. Terry continued looking to the racks, absentmindedly browsing for potential new items for Lucy. The one thing that Joseph had been surprised about was how fast his daughter grew out of her clothes. Yes, he had heard the stories, the old refrain of 'they grow up so quickly, don't they' but he had always thought that referred to how quickly time passed, not the speed in which a child could grow.

He looked down at his daughter and felt a swell of emotion. He loved her, unconditionally. It came over him strongly, like a wave. He put his hand on her small head and felt as his fingers moved through her beautifully soft black hair. She had her mother's looks, the round Welsh face and the slightly pinched nose, but she had his complexion. He had been born in Iran, leaving and coming to the UK when he was only six. His parents were Muslim but he had left that behind in his teenage years, fully embracing his new home. He had never really discussed it with his father, although he was aware that they knew he had fallen away. When he had met and fallen completely head over heels with a Christian, they had accepted it and had beamed with pride throughout the very non-religious ceremony at the registry office. When Lucy was born three years later, a mop of black hair on top of a mass of wrinkly skin, they developed a new zeal for life. He was their only son and now they had a granddaughter!

He stooped to look at her, to stare into her eyes and tell her he loved her. His heart filled with a love which, given the heaviness of the night and his inability to rest, was a welcome relief. He didn't know where this feeling was coming from this late at night, but he wanted to embrace it and indulge in it as much he could.

However, as he crouched down, he noticed that she wasn't looking at him. She was staring past him, down the aisle with a playful smile on her face.

He followed her gaze, curious to see what it was that so interested her. When he saw the big man walking slowly, deliberately towards them, his eyes fixed on Lucy, the same overfamiliar smile that Lucy gave him, all Joseph's warm feelings scurried away like a mouse in a kitchen as you turn on the light.

Joseph stood up and placed himself in front of Lucy, slowly pushing her back with his hands.

The big man stopped as if seeing Joseph for the very first time. He glared at the father and the smile he had for Lucy disappeared, to be replaced with a sneer.

Neither man said anything. They just stood there watching each other, as if waiting for the other to make the first move. Behind him, Joseph could feel Lucy trying to push past his hands and step from behind him. She squirmed as he used more force to control her, until she finally cried out, 'Daaaad!'

Terry turned to her daughter and noticed the big man for the first time. Joseph was aware of her change in demeanour and then heard her gasp. She instinctively stepped behind her husband and reached down, pulling her daughter closer to her. Lucy continued to squirm, her complaints beginning to turn into a cry.

The big man's face changed again, this time looking vaguely like concern. He reached out to the little girl, then stopped and looked at Joseph one more time. Then he relaxed, his arms dropping to his sides.

'Don't cry,' he said. His voice was deep and raspy with the hint of an accent that Joseph could not place. The man smiled at Lucy and winked. Then, with one last glance at Joseph, he turned and began walking away, down the aisle before turning the corner and disappearing from sight.

Joseph breathed heavily, aware for the first time of the pounding in his heart. His mouth was dry, and his bowels felt like they could loosen at any moment. His shoulders slumped and he turned to his wife and daughter. Terry's face was white, furrowed with concern. Lucy had stopped her protesting but continued to whimper.

'Who the fuck was that?' he asked Terry, quietly.

His wife shook her head then crouched down to Lucy.

'Sweetheart,' she said, trying to keep her voice level. Joseph could see her hands shake as she gently took hold of her daughter's shoulders. 'Have you seen that man before? Do you know who he is?'

Lucy stopped whimpering and looked forcibly into her mother's eyes.

'Of course, I do,' she replied. 'He's my friend.'

***

Morgan would remember later that he was just about to pick up a bottle of Ketchup when he saw the big man again, this time charging passed the milk at the end of the aisle. People seemed to intuitively step out of his way before the man even came close to them, like the Red Sea parting before Moses. Most people, Morgan noticed, didn't even bother to look at him, although Morgan surmised that was probably out of the desperate need not to have anything to do with this beast.

However, Morgan couldn't help but watch. Maybe it was because he was a safe distance away and he felt courage he lacked only a short time ago. The man seemed to know exactly where he was going, as if he had been here before, although Morgan was sure that he would remember if they had previously crossed paths.

As the man passed the end of the aisle and disappeared out of sight, Morgan felt compelled to follow. He gripped the trolley handle tightly again and pushed it quickly down passed the ketchup and other sauces until he came to the junction. This aisle was now almost completely devoid of people as they scurried out of the way. The man stopped at an entrance that Morgan assumed led to the warehouse. There were scuffed transparent plastic flaps that descended in long strips from the top of the entrance down to the floor, partially obscuring what was behind whilst ensuring that any goods could be transported onto the shop floor quickly and easily.

There was possibly the briefest of pauses then, with single-minded resolve, the man pushed through the flaps and disappeared on the other side.

Morgan was in two minds. On the one hand, he didn't want to go anywhere near this beast of a man. He was obviously trouble, it emanated from him like a bad smell. Yet, at the same time, curiosity compelled him forward.

He forgot about his trolley and stepped tentatively towards the entranceway. The flaps still swung after being pushed aside by the big man. Morgan hesitated. His mind was telling him to turn around, to leave his shopping and to run out of the store now. Maybe even leave Trehenri and not come back. To stay away, to flee.

He reached out and pulled one of the flaps aside. Compared with the bright lights of the supermarket, the interior of the warehouse seemed almost black with shadow. Morgan considered the possibility that his prey (really? *His* prey?) was waiting for him on the other side, aware that he was being followed. Yet Morgan took a step forward, then another. He pushed the flaps out of the way and stepped through the gap.

The warehouse was indeed bathed in shadows, illuminated not with the bright fluorescent of the store, but with a scattering of weak bulbs from which generated a stale yellow glow, like watered down urine. On his left, there were long racks of shelves filled with boxes and bags of stock waiting to be carried into the store for sale. On his right was an open area lined with the large trolley cages that the staff used to transport the goods to the store itself. Beyond that, there was a large room with a heavy closed door on the front. The freezer, Morgan guessed. In the distance there was a corridor which seemed to lead around the freezer, disappearing out of sight.

The big man was nowhere to be seen.

Morgan stepped further into the vast room, looking right and left, his eyes darting from one side to another. His breathing had stopped, and his heart seemed to be working overtime.

The man was gone. Although the corridor seemed a considerable distance from the entrance, the man must have run over to it before Morgan had entered the warehouse, he thought.

He started to relax. Whilst he couldn't be sure exactly where the man had gone, it was obvious that he wasn't here now. The search was over.

But what the hell was he doing? he thought. What in God's name had compelled him to come in here searching for someone who he was so obviously petrified of? And what was he going to say if the man had been waiting for him? Was he really in any position to confront him? Of course not.

'Oi! You!'

The words rang out through the room and Morgan jumped. He frantically looked around, finally seeing a man's silhouette, standing in a shadow with the light of the corridor behind him. There was a moment's pause as if the silhouette was expecting an answer, but Morgan couldn't say a word, his heart beat too loudly in his head, his throat contracted.

'You are not supposed to be in here.' It wasn't the big man, Morgan realised. Just an employee.

'Shit!' He exclaimed, becoming fully aware of the relief he was feeling.

'You can't come here,' the man repeated.

Morgan took a few deep breaths and smiled, a fully satisfying 'I just looked death in the face and I only marginally shit myself' kind of smile.

'I'm sorry...I...' He trailed off and began to turn back to the flaps and the safety of the brightly lit store, the worker following closely behind to ensure he left the warehouse. The light seemed welcoming; almost normal.

He pushed one of the flaps aside and then turned to the worker.

'You didn't see anyone pass you down the corridor, did you?'

The worker looked at him agitated. 'No, I didn't.'

'Are you sure?'

'Look, sir. Only Employees are allowed back there.'

'I know', Morgan persisted. 'I was just wondering.'

'No, there was no one there but me. I've been there for about twenty minutes.' He glared at Morgan and held up his hand to indicate it was definitely time to go.

Morgan relented and passed through into the store once more. As the flaps fell back into place, he heard the shop worker mutter: 'Stupid fuck'.

Charming he thought, whatever happened to the customer always being right?

He looked around the shop, but no one was looking at him. They all seemed to be going about their own business, oblivious to anyone else around them.

***

Joseph paused at the entrance for a moment and looked around. There were still a lot of people milling about but that huge freak was nowhere to be seen. As soon as they had gathered their wits back in the clothes section, he had decided to go home immediately. This place obviously wasn't safe. They would also have to look for another supermarket to do their shopping in the future. Maybe he should complain to the management or make a report to the police. That was probably the best thing to do, but it would have to wait until tomorrow. Right now, all he wanted was to take his family out of this damned place and get them home to the familiarity of their own house. He would lock the doors and windows; they would put the lights on and watch TV until they fell asleep. In the morning, they would be full of the aches and pains of uncomfortable sleep, but that was a price worth paying.

He held on to Lucy's hand tightly and the girl didn't protest. He was dismayed that the only reaction she had was not the fear of being confronted by the freak, but because she had been told she couldn't talk to him.

Had they met before? Joseph certainly had never seen him

before. The size of the man, the coldness of his gaze, was certainly something that would have stayed with him. So where would they have met?

It wasn't in the park, or anywhere else that he or Terry took Lucy to play – they would have seen him – and the school hadn't reported any suspicious activity; yet his daughter didn't seem frightened at all. In fact, she seemed at ease in his presence, as if she were familiar with him.

Joseph shuddered at the thought. He would definitely report the man at the police station in the morning!

'You ok, honey?' Terry looked at him expectantly. She stood the other side of Lucy holding their daughter's left hand just as he was holding her right. He had to be strong for them, he thought. They needed him right now just as much as he needed them.

He nodded then glanced around the car park once more. He could see their car, just below a bright lamp, and he quietly thanked the God he had forgotten about for so long, that it was so. There were loads of shadows in the area, especially by the nearby bushes, but the car was brightly lit.

He took a deep breath and tried to put on a mask of confidence that he didn't really feel.

'Fine,' he replied. 'C'mon, let's go home.'

He smiled at his wife and she smiled back. She would have known his fears, but she was doing her best to convince him she had the same confidence in him as he pretended to have in himself. He loved her for it.

'Alright, chick?' he said to Lucy.

His daughter looked up at him and nodded. There was no fear in her eyes, only a sleepy annoyance at what was happening to her in the middle of the night.

They crossed the road, passed a couple of old people who held hands and looked like they were still in love after a hundred years of marriage. Joseph hoped that he and Terry would look like that one day.

They got to their car quickly and Joseph couldn't help but

sigh in relief. They had made it. He fished out the keys and pressed the button to unlock the doors; then he opened the back door to allow Terry to put Lucy into her child seat. She lifted the child up and into the car.

It was as Joseph turned to the driver's seat and reached to the handle to open his door, that a huge hand grabbed him tightly. Joseph looked up. The big man, the freak from the store, stood over him, glaring down on him with malevolent contempt and undisguised hatred. Joseph tried pulling his hand away, but the grip was far too strong.

'Let go of...' He couldn't finish, his words faded as the man's grip grew tighter. Instead, he let out a garbled cry. With his other hand, the man grabbed the front of his jacket and pushed Joseph against the car. He let out a loud 'uff' as his breath left him. Then the man lifted him into the air with one hand and threw him to the ground. He landed heavily, pain cascading through his body as his head violently hit the tarmac and the skin on his hands was scrapped away, replaced by dirt and tiny bits of stone. Yet he tried to stand up, the safety of his family was at stake, he couldn't let them down.

The big man stood over to him and then stepped onto Joseph's throat with a giant boot. The last thing Joseph Farhadi saw before the crushing weight of his assailant's foot took the last of his breath away, was his wife being grabbed by the hair and pulled close to his killer. As the world faded and his life dissipated, he was filled with a feeling of utter despair and grief.

***

Shadow grabbed the woman, pulled her closer to him so he could smell her perfume, and then pushed her hard against the car. He pulled open her coat and roughly grabbed her breasts. He squeezed tightly and she let out a gasp of pain.

He wanted her so much. His entire being yearned for her but he knew he had to control it. There was a job to do.

Yet he couldn't resist. He grabbed her jeans and pulled them until the button popped and the zip loosened. Then he reached down inside her panties and felt the pleasure of her womanhood. Warmed wetness covered his hand and he realised she had pissed herself. But that was ok. That was part of it. He liked it like that.

The woman cried softly, although her body was now going limp and he had to hold her upright. He felt himself go hard and wanted to unleash himself and take her here and now. He could do it, he knew. He cared little if he was seen because no one would be able to stop him. Not when he was in full flow.

'Ay!' A voice came from behind him,

He became aware of the world around him and turned to see a young man walking towards him. Behind the young man was a woman with a phone to her ear, talking frantically into it. Another person held up his phone as if to take a picture or video.

Shadow sighed and loosened his grip on the woman. She fell to the floor in a heap and he kicked her aside with his foot. He then stepped closer to the approaching young man and shook his head.

'I wouldn't,' he growled.

The man hesitated. 'We're calling the police. Let them go now.'

The big man sneered then began to laugh. It bellowed, the sound echoing around the car park. A crowd was gathering, getting closer, emboldened by each other.

Shadow dismissed them with a wave of his hand and turned back to the car. He stepped over Terry's body and reached into the back seat. Lucy looked up at him with frightened eyes and he smiled reassuringly.

'Don't worry little one,' he said. 'I'll protect you, come with me.'

He lifted the little girl delicately from the seat and wrapped her in his arms. As he stood to full height, the crowd saw what he was doing and started screaming to each other. Men rushed forward to stop him but he just walked away, his pace picking up so he reached the shadows before the crowd reached him. All along, he sang an ancient song, as old as time itself, to his new charge. He could feel her holding him back, holding him tightly and lovingly.

Someone grabbed his arm from behind him, but he swatted them away with violent ease. Then the shadows enveloped him, and he was gone. A half a second later, others arrived in the shadows of the trees, but the big man and the girl he had taken from the car, were nowhere to be seen.

CHAPTER 10

The phone belonged to one of the witnesses and Gareth stared at it intently.

The images were shaky but were still quite clear. He saw the big man walking quickly to the wall, he saw the bystander reach him and try to grab the man as he carried a child in his arms. The bystander was thrown, almost nonchalantly, aside, as if he were nothing more than a crumpled-up piece of paper.

Then the big man in the strange clothes, walked into the shadows by the wall and... what?

Gareth paused the video and looked up at the wall, which was now illuminated by the headlights of three cars, the best they could do before the forensics team arrived. There was nowhere to go. It was an old-fashioned wall, made up of large misshapen stones. Weeds had taken root in some of the cracks, a bush overhung from the road above. It was a completely unremarkable wall; the type you would find all over the valleys and beyond.

He looked down to the phone again and pressed the play button.

Almost as soon as the man disappeared, a group of eight to ten people crowded into the small area. One ran straight into the wall, violently bouncing back and falling to the floor. The others seemed lost; they pushed their way through the bushes, throwing branches aside. One woman used the torch app on her phone to get a better look. The sound was a cacophony of confusion, screaming, wailing, and crying.

He pressed pause again and sighed heavily. There was no way forensics were going to find anything. No way. The crowd had trampled on everything, touched just about every stone on the wall, brushed against every leaf on the bush. Not that it would make much of a difference, he supposed. He had the feeling that this wasn't going to be solved that easily anyway, and he doubted there was much in the way of evidence here.

Who was this man?

For one thing, he was truly huge. Gareth rewound the video to study him one more time. His back was to the camera so the only detail worth noting was his clothes – his odd jacket which hung passed his backside on towards the backs of his knees – and his size. His head was higher than the bush to his right making him almost seven foot tall, and he seemed just as wide and muscular as he was tall. A real beast of a man both in appearance and in purpose, Mann thought.

Gareth Mann was a confident man - someone who had built up years of experience by getting on with his job, applying a keen sense of logic and an ability to see beyond the ordinary. But right now he felt a tremor at the pit of his stomach, telling him that maybe nothing in his years on the force could help him here. Whatever this was, it was nothing he had seen before.

'Sir?'

He turned to DC Tina Harris. Harris was a young woman who looked younger. She was eager and very bright. Probably could go far if she wanted to, Mann had always thought.

'We have found someone who saw the kidnapper in the store.'

'In the store? He was stalking them?'

It was something he had been thinking about. A frightening possibility that this monster had chosen his prey and hunted. This was the second kidnapping of a child in the last few days. The second child named Lucy to be taken. That could not be a coincidence. Lucy wasn't an unusual name, but it certainly wasn't common in these parts.

Harris only nodded.

The night was illuminated with the flashing of the ambulance lights and the creeping light of sunrise. There was a restlessness in the air that they all felt. People milled about, watching the scene unfold, and there were PCs doing their best to organise the crowds behind barriers of yellow tape. There were far too many people here for this time in the morning, people who should be in bed, restfully sleeping, their alarm clocks not due to go off for another hour or two.

Mann sighed heavily. He too had been up, sitting on the porch of his house drinking coffee, when the call had come in. They told him there had been another kidnapping and he had thrown the remnants of his drink onto the lawn, hurried into the house to get his jacket and his car keys, and come straight here. It was as if he had been waiting for something, he thought.

'He's over by the entrance. His name is Morgan Williams.' Harris said eventually.

'The teacher?' Mann asked.

Harris shrugged. 'Sorry sir, I didn't ask.'

Mann turned to the store and started walking. He tried to be brisk, to show some confidence, to project momentum that he was in charge and knew exactly what he was doing, that a plan was in place. But in truth, it was a struggle to keep his shoulders from slumping.

He saw Morgan talking to a constable by the entrance of the store and smiled slightly. He liked Morgan, they had grown up together, and although they didn't see each other very often anymore, they still remained friends.

The bright lights of the shop made him squint a little, and he wondered how such a heinous and mysterious act could occur in a place as incongruous as this.

'Morgan,' he called when he was only a few yards away.

Morgan turned and saw him and smiled. Mann stretched out his hands and they shook warmly.

'I was wondering if you would show up,' Morgan said. He said this amiably, but Mann could see the tiredness in his friend's eyes, the sunken shadows of his sockets and the pallid tone to his skin. Mann knew that the bright fluorescent lights were part of the story but not the whole. Everyone was feeling the same, he thought. We all do and that is why so many people are here in the middle of the night.

'DC Harris tells me that you saw him. The big man?'

Morgan nodded thoughtfully. 'Big man. He certainly was big, a giant of a man. I saw him first standing by the clothes aisle.'

'Can you show us?' Mann asked.

'Of course,' Morgan replied.

Morgan led them through the store to the clothes section. The store had been cleared of customers although the occasional staff member could be seen trying to get a glimpse of any action. Gossip would be ripe for a couple of days, as tiny pieces of information and conjecture were assembled and given life. That was the nature of the beast, Mann understood.

'I came up this aisle and was wondering which way to go next, when I saw him standing over there.' He indicated to the children's section.

'How come you were out this time in the morning?' Mann asked. 'You're not usually a nighttime shopper, are you?'

'No way,' Morgan answered emphatically and Mann couldn't help but smile. 'You usually have to drag me out of bed only...' He paused for a second as if to collect his thoughts. 'I dunno. I just couldn't sleep. I had to do something; it was as if there was something in the air, some anticipation.' He shook his head then continued:

'I know that makes no sense but when I got here the place was buzzing. There were people everywhere and I could see that they felt the same way. I'm not making much sense, am I?'

Mann nodded, thinking of his own inability to sleep tonight.

'There's certainly something odd tonight,' he said. 'What happened then?'

Morgan shuddered. 'I have to admit, the man freaked me out. He was like a giant, a roider certainly, completely out of place, and his clothes were really odd. I remember thinking he looked almost Victorian, like an undertaker. So, I went that way. I didn't want to be anywhere near him.'

'And you saw him again?'

'Yeah, I was over by the ketchup and I saw him walking really quickly like, passed the top of the aisle. I guess I got curious, so I followed him to the warehouse.'

***

Morgan led Mann, Harris and the constable to the entrance-way with the plastic flaps hanging down.

'He went in there,' Morgan continued. 'I was a bit reluctant at first, but then went in after him?'

'Why?' Harris asked.

Morgan thought for a minute. 'I can't tell you precisely, I was just really curious. This man didn't belong here. He looked completely out of place. In fact, I can't think of where he would fit in. He reminded me of a cartoon bad guy, just so much bigger and more real.'

Mann walked past them and into the warehouse. There were shadows everywhere and he wondered if the warehouse was always this dark. There were no windows he could see, just rows of shelves partially full of boxes, cages to his right and then the freezer. He crossed the open area towards the freezer and to the corridor behind it. He saw that it was about thirty feet long with more shelving on one side and a couple of desks on the other. Probably where the staff completed their paperwork, he assumed.

He could hear the flaps moving behind him as the others follow him in.

'Where did he go then?' Harris asked Morgan.

'I dunno, he was gone by the time I arrived.' Morgan replied.

'Gone? How long did it take for you to come in here?'

'Dunno, not more than 5 seconds, I think. He was gone by then. I couldn't see how he could have disappeared, although it was conceivable that he made it to the corridor over there.

But that's when I saw the staff member who told me that he saw no one. He told me off for being out here in the first place, so I left.'

Mann listened, looking around as he did so. He walked slowly further into the warehouse towards the far end and turned towards the corridor. There was a desk which was covered with paper, with half a mug of cold coffee precariously close to the edge. It was an unremarkable workstation. At the far end of the corridor there were a few more doors, one marked Manager, another Canteen, then two more with the standard male and female symbols for the toilets. There was no way for someone to escape down this way without being seen by anyone who was already in the corridor.

Mann turned around back to the warehouse. There were a set of double doors behind him, unseen from the entrance from the shop, with an 'emergency exit' sign above them. He made a mental note to check if they had been opened recently.

The others joined him and stood silently as they surveyed the area.

'Doesn't make any sense,' Mann said eventually. 'I can see how the man could cross the corridor before you came in here, Morgan. It's easy to misjudge time when you were apprehensive.'

'Apprehensive' Morgan said. 'I was shitting myself.'

'Let's just assume that the staff member was completely consumed in his work and somehow missed the man rushing passed him - we'll find out more when we speak to him - but it seems to suggest that this fella knew the place, that he knew where to go, where he could hide. Did he ever work here? Again, we can find that out later.

'But then it gets weird. How did he get out and around the front in time to intercept the Farhadi's as they left? The timing is all wrong. It happened much too quickly! And why would he choose this route. It would have been easier to go straight out the front door. Especially if he was stalking them.'

'Stalking them?' Morgan asked.

Mann stared at his friend keenly. 'Morgan, I know I can trust you, but I must say this. I don't want you talking to anyone about this. There are going to be a lot of rumour and speculation over the next few hours. I don't want you adding to the fire.'

Morgan nodded, and Mann could see how much this was affecting him.

Mann then turned to Harris and the constable. 'I want to know who the staff member was, and I want him brought here in the next five minutes. Morgan, can you go with them to find him? I then want you to make an official statement to the constable before going home and getting some rest. You look like you need it. I also want to know if forensics has arrived. I want to speak to them. OK?'

'Yes, sir,' Harris and the constable said in unison.

'If you will come with us please?' Harris said to Morgan. Morgan just nodded again and let himself be led away.

Mann stayed in the warehouse alone for a few moments. He then decided to quickly check out the offices, the canteen and the toilets before they returned with the staff member.

There was just too much here that made no sense. How could a man like that disappear into thin air? Perhaps twice! If he was indeed stalking the child, why come this way? The warehouse was in the opposite direction of the car park. And why was he after the children? It couldn't have been a coincidence that they shared the same name, so why was he after young girls called Lucy? Was there another link beside their names and the general area that they lived in? Were there any other girls called Lucy in the area and were they also potential targets?

This last thought sent a shiver down his spine. However remote the connection, it was one that he had to investigate.

There were just too many questions that didn't seem to lead anywhere yet, and for the second time since he arrived here, he felt that awful sinking feeling that maybe this was beyond him to solve.

CHAPTER 11

Catryn would say later that she awoke just after six, but in truth she hardly slept. She didn't know what it was, maybe the strange bed with unfamiliar surroundings made worse by the shadows of night. Maybe it was the thought of running away but not really knowing where it was she was really going. It could have been the mere act of returning to her parent's home, a different home to the house she'd grown up in, a house without her mother. A disconnected feeling of the familiar and the unfamiliar vying for the same place in her heart and her mind.

She had gone to bed late with a melancholy and, she would not admit aloud, still feeling the scary uneasiness of her trip to the clearing, followed by that awful phone call.

Eventually, she got up, creeped downstairs and made a cup of tea. She craved coffee, something stronger to give her a kick up the arse in preparation for whatever the day brought on, but neither her parents ever drunk it. She sat in front of the television and watched an old episode of Frasier but not really taking anything in. Her head felt heavy, her eyebrows leaden like storm clouds. She sat there for almost an hour, not moving – feeling almost comatose within the cocoon of her misery.

She had so much to sort out; what she wanted, where she wanted to be, how she wanted to live. She wasn't yet convinced that she wanted to be here. Yes, she had run into the arms of the one person that daughters around the world, whatever their age, always run to – her father. His old face and broad smile had made her feel welcome, not the house. It was the man.

She heard a creak from upstairs and knew that her father was getting up. She wondered if he had heard her or if he was an early riser? There was so much she didn't know about him. He had always been there for her; he wasn't the unreliable type, although her mother always claimed he was. It was all in jest, Catryn understood. They had loved each other dearly; whatever love was of course. Maybe, after all the years they had spent together, it was just that they had got used to being around each other. It wasn't a particularly original thought but Catryn guessed it was true. And now that her mother was gone, he was alone. Like the amputee who believed his leg was still intact, Catryn knew her father had moments when his wife of so many years was still here.

She felt a jolt of pain in her stomach, a spear through her gut, as she thought of her own predicament. It looked like she would never experience that feeling, that casual bond between two partners, two lovers.

Another creak of the floorboards.

Catryn stood up and crossed to the hallway; she put on her jacket and made sure she still had the key her father had given her the night before. She couldn't face him right now. Those eyes full to the brim with love and concern. She knew what he saw when he looked at her and it pained her to know what she was putting him through. At least if she had stayed away then he would have been protected by distance. The remoteness between them would have acted like a comfort blanket to him. He could have easily lived with the illusion that everything was ok, she thought.

She quietly opened the front door and stepped out into the morning. There was a covering of low hanging cloud in the sky obscuring the sun, which fought vainly to break through. It wasn't very cold, but the wind was a little sharp on her face.

She closed the door quietly behind her then took her phone out of her pocket to check the time. It was just gone seven a.m.

She crossed the street and continued down to the foot of

Henry Hill, then onto Main Road. The clean air felt good for her, each intake of breath felt clean. This was one thing about living in the city – you got so used to the fumes from the car engines and the dry heat from the concrete all around you, that you began to believe it was real, that this is what the body needed. It wasn't until you were away from it that you realised how wrong you were.

As she walked down Main Road, she again felt the sense of nostalgia she had experienced the day before. Her childhood was here, in these streets. Some of the shops had changed but everything else was there. She was aware of a difference though. It looked at once both familiar and muddled, and the further she walked the more she felt it. Maybe it was as simple as growing up, she was seeing it all through different eyes, through a veil of different experiences.

She paused for a moment as she saw the sign for A Cut Above Hairdressers and she was immediately transported back almost thirty years. Back then, the shop had been called Anne's Hair and was run by a rotund and loud creature – Anne Evans. When she was growing up Catryn had very long hair, straight and fine stretching all the way down her back to her waist. For years she had loved her hair, it was a badge of honour, something that belonged only to her. Then one year, she decided she wanted it cut. Her mother had been appalled when she was first asked but Catryn had insisted. All her friends had shorter hair - Leanne's was no longer than her shoulders – the the bouncingand, to make things worse, some of the boys would often grab hold of it in the school corridors and give it a yank. She was convinced that she needed it cut, to be just like her friends and to lower the possibilities of bullying.

Eventually her mother had taken her to Anne's and the old hairdresser seemed both shocked that Catryn wanted to get rid of it, and gleefully delighted at the prospect of chopping it off.

After it was all done Catryn had felt completely wrong.

It was as if a part of her soul had been stripped away. As she walked through the school gates that Monday morning, she could hear some of her classmates audibly take in their breaths. They looked at her as if she were an alien. And, if truth be told, that's exactly how she felt.

The weight of her hair that had always been with her was now gone, when the wind blew she could feel it caress her neck making her shudder each time. Her friends overcame their initial surprise and insisted they loved it, and there were no more hair pulling by the bullies, but that night she cried herself to sleep. It was so strange how such a simple thing could change you, not just how you looked but how you felt internally.

It was similar, she thought, to how she was feeling now.

Now Anne was gone, and she knew that her old friend Leanne had started working here as an apprentice of sorts to the new owner – Jean Stewart. That was about the last time she saw Leanne; their lives had diverged, and they had grown apart like school friends often did.

She noticed a light was on and stepped up to the window. She couldn't see much, although there was definitely someone in there.

Could it be Leanne?

She leaned closer and cupped her hands to get a better look, hoping that no one would see her and think she was staking out the joint. At the front of the salon, there were three seats, with all the adjustment knobs and levers typical of a hairdresser. In front of them, there were basin and mirrors. Everything looked sparkling clean with a chrome and white finish. On the opposite side of the room were several huge hair dryers. At the back of the salon was the reception desk and till, and opposite that was a very large and comfortable corner sofa. On this sofa were two people. She couldn't make out their features but judging by their sitting positions, Catryn guessed that they were lounging with a drink in their hands. One of them was moving their hands animatedly, as if trying to make a point.

The lights were too low for her to know if one of them was Leanne.

She stood away from the window before anyone saw her and took a step back. She thought about knocking the door and asking. If Leanne did work there then they could have a brief reunion, if not she could possibly get some information as to what happened to the girl who was once her best friend.

She stood back and surveyed the shop for a moment, hesitating and not really wanting to commit to anything. Yes, she wanted to see her friend again but, she was also afraid of any more nostalgia, anything else that didn't live up to her memories.

A car passed behind her and she could hear the bump bump bump of some piece of dance music. She had liked that type of music as a kid, she and her friends would often turn the music up loud in Menai's car as they cruised the streets of Trehenri and drove up to McDonalds in Llwynypia.

Today though she knew that her musical tastes had changed. She preferred a good soul ballad now, loved Etta James, Whitney Houston or Aretha Franklin – big women with bigger voices. She hated the thought of sitting in a car now and listening to that awful repetitive din - all beat, no rhythm. They called it R'n'B, Rhythm and Blues but, as far as Catryn was concerned, it was all rhythm and no blues whatsoever.

She lifted her head to the sky as if looking for inspiration. All she got back was an emptiness, as if there was no answer to be had, and she made up her mind. The past was the past and, for the time being at least, she was happy to leave it there. She didn't want to face anymore change right now, she was completely wound up with the last few days, the tension she had been feeling had balled up into a knot in her neck and extended down her back.

At last, she turned on her heels, turning her back on Nostalgia Lane and headed back what to was now her home. One change at a time maybe.

CHAPTER 12

Jimmy was aware that something was wrong as soon as he stepped into the chapel. It was the smell, a fetid noxious assault on the nasal membrane. The Calvaria had been his second home for almost fourteen years now. It was the place he worked in, preparing his sermons and writing his various articles for Gospel News Weekly, and it was also the place he changed his mindset from the relaxed cinephile he was at home, to the focused shepherd of a congregation of almost four dozen.

He always entered from the back door, which was about halfway down an alleyway. It certainly wasn't glamorous, but he never entered the faith for the glamour. It was a calling he had felt for as long as he could remember, and there was only one life for him. Growing up he had always wanted to be a film director, but that never really seemed reachable. He started off working as an assistant at the Temple in Cardiff, until one day Gwynfor James, the minister of Calvaria suffered a heart attack and died. Jimmy was devastated as Gwynfor had been his pastor when he was growing up, but when the elders called upon him after the funeral to take over the ministry, Jimmy couldn't help but thank God for his fortune. He never felt bad about the circumstances either as he believed that Gwynfor was where he needed to be, at God's side.

The years had flown and now he couldn't imagine being anywhere else in the world.

However, today it was all wrong.

He reached to turn on the lights as the entrance way had no windows, then he closed the door behind him. The stench was so bad he felt sick to his stomach, as if the odour was reaching down into his innards and sloshing about his intestinal juices.

He crossed the small hallway to the doors to the meeting room. Normally he would ignore these and turn right up the stairs to his office, but he seemed to know instinctively where the smell was coming from.

The meeting room was a small room, about thirty feet long and fifteen wide. It was used for prayer meetings, Bible studies, and other church get togethers. A few members of the church used it to hold sewing clubs (Wednesdays) and Welsh Language Study (Thursdays) and he had often thought of setting up a small film club. However, he always resisted as he wanted to keep his leisure activities and his professional life separate. The thought of having Robert de Niro effing and jeffing right next to the church also made him feel more than a little uncomfortable.

The room looked ordinary, nothing out of place. In one corner, was the stacks of chairs that were used in the meetings, in the other corner, the small tables that the clubs used were also neatly piled. At the far end was a small lectern that Jimmy used when leading his prayer meetings. Opposite that was a piano, a guitar and a few other instruments that were often used by the small choir they had.

It all looked as it should have, yet the stench prevailed. With a heaviness in his step, Jimmy closed the door and reached to open the entrance to the main hall.

He pulled the handle down slowly, then pulled the door slightly ajar.

The intensity of the stench hit him as if it were a physical object. It slammed into his face and he was forced to pause for a few moments before proceeding.

He didn't want to breath, afraid of what poison he would be taking into his lungs. Yet he knew that he needed to breathe to confront whatever it was that was on the other side of the door.

He closed the door again, paused for a second then took

a deep breath. Then another. He was aware of the trembling in his hands. In fact, he trembled all over, absolutely terrified of what was on the other side.

He'd had an awful sense of unease all night. He was unable to sleep properly, tossing and turning yet determined not to give in to the temptation to admit defeat and get up. Carys felt the same too. At around three that morning they had held each other tight, whispering to each other in the darkness. They spoke about nothing of consequence, just trying to keep each other company, knowing that together they were stronger.

When they eventually got up, they were both lethargic, too tired to do anything other than the basic morning routine. Breakfast, a cuppa, a shower.

Then he decided to come to work, to try and to focus his mind on something productive.

As he walked down to Calvaria, he could see the police lights flashing down by the supermarket and he knew that something had happened, that the restlessness of the night before was just a symptom of something bigger.

And now he was here, delaying the inevitable.

With one last breath he pushed the door open again and, as quickly and determinately as he could, he stepped inside.

The doorway opened to the left of the large ornate pulpit that dominated the room. The church took a great deal of pride in their hall, keeping everything immaculately cleaned and maintained. Not that you would have known it now.

It looked like a great force had been loosed in the hall. The pews were piled in the four corners, as if they had been thrown casually out of the way. They were broken, their wood smashed with splinters scattered across the floor. They seemed to have been organized in a rough circle around the center of the hall.

There was something in the middle of this circle and for a moment Jimmy couldn't work out what it was, not because it was undefinable, but because it looked so incongruous in this place of worship.

On the bottom was a sheep, its legs were splayed, broken and pulled out at unnatural angles. Its head rested on the floor; the bottom of its jaw lost in a pool of thick congealing blood. Its throat had been cut and it had bled out in that spot. Its tongue lay on the floor about a foot in front of it, ripped out of the creature's mouth.

Resting on the back of the sheep was a large dog. It had been posed to look like it was in the middle of a sexual act, a dog humping a sheep. How it still stayed in that position, Jimmy couldn't determine. It seemed perfectly balanced, as if a whisper of wind would knock it over. It was raised slightly on its hind legs and Jimmy could see the shaft of its penis sticking into the back of the sheep. There was no sign of blood from this animal, no viscera or gore that was obvious.

He felt dizzy for a moment and had to reach out to the doorway to get some balance. He wanted to vomit, to bring up what little breakfast he had managed, and deposit it amongst the wreckage and the blood.

He turned away from the image again and tried to breathe. He had to focus but the image of the dead animals before him wouldn't leave his thoughts.

'Lord help me,' he prayed aloud. 'Strengthen me, hold me up and carry me.'

He was aware that tears were running down his face and he could taste the salty flavour as they touched his lips. He wanted to go somewhere quiet, somewhere away from all this sacrilege and hide beneath a duvet. He wanted Carys to hold him, to carefully remove his clothes and to make love to him. He wanted the tenderness of her caress, not the vileness of this moment.

He turned back to the carnage and took a step forward. He had to force himself, one leg at a time.

The sheep's blood had spilled, creating a shallow pool of about one meter. There was nothing else on the floor, and Jimmy became aware that he was looking for some sort of pentacle or other symbols of witchcraft. After all, what else could this be about?

He'd heard of this sort of thing before. Youngsters looking for a laugh, ganging together and pretending to worship the devil. A way to feel naughty, and to reject the Christian church and whatever that meant in their household or their community. He would report this to the police and, chances were, they already have someone on their radar, someone they had come across before. This sort of thing wouldn't have been a first offence, he was sure. The culprits would have done other, lesser, things which nonetheless would have become known to the authorities.

It would be sorted quickly.

He stopped as close as he dared to the abomination and leaned forward. There was something odd about the dog. The fir didn't have a natural look, as he supposed a recently killed animal would have. It looked older, and parts of it looked worn.

He reached out and, with unsteady hands, lightly touched it. It felt hard, as if the fur was not covering a deceased animal but...

And then it came to him. This had been an animal once, probably a pet, but that was a long time ago. The dog had been stuffed. This was an ornament. It may have been a dog once but now it was nothing more than a decoration.

He pushed it ever so slightly and the dog seemed to move. He pulled back his hands, conscious that this was a crime scene and he didn't want to disrupt it.

He stepped back, reached into his jeans pocket and pulled out his mobile phone. He switched on the camera and started taking video, starting with the dog and then moving around the sheep, careful not to step in the blood.

Then, as he stepped back further to try and get as much detail in as possible, he saw the graffiti.

Above the alter, unseen from the doorway but obvious to anyone who sat in one of the pews, were three words:

LUCY FOR
EVER

His hand went to his mouth and he almost dropped the phone.

'Oh, lord,' he muttered, thinking about that baby who had been taken only a few days before. 'Oh Christ.'

Turning the camera off, he pressed the button for the phone and on the keypad he pressed 999.

***

As Gareth reached out to shake Jimmy's hand the priest couldn't help but be struck by how tired his son-in-law looked. He had only seen him the night before and, although the strain was obvious then, now it was etched in every crease of his suit.

Gareth's eyes seemed to have sunk into his skull, his skin looked pale and there was no trace of warmth or humour at all. His hair was a mess, although this was probably because of his habit of ruffling it when he was concentrating.

Jimmy was struck by how hard this must be on Gareth and, by extension, Jenny. He felt a prang of apprehension at the pit of his stomach. Jenny was a tough nut to crack sometimes, she had to be. The daughter of a priest was often picked on in school, especially around Christmas and Halloween. People rarely realised this. At Christmas when all her friends were talking about Santa Claus and Christmas lists, Jenny sat quietly. She had been taught to keep her mouth shut or face the wrath of her friends who believed more in the fat man with some reindeer than they did in Jesus. And at Halloween when everyone else was dressed up, Jenny stayed at home as they ignored the knocks on doors by the trick or treaters. Jimmy knew that the other children would talk, especially at school, but Jenny had soon learned to be strong and stoic. It was probably good practice for being the wife of a detective and a manager at a day center for people with Learning Disabilities.

But seeing Gareth now worried Jimmy.

Gareth looked passed Jimmy with a vacant look in his eyes.

'Everything alright?' Jimmy asked.

'Long night.'

Gareth stepped passed his father-in-law and surveilled the scene. Jimmy could see the younger man's eyes stare intently at the sheep and the dog before lifting his gaze up to the graffiti.

'Lucy forever,' he muttered.

'No,' Jimmy said.

Gareth looked back at him. 'No?' he asked.

'The way the words are written,' he said, 'it reads LUCY FOR... EVER.'

'That means something to you?'

Jimmy shifted on his feet. This wasn't his area and suddenly he was aware that his initial thoughts could be completely wrong. This wasn't just a police officer; this was his daughter's husband. A man he had known for eight years, who visited regularly but rarely shared any stories of work.

'Jimmy?'

'Um...well, when I first saw that,' he indicated the abomination with a tilt of his chin. 'My first thought was kids, pretending to be devil worshippers. You know, you see it on TV.'

Gareth nodded.

'Well,' Jimmy continued. 'When I first saw the words, they didn't mean much to me apart from that little girl that was taken, but when I said them out loud, they sounded like they were actually LUCIFER, Ever.'

Gareth turned back to the writing and Jimmy could see his lips moving as he read them. Finally, he said them aloud, just as Jimmy had.

Gareth nodded and smiled, although there was very little mirth.

'Does it mean anything to you?'

Jimmy shook his head. 'I don't think so. Nothing I can think of. It just seemed like a play on words. You know, because of that baby who was taken.'

Gareth nodded. 'There was another kidnapping last night,' he said.

'Oh, good God, no.'

'Up at the supermarket.' Gareth continued. 'A four-year-old girl.' He paused then said: 'We haven't released the details yet, so this is just between you and me, confession like.'

Jimmy thought of pointing out that, as a Baptist, he didn't take confessional, but he kept quiet. A voice in his head told him that this was important. It wasn't often that Gareth wanted to talk and if he did today then that was ok. Jimmy would listen to a confessional and keep it completely sacred.

'Of course,' he said.

'Lucy Farhadi, you know her?'

Jimmy nodded, any remaining colour he had dissipated from his face. 'I know her parents, Joe and Terry. They live up on Heol Fawr. He works down in that DIY place on the way to Ponty. What happened?'

'The strangest thing. Vanished into thin air.'

'You'll have him on CCTV, surely.'

Gareth nodded. 'And about a dozen camera phones. This ape of a man, huge bastard, attacked the parents then reached into the car and took the baby. Then disappeared into a fucking wall.'

Jimmy ignored the curses. Listening to it here in the church made him feel uncomfortable but he understood what Gareth was going through.

'You'll probably be able to see it on YouTube already,' Mann continued. 'Damnedest thing I've ever seen.'

Jimmy reached out and held the detective's shoulder but couldn't think of anything to say. What he was hearing made no sense whatsoever, yet he knew not to dismiss it. Instead, he let his thoughts linger on the little girl.

'Poor Lucy,' he said eventually. 'I can't imagine what Joe and Terry are going through right now.'

Gareth looked him directly into his eyes and Jimmy could see the hurt that had taken up residence there. Then it hit him what those eyes were telling him.

'Oh no. They're dead, aren't they?'

Gareth nodded. 'Mr Farhadi died at the scene, his wife died about an hour ago down the Heath Hospital.'

Jimmy turned away from those piercing eyes and leaned against the wall. He felt the vomit in his stomach rise again.

'Who would do such a thing?'

Gareth didn't answer.

Jimmy turned to him. 'You will catch him.' It was a statement, not a question.

Gareth nodded, an expression of grim determination on his face.

He held Jimmy's stare for a few seconds, then he stepped forward leaving the priest alone.

Jimmy wanted to leave. He didn't want to see this anymore. He wanted rid of it.

Action, that's what was required. That was how he worked things out, by working them through. That was one of old Mrs Singh's sayings and it had always stayed with him.

He needed to phone some of the elders and the deacons, to arrange a meeting to discuss this and to arrange a clean-up-squad as soon as the police were finished and had removed the offending items. The church had to be cleaned completely, then, once that was done, cleaned once more.

He left the hall and took the door to the hallway and onto his office. There was a lot to do but, if he was entirely honest, first he wanted peace, quiet and solitude. He wanted to go somewhere without people. Somewhere he could weep, somewhere he didn't have to be strong.

CHAPTER 13

By the time Morgan got home, he was exhausted. His body ached from the lack of sleep, and his mind and soul cried because of the terrible things he had witnessed. As he closed the front door behind him, he slumped back onto it and closed his eyes.

Images of that man flooded his thoughts and he had to force his eyes open again. He didn't want to see him, didn't want to think about him. To think he had chased (*chased - was that the right word?*) such a beast, someone who had gone on and attacked two innocent people, then kidnaped a poor child!

What had compelled him to do such a thing? He couldn't say. He knew that there was something about that man that repulsed him, something that had told him from the very first glance that the man was trouble. Yet, there he had been charging after him like a hound dog on the trail of a fox.

The man was obviously a threat and, if it had come to a confrontation, he could have crushed Morgan's skull with one hand. Morgan would not have stood a chance. So why did he do it?

Morgan didn't have any answers.

As he stood in the hallway of his small house, he suddenly felt very dirty, almost tainted by the events of the evening.

He ran upstairs and stripped off his clothes. Then, before he stepped into the shower, he closed the bathroom door and closed the latch, locking himself in.

He turned the water heater up as high as he could stand it, happy to feel the thousands of pin pricks of heat attack his body. He wanted to be cleansed.

Later he lay in bed. It was still morning and he left the curtains open wide, not wanting to be in the dark. He had the irrational thought that the man was hiding in the shadows themselves, and he remembered both the semi lit warehouse and the copse of trees in which he had disappeared. It made no rational sense, yet, at some basic fundamental level somewhere in his DNA, he was scared. He had never felt anything quite like it before.

He knew that he was essentially a coward. He was not a big man; he didn't work out and all his self-defense training had come from watching The Karate Kid when he was just a teenager. That was it. There was no chance that he could have faced up to an adversary as big as the kidnapper.

Years ago, he had witnessed a man punching a woman in the face. It had been on a quiet lane on his way from home. He had turned onto the lane as it was a short cut to his house. As he rounded the first corner, he had heard raised voices. He had edged the way forward and saw a man and woman arguing. He stopped by a bush for a few seconds as the tempers and the voices increased. Then, suddenly, the man had lifted his hands and punched the woman square in the jaw. The woman had screamed and almost fell to the ground. The man continued shouting and the woman began crying. She repeatedly cried that she was sorry, that she would never do it again.

Morgan knew that he should have stepped in. He knew that he should have confronted the man and tried the protect the woman.

But he hadn't.

The fear in his stomach had grabbed hold of his balls and pulled him away. He had felt pathetic. He was pathetic, even now twenty years later. A coward who could have saved the woman but chose not to.

It was a shame that he still felt to this day.

Maybe that was why he followed the kidnapper. Of course, he didn't know that the man was a kidnapper at that time, but he knew there was something off about him. Maybe somewhere in the recesses of his soul, something was compelling him to confront that shame and do something about it.

Or it could all be bullshit.

There was a tiny mote of dust floating across his bedroom, illuminated by the rays of sun that were shining through the window. He followed it as it moved and for a moment it consumed his mind completely. Then it disappeared into a shadow and the troubles of the day returned.

Morgan realised that it was useless laying there. No matter how tired he was, his soul was too troubled to rest.

He sat up on the side of his bed and rubbed his eyes in his hands. He didn't know what to do. He looked around the room absently and spotted the book that he had been reading, The Temporal Void by Peter F. Hamilton. A huge tome which was the second part of a trilogy. He thought of picking it up and trying to read but knew that it was useless.

Finally, he got up and put on his jeans. He would go for a walk, he thought.

***

The sun shone and there was a hint of warmth in the early morning. A suggestion of a breeze caressed Morgan's hair as he strolled up the Main Road. The street was rather quiet, especially for a Saturday afternoon, and it occurred to him that the supermarket carpark was busier last night.

This thought did nothing to lift his mood. The memory was still as fresh as the fatigue in his muscles and joints. The one thought that seemed to continuously rattle in his brain was how the kidnapper had managed to disappear. He knew that this question was gripping anyone who had seen the video so far which, as this was the 21th century, was probably half the world already.

The other mystery was the girl - Lucy. What was the chances of two children of the same name being kidnapped in such a small area? Did it mean that the kidnapper was targeting Lucys? Why would anyone do that? It made no real sense.

But then again, did any of this make sense?

He remembered the images of the man carrying the child almost nonchalantly towards the bushes and the trees. There was no rush, no worry that he could get cornered. He obviously knew that there was a way out. And then he had entered the shadows and disappeared.

God, I hate this supernatural shit, he thought. It was a thought that struck him. The idea that any of this maybe supernatural hadn't occurred to him until now, yet there it was. The man had disappeared from the warehouse as if by magic, and then again in front of the crowds of people in the car park. Again, as if by magic.

Morgan knew very little about magic or illusions. He watched the occasional performer on TV now and again but that was it. However, deep down he seemed to know that this wasn't an illusion. It was something more, something darker.

He had just turned the corner onto Porth Road when he heard the call.

'You ignoring me Morgan?'

He turned and saw Glyn Evans on the other side of the road. He was carrying two shopping bags of groceries and was trudging up the hill. On that side of the road, the bushes from one of the steep gardens leading up the hill were overgrown, and Glyn had to duck to get passed them.

'Hiya byt,' Morgan called and crossed the road, checking for traffic as he did so. 'You got your hands full.'

He took the bags off the old man who seemed to physically relax.

'Thanks,' Glyn said. 'You ok? You seem to have your head full.'

Morgan lead Glyn across the street to the other side where terraced houses replaced bushes.

'I'm alright. Just a little tired.'

'Same here. Couldn't sleep a wink last night.'

'You and about half the valley, I think. I went shopping at

three this morning - it was pretty packed, especially for the crackend of the day.'

Glyn reached and touched Morgan's shoulder. 'I just heard there was another kidnapping.'

Morgan tensed. 'I know. I was there.'

Glyn paused and looked at the younger man with concern. 'You OK? I heard it was pretty bad. Two people were killed.'

'Aw shitting hell.' Morgan exclaimed. 'Mr and Mrs Farhadi. I knew that Mr Farhadi had been killed but Terry was still alive when I left there.'

The pair resumed walking.

'Farhadi?' Glyn mused. 'That's that Arab couple down the bottom?'

'Iranian.' Morgan corrected. 'Or a least he was. She was from around here. Shit. They were a nice couple.'

Glyn grunted, and Morgan smiled to himself. Glyn was typical of the older generation; they could like anyone and everyone on a personal level but at a distance there always seemed to be a tinge of racism. It wasn't hatred, just a dismissal of anyone different.

'I just heard that the Church was vandalized this morning as well. Some kind of witchcraft thing,' Glyn said.

'Witchcraft? In Trehenri?'

'Yep,' Glyn answered pensively. 'Probably just kids, they hear about the kidnappings and their destructive imaginations run away with themselves. You know how it is, being a Teacher an'all. It's probably one of your kids up the comp."

'Dunno,' Morgan said, although he couldn't think of anyone who would do such a thing. Of course, there was always the usual bunch of miscreants and troublemakers but none that he would have thought had sufficient imagination or balls to break in to a church.

'Probably all these horror films you see on the TV.' Glyn lamented. 'What's the world coming to?'

They walked on for a few moments without saying anything until Glyn changed the subject completely.

'You remember my daughter?' he asked.

'Catryn? Of course. We were in school together. She was the lucky one that got out. Why? What she up to?'

'She's home. She's staying with me for a little while.'

'Cool. Must be nice to have her back. Is she changing jobs? Coming home to stay?' Morgan said then added: 'Sorry, too many questions.'

'That's OK. I'm hoping she'll be staying. She was married to a real bastard. Don't mention it to her though. It's still raw.'

'I won't.'

They walked further up the hill until it leveled out to become flat. The gardens on the opposite side gave way to an open expanse from which you could see all the way down Main Road and beyond to Porth.

'Thanks for helping,' Glyn said finally. 'Now come inside and have a cuppa. You can catch up with Catryn and tell us all about your awful adventures last night. I know it's distasteful and I know that you might not want to go over it, but it'll do you good to share. Besides, we all like gossip, however salacious.'

Morgan hesitated. He really didn't want to go over the events again but the idea of meeting Catryn after so many years gave him what could only be described as warm butterflies. He had fancied her as a teenager even though she was way out of his league for so many years. They had always been friendly, however, and after they left school they had started hanging out in the same group. His crush had always remained, but he was too scared to ask her out. This fear seemed to get worse as they got friendlier. He sometimes had to wonder how he ever managed to ask Chantel out.

Glyn opened the front door and stepped inside gesturing for Morgan to follow him. 'C'mon' he said.

Morgan stepped over the threshold and into the cool darkness of the living room.

'Catryn?' Glyn called out.

'Dad?' Morgan heard that unmistakable voice as he stepped

into the room.

'Look who I found.'

Morgan saw Catryn turn around and watched the recognition spread with her smile across her face.

'Morgan?'

The smile was genuine, but Morgan noticed a hint of apprehension on her face, like she was caught off guard doing something she shouldn't be doing.

'Hi Cat.' He took a few steps toward her and held out his hand to shake hers. Instead a change came over his old friend and she seemed to relax visibly. Her smile grew, and she moved past his proffered hand and put her arms around him.

'Morgan!' She said again, this time with more affection.

He held her tightly for a moment and the old crush returned with a rush. He was so glad the room wasn't very bright otherwise they would have seen the flush on his face.

Catryn stepped back and looked at him. 'You've grown old,' she joked.

'Catryn!' Glyn admonished from the kitchen where he was dropping the shopping bags onto the work surface.

Morgan smiled. 'You haven't,' he said.

Catryn returned the smile and hugged him again. 'You liar,' she said.

She moved back again and indicated for him to sit down. In the kitchen Morgan could hear Glyn filling the kettle and bring out a few mugs from one of the cupboards. He heard this but didn't see it as he could hardly take his eyes off Catryn. He had meant what he said. Yes, she looked more mature and there were some obvious lines on her face which had not been there when they last met, but she still looked as beautiful as she always did. It hadn't changed. The contours of her face, the round eyes and the auburn hair. Everything that had caught his attention twenty years before was still present.

'There's been another kidnapping,' Glyn said from the doorway. 'Morgan was there.'

Catryn put her hand to her mouth. 'Oh no. Another baby?'

'Almost, she was four.' Morgan replied.

'Oh, those poor parents.'

'They were killed at the same time,' Glyn said.

'Killed? How? By who? Do the police have any clues?'

'They have lots of eyewitnesses, lots of camera footage,' Morgan said. 'It's just so weird.'

'Why, what happened?'

'Hang on there for a moment, cariad,' Glyn said turning back into the small kitchen. 'Let me make a cup of tea for us all and Morgan can tell us then. You get some biscuits for our guest. I think the telling of this story might be good for him.'

***

An hour later, Morgan and Catryn leaned on the fence opposite Glyn's house watching the traffic of Main Road and the Bypass further on. Morgan had to admit that telling the story had helped and he felt a little lighter, although if truth be told, it was probably more to do with the fact that Catryn was listening. He had started hesitantly, aware of the promise that he had made to Gareth, but he knew that he needed to get it off his chest. Besides, he was loath to admit, he also wanted to impress Catryn.

A breeze had risen slightly, and he couldn't help but feel a chill but there was no way he was going to leave this place until he had to.

Catryn had listened to him throughout, enraptured by the horror she had returned home to, and he had felt a perverse excitement at ramping up the tension of the story.

'This might sound odd,' she said, not looking at him. 'I went for a walk last night up to the old clearing. You know, to see if it was still there.'

'Wow, I've not been up there for donkey's years. Is it still there?'

Catryn nodded and paused for a few heart beats.

'It is. The strangest thing happened to me. I was all alone and it was getting dark, so you can tell me that I am just another sacred little girl but...' She trailed off.

'But?' Morgan prompted.

'I dunno. I just felt that there was someone else up there, hiding in the shadows, watching me.'

Morgan turned his body to her. He could see the fear etched onto her face.

'What do you think it was?'

She shivered. Morgan reached towards her and before he knew what he was doing, he pulled her close to him.

'Probably a cat or a fox, I suppose. It just felt....'

'Like it was something more, something dangerous.' He was thinking of the man, the giant kidnapper who he had chased after. He had felt exactly the same the night before.

She looked at him intensely, her eyes seemingly burrowing into his soul.

'You really did feel it, didn't you? When you saw him.'

He nodded but couldn't think of anything to say, afraid that his words would stick in his throat.

She turned back to survey the valley, although she remained close to him. He could feel the heat of her body next to him, warming him up. Just over an hour ago he hadn't thought of her in months, maybe years, and when he had it was through the distant lens of memory and nostalgia. Yet, here they were, close to each other, drawing comfort from each other. He got the feeling that she needed something, that she had been looking for a connection to the past and that was what he was to her.

The slip back into friendship was easy as a warm knife through butter. It seemed natural, yet he was afraid of falling into the trap of believing it was anything else. He knew that he would think of her later, he was a lonely man and he was probably searching for a connection as much as she was. He had to make sure he tempered the feelings, to not let his imagination grab hold of him.

They stood there for about five minutes before she turned to him.

'How's Chantel and the kids?' she asked. 'They must be growing up real fast.'

He smiled. 'They are, although I don't get to see them as much as I should. Chantel and I split and now she's living in Cardiff.'

'Sorry,' she said. 'I didn't know, I wouldn't have said anything...'

'That's OK, you kind of get used to it. I keep myself busy and I get to see them every two weeks. At the moment, I'm the good guy. I never get to tell the kids off, never shout at them. I think that Seren is really using it for her advantage.'

Catryn smiled. 'I bet. Little girls can be crafty.'

'She's a good girl, just grappling with a difficult situation, that's all.' He said.

The wind blew a single gust and the bushes and the grasses on the hill rustled.

'Look,' he said. 'I've been thinking. There's an old man up Henry Hill that I visit a couple of times a week. He's a gruff old bastard but if there is anyone who knows more about Trehenri I'll be surprised. I'm going to see him tomorrow afternoon and I thought I might ask him if there is any significance to the fact that the two girls kidnapped were both named Lucy. If you want to come, I'll be more than happy to take you.'

Catryn nodded. 'I was going to go to church in the morning with dad. But after that I'll be free. Would about 1.30 be OK?'

'Perfect,' he said.

He could see the apprehension in her eyes again but this time it was matched by a determination that seemed to radiate from her.

'I've got to go in, fix Dad some tea. He thinks he's looking after me, but I think it's going to be the other way around.'

Morgan nodded. 'Thanks for inviting me in today. Your father was right, talking really did help.'

'No, thank you for coming. It was good to see you. You are the first person from the old days for me to speak to and, you know, I was glad it was you.'

She reached up and kissed his cheek. When she pulled away from him again her eyes were moist.

'You OK?' he asked.

'No,' she replied. 'But I will be.'

She didn't wipe the burgeoning tears away, instead she turned on her heels and crossed the street. He stood there watching her, his emotions churning inside him. There was something there, something that was hurting her, something that she was struggling to free herself of.

As she got to the front door, she turned to him.

'See you tomorrow, Morgan Williams,' she called to him. She gave a brief wave which he returned. Then she entered the house and closed the door behind her.

Morgan remained, fixed in his spot for another few minutes watching the door. In his mind's eye, he was a teenager again and she was his crush.

That was a long time ago though. He was now in his late thirties, with an ex-wife and two growing children. He wasn't the same person anymore. Then he felt a stab of bitterness in his heart and thought once again that he was a lonely man who filled his time seeking importance at the historical society and visiting a grumpy nasty old man.

He sighed heavily and began the walk back home.

CHAPTER 14

Saturday was a very long day for so many people. News of the murders and abduction spread quickly. Before it even appeared on the television people knew. The streets became quiet, the playgrounds emptied. Although the day was bright, there was a cloud hanging over Trehenri more brooding and dangerous than any storm.

Rumours spread and people were blamed. Pedophiles and Immigrants, an escaped convict which the authorities were keeping out of the news; people known to have learning disabilities or mental illness were watched carefully. No one seemed to care for the facts.

There was anger and frustration that nothing seemed to have been done to catch the killer. The police weren't doing enough; they couldn't because of government cuts; someone in power must be involved for the killer to get away like he did. In the absence of facts, take whatever you are worried or suspicious about, and multiple it by a factor of ten.

Soon the video of the incident began to spread. They saw the huge man in the odd clothes, and they saw the disappearance. The shots of him killing Joseph and Terry Farhadi were edited out but everyone saw the face. A face, they said, of evil. Reporters from the TV news channels arrived in droves and quickly the small town of Trehenri was making international news. The face of the giant who had stolen two children was plastered on every TV channel, on every TV. If he showed up again there would be no doubt that he would be seen.

Members of the public were urged to stay away from him

because he was known to be highly dangerous. They were to lock their doors and windows and report anything suspicious, however trivial. Of course, most of it was trivial and the police were soon inundated with eyewitness accounts. He was seen walking down the Main Road, shopping at a bakery, driving through Porth; others caught glimpses of him as far as Cardiff and even Bristol. Police were being brought in from nearby forces and there was a rumour that the London Met were about to send some sort of expert down to assist the local force.

The fear spread, fueled by gossip and hearsay.

In the shops, notices were put up informing customers that they were shutting up early. No one wanted to stay out late, the shadows of night giving everyone the chills.

In the Church Jimmy waited patiently for the police to finish their investigations only to be told that the Sunday service would have to be held elsewhere. He spent hours with his fellow elders in his house discussing what exactly to say in the sermon the next morning. It was proving the hardest sermon he had ever written, and he knew that whatever it was, would be terribly inadequate.

Morgan Williams stayed home alone trying desperately to sleep until it crept up on him silently. He dreamt of being lost in a vast warehouse filled with the darkest shadows. The Shadowman would appear, grinning at him, playing with him like a cat toys with a dying mouse. He awoke later in a sweat, his heart pounding in his ears and a wet stain expanding around his shorts. He spent the rest of the day cleaning, first the bed, then anything else he could find to occupy his mind.

Catryn and her father stayed home, the TV continuously tuned to the news channel. The reporters talked a lot but very little was actually said. Catryn wanted nothing more than to hide away from the terrible things that were happening outside. The memory of her fright the previous night stayed with her, gnawing at her bones. She understood it was irrational, yet she could not shake the fear she felt. She didn't tell her father this, afraid to vocalise the fear as if it would make it all the more real.

At 28 Heol Gwynddu, one family had perhaps the most to worry about. It was the home of Emma and Kyle Morris, and their ten-year-old daughter Lucy. As the news that both children taken so far shared the same first name, Emma and Kyle grew increasingly anxious. At 4.30 that afternoon police knocked on their door. A very tired and gruff looking man who called himself DCI Gareth Mann introduced himself and two officers – Shane Blackheath and Rhys Evans. He wanted Blackheath and Evans to stay the night with the Morris's, maybe two. It was purely a precaution, they were told. This was standard procedure they were reassured. In addition, the street outside their house would be constantly monitored. There would be no repeat of the failings of the first kidnapping.

The Morris's were both reassured and terrified by the intrusion, but they accepted it gladly.

As night fell, the sense of dread flowered as if it were a living organic thing. It pervaded every heart, its smoky tendrils drifted into every home. It was as if the town itself was suffering from a panic attack.

As darkness won its daily battle with light, the air was thick with anticipation. Sleep only came when exhaustion became too strong and people's dreams were filled with the thickest, blackest secretions.

The town was hoping for morning but waiting for an endless night.

Sunday

CHAPTER 15

Jimmy had taken a long time to wake up that morning which was not normal for him. He and Carys were two very different people in the morning. She liked to take her time, to wake up gradually, to drink a cup of coffee and wait to come around. She could be happy and bubbly throughout the day but in the morning, she could snap without the slightest of provocations.

Jimmy, however, could jump out of bed and start singing to himself before her got to the bathroom. The first thing he would do each morning was urinate and brush his teeth, and each one would be accompanied by its own song. He would often make up his own lyrics describing each action, sometimes to a blues tune, sometimes to a showtune. It could change each morning.

But today his legs felt leaden; his heart heavy with fear and anxiety. He swung his legs out of bed slowly and lifted himself up to a sitting position where he stayed for several minutes. Carys reached over to him and rubbed the small of his back.

'You ok?' she asked, her voice gruff with sleep.

Jimmy nodded and sighed. 'I didn't sleep too well.'

'Neither did I, and when I did, I kept having some horrible dreams.'

He nodded again. 'Same here.'

He shifted so he could look into her eyes. Although they were brown, they always struck Jimmy by how clear they were. It probably wasn't something other people would be able to see, but to him, her eyes were as beautiful as the rest of her. He was, he knew, very much in love with her.

Carys lifted herself up and moved closer to him, sitting directly behind him. She wrapped her legs around his waist and her arms around his shoulders. He held her hand tightly. Carys kissed his neck and then rested on his back.

'There's going to be a lot of scared people out there today,' she said.

'I know.'

'I know you think your job is a doddle – giving the odd speech and watching films all day – but this is really the reason you are here.'

He nodded again. It was true, he supposed. You couldn't really train for this but ultimately this was what he was here for. He had held many hands at funerals and in hospitals, and this would be no different.

'And I know that you can do it,' Carys continued. 'This is actually what you are good at. Being there for people.'

She squeezed him tightly and kissed his neck again. He leaned back towards her, letting his wife support him for a moment.

Her hands wandered down his body and lifted up his tee-shirt. They then continued around his stomach and back up to his chest. She squeezed him gently.

'You're getting man boobs,' she giggled.

Jimmy sniffed a laugh. 'I think they are called moobs,' he said.

'Moobs?' She squeezed him again. 'Yeah, I like that. My man has moobs!'

'Perhaps I should go on a diet.'

'Well, right now you need to get off your ass and get in the shower. You've got work to do.'

They sat there for a few heart beats before Jimmy stood up. He turned around and revealed his erection pushing at his shorts. He smiled at her and raised his eyebrows. Carys snorted.

'If you want anyone to play with that this time in the morning, then you'd better do it yourself in the shower, you dirty old man. Now go on, take your manhood and your man moobs and get going.'

Jimmy smiled. 'Perhaps I'll save it for later.' He said. Then he turned and left the room. His mood wasn't quite as good as it usually was in the morning, but it was slowly getting better.

***

At 11 am Jimmy walked out in front of a very packed hall in the Girls and Boys Club, the best replacement that could be found at such short notice. He glanced around at the congregation and noticed a lot of faces that he would never usually see in his church. Some were people who he often saw around town, others were completely new to him. Some, he was told, were from the media although whether they were there because they were believers or because they were looking for an angle, he didn't know.

But it didn't matter, he thought. Most were there to hear something to lift the gloom, to make them feel better and possibly get some answers. Unfortunately, he didn't think he could provide these answers and feared that many of them would be going home without the comfort they needed.

The elders had taken over the front rows - as they always did as they were usually the first to arrive - having a good gossip amongst themselves first. They always seemed to know exactly what was going on, especially Reg Williams, which was particularly strange given the fact that he was in his late eighties and never seemed to leave his house from Monday to Saturday. Further back he saw Glyn Evans and his daughter Catryn. He had seen her earlier at the hall helping out with the preparations, but they hadn't had a chance to talk yet. He was struck by just how old she was beginning to look. Not her face, she had always been attractive, but her eyes seemed to have been witness to just a little too much experience. He was reminded of the line in Raiders of the Lost Ark when Indy explained his aches and pains by saying 'It's not the age, it's the mileage.' He made a mental note to find some time to visit them later and find out how she was.

He climbed onto a cramped stage area where a small lectin had been put in place for him. He had a few notes and spent a few seconds putting them down neatly in front of him. The crowd became quiet.

'Let us pray,' he said. He bowed his head and paused to ensure everyone else had time to do so too.

'Our Lord God, we come to you today from this hall to worship and to ask that you reveal your presence to us at this most terrible time. You are the Lord our God, the one true God who sent His Son down to us to experience the trials of mortality, to live that most perfect of lives and then to return after death, in glory, to free us all of the bondage of sin. We ask that the Lord Jesus intersect for us at this time, a time when we are in desperate need for your comfort, for your guidance and your healing upon our community. It is in His name, the name of the Son Jesus Christ we prey, amen.'

A chorus of 'Amens' could be heard from the gathered crowd, and Jimmy opened his eyes and lifted his head to look at them all. He paused for a minute, not sure what to do. He shuffled the notes in front of him then decided to abandon them all together.

'Normally in our Sunday services,' he began, 'we would spend the first half an hour in prayer and song. It's our way of worshipping and of talking directly to God. It is a quiet and solemn time when we reflect on our relationship with God, asking Him for forgiveness, for His mercy and grace to shine down on us.

'I have always been wary of tradition as sometimes it can become more important than the worship. People often think that the tradition, the order of events, becomes worship. They don't. Yet we do, I admit, follow the same pattern week in and week out. It becomes comforting. You know where you are and that can be very nice. For some, it may act like a clock, so they know how much more they have to endure.'

There were a few smiles on the faces in front of him.

'You can often forget the importance of what you are doing because you are too comfortable in the way you are doing it.

'Then something happens. Unfortunately, it is often something tragic. It pulls us out of our comfort zones and reminds us of the horrors that surround us. This is what has happened to us now.

'For us, the disgust we feel for what has happened to our church is a minor inconvenience to what has happened to our community and, more importantly, to two families, to their friends and their colleagues.'

Jimmy took a deep breath and scanned the room. Some fought their tears, others let them flow, whilst others again looked at him with stern, hateful eyes. They were the ones who wanted to strike back, to hurt someone for the injury inflicted on Trehenri and the wider Rhondda. He wondered what they were doing here this morning. Did they want a call to arms? Permission to strike? But who would they strike out against? he thought.

'I wonder how many people here - and there are so many new faces - believe in God. Are you here to find inspiration? An answer you are unable to find yourselves? Or just comfort? There are, I can see, a lot of fearful hearts and my message to you is to be strong. God will protect you. Isaiah 35 verse 4 says this very thing – "Be strong, do not fear; your God will come, he will come with vengeance; with divine retribution he will come to save you." Is that enough for you? If you believe, if you really believe, then these words will comfort you. But if you need more then how about John 14:27 "Peace I leave with you; my peace I give you. I do not give to you as the world gives. Do not let your hearts be troubled and do not be afraid." Or Joshua 1:9 "Have I not commanded you? Be strong and courageous. Do not be afraid; do not be discouraged, for the LORD your God will be with you wherever you go."

'We all feel fear, that is the human way. For some that fear is so overwhelming that they have trouble experiencing anything else and that is why faith is so important because if you have faith, then that fear loses its power. It doesn't go away; we are human after all. But there is something else as well, a promise by God to be there for us, whatever the situation, even one as dreadful as this.

'I knew Joseph and Terry. I had met Lucy on a number of occasions. I have also met Mr and Mrs Downs. These tragedies are personal to me, just as they are to so many others here today. You cannot live in a community as small as Trehenri without lives intersecting, without paths crossing. When it's personal, it hurts more, the pain is greater, the fear is greater. We feel it deeper and it becomes more imperative that we remember that God is on our side. He's here in this room right now, standing beside us, among us. He knows what we are feeling, and he is doing something about it. He will protect us with divine retribution, He has told us to be strong and with Him and through Him we can be. These are not empty words, although they may seem to be by some people, even believers. So, my prayer today is for each of you to think of this message, to open your hearts and your minds to faith and, I promise that you will feel better with Jesus by your side. Some will not want him, some will have already rejected him, but for the rest of us, this is God's Promise.'

He stood back from the lectin and bowed his head for a quick prayer. There was so much he wanted to say but didn't know how, and he hoped that what he did say would speak to some. Then he picked up a hymn book and opened it to the prearranged number.

'Please, open your hymn books to hymn number 31. Maxwell, if you please.'

A young man stepped over the small organ that had been set up for the service. It was his own keyboard he had brought in from home, and Jimmy said a quiet thank you to God that there were people like Maxwell who gave so much of their time and energy to maintaining the church.

CHAPTER 16

In the shadowlands between reality and dreams, in the darkness that exists in the memory of time and the obscurity of destiny, a man roared.

The frustrations he felt were consuming him, eating at his soul and devouring his self-control. His hands went to his face as he bellowed into the echoes. His fingers were gnarled like a raptor's talons. Every fibre of his being, every strand of thought, restricted with rage.

The sound cascaded in the absolute darkness and reverberated back at him, mocking him with his own rage.

A laugh broke from that darkness, a chuckle of merriment and delight. Unlike the man's screams this laugh did not echo, it surrounded him internally, emanating from within him.

The man cried out again, trying to drown out this murderous and ornery sound.

'STOP!' He raged.

The laughter continued, insulting him with its malice. It continued unabated, a steady humourless laugh that mocked rather than celebrated.

'Stop!' The man said again, although this time with less conviction.

The laughter faded as if it were a recording which had its volume slowly turned down.

The voice faded, crumpled to the blackness. There was no ground, no sky, no walls or ceilings. Just an obsidian blackness where no light could penetrate. The fact that the man felt he could see, felt he could hear, were just figments of an imagination which couldn't help but fill the gaps where the senses should exist.

When the voice came, he looked up even though he knew there was nothing or no one there to see.

'Quod hodie venit,' it said. 'tempus adest mortum.'

'The time is now?' the man asked. 'The time for the dead?'

'Yes.'

The man hated it when his master spoke Latin. He spoke Latin, of course, it was the language of the dead, but his master had no skill with it, no understanding. The man wanted to shout out at the voice in his head, to challenge his master, to ridicule his attempts to speak it.

'The darkness is our god,' the voice continued. 'The blackness of the human heart, the fears of the weak and the quaking of the cowardly are our amber and our nectar.'

The man couldn't help it, he had to respond. 'Yes, my master.' The grip his master had him in was just too strong, the fist too tight. It spellbound him, crushing any resistance.

'Soon my love will help me return, we will rise and you, my faithful vassal, will be rewarded for your service. You will be at my right hand and you will have vast power.'

The man wanted this but the yearning he felt still gripped him. The master noticed the hesitation.

'Yet you are not happy. Is this not what you want?'

'Yes, my master.'

There was that chuckle again.

'I know what you want, you want more, you wanted that woman, you wanted to fuck her, to violate her, and molest her soul and body, yes?'

The man looked up with a prang of hope in his heart. Would his master allow this?

'NO!' The voice barked. 'You endangered the hunt. You put your own petty urges before your mission.'

'I...I' The man stammered.

'No? NO! You are proving yourself to be quite useless, Shadow.'

The man bowed his head in deference, unable to stand up to the accusations.

'I am sorry, my master.'

'Your job is almost complete; you will not let me down.' This promise was told as a threat, daring the man to do anything but succeed.

The voice chuckled again, this time it was almost paternal.

'Control yourself, Shadow. You know what you must do, you know how to do it. You will be unleashed once it's complete. You will have your women, you will do with them as you please, but first, you must be patient and focus on this job at hand. I brought you to me because you have always been loyal. Would you have preferred to continue living in the flames?'

'No, My Master.'

'Soon, my vassal. Very soon.'

CHAPTER 17

When Morgan knocked Glyn's door at three that afternoon, he actually felt nervous. It was ridiculous, of course, but he knew that he would feel like this whoever the woman was. That's what loneliness did to you. It bred desperation, a flutter in your stomach anytime a woman looked in your direction. He would fantasize about the mother in the supermarket, how she was obviously lonely too, how her husband or partner had been a right bastard who treated her badly, but now she was free of him and looking for someone to treat her right. It was often a random woman but more than occasionally it was Jean in the Library, the intelligent but hot type who he was convinced flirted with him once.

Of course, she hadn't. She had just been nice and in his head, he knew this; but sometimes in his heart, he had wished it to be something else.

Now it was Catryn.

Of course, he had always had a crush on her, going all the way back to school, but that was only because she was stunning, and he was a geek. He recognised that this was all there was to his feelings now. The desperate need for someone, preferably someone incredibly good looking.

He might be desperate and lonely, but he was still a man, he thought,

The door opened and Catryn gave him a big smile which just made him feel much worse. How was he going to control his yearnings and his anxiety if she looked at him as warmly as that?

'Is anything wrong?' Catryn asked.

Morgan spluttered. 'No, I er, was just daydreaming and... you know.'

Catryn stepped out and closed the door behind her. 'You were in another world and now it's time to come home? I know what that's like.'

Morgan flushed. 'Caught me.'

'So, where we going?' she asked, then smiled realising she had spoken like a local, missing the 'are' in the sentence. It was so easy to slip into the old cadences.

'Up Henry Hill.' Morgan answered.

'Ok, let's go.' Catryn turned to start the walk up the street.

'How you been?' he asked, although inside he wanted to ask – have you been thinking about me?

'All good. I went to Church this morning with dad, first time I've been there in twenty-odd years.'

'Was it good?'

Catryn frowned. 'It was very sad. It was in the Boys' and Girls' club and it was packed. Of course, there was only one thing on everyone's mind. Did you know Jimmy Bevan, the priest?'

'Yeah, Jimmy. He's a friend of mine. You know him?'

'Yeah, his father was a friend of my father, so we used to see each other a lot growing up.'

They walked on, turning the corner before ascending the road that passed the farm entrance and Morgan could see an unease in Catryn's eyes. She stared at the entrance as if it were something unholy.

'You ok?' he asked.

She looked at him and smiled. 'Fine,' she said.

'Still creeped out?'

She nodded but didn't say anything.

They continued silently until they came to the entrance of the long steps.

'Ok,' Morgan said. 'We can go the long way or cut through here to the top; however - ' he paused for a second for effect, '- by the time we get to the top I will show you how absolutely unfit I am. If I do, you must promise not to laugh.'

Catryn looked at the steep set of steps and smiled.

'Ok,' she said. 'We'll take the steps and I promise that if I have any breath left at the top, that I will absolutely laugh.'

'Aye!' He protested. 'Perhaps we should go up the road.'

'No way Jose!' She laughed again. 'This is a challenge and if we make it, then it will be worth the laugh!'

Morgan sighed theatrically. 'OK, but if you make fun of my lack of lung power, I am not sure if I could forgive you.'

Giggling lightly, Catryn grabbed his arm and steered him towards the steps. The contact was like electricity pulsing through Morgan's body.

Shit, he thought. It felt very good but shit all the same.

***

'I've forgotten these places,' Catryn said halfway up the steps. 'I'm not sure if they are unique in the world but I've never seen them anywhere else.'

'I suppose you see them in any hillside community,' Morgan replied. 'Just think of the favelas in Brazil.'

Catryn laughed. 'I'd hardly compare the Valleys to the slums of Brazil.' She said. 'I have often derided Wales but never would have thought of that comparison.'

'Why have you derided Wales for?'

Catryn took in a steep breath. They were almost to the top and she was certainly beginning to break out in a sweat.

'When we were growing up I always wanted to leave.' She answered finally. 'I always thought that people around here were, I dunno, not very sophisticated.'

'We're not, but there's nothing wrong with that.' Morgan too was sweating. He pushed an overhanging branch out of the way and let Catryn pass in front of him.

'I know,' she said. 'But when you are younger and have dreams then it does matter. The whole idea that Wales seems to really like itself sometimes despite what I thought of its smallness, infuriated me. It was as if the people here have delusions of grandeur. That Wales was too far up its own arse.'

Morgan chuckled. 'I always thought the opposite. I have always thought that Wales lacked any real confidence or pride. We make fun of our own accent, mocking people for sounding too 'Welshy'. I hate that phrase. If someone has a problem with my accent then it's their problem, not mine.'

Catryn laughed.

'You certainly do have a strong accent. When I first went to London for college people used to make fun of me all the time. There was a minibus driver that would drive people between the campuses, every time he saw me, he would ask what I was doing that night. "Down the pub, is it, boyo?" He thought it was hilarious and I'm afraid to admit it but it made me feel even more ashamed. I worked really hard to get rid of my accent.'

'Well, it almost worked.' Morgan said. 'You don't quite sound like a cockney but you probably could get a role on Eastenders. "Get out of my poob, Yew hain't my mover!"'

Catryn snorted. 'That is the worst London accent I have ever heard. You make Dick Van Dyke sound like the real thing.'

'Whatever,'

They had reached the top, their breathing heavy but Morgan worked hard to control it, careful not to show off too much weakness. An old woman standing on the doorstep of the terraced house raised a hand and waved.

'Hello, Morgan,' she called.

'Hello, Irena. How are you today?' Morgan called back.

'All good. Nothing a nice sherry won't solve. Are you up to the old man?'

'Yeah, just popping in. Shall I tell him you were asking about him?

The old woman waved her hand in dismissal.

'The old goat won't take any notice if you did. Don't you stay long with him, he might infect you.'

Morgan laughed. 'I won't. See you later Irena.'

'You're in with the old ladies aren't you.' Catryn said as they

146

continued up the hill to Tal's house.

'You don't remember who that was? Irena Reed, our English teacher back in school.'

'Mrs Reed? That was Mrs Reed?'

'Yep.'

'Shit, she has gotten old. I didn't recognise her. She was a right bitch.'

Morgan smiled. 'She's a lovely, if lonely, old woman. Her husband Tony died about ten years ago.'

Catryn nodded. 'I was terrified of her. I really hated her classes.'

'She's not like that anymore. Probably never was.'

***

When they reached the house, Morgan paused for a second before going in.

'Look, Tal is a very strange individual, ok. He will say things that just might offend you. He'll do it on purpose.'

'Ok, you've got me nervous now.'

'Don't be nervous,' Morgan replied. 'He'll notice and he'll probably use it somehow.'

'Who are we seeing? Hannibal Lector?'

'Much worse; much, much worse.' He said smiling.

***

'Are you fucking her?'

Morgan looked at Tal reproachfully, as if trying to convey his feelings through looks alone. Catryn stared at the old man in the large chair and gawped. She didn't quite know what to think outside when Morgan had warned her. She thought he had been joking but here they were confronted by the rudest old man she had ever met.

He was a skinny old man, sitting on an oversized chair covered in blankets despite the oppressive heat in the room. He seemed to have most of his teeth missing and a couple of days stubble covering his chin. He looked at her lasciviously as if seeing her naked under her clothes. She felt distinctly uncomfortable and instinctively crossed her arms across her chest. She looked over to Morgan who returned her look with a silent apology. His face was flush with embarrassment.

'Tal, you are a disgusting old man,' he said

'It's a straight question. You are obviously sexually frustrated and tired of using your right hand for a girlfriend, then you bring this beauty to see me. What else am I supposed to think?' Tal turned to Donna who stood at the kitchen door shaking her head.

'What do you think Donna?' he asked her. 'Morgan obviously needs to get laid, doesn't he.'

'If you carry on, he's not going to come and visit you anymore.' She answered.

Tal sighed heavily then turned back to Catryn.

'Well, if you two are not playing gardener with his cock, what are you doing up here? I was watching Diagnosis Murder.'

Catryn found that the words just didn't want to come out. She wanted to leave this vile old man right now, to go back to her house and have a long shower.

Sensing her displeasure Morgan said:

'Look, you crusty old bastard. Just because you haven't been able to get it up for a few decades, don't project your limpness on anyone else. '

'I ....'

'I don't give a flying fart. Catryn is here as my guest so you will treat her with respect.'

Tal sighed heavily. 'What do you want?' he asked haughtily.

Morgan turned to Catryn and smiled reassuringly. She couldn't help but feel thankful that he had stood up for him as he did. He then turned back to the old bastard and sat down on the chair opposite him.

'History,' he said. 'We need history.'

'You are the historian.' Tal was acting like a spoiled child.

'I know you know something about these kidnappings and murders?'

'What? What could I know?'

Morgan paused and stared at Tal. Catryn could almost count the heart beats.

'Lucy, both girls are called Lucy.'

Tal matched Morgan's stare then sat back and relented. A little saliva escaped from the corner of his mouth and his tongue darted out and lapped it up. Catryn looked down at her hands, not wanting to look at him.

'1816, Charles Henry bought a plot of land and invested in a coal mine. It was one of the first in the Rhondda at the time. Only the mines at Dinas had been sunk then.'

Morgan leaned forward, his hands together as he leaned on his knees. 'Yes,'

Tal looked back between Morgan and Catryn. She noticed that his face had changed, he seemed calmer, more at ease and less in a confrontational mood.

'That's how these places got their names. Wattstown was named after Watts & Company, Treherbert was given the name by the Marquis of Bute after his ancestor Herbert, Earl of Pembroke, Hopkinstown was named after Evan Hopkin. It seemed that every coal baron wanted to leave their stamp on the valleys. Well, Trehenri was originally called Henrytown before the Welsh brigade decided to change its name.

'Charles Henry was a right bastard. He treated his workers like shit. He wasn't the only one, of course. Up in Merthyr, there is a gravestone with 'God Forgive me' written on it where Robert Thompson Crawshey is buried. His family built a clock tower with a clock on three sides. The side without a clock face? The one facing the steelworks. The bastard didn't want his workers to know the time so he could extend the working day without any of them knowing. Of course, none of them gave a fuck about the workers really but some were particularly worse.

'Well, you know about the affair Henry had with Mary Smithfield. She was a right bitch too. Her husband came to Wales for Taxes, left with a limp dick and a scandal. Henry and Smithfield were a right pair. You see, Henry had this thing about witchcraft and such shit. He believed that if you worshipped the devil then you could live forever, just like those silly Christians believe. He became an expert at conjuring demons, and it was said he could turn people into zombies. His servants worshipped him, they would do whatever he wanted, like they were under his spell or something. There was talk of a devil chapel in his house somewhere. Ironic really.

'Why?' Morgan asked.

'Because people back then were big on their God, always fighting each other over which version was the best. The official religion was Church of English Bastards, or whatever you call them, but these mountains are full of old chapels that people built so they could worship in Welsh when the language was banned in town. They used to traipse for miles into the wilderness for privacy because the coal barons didn't want the language spoken. They were effectively hiding from their bosses and then there's one boss doing the same thing to hide from his workers. There would have been riots if they discovered a Satan worshipper in their midst.'

'I heard that Henry was particularly weird but beliefs like that were not really unusual at the time,' Morgan said. 'It was particularly popular with the French, the Marquis de Sade used it in his writings. Henry could have picked up these beliefs at any time.'

'I'm not talking about believing,' Tal said with emphasis. 'I'm talking about doing. Somehow Henry had managed to cross that divide and actually make things happen.'

Morgan nodded. Catryn caught his glance. She didn't know what to think. It all seemed a bit silly, yet she found herself enraptured.

'Anyway, Georgie and Scary Mary had an affair which resulted in a child, a baby girl called Lucinda – Lucy for short. They weren't exactly what you would call good parents – she was never allowed out, never seen in public and most historians' he said the word with undisguised contempt, 'refuse to believe she actually existed. But she did. The rumour is that they ultimately sacrificed her to the devil in return for everlasting life.'

'They did what?' Catryn blurted.

'Sacrificed her. Killed her. Ritual killing. I don't know. The only people who were there at the time was Henry, his mistress and their zombies. No real witnesses so I can't say for sure.'

Tal coughed loudly and reached around to the side of the chair for a cloth hankie. He then put it to his mouth and spat.

'Did it work?' Morgan asked.

'It didn't work for Mary, she died of TB a few years later. Henry died not long after. It's a good thing he did. There was no way he could fuck off back to London after his dick accidentally fell into the minge of some lord's wife.' Tal replied laughing.

'So, what has this got to do with what's happening now?' Catryn asked.

'Well, I'm not going to pretend I haven't thought of this,' Tal said. 'But if the story is true, I would say that Henry is back somehow.'

'He's dead,' Morgan said.

'That's probable,' Tal said, 'this all happened two hundred odd years ago.'

'So....'

'Well, if you buy into the eternal life crap,' Tal said. 'Then the next logical step is he didn't die. At least not in the traditional sense.'

Morgan leaned back in his chair. Catryn looked back and fore between the two men. Morgan obviously trusted the old man's story and, despite how unbelievable it sounded, she admitted there was a part of her that maybe wanted it to be true – if only because of some attraction with the extreme.

'So, he's come back?' Morgan asked. 'Because...?'

'There's the question. I think the answer is the little girls that are being taken. He was suspected of kidnapping children back in his day.'

'Lucy' Catryn said.

Tal winked. 'She's got it,' he said.

Catryn shook her head. 'It makes no sense. I don't believe in witchcraft or eternal life. It's all, I dunno, bullshit.'

Tal laughed heartily, which turned into another cough. He spat into his hankie again.

'So, what do you think is happening, Tal?' Catryn asked.

'What does it matter what I think?' Tal asked. 'The fact is I'm an old man whose pants are running up my arse. All I can tell you is the stories and leave the rest to you. Not that you can do anything about it. Look at you.'

'How could he do this?' Morgan asked.

Tal snorted. 'What a stupid question that is. If you believe that he is somehow still alive at two hundred and fifty years old, and that he once sacrificed children, including his daughter to live forever, then surely you can accept he has a plan.'

'I don't believe any of it,' Morgan said.

'Yet here you are. I should be watching Dick Dyke solve murders but no, you had to disturb me.'

Morgan rose from his chair, stepped over to Tal and patted him on the shoulder.

'It's Dick VAN Dyke,' he said.

'Van makes him sound like a foreigner. I prefer dikes!' Tal snorted loudly, holding his belly as he laughed.

Catryn rose with Morgan and looked towards Donna.

'It was nice meeting you Donna,' she said.

'What!' Tal shouted. 'No nice words for me. If I was any younger, I'd grab you by your pussy and carry you upstairs.' He laughed then coughed once more.

'You wouldn't have been able to keep up, old man.' She answered icily.

'Ha! I like you! Morgan, when you get her home don't forget to give her a good rogering. Neither of you are entirely damaged goods and both could do with a bit of porking the pig! Forgive me if I don't get up, my dear.'

Morgan shook his head. 'Well, that's a first. He likes you.'

'I'm honoured,' Catryn replied dryly.

They moved towards the door, Donna following behind.

'I do like you!' Tal called to them. 'You have a great rack and a real nice arse!'

As they opened the door into the early evening, his laughter followed by another bout of coughing, trailed them.

As they stepped out into the street Catryn asked Donna:

'What a peculiar old man. How do you put up with him?'

Donna smiled. 'Drugs, alcohol and dreams of smothering him in his sleep,' she said.

***

'So, what do you think?' Catryn asked.

They were walking down the road having chosen to avoid the steps because of the growing late afternoon shadows. They passed houses, all terraced, each door opening directly onto the pavement. The street was narrow, made narrower by the cars that seemed to be parked everywhere; it would be impossible for two vehicles to pass each other if they were coming in opposite directions. This is one thing that had struck Catryn over the last few days. Surely there hadn't been as many cars here when she was growing up.

'Dunno,' Morgan replied. 'He may be a horrible old man, but he tends to know what he is talking about.'

'How does he know all this?'

'He used to be a journalist and local historian. Always told me that it was better to talk to people than to try and read ridiculous books. He was always a huge proponent of oral history. That way you could pick up the local legends and gossip, instead of just the official versions of history.'

'That leaves a lot of room for interpretation and error.' Catryn said.

'Yes, but you also get a different side to things and in cases like this, more detail.'

'So, you believe him?'

Morgan fell silent for a moment as he considered this question.

'It's way beyond my experience or my learning, however, I won't discount that these things happened.' He said. 'Lots of people had strange beliefs at that time.'

'Yeah, but he was talking about more than just belief.'

'Well, this is way beyond me,' Morgan sighed. 'I've no real idea. To say it happened two hundred years ago is one thing, to say it is happening today, here in Trehenri, is a whole new ball game.'

'Let's pop down to Jimmy Bevan's house,' Catryn said as if deciding something.

'You think he'll know just because he's a priest?'

'He'll know more than us and, besides, if he hasn't changed over the last few years, if he doesn't have any theological answers, he's probably seen a film about it.'

***

They walked together down the hill as the sun was already starting its descent down behind the surrounding hills, and the shadows were growing longer. The night would not be long coming.

CHAPTER 18

Gareth Mann sat on a chair in the church hall. It was a folding chair he had found in the office upstairs. He had carried it down and placed it within a few feet of the monstrosity that dominated what was supposed to have been a room for God. The forensics team had been and had meticulously checked the place over, and now they were waiting to take it away so a more thorough analysis could be conducted. So far, no clues were found.

He was waiting for some expert from Cardiff University to see it, and they were due any moment now, so in the meantime he just sat and stared.

They had decided to leave the thing intact overnight before taking it out. This was partly because they were currently extremely stretched and tracking the Shadowman, as everyone seemed to be calling him now, was the priority. Deep down, Mann knew that this was linked, but not everyone agreed with him. They seemed to think it was just kids who had been inspired by the events overshadowing the village right now.

DC Tina Harris stood opposite him in the doorway, leaning on the frame. She watched him intently. He understood that she was focusing on him because she didn't want to look at the dog and sheep thing before her. She had told him earlier that it gave her the creeps; why would anyone want to do something as sick as this? It was beyond her realms of experience.

Mann agreed. There had been nothing in his life that could have prepared him for the last few days. Nothing he had learned, nothing he had ever imagined.

He knew that he was a small-minded man. Not in the

petty, self-righteous way that some people are, but because of the simple fact that he had been born in this village, he had married in this chapel, that he had lived his whole life in these valleys. He had travelled, mostly to Europe, and he had always insisted on leaving the pool area and experiencing the country, to explore the towns and the villages that most tourists ignored. Jenny was happy to relax, to catch a tan and to read a few books, but that would have bored him senseless. He was also fairly well read, having had a few years in his late teens and early twenties when he devoured the classics – Dickens, a few Russians, some gothic masterpieces.

Yet, despite all this, he understood that his outlook was very limited. And that was fine.

He had found and married a fabulous woman – a valley's girl just as he was a valley's boy. He had never had any desire to move, to live anywhere else. Yes, he admired those who upped sticks and went down under – the sun, the surf and the sand certainly looked appealing - but not enough for him to imagine making such a move himself.

This was who he was: a small-town man with a small-town mentality.

Yet, small towns weren't supposed to be like this. This giant who could disappear into walls; kidnappings and murders; sacrilege and fear.

The south Wales valleys were certainly not idyllic. No one living here would ever claim them to be such a thing. There was too much poverty, too many social problems, too many drugs and the crime that came with it. People knew this and, whilst not happy with it, they still accepted it. They lived with it.

These crimes, these problems, were what he had been trained for. Murders were rare but usually solved very quickly – the victim invariably knew their killer. You could see the clues, you could process the scene, you could get a pretty good handle on the situation very quickly. But this...

This was beyond him.

He felt like he was floundering, he was completely out of his depth. He wasn't in charge anymore. The London Met had sent down a team to assist and, even though they insisted their job as to back him up, he knew that it was his job to keep out of their way. And that pissed him off even further.

He looked over to Harris and saw the same feelings, the same thoughts in her eyes. They had gone over the videos of that man disappearing time and time again. From numerous angles, phones and qualities. None of it made any sense. A digger had been brought in and part of the carpark wall had been removed, causing havoc to motorists on the bypass above it, but there was nothing there. This inability to comprehend was even more terrifying than the crimes themselves. He had seen murders but never this. This wasn't reality, it was the supernatural.

He reached up to his tie, and straightened and tightened the knot. This was his habit. He could wear the same suit for days on end and wouldn't care if it was rumpled or creased, but his tie was always perfect. He even kept a few replacements back at the station. When he had first left school, he took a job as a door to door salesman. Basically, his job was to knock on doors and try to convince people to buy into a scheme which would give them discounts at restaurants etc. It was a bit of a scam, he supposed but he was good at it and, for a little over six months, he had made as much of a living out of it as was needed by someone so young and without any responsibilities. The man who trained him – a very slick fella by the name of Carson Williams – would always straighten his tie just before he knocked on a door and insisted Mann do the same. The first time he had knocked a door himself he got a sale and the tie thing became good luck. This soon turned into a habit and it had remained with him to this day.

He heard the entrance door open and Harris turned around, her posture immediately on the defensive. She left the room for a moment and came back with a small but immaculately dressed man. He was completely bald, and his head had a bit of a sheen to it that seemed to catch the overhead lights. He wore a dark business suit and a bright red tie, and Mann couldn't help but be reminded of Donald Trump – at least from the neck down.

'Boss, this is Dr Bedford, from Cardiff Uni,' Harris said.

'Medford,' the man said, thrusting out his hand with purposeful energy. 'Harold Medford. Nice to meet you.'

Mann took his hand and shook it. Medford's grip was strong, and the shake was vigorous. The doctor then turned his full attention to the display in front of them.

'Oh my,' he said.

He walked around it with his hands behind his back, stooping occasionally to get a better view. The silence dragged on for a second and for some reason Mann felt annoyed with it.

'We figured it was some, I don't know, Satanic message or something,' hjinne said.

Medford didn't say anything. He just carried on inspecting, occasionally grunting but nothing else. As he finished his inspection he stopped and stroked his chin.

'There is also the message on the wall,' Mann said pointing behind the altar.

Medford frowned and slowly walked towards the writing.

'It was written in the sheep's blood?' he asked.

'Yes,' Mann replied. 'We were wondering if it was a play on words.'

Medford turned to the detective. 'How so?' he asked.

'Well, as the girls who were taken were both named Lucy, we also thought that the comma after the word 'FOR' makes the message read 'Lucifer, Ever.''

Medford nodded. 'Yes, very clever. However, based on what I can see, I don't think this is Satanic. Demonic maybe, but not Satanic.'

'Is there a difference?' Mann asked.

'There is but to a layman it may sound like we are talking semantics. The devil, it is said, was – or is, if you believe that sort of thing – an angel who fell from heaven. Some say he was, as other angels are supposed to be, a figure of goodness and of love but became foolish with pride and, instead of serving God, he became "the adversary". In fact, that is what the word "Satan" means. He became an opponent of God. This is why he seduced Eve in the Garden of Eden.

'That didn't stop him talking to God though, in fact, in the Book of Job, God and Satan have a conversation about Job, and Satan, in effect, bets God that he could make a good man renounce his faith. God even gives Satan permission to try this. Of course, he failed, and Satan is sent away in shame.

'Demons, on the other hand, can mean many things. They are sometimes depicted as bodiless, yet very intelligent beings – Jesus himself came across them on multiple occasions – you know the story of Jesus casting out the demons from a man and into some pigs and then driving them into a lake where they drowned? It's in Mark, chapter 5, I believe.'

Mann nodded. He knew the story and remembered discussing it with Jimmy. The ending of the classic film The Exorcist was loosely based on it.

'Many people think that demons are basically the Devil's army, but this is not always the case. Sometimes they are just evil spirits without any direction or purpose other than to cause trouble. Various forms of them turn up in all the major supernatural religions – in Islam they are sometimes called Jinn; in Hinduism, they are often the disembodied souls of people who, in their previous existence, did extraordinarily bad things. I'm not an expert in demonology as there are a vast number of interpretations, however, judging from what I can see here, I can confidently say that this is not about Satan.'

'So, the words mean nothing?' Mann asked.

'I'm not saying that. It is entirely possible for a demon to pretend to be Satan. It's entirely within character, so to speak.'

Mann nodded again.

'The demon in the film The Exorcist claims to be the devil at one point, if I remember correctly,' he said.

Medford shook his finger at the detective. 'That's right. Are you a fan of that film?'

'My father-in-law is; he's a film buff.'

'Ahh,' Medford stepped back and seemed to survey the church hall. 'It feels a little odd talking about these things in a hall like this, doesn't it? Best not tell the minister what we're discussing The Exorcist. He might have a funny turn.' He laughed, obviously enjoying his little joke.

Mann couldn't help by smile. 'My father-in-law is the pastor of this church,' he said.

He glanced at Harris who was also smiling.

'Oh,' Medford said. He seemed a little flustered for a moment and busied himself by studying the display again.

'So, this is not Satanism?' Mann prompted after a few moments.

'No. This might sound a bit strange so please bear with me. Imagine, if you will, that demons are real, yes?'

'OK.'

'Well, this sort of thing could easily be done by a demon, one that was trying to assert itself. The sheep would represent God or one of His flock. The Bible is replete with images of God as a shepherd and the people as His flock. The dog is more interesting. History is full of images of demon dogs from Cerberus the three-headed dog that guards the entrance to Hades, to *Okuri-Inu* in Japan. Even in Britain, we have our own versions, like the Mauthe dog on the Isle of White. The positioning of the dog is significant. It looks like it is raping the sheep and is, therefore, raping the people of God. You could take it further and say that the attack is actually on God Himself.

'The words to are a way of asserting the demon's will on the situation. It is claiming that it has the power of the devil, that it is equal to Satan itself. You were right to say that it is a play on words, but it is also much more. It is a declaration of some sort.'

Mann frowned.

'Ok,' he said. 'Everything you just said probably makes some sense if demons existed. However, they don't. The perpetrator is obviously human. So how would you account for that?

'Well,' Medford replied. 'I am a Semiologist, not a psychiatrist however, does that really matter? I mean, if a person believes in this sort of thing, then surely it is possible that he may see himself as a demon. If that is the case, then it doesn't really matter if demons exist at all. Throughout history, the deeds of man have been accredited to the supernatural. It is a legitimate way for people who have little learning but a lot of fear, to explain anomalies in human nature.

'Think of the famous Salem Witch Trials in Massachusetts. That all started with two young children experiencing what was probably very severe epileptic fits. It was beyond the experience of the people of that small and very religious town. This was a time when the unexplained became the supernatural and to explain it in any other way would have led to you being denounced as a heretic. To deny the existence of the devil is to deny the existence of God himself.

'Surely, a deranged individual with a belief in the supernatural could do such a thing. He doesn't believe he's the devil, but he does want to assert himself somehow and this could be it.'

'So, you are saying that someone believing they are a demon, is kidnapping children and killing their families?' Harris asked.

'I'm not saying that precisely.' Medford waved his hands in front of him. 'I'm just giving a possibility based on the symbolism in front of me. It is obviously linked to the kidnappings, even if all this was done by someone inspired by the strange images on TV of that man disappearing, and not by the man himself. By the way – is that footage real?'

Mann nodded but didn't say anything. He reached up and adjusted his tie again.

'My goodness,' Medford continued. 'Without seeming facetious or flippant, it is almost as if the man is supernatural after all. Not that I believe in that sort of thing, yet...'

He trailed off and silence fell on the wall. Mann looked up and saw Harris looking at him. She tilted her head slightly to the professor. Mann nodded.

'Dr. Medford?' Harris asked. 'Thanks for coming today. You have given as a great deal to think about.'

'Oh my.' Medford said, 'Anything I can do, anything at all.'

'If you'll just come this way please?'

Harris led Medford out of the church hall leaving Mann alone. He looked at the dog astride the sheep but in his mind's eye, he just saw the image of the killer disappearing into the shadows.

Maybe he really is a demon, he thought, but if he was trying to assert himself, the obvious question was against who?

CHAPTER 19

Jimmy didn't hear anything when the doorbell rang. He sat on the settee, his feet up on a rest, headphones covering his ears and watching the television. Carys sat beside him reading a book. This was often the ritual for the couple; he would take over the TV and watch one of his several hundred DVDs or Blu-rays, headphones on so as not to interrupt his wife who liked nothing more than curling up with a good potboiler. It suited them both, allowing them to indulge their hobbies whilst staying close together.

Occasionally Carys would watch a film with him but not very often. His taste was often a little too niche for her, liking as he did foreign, old and sometimes incomprehensible films. She preferred a straightforward plot, something with a few twists maybe and a good finale. Silent Japanese or Avant Garde French films were just too far for her simple tastes.

Tonight, Jimmy needed the familiar ritual more than ever. The disgusting vandalism of the church and the violence that had erupted in his village had rocked him to the core. He was tense; when standing he paced, when sitting he fidgeted. He didn't want to put on a film, it was Carys who had persuaded him. In fact, she had to manoeuvre him to the sofa and forced him to watch something. She had even selected the film for him too, knowing his love for the Japanese Master Yasujiro Ozu.

And it had worked. As he began watching the slow, methodical precision of Ozu and began laughing at the antics of the three businessmen around whom the story revolved, his body began to uncurl, his muscles started to relax. He wasn't fully aware of this – he was soon fully immersed in the film – but, subconsciously, he could feel it.

He was barely aware of Carys getting up, methodically placing her bookmark in the right place before setting it down on the coffee table and leaving the room. He wasn't aware of her returning a few moments later until she reached down to the remote control beside him and paused his film.

'What?' he turned around, feeling a little confused, then felt more bewilderment when he saw Morgan Williams and Catryn Evans standing in the doorway looking a little sheepish.

'Oh, hi,' he said, as he slipped his headphones down around his neck. 'Catryn, Mogs. Come in, come in.'

The two guests entered the room and Carys told them to sit down.

'Shw mae, pastor,' Morgan said. 'Sorry to disturb your film.'

'Don't worry about him,' Carys said from the doorway. 'He's seen this one hundreds of times. I've never seen it but I could tell you all about it.' She smiled.

'Don't mind her,' Jimmy said. 'She hasn't got any taste. Smw mae Mogsy, Catryn welcome. What brings you to these parts?'

'Just needed to ask you a few things if you don't mind,' Carys asked.

'Can I get you a cup of tea,' asked Carys.

The visitors both said yes, and Jimmy asked for water. Carys then left the room, leaving the three of them to chat.

'What you watching?' Morgan asked.

'Late Autumn,' Jimmy answered.

'Not heard of it.'

'It's a real classic. It's about three old businessmen who set out to find a husband for the daughter of an old friend of theirs' who died a few years previous. Things get complicated when it turns out that the daughter doesn't want to marry because she doesn't want to leave her mother alone, so they set out to find the mother a husband as well. I love it, the director is one of my favourites.'

'It looks old.'

'1960' Jimmy said. 'If you have come here to talk movies then you'd better bring a sleeping bag because I could go on all night. However, as I'm the only person I know outside of Twitter that loves these movies, I would imagine you are here for another reason.'

There was silence for a moment, and then Morgan asked: 'You're on twitter?'

'Yes, it's the perfect place to speak to cinephiles around the world.'

There was more silence.

'We've just been up to see Tal, up on Henry Hill.' Morgan said.

Jimmy smiled. 'Tal? How is the old curmudgeon? Was he all sweetness and light as usual?'

Morgan smiled. 'He is who he always is.'

'And how did you find him, Catryn. He's a very singular person, isn't he?'

Carys didn't even try to hide her disgust at the old man.

'He's a filthy, vile old man,' she said.

Both Jimmy and Morgan laughed.

'He certainly is,' Jimmy said. 'Always has been and if you said it to his face he would probably take it as a compliment. That's who he is. Suffice to say that he and I don't get on but then again, I don't think he gets on with anyone. Both Mogsy here and Donna, especially Donna, are modern day saints for the abuse they put up with from him.'

'You get used to him,' Morgan said.

'But why would you take Catryn, a novice to the seductive charms of old Taliesin?'

'We wanted some information about the connection between Trehenri and the name Lucy.'

Jimmy became serious in an instant. The calmness of only a few moments earlier seemed to dissipate almost immediately.

'Well, I didn't expect that, although I suppose Tal is the right person if you want to know the history of Trehenri.'

'He told us a lot,' Catryn said, 'I'm not sure I believe any of it, but it was certainly interesting.'

Between them, Catryn and Morgan recounted the story that they had been told earlier in the evening. As they spoke Carys left and returned a few minutes later with a tray of tea and biscuits. She sat next to her husband and listened to the story.

'Well, ok,' Jimmy said at the end of it. 'That's quite a story. And you two seem to believe it.'

'I'm not sure. Some of it seemed ok, but other parts were, I don't know.' Catryn said shaking her head.

'I've heard a lot of strange stories about Charles Henry,' Morgan said. 'I can believe that he had a daughter. And I know he had some, shall we say, unorthodox beliefs. Obviously, the rest sounds like a horror story.'

'I can tell you one thing,' Carys said. 'That old house is odd. I went up there for a walk once with the dog but we stopped before we got too far, and he refused to carry on. We turned back without me being able to see much but, I don't know, it felt odd.'

Jimmy nodded. 'Yeah. I've lived in Trehenri most of my life and only ever went up there once. I used to visit a member of the church up there. You remember Mrs Cranley?' he said to his wife.

She nodded. 'Flora.'

'That's right. I used to go up and see her occasionally-, after she got too ill to leave her house. She used to live at number 1 Henry Hill, right at the top at the point where the road ends and the lane to the Hall begins. There's a gorgeous view up there, you can see for miles down the valley. It's stunning. She had lived there almost all her life. She was born there, moved away briefly when she got married but when her father passed, she and her husband moved in to look after her mother. I remember mentioning to her how beautiful the area was and how lucky she was to live in a place on the very edge of the countryside. I said she probably had run up and down the lane as a child, playing hide and seek and stuff.

'I remember her face turned harsh and she almost spat her words out. "No one plays up by the hall," she said. "No kids would ever go near it."

'I laughed and said something about that being hard to believe and she grabbed me by the arm and said that I should take a look for myself. "The place is evil," she said. "You go see yourself!" Then she shook her head and told me, on second thoughts, not to go there at all. It was all very dramatic and, I hope this is not too unkind to old Flora because she was a lovely woman, but it was also so very clichéd.

'So, being a lover of drama, that afternoon I felt I had no choice, so I took a stroll up there to take a look for myself. It certainly didn't look like it had been abandoned for two hundred years or so. It looked odd. On the one hand, it looked as if someone had maintained it, but, at the same time, I remember one window was broken and a tree branch has extended into an upper room. But that was the only one. All the other windows were intact. What's the chances of that? Think about it. How many old abandoned houses survive the flying stones of naughty kids? None. Yet Henry House was almost completely intact.'

'So, are you saying you believe there is something supernatural going on?' asked Catryn.

'I didn't say that; however, I'm a priest. My job is supernatural. My whole belief system is based on something which cannot be explained in ordinary terms.'

'Yeah, but this is not right. This is not a belief in God but in something, I dunno, just unbelievable.' Morgan said.

'If you believe in God then you must believe in the Devil. If you believe in the Devil, then you must believe in the rest.'

'Aren't there some people out there who believe in God but not the devil? Morgan asked.

'Yes, there are,' Jimmy replied. 'Some people see the devil as a created entity to explain a huge number of ailments. Depression, epilepsy, disabilities, whatever. I've never liked that idea because then you can just as easily say that God is a created entity to explain just about everything else. I believe in God – it's not just my job and I certainly don't do it for the money – and I also believe in the rest. Not everything – ghosts, I'm not too sure about. They are not mentioned in the Bible which could be because they don't exist, or it could be because no one mentioned them. Spirits are mentioned, and they could certainly be a form of ghost, but hauntings, no.'

Morgan took a sip of his tea and thought for a moment.

'So, with everything that's going on at the moment – a man who can disappear into nowhere; a possible link, however tenuous, to the past; another possible link with Henry House – are we saying that we think that there is something supernatural going on here?' he asked.

'It scares me just thinking about all this,' Carys said. 'I've lived here all my life. The Rhondda is home for me and to think that something like this could be true disturbs me.'

'A few weeks ago I would have never dreamed of having a conversation like this,' Catryn said. 'But here we are.'

'Someone needs to go up to that house,' Morgan said. 'To take a look around.'

'I'd go,' Jimmy said. Carys looked at him with concern but didn't say anything.

'I'd go too,' Catryn said after a brief hesitation.

'Tomorrow morning,' Jimmy said. 'It's too late now and, if I'm going to be completely honest, I'd prefer to do it is bright daylight.'

Catryn laughed. 'I second that, your honour.'

'I can't go tomorrow,' Morgan said. 'I have work.'

'So do I,' said Carys, although she almost sounded relieved.

'That's OK,' Jimmy said. 'Me and Cat will go and report back tomorrow evening. If that's ok with you?'

Catryn nodded. 'One of the benefits of being between jobs,' she smiled.

'Perfect,' said Jimmy. 'Knock the door about 10:30 to 11, bring some good shoes and water.'

'Wait a minute', Carys said, finally. 'There's a killer on the loose. A murderer, here in Trehenri. What if he is hiding out in that building?'

Silence descended on the group for a moment.

'Nah,' Jimmy said. 'There are a million places to hide in the Rhondda – if he is still here. Besides, that house is over two hundred years old. Despite what it looks like on the outside, it will probably be a wreck inside. Plus, there is only one way in and one way out. I think people would have noticed that big fella traipsing up and down Henry Hill, don't you think?' '

Carys shook her head. 'Perhaps you should call Gareth first,' she suggested.

Jimmy took her hands in his and smiled at her.

'There's no one there,' he said. 'However, if we see any sign of activity, we'll get out of there faster than a bull in the streets of Spain.'

'He might be there,' Carys persisted.

Jimmy shook his head. 'Look, all it will be is a bit of an adventure and I've always wanted to have a look around.'

Carys shook her head and pulled her hands away.

'Whatever,' she said testily. 'But if you go up there and get yourself killed, don't be running back to me for sympathy.'

***

Later, as they stood outside Catryn's father's house, Morgan looked at his old friend with concern.

'Are you sure you'll be ok tomorrow?' he asked.

Catryn smiled. 'Don't worry about me. I'll be ok. I have a priest to look after me.'

'I know, but if there are any rotted floorboards or chandelier's ready to fall on top of you, then there is nothing that Jimmy and his faith can do about it.'

'Why, Morgan, I would swear that you are worried about me.'

Morgan blushed and even in the dimmed light of the long shadows that often fell on the valleys, it was obvious.

'I don't want you to come home after all these years then end up dead or in hospital, that's all.'

She had to laugh at this but there was one word he used which did hit her. Home. She hadn't been here for all these years and when she was here, she had wanted to leave for as far back as she could remember. It was a place that she always felt held her back, as if her dreams were too big to be confined to such a small place. Yet here she was, back in the old town, back with an old friend and she felt comfortable.

The events of the last few days, the strangeness of her conversations this afternoon, the fear she had felt on her walk the previous night, none of it seemed to have taken that feeling away. It was if everything that had happened over the last year, everything that had led her to return, had worked to prepare her for a homecoming.

She looked into Morgan's eyes and could see a desperation in them that she recognised. He was a lonely man, she realized. Someone who missed having company to sit next to at night and watch TV, someone to plan a weekend together, to cook and eat together.

She knew what he was missing but didn't know if she wanted to be the one to give it to him. She had enjoyed hanging with him today, not just because he reminded her of the past, but because he gave her an excuse to go outside. This was something she had missed too.

But was this enough to cover everything she had gone through? She wasn't sure.

'You OK?' he asked.

She nodded, then reached in close to him and kissed his cheek.

'Thanks for a very interesting afternoon,' she said. She then opened the front door and quickly went inside. She closed the door and leaned against the wall. She knew that he would still be out there, not moving, at least for a few moments and she could imagine how he felt. She didn't know why she had kissed him. It had come out of the blue for her too.

'Cat?' her father's voice called out from the living room.

'Yes, Dad. I'll be there now in a minute.' She said, aware that she was using another local phrase that she hadn't used for a long time.

What she was doing? It was too soon, and things were a bit too weird. But she had kissed him, and she knew what he would be thinking. If she had been in his place right now, she would be going through turmoil. She had started on a path which could result in her hurting a friend, but it seemed right.

She sighed heavily and went in to join her dad.

CHAPTER 20

That Sunday night would always be remembered. For many, it was the moment the horror came into people's homes. They would say that it started with a howl.

Everything that preceded the deathly scream in the night was remote. They saw it on TV, they talked about it in their homes, at work or whilst shopping, but it had all happened to someone else. It could have been in the next street, but it could just as easily have occurred in London, or Paris, New York or Brisbane. But the noise that resounded up and down the streets of Trehenri and the surrounding villages that night, was heard by all. They couldn't deny it. It was loud enough and lasted long enough that there was little doubt as to its existence.

What's more, it didn't seem to be confined to the sound-waves that surrounded them. It seemed not to exist externally, but internally; not as a reaction on the eardrum, but a tremor on each and every individual's mind.

It seemed to explode from every synapse in each person's brain.

Jimmy was sleeping, yet the scream was enough to grab him roughly from his dreams and wake him. Carys sat up in the bed next to him and, in the silver glow of the moonlight, he could see her chest rise and fall as if she was hyperventilating.

'Did you hear that?' he asked her and became aware that he too was breathing heavily.

'I heard something,' she replied. 'I thought it was just me, I thought I was dreaming.'

'It wasn't a dream,'

They sat together in bed, feeling wide awake, listening to silence, waiting for the sound to repeat but it never did. Jimmy propped himself up, the pillow lifted to support his back behind him. Carys moved closer to him and rested her head on his chest. He put his arm around her and pulled her close, taking comfort from her weight; the heat of her body made him feel safe.

'What do you think it was?' Carys asked eventually.

'Don't know, with everything that has been happening here recently...' He trailed off, not knowing what to say.

***

In the bedroom of her father's house, Catryn also heard the grim cry piercing the night. She was awake and had been for a while. Sleep had a habit of being a bit slow arriving recently. She too was propped up on her bed, a copy of the latest Michael Connelly book in her hands, the room dimly lit by one small bedside lamp. Harry Bosch was listening to a piece of jazz, going through a murder book, a drink in his hands and a scowl on his face.

When she heard the sound, she sat bolt upright; her eyes darting back and forth as if the sound had emanated from her own room. Not that there was much room to do anything in this little box. Its length was barely enough for the bed, with only enough room at the end to fit another small cabinet. Next to that was a cupboard. It had once been a flat pack and was now suffering the same problems that many such wardrobes had – the back bulged, the tacks that held the flimsy board were loose. On the front, one of the two doors were slightly out of lineament and wouldn't close properly. It was the type of wardrobe that no self-respecting boogie man would have ever be caught in.

She pulled back the light duvet, swung her legs around and stood at the edge of the bed. She waited a few moments to see if the sound would repeat itself. Nothing except the noisy springs of her father's bed. She could hear him get up and open his bedroom door. She crossed the short distance to her door and opened it carefully. Her father stood on the top of the stairs, dressed in just a pair of boxers and an old tee-shirt.

'You OK, Dad?' she whispered.

'I heard a sound,' he replied. 'You OK? You were having a bad dream, were you?'

'It wasn't me. I heard it too.'

They paused for a second, waiting for it to happen again. After a moment, Gwyn shrugged.

'Oh well, it's probably just cats.'

He turned and disappeared back into his bedroom. Catryn couldn't help but smile, even though the noise had unsettled her. She loved her father's capacity for pragmatically accepting things. He had always been the same. It had frustrated her in the past, especially when she was a teenager. Most of the other fathers seemed to have a great sense of humour but not her's. His humour was too dry for a teenager and his apparent lack of imagination had driven her nuts on many an occasion. But now that she was older, and when so much that she had taken for granted had been flipped completely upside down, she couldn't help but think of it as a talent.

She returned to bed and tried to focus on the old, and many ways mysterious, man in the other room. There was so much she had forgotten about him, so much she would have to learn again or learn for the first time.

***

In Llwynypia Terrace, right at the bottom of Trehenri, just a stone's throw from Ynyshir, John and Margaret Mayhew were making love when they heard the noise. He had only returned home less than an hour ago, having just called it a night in his role as a Taxi Driver. He didn't usually work on Sundays, but the recent kidnappings and murders had caused an influx of people from all over the UK. Media people mostly but also those who had come just to be a witness to the terrible events. These people were sick, but they seemed to spend a lot of money in the local pubs and were more than willing to pay his ever-so-slightly inflated fares, so he didn't really care. He was 68 years old and didn't have a decent pension. The State Pension was a joke, how people could live off it he didn't know. So, he worked long and hard hours, ferrying people around the valleys.

He had arrived home long after dark, at a time when the predominant colours were the black of night and the sulfur of the streetlights. Margaret was in bed with the light on and a book in her hands. He walked into the room and saw her there, and he felt that familiar attraction that had been there since they were married only three years before.

He showered, put on his satin shorts and joined her in the bedroom, moving close to her then on top of her. When his children found out that he, a widower of fifteen years, was getting married again they were confused, and he knew that part of it was the idea that their old man could want a sex life. Well, he did and Margaret, who was only a few years younger than he was, wanted it too. She was energetic and vigorous, and he still was capable of maintaining an erection without the help of medication. If this became an issue, he would just make a trip to the doctor and tell them straight - 'Doctor, I want something that will give me a boner!'

Until now, it had never been an issue with him but when he heard that scream, he went as limp as a soggy biscuit. His energy died; his sex drive drove off. And for some reason, he felt ashamed. Margaret tried to comfort him, reassuring him that she too heard the noise and it gave her the creeps, but he won't listen. He got out of bed and walked heavily down the stairs and spent the night in front of the TV, a pillow on his lap to cover his nakedness and the evidence of his failure.

***

Further down the hill on School Street, Megan Edwards woke with a start. At 14 years old she was usually a heavy sleeper but the last few days she was having difficulty. She reached over to the night light and looked around the bedroom, not really knowing if the noise was real or not. Everything was where it should be – her Ariana Grande posters on the wall, the globe on her desk on the far end of the room, the bookcase next to the desk with all her Dork Diaries and Wimpy Kid collections. It was all real, all familiar, yet she still felt odd, like the air itself was wrong.

She pulled the Unicorn duvet closer to her for comfort, but it didn't seem to help. She even picked up her photo of Iestyn that she kept on the bedside cabinet, and stared into his lush and beautiful eyes, but their magic seemed to elude her for tonight.

Finally, she gave in to the urge that she was feeling and got out of bed, crossed to the chest of drawers and opened the bottom drawer. She reached in, searching with her hand for the prize inside.

Then she found it.

She pulled out an old ragged teddy bear, its ears frayed, and its clothes damaged by years of being dragged on the floor and dumped wherever and whenever. She then crossed quickly to the bed and got beneath the covers, holding Bubbles as close to her as possible. Finally, she fell asleep before waking up embarrassed that she had succumbed to such a childish impulse the night before.

***

Up on Henry Hill, Taliesin Jones heard the scream as he lay awake in bed. He snarled in defiance at the darkness around him.

'Fuck off, you ghost cocksucker!' He muttered.

***

In the Darkness, Shadow raged. His body ached with want, with desire, with need. He knew he had to control it. He had to fulfil his master's commands, but the urges were too deep. He had screamed with rage, with anger, with impotence. The time had to come soon.

It had to.

STEPHEN AMOS

Monday

CHAPTER 21

Morgan awoke with a feeling that he normally would have said was a hangover. It wasn't of course. He'd had a few drinks but nothing too heavy, yet is head felt almost cumbersome, as if it were something he wasn't used to carrying around with him. His eyelids were determined to stay closed and, when he finally managed to lift himself up off the bed, the room swam around him as if he were trapped in a whirlpool, spinning rapidly, probably drowning.

His legs felt laden, and each step was a battle against vertigo and gravity.

He had stepped into the shower and, although he didn't normally like it cold, he turned the switch down until he was barely able to stand it. Each drop of water slammed into him like a poisonous dart from the blow straws of a forgotten Amazonian tribesman.

He almost fell over getting dressed, unable to get his leg into his underpants nor into his trousers. He put his shirt on and was halfway downstairs before he realised he hadn't put any deodorant on.

He ate his breakfast – Weetabix with far too much milk, spilling a drop down his chin onto his stubble. He knew he hadn't shaved for a few days and didn't care. He doubted anyone else would either.

As he stepped out into the bright morning, he had the overwhelming urge to turn around and go back to bed, to hide under the duvet and pretend the day didn't exist. To find solace in the comfort of his sheets where the world was nothing more than the remnants of a nasty dream.

It was Monday and the weekend was over. The horrors of the last few days, the excitement of being with Catryn and the freedom of not having to work, were all lost in the inevitable routine of working life. Every terrible thing that had happened was to be reduced to chatter in the staffroom.

There was only a ten-minute walk to the school, just down the Main Road, turn left passed the old bingo hall and across the bridge at the end of School Street. As he started down the hill, he joined the students gathered in small groups, some laughing, many zombie-like. A few saw him and called out 'hello, sir.' Most ignored him. He was just another lost soul called to this undignified temple of learning.

He sniffed at this last thought. A Temple of Learning? More like a toilet bowl for the piss strings of humanity.

Ok, that was too harsh, yet these swings in mood and the turbulence of his thoughts summed up exactly how he had felt the last few days. Now he felt like the crud in a toilet bowl, but yesterday with Catryn, he had felt as if possibilities actually did exist.

He had thought about her a lot that evening and this morning. He had tried to restrain these thoughts, not letting his loneliness get the better of him. He knew that if he let it, he would start dreaming of romance, of marriage, of children and old age together. I'm just a pathetic loser, he thought.

He wondered what she had done over the last few years. She clearly hadn't wanted to talk about it, it didn't take a genius to realise that. She had not mentioned it to him, had avoided the subject when their conversations had come close to it, and she generally seemed content to play make-believe, as if she were immune to whatever had happened.

Was she on the run? From what or whom? She had been an accountant – how much trouble could an accountant get in to? Then he had thought of organised crime, of money laundering and tax evasion. If anything, this sense of intrigue actually made her sexier, more alluring.

Stop it! Damn it!

He hardly noticed as he crossed the bridge and walked through the school gates before turning left past the swimming pool towards the staffroom. He was in a daze with only muscle memory and instinct guiding him. He entered the building and moved through the crowds of pupils. In his periphery, he was aware that no one was taking any notice of him; they too looked like they were fighting a battle to remain awake, to remain aware.

The staffroom was busy as the other teachers hung up their coats, put their lunch boxes into the fridge that they had all chipped in together to buy, and generally going about their business like Zombies.

As Morgan took his jacket off, the headmaster - a short, rotund, bald man who looked like the American comic, Don Rickles - walked into the centre of the room and held up his arms in a theatrical gesture.

'Everybody, please? Everyone. Can I have your attention, please?'

As the room quieted Morgan slowly came out of his reverie.

'There will be an assembly first thing this morning,' the headmaster continued. 'We will have members of the Police here who will speak to the students in order to help them feel safer. I know there are lots of rumours going around so hopefully, this will help to control them.

'I would be grateful if you take the registers quickly, then escort your classes to the hall in a quiet organised manner. Judging from the subdued atmosphere in the halls this morning, that hopefully shouldn't be a problem. The police will then spend the day going from class to class to discuss the events of the last few days with the children and answer any questions.

'It's not an easy time but the school governors have decided that we remain open as usual for the moment and we'll monitor the situation daily. Thank you, everyone, I'll see you in about a half hour.'

With that, he turned and left the room quickly. He was

normally a relaxed man whose tough exterior hid a cool, dry sense of humour, but this morning Morgan couldn't help but think he looked haggard and stressed. As if he had hardly slept a wink.

Morgan hung his jacket up without talking to anyone. He knew exactly how the headmaster felt because he felt exactly the same.

The staffroom was quiet and everyone looked morose. Each left to their classes almost silently, like soldiers on the way to the execution grounds. Morgan couldn't help but wonder on which side of the ground they would all gather.

CHAPTER 22

As Catryn left her father's house that morning, she felt almost conflicted inside. The night had come with little sleep and her whole body felt exhausted, yet she was actually looking forward to her little expedition. She was happy to be around her old friends and felt relaxed knowing that she was in the company of people who wouldn't judge her. At least not yet.

The recent past, for the time being at least, was well and truly in the past, which was ironic really considering where she was. Her time in London, her time with Joe and the bad memories that came with him, were gone. Well, maybe not gone, but she was happy that there were other things for her to concentrate on right now.

Returning home despite all her feelings of resentment she had held onto all this time, had been the right thing to do. What's more, she was felt at ease separating the awful events that were occurring here over the last few days, from the town itself.

This might not be easy for some, and she knew that to the media, Trehenri, and possibly the Rhondda as a whole, would be forever linked with the terrible murders and kidnappings. It was a stain the town would be forever associated with, which was a pity but for those living here life would go on, she knew it.

Just as she knew that Trehenri was home. These streets, the hills and the mountains, the lanes and the steps. The terraced houses that snuggled into the hillsides and the gardens that sometimes seemed to rise at ninety-degree angles. All those things she had once run away from were now wrapping her up like a warm comfort blanket. It was what she needed. To see people like Morgan or Jimmy and Carys, and to stay with and talk to her Dad in a way she had never really done as an adult; it gave her a sense of peace that the town itself was missing at the moment.

She had thought about it all night. As she lay in bed, unable to sleep after hearing that strange scream, she had gone over the dirty old man's story and wondered what it was that had convinced her so much when she first heard it. Maybe it was simply getting caught up in it all. The giddy excitement of being a part of something so big and serious, mixed with the whirlwind of change and memories. So, here she was, intent on further delving into this madness.

She couldn't help but smile. The feeling she had was not dissimilar to the way she felt when involved in the organised crime investigation the previous year. To be part of a mystery; to try and unwrap it, had made her feel the same way. She loved this sense of excitement. But more than that, it made her feel like she belonged, like she was part of something bigger and better than she was by herself. This mystery had brought her to Morgan and Jimmy, it had introduced her to the old bastard Tal, a man who she would never had met in any other circumstance. Without his knowledge, whether was it real or the ravings of an old man with an overactive imagination who just wanted company (and the shape of a breast to ogle over), she wouldn't have been walking up the hill right now.

Her feelings - the situation she was in at the moment, the feelings of both contentment and horror, the return to a home which was being violated - were certainly a potent mix and she was aware of the disparity within, of the contradictory and paradoxical mood she was in.

She walked up the terraced street to Jimmy's house, glancing absentmindedly into people's windows. Every house was identical, each one over a hundred years old. Built with brick quarried from the nearby mountains which were still scarred all these years later. Inside people decorated them in individual styles but outside there was only the odd lick of paint to discern them from the neighbours. The pavement was cracked, the flagstones broken with moss or weeds growing out of the gaps. Not outside every door, of course, some people took more care and pride in the pavements at their doorsteps than others did, but these were mostly older people with more time on their hands.

She found Jimmy's house and knocked the door. She had to wait a few moments before he answered and she observed that his pavement was immaculate, the stonework around the windows was perfectly painted.

As he opened the door, Jimmy smiled at her. He was putting on a small jacket and over his shoulder was a small rucksack.

'You are coming prepared,' she said.

He smiled genially. 'Used to be a boy scout,' he said. 'A long time ago,'

He closed the door behind him and turned to her. 'How are you this morning?' he asked.

'Tired, didn't sleep all that well last night, but up for a mystery.'

'Same here. I'm not sure if our talk last night had ignited my imagination, or if there really is an oppressive atmosphere hanging over the valley, but something is a wee bit off. '

'Yeah,' Catryn said, 'I heard this really weird scream last night. My dad said it was probably just cats fighting but it really freaked me out.'

'It wasn't cats,' Jimmy said. 'We heard it too. Freaked us out as well. The whole thing gives me the chills.'

They began their walk up the hill and the conversation turned to the banal chitchat that two people rely on when they were not too familiar with each other. They had known each other for many years before Catryn had left for London although they had never been what you would call real friends. Probably an age thing as Jimmy was over a decade older than she was. That kind of age gap makes a difference when you are younger but now she felt comfortable and relaxed in his company.

As they walked up Henry Hill, having taken the steps again, Jimmy pointed out Tal's house,

'So, what did you think about him?' he asked.

'Tal?' Catryn thought about it for a few seconds. 'Part of me thinks that he's a dirty old man who wants the pleasures of the flesh that he was able to indulge in as a younger man but now can't. That it made him, well disgusting. But listening to what you and Morgan were saying last night; I get the feeling he has always been that way.'

Jimmy nodded. 'I've known him for about thirty years and he's always been a nasty piece of work. Never had a kind word to say about anyone and always too eager to point out details about the women around him.'

'I feel sorry for his carer.'

'Donna. She's his niece. She has a heart of gold and the patience of a saint. I honestly don't know how she puts up with him as he seems particularly nasty to her. But she's there every day. Without her, he would have died years ago.'

'I noticed last night.' Catryn said. 'He's certainly able to tell a tall tale though.'

'So, you've changed your mind? You seemed pretty convinced last night.' Jimmy replied.

Catryn shook her head. 'I'm here aren't I?'

They passed Tal's house and continued. The road levelled off and, in the distance, Catryn could see where the street ended and the lane to Henry House began.

'The thing is,' Jimmy said. 'Despite my reservations about the man, he does know what he's talking about. I'm not talking about the supernatural stuff although, as we discussed last night, I'm willing to accept that possibility. But history? He knows his stuff. Always has.'

At the end of the street, Jimmy pointed to the first house.

'That's Mrs Cranley's house. The old lady I told you about.

She's gone now but her family lived there for generations. Last I heard was her son had sold the house. Don't know who lives there now.'

Catryn could sense an edge of sadness in his voice as if he were lamenting the end of a tradition that would be gone forever.

'And here,' Jimmy continued, 'is the start of the lane to the mysterious Henry House. As we cross the threshold from the street and onto the lane, you will notice a shiver running down your back,' he said playfully.

There was no shiver but Catryn was aware that they were heading into a mystery. They both fell silent as they left Henry Hill and headed down the path.

The lane was like a glimpse into the past. The path was cobbled, the stones shiny and worn as if from constant use. It was just wide enough for one car to drive along at any time. Not that cars were an issue when the house was built; that was back in the horse and carriage days. Each side was overgrown with bushes, nettles and weeds. Catryn didn't have a clue what any of them were actually called. There were brambles, they were obvious, as were the stingy nettles which rose a few feet into the air, and dock leaves that crowded the ground. That was one thing she could remember: if you ever stung yourself with a stingy nettle then rub a Doc leaf into the infection and it would ease the pain. She didn't know if this would actually work but it seemed to be widely recognised knowledge, so maybe there was some truth to it.

The lane twisted to the right at a leisurely angle but the house wasn't immediately in sight as trees obscured the view.

'Considering all the things you've said about this man and all the things implied about this house, it doesn't seem that scary,' Catryn said.

'No, it kinda helps that it's a beautiful morning.' Jimmy replied.

'It's difficult to believe that kids don't play up here. It gorgeous.'

Jimmy nodded. 'Look around. A place like this should have some signs of humanity. There should be shattered glass, crisp packets, discarded condoms.'

'Discarded condoms? What type of priest are you?'

Jimmy laughed. 'Firstly, I never refer to myself as a priest. I'm a pastor, or, as my church calls me, Jimmy.'

'Are you one of these new aged religions, then?'

'No, I'm very strict I suppose, but I do live in the real world. Catholics may shy away from sex but I've got two kids. I know all about how the birds sing and the bees sting.'

Catryn laughed. 'I hear what you are saying but it feels a bit weird being told this by a, um, pastor.'

'Possibly, but I think that says more about you than it does about me. I don't think you've really had much contact with the church as an adult, have you?'

'No, not really,' Catryn confessed. 'I bet you hear this all the time, but I never seemed to have the time.'

'Life does get in the way of so much sometimes. I understand. Don't feel you need to make excuses. I'm not going to judge you.'

They fell silent for a few moments more. They were walking very slowly now; their previous determination had turned into a lazy amble.

'I kind of just fell away, I suppose,' she said eventually. 'A lot of people go to church when they are kids but stop going when they grow up.'

'They do. People's priorities change as they get older. They decide to leave the church.'

'Recently I feel the church left me,' she said, sadly.

'The church is always there for you. If you decide to leave, that's not the church's fault.'

Catryn felt a surge of argue. When she went through everything with Joe, where was the church? Where was God? Jimmy was a few steps in front of her and, instead of saying anything, she snarled silently at him.

Then they fell into silence again and continued walking on

slowly, each step taking them closer to Henry House.

CHAPTER 23

Henry House wasn't as big as they thought it was going to be. Certainly, nowhere the size of Cyfarthfa Castle or Llancaiach Fawr - two stately homes about 15 miles away that today housed museums - but it was obvious it had been built by someone with money and power. As Catryn and Jimmy rounded the last corner, the house came into full view, not looming as they imagined it might, but still imposing. It was built with a grey-white stone, aged like old gravestones. It seemed to have been in 3 sections: a central block which housed the main entrance and a number of small windows, and a wing block on each side. Each wing had six windows on the ground floor and another six on the first floor.

As Jimmy had remembered the previous afternoon, there was an old, craggy tree growing up on the left wing, and one of its skeletal branches has broken through into an upstairs window. The branch looked like an emaciated claw of some hideous Lovecraftian monster frozen between dimensions. Most of the windows had closed shutters protecting them, but two on the upstairs right wing were open. How the glass inside was still intact after so many years, Catryn couldn't fathom.

The path up to the house was overgrown and untidy, as was the house itself. It certainly looked old and in need of some repair, yet, it didn't look in nearly the state of disrepair that it might have been. The walls were weathered but showed no sign of deterioration, as if they had been maintained or protected for the two hundred years the building had stood. Even the path leading up to the door seemed devoid of any weeds, although away from the path the area was over-grown.

'You were right,' Catryn said, her voice breaking the silence and sounding far too loud even though she has whispered. 'It looks too tidy to have been disserted for so long.'

Jimmy nodded and walked up to one of the windows, his footsteps loud on the brown and dying brambles and stingies that had sprouted along the wall. He reached up to the shutters and with a yank, he pulled one open. It made a popping sound that dissipated as soon as it was heard, as if the sound had died on the spot. He then leaned forward and peered through the glass, his hands cupped around his face to block out the sun.

'Can't see anything,' he said. 'It's too dark.'

Catryn walked up to the door and turned around to survey the surroundings.

'You know, if those bushes and trees were missing,' she said pointing to the copse opposite the front entrance, 'you'd probably be able to see most of Trehenri from here.'

'Yeah, you are right.' Jimmy replied. 'I suppose that's why the house was built here. A way of keeping an eye on the riff-raff whilst affording enough privacy that you could pretty much get away with anything up here.'

'From the sound of it, he did.'

She turned back to the door and gave it a little kick. The door opened slowly with a loud creak.

'Shit!' She exclaimed loudly, stepping away.

Jimmy laughed. 'Didn't expect that, did you?'

Catryn held her hand to her chest and laughed with him. 'No, I didn't. Sorry for the language,' she said apologetically.

Jimmy waved his hands to dismiss her concerns.

'I'm a valley's boy, I've certainly heard worse.'

There was a moment's silence, save for the rustling of a light breeze moving the surrounding branches. That and the sound of her heart which thudded in her ears.

'So, what do we do now?' she asked.

'We have a look inside,' Jimmy said.

Catryn looked at Jimmy, frowning. What if the killer was

living here? What if he was using this as his base? The worries which seemed remote last night, all seemed very real now.

'You sure?' she asked.

'Not entirely,' Jimmy replied. He stepped back and took another look around. 'There doesn't seem to be any signs of life here. Look at the door, there is dust all over the floor but no footprints except for your own. No one is here.'

'Ok.' She stepped forward again and reached out with her foot to kick the door open wider. She looked down at the ground and saw that Jimmy was correct. This door hadn't been opened for a very long time.

'You're a film fan, yes?' she asked.

'Uh-huh'

'So, faced with an open door of an ancient house in which the owner is believed to do a bit of devil worship, and given what is happening in town right now, what do the movies tell us to do?'

Jimmy smiled. 'Oh, that's easy,' he said. 'Run like hell. You ever see Salem's Lot, the TV series?'

'The Stephen King thing with the boy tapping the window?'

'That's the one. Frightened the living daylights out of me as a kid. The house in that one was a lot different to this one, but the gist is the same. Ye be vampires.'

Catryn took another step closer and tried to look inside.

'You are not helping, you know,' she said. 'Just to let you know, I'll probably be swearing a lot in there.'

She reached into her pocket and took out her phone, turning on the torch. She lifted it up to shine into the building then took a step inside.

It was a large reception area. In front of her was a staircase, which rose up to the first floor and a landing which seemed to connect the two wings, but she couldn't be absolutely sure as it was too dark. Behind her, she could hear a creak of a step as Jimmy stepped in next to her. He had taken out a torch from his bag, the beam much brighter than her phone and she cursed herself for not thinking all this through.

She glanced down to the ground and saw dust everywhere and, more importantly, no other footprints. The hallway was too dark and foreboding; although Catryn would have been the first to admit that it was probably her imagination, which was working as hard as her heart was beating.

Jimmy moved passed her and stepped to the right where there was a large open door. The room on the other side of the door was dimly lit, and Catryn remembered that he had opened one of the shutters outside.

As their eyes began to adjust slightly, more details could be seen. There were doors at both left and right sides of the main entrance, about ten feet away. There were also corridors on each side of the stairway. At the entrance to the wings there were tables, where Catryn imagined flowers may have once been placed, but now only held more dust. The furniture seemed particularly curious to Catryn. How could anything survive here for all this time? Surely, they would have rotted in a building without any heating for so many decades. This house had been empty for almost two hundred years yet, even in the gloom, she got the sense that it had somehow been preserved.

This only increased her unease. She had expected the place to be scary – it was an old house with a very bad reputation after all – but not like this. It was as if the building had been caught in a time capsule.

As these thoughts fluttered through her mind, a shiver run down her back and she suddenly became aware of the need to pee. She scanned the light around, not sure what she was looking for. Something to make her feel more at ease, perhaps? She was breaking and entering into a creepy old house, what could possibly make her feel at ease?

'This place gives me the creeps,' Jimmy said, coming towards her. She was glad that he was feeling the same way, not because she was afraid of being perceived as a coward, but because she needed confirmation that it wasn't just her imagination.

It was almost as if the shadows were bearing down on her. The natural gloom of the place (for it must be natural, she supposed) seemed to make things worse.

'What should we do?' she asked.

'Dunno, shall we look around?' he asked.

'What if there is someone here?' Catryn asked, trying to keep her voice calm and even.

'I honestly don't think there is.'

'Look around!' She shone the light in a wide arch. 'Does this look like a place that has been abandoned for a century?'

'No, it doesn't,' Jimmy replied. Then: 'Hello?' he called out loudly, his voice echoing in the darkness.

'What the fuck are you doing?' Catryn hissed, trying to keep both her voice and her anger down. 'There could be a fucking murderer here!'

Jimmy shone his torch up to a wall, and then moved it around the reception.

'Look,' he said. 'No electricity. The last time this place was used was during the age of candles.'

Catryn shook her head. 'Yeah, maybe the bastard has been using candles. You think of that?' She found herself moving back towards the front door as if the daylight could offer some protection.

'No,' Jimmy said. 'I've been thinking a lot about this since last night. I've seen the videos, heard the stories, I think that all this, the killings, the kidnappings, this house, I think it's all supernatural. There's no one living here, no human at least.'

'How can you say that? You're a priest for God's sake. You can't believe in all this shit! Where in the Bible does it mention ghosts that kill and do housekeeping?'

Jimmy laughed.

'Housekeeping? Pretty lousy housekeeper, leaving all this dust.'

'Yeah,'

'I would fire her for not dusting.'

Catryn smiled, she could see the absurdity of it. Her smile

also turned into a laugh and she could feel the tension easing slightly. Jimmy moved to the door and put his hand on her shoulder.

'Look,' he said, trying to become serious. 'I've got a very active imagination. When you have seen as many films as I have, you learn to suspend your disbelief. That, coupled with my day job, means I'm more open to these sorts of things than some people. Or, it could simply be because of something else, something deep inside me, something searching for more than I can see and feel. I don't know why, but I believe.'

'Ever think it could be because you are just simple-minded? Catryn asked.

'That could be true too,' he said. 'Either way, I would like to have a look around. Let's just say it's to satisfy this curiosity or because I'm too simple-minded to recognise the danger. Or, it could be, I'm in denial of the danger. The thing is, however much I want to do this, I will admit that I'm also a little scared. I would prefer to have someone with me.'

Catryn took a deep breath and looked around the reception area once more. The place certainly gave her the creeps and she wasn't sure she believed any of the supernatural bullshit, but she too felt a morbid curiosity. She wanted to know.

'Ok,' she said finally. 'We carry on. But the first sign of ghosts and I'm outta here. Quickly.'

'If we see ghosts, you'll have to race me.' Jimmy replied.

***

From a long way away, a presence became aware of another. Its sanctuary had been invaded; its home had been opened by unwelcome interlopers.

This was not acceptable. This was something that didn't happen. The presence had worked to protect its home from anyone on the outside. It had cloaked the house in solitude and fear. It had ensured its privacy for decades, probably more. This was its temple, and soon it would be its dwelling once more.

It felt a rage encase it, like a shell of red hot fire. It enshrined it in flames and it wanted nothing more than to find them, to rip through them, to attack every cell in their bodies until they called out in unimaginable pain. It wanted to make pain their home, their eternal cell.

But it could not. Not yet. Its work was too important, the result too glorious. And there was too much left to do. Secrecy had to be maintained.

So, it waited. It had no choice.

But they are there, its anxiety overwhelmed it. Why were they there? What did they want? How could it ensure they never returned, or at least didn't return until its rebirth?

'Shadow,' it called.

And Shadow came. The presence of the big man made itself aware before him.

'Yes, my master,' Shadow replied reverentially.

'There are intruders. In our house.'

It could feel the heat begin to emanate from his servant. It knew of the rage its slave possessed.

'I shall ripe their hearts from their body, I will drink of their life's blood.'

'No,' it replied. 'If they die more will come. Run them out, astound them, demoralise them, horrify, dismay and dishearten them. Loosen their bowels and they will never come back.'

'They might still,' the man in the shadows said.

'After tonight, after the final sacrifice, nothing will matter. Now go!'

***

'Which way first?' Catryn asked. Her voice had reduced to a whisper although she didn't know why. It was certainly not out of respect; she was starting to really dislike this place.

'This way,' Jimmy replied, shining his light to the right.

They crossed the small area to the first set of doors which were already open. The room they entered was the size of an average sitting room. An old sofa faced the window, through which an orange unwelcoming light seemed to glimmer. Their torches cast dancing shadows as they moved which did nothing to help calm Catryn's nerves. Each shadow seemed as black as pitch and not even the wan light from the window seemed to help.

Jimmy moved into the middle of the room where there was a small coffee table. Or at least that what she thought it was. It could have been a brandy table, for all she knew.

The room as interesting but unremarkable. If she had seen it reconstructed in a museum or at St Fagan's Museum of Welsh Life, she probably would have 'oooed' and 'ahhed' at it all, amazed by this demonstration of how people lived so many years ago. But here and now, she was happy that there was nothing of real interest. Just a room in a house. Nothing scary.

Jimmy moved toward the sofa and put his hand on it, dragging it against the material. He then lifted his finger up and shone the light onto them, rubbing them together. He then gave the back of the sofa a hard whack. A cloud of dust rose into the air forcing him to take a step back.

'Whatcha do that for?' Catryn asked.

'Curious,' he replied. 'Just like the entrance way, the house seems so well maintained and yet...' He waved his hands in the air to indicate the small cloud that was dissipating into the air.

'What does it mean?'

'Don't know. Just another item on the long list of oddness.'

'And another reason to fire the housekeeper?'

'Uh-huh,' Jimmy said. He crossed to a set of cupboards at the far end of the room and run his fingers on the wood.

'This house could be renovated, fixed up nicely,' he said. He opened one small door and shone his torch inside. It was empty. He then began opening other doors and drawers randomly, but they too, were all empty.

Catryn lifted her light to the ceiling, following the tops of the walls.

'Considering the amount of dust here, there are no cobwebs, no spiders, nothing,' she said. 'It's almost as if the creepy crawlies are too creeped out by this place to set up shop.'

Jimmy looked up as well and nodded.

'Except that creepy crawlies don't generally get creeped out,' he said.

They moved together to the far door and Jimmy reached out to open it. It was stiff but, after a good pull, it gave way and opened with a loud creak.

'Shit,' Catryn said. 'Why do they have to the creek?'

'If this were a film set, then everything would creek,' he said grinning.

Shining their lights in front of them, they stepped into the next room. This room was almost completely black and Catryn was again aware of the pounding in her chest. Her breathing had become rapid and she took a moment to try and calm herself down. She took a deep breath and held it for a few seconds before releasing it. She then repeated the exercise a few more times until she felt more comfortable. Not at ease, the only way she was going to feel at ease was when she was out of here, back home with her dad watching the evening news, which would be full of the reassuring reports of war, murder and economic devastation. Anything was better than this.

It was a long room, stretching away at a ninety-degree angle from the door. In the centre of the room was a long bare table surrounded by chairs. As Jimmy shone his light on the walls, they could see it was lined with numerous paintings. They seemed like the standard stuff for this type of room - women holding bouquets, men on horses surrounded by hounds. On the wall to their right there was another window and below it a long, narrow table.

This room was creepier than the previous one. Here, the light from the torches just didn't seem to carry more than a few meters before disappearing into a grey gloom in the distance. The shadows seemed deeper, as if they were actual physical objects rather than just the absence of light.

She moved to the table and forced herself to touch it. She wanted to know that the room was ordinary, that it was filled with everyday objects. There was nothing supernatural about a table.

'So, why return home now?' Jimmy asked.

The question caught Catryn off guard. It wasn't something she would ever have expected in a place and a situation like this.

'What?' she asked.

Jimmy was standing near the wall opposite the door. His light revealed another shuttered window and a picture of a rather stern looking woman dressed in frills and lace.

'What brought you home now? After all these years?'

'Why do you ask?' She knew her voice was shaky but she couldn't decide whether it was because of the fear of the situation or of the fear of revealing the truth behind her move back to Trehenri.

'Because I don't want my entire thought process focused on how scary this place is,' he said, with forced lightness that Catryn could see through in the dark.

'I got divorced,' she said after a few very loud heartbeats. 'I needed a complete change but didn't seem to have many options.'

Jimmy bent down and shone his light under the table. The area nearest her was suddenly filled with long shadows, moving across the walls, floor and ceilings. It reminded her of the bars to a prison cell in an old film noir. It also reminded her that the darkness surrounded them like a hoard of ghosts and demons, but she decided not to focus on that.

'What's your favourite film?' she asked, seizing on the idea of film noir.

He stood up to full size and shone the light towards her. She held up her hands to the light, temporarily blinded. He moved the light away from her quickly and apologised.

They began to move down the long table, Catryn on its left, Jimmy on the right.

'Cinema Paradiso,' he said finally.

'What?' she asked. The table was bigger than she initially

thought, almost fifteen feet long at a guess. She counted ten chairs on each side and two at each end. A feast for twenty-two people. She wondered if it had ever been used.

'My favourite film. Cinema Paradiso. Or at least that's what I tell people.'

'Is it not the truth?'

'Oh, it is, except I have a lot of favourites. Carys always jokes that there are at least twenty-five films in my top ten.'

'Does she like films as well?' Catryn came to the end of the table. There was a large gap of about ten feet, then another wall with one door on the far right side and another on the same wall they had come in by. Between the two doors was a large cabinet crammed with what looked like stuffed animals. If was the only decoration they had seen aside from the paintings.

'She enjoys a good film and puts up with my choices occasionally. But not to the extent that I do.'

Jimmy moved towards what looked like an owl. As he moved his light across it, the eyes seemed to move and Catryn had to look away. It looked as if it were alive.

There were four animals altogether – the owl, a fox, a hawk and what looked like a stoat. She didn't want to go too close to them, afraid the effect the shadows were having on their glassy eyes and her imagination.

'I've seen Cinema Paradiso,' she said. 'It's the one with the little boy and the old projectionist. It has a lovely soundtrack.'

'Ennio Morricone,' Jimmy confirmed. 'I absolutely love it.'

She crossed to Jimmy and shone her light on the door at the far end.

'This one?' she asked.

'Ok,'

He reached out and took hold of the door handle again. Catryn aimed the light at it as he gave it another tug. The door opened easier than he thought and he stumbled backwards slightly, away from Catryn and into the corner.

The door swung open and Catryn saw the white face of a

large man grinning down at her. His eyes were wide, his teeth were black. His hands reached out in front of him as if he was going to grab her.

She screamed loudly and fell back towards the table. Her phone fell from her hands, the light of the torch going out. The man disappeared in the darkness. Jimmy shone this light towards her. The light frantically moving across the floor.

'WHAT IS IT?' he called out.

He stepped away from the door and moved towards her.

'No, the door! There's someone there.' Catryn was panting wildly, and she could feel herself losing control. A thought cascaded in her mind that she might just piss herself. Strangely it made her feel ashamed, the thought of leaving this godforsaken place with a wet strain around her crotch, making her feel fleetingly angry.

Jimmy crouched down beside her and lifted the light up to the doorway.

There was no one there.

Catryn tried her breathing exercises again but this time it was much, much harder. Her hand stretched out as she tried to feel for her phone, all the while not taking her eyes away from the doorway.

'My phone, my phone,' she panted.

Jimmy shone the light across the floor and saw it had fallen across the threshold and into the other room.

'Oh Lord,' he whispered. 'Guide my steps. Watch over me in this awful place.'

He stood up and stepped towards the door.

'Don't go in there,' Catryn almost cried.

'It's ok,' he said.

He took another step and Catryn lifted herself up to a crouching position. She wanted to be able to run, to escape into the daylight, in a heartbeat.

Jimmy reached the threshold of the door and shone the light back and fore.

'It's a kitchen,' he said.

'What?' Catryn hissed. 'I don't care what the fuck it is. How about the man? Where is he?'

Jimmy stepped into the room and all Catryn could see was his silhouette as the light moved around the next room. She could see him crouch down and direct the light under what looked like another table and chairs. He then took a step backwards and leaned down to pick up her phone. He touched the screen and a dim light came on.

'There's no one there,' he said.

Catryn stood up. Where was he gone? There wasn't enough time for him to go anywhere. Surely it hadn't been her imagination? It was real. The face and the hands, they had moved, as if they were reaching for her.

'He's there somewhere,' she said. 'I saw him; he was only a few feet away.'

Jimmy disappeared further into the room and all she could see was a calamitous battle between light and darkness. There was no grace, there seemed to be only violence in the movements. The lights flickered and dimmed and brightened and strafed, but the dark always seemed to hold sway.

He was gone for seconds stretched into hours, she could hear him move close by, yet he seemed as far away as the earth could take him. She felt a fear inside her guts that was familiar and mundane yet spellbinding in its malevolence. She had felt it before, not so long ago, sitting on the bed in her house in London, her legs close to her chest, her arms holding them in tightly. The fear sometimes lasted for hours, and sometimes for minutes. Those were the worst times because they were the times she would be hurt, when the internal horror would be translated into punches and blows with a belt.

A tear escaped down her cheek. It burned her skin like a path of fire rushing to a keg of explosives. She brushed it aside robustly, determined to control its path. It was a small thing but it was all she could do.

As she stood in front of that door, her fear was not of a ghost or of a supernatural being coming to feed on her soul. The horror she envisioned on the other side was Joe, his fists clenched, spit flying from his mouth as he called her a 'fucking lying bitch!' As the belt struck her arms and her back time and time again, until her crying would stop, until she had nothing left inside her.

All the time, he would shout and scream at her. 'I saw you talking to him, I saw you flirting with that motherfucker. You're nothing but a cocksucking whore. A vile bitch who deserves

[Whack]

'Every fucking thing

[whack]

'You get.'

[Whack]

And she believed him. There were times she knew that everything he said was the truth, that she was worthless, that she was a whore. And that was how she felt right now. Small, insignificant, shameful.

One night, after his energy was spent, after his arm ached from the beating he had given her, as she lay below him whimpering quietly like a dog, he had unzipped his jeans and pissed all over her.

As she stood in front of the door now, she could still smell the urine.

'There's nothing there,' Jimmy said.

She looked up at him and saw him standing in the doorway. She couldn't speak for a moment and just stood there shaking. He shone his light at her.

'Cat?' he asked. He must have seen the fear in her eyes as he rushed to her and put his arms around her.

'My God, you're trembling.'

He guided her to the table and pulled a chair out for her. He manoeuvred her down to a sitting position and leaned close, holding her tightly.

'It's ok,' he said. 'It's OK. You've just had a fright, that's all.'

His arms comforted her. In all the times she lay on the

kitchen floor, smelling of piss and fear, she never had anyone to hold her. Those times she had felt like a child, when her parents were superheroes who could hold back the monsters under her bed.

'Look at me.' She heard Jimmy's voice and did what he asked. His face was pale in the wan light, his cheekbones deeper than normal. His eyes were almost in shadow yet there was still a reflection of light shining from them as he moved.

'What?' she asked.

'I think we should leave. You've had a terrible fright, we should leave.'

'No,' she said in a small voice, and she meant it. The fear she had lived with for all these years would always be there. She knew it, the psychologists had told her as much. They said it would seem to ease until sometimes she would think it was gone. Then something would happen, and she would be reminded of it. But she could not let it control her. It was the past, he was gone. There was nothing he could do with her anymore.

'No,' she said again.

'Cat...'

'No.' This time it was more forceful. She felt strength from the word. An act of defiance that fed further defiance. 'I'm jumpy, that's all. I imagined it.'

She stood up and checked her phone. 38% battery life. Enough to last a good while yet, she hoped.

'Come on,' She started to walk towards the kitchen. Her knees were unsteady, her legs lacked the strength they normally had. She felt heavy as if she had been in water for hours and had grown used to the buoyancy, but now was on solid ground and had to fight the full force of gravity.

'Catryn, we don't have to do this.'

She turned to Jimmy and smiled, although she wasn't sure he could see it in the dark.

'Let's just check this room and circle on back to the front door. If we don't do it now, there is no way in hell I'm coming back.'

'I'm with you there,' he said. 'Lord, a few more minutes please.'

'Do priests all talk to God like that?' she asked.

'I don't. But at times like this, I want him to know I'm here.'

Catryn actually chuckled. She still didn't feel better but she understood what he meant.

***

A chuckle echoed around the corners of the cavernous space where it lived for the time being. It felt good, to feel the intruders panic, to feel them scared almost to death. It couldn't see them, not yet. That would be coming very soon but it could feel their fear and it felt very, very good.

It liked this feeling. It had spent so long in the darkness, away from life, that it had almost forgotten the ecstasy of fear, of hurting the living. And this was just a glimpse. Tomorrow it would feed off the anxiety and despair of hundreds, maybe thousands of souls. Tomorrow it would rise again and the power it had felt all those years ago, would be its again.

It felt the presence of Shadow again.

'Very good my friend,' it said.

'That was just the start,' Shadow replied. 'But...'

Shadow trailed off then didn't say anything.

'What is it?' It asked.

'My Lord, the man, he is a man of God. A priest.'

It chuckled again.

'So, what of it?'

Shadow seemed to falter.

'He is a man of God,' he repeated, unable to express his feelings.

'Yes, a man.' It reassured him. 'A man of God maybe, but a man just the same.'

'But he is protected. I cannot touch him.'

'No Shadow, our lord is stronger that his. Do not fear him or his god.'

Shadow went silent for a moment. 'But he is protected...' he said quietly.

'No, Shadow. Listen to me. You have nothing to fear. You do not need to touch him, just scare them out of here.'

'My Lord -'

'Go Shadow, get them to leave. I do not want to see them here again.'

Shadow, the servant, acquiesced, and it could feel the faith and love that he felt for his master. He disappeared and it chuckled once more.

***

The next room was indeed a kitchen but what she had assumed was another table and chairs was a workstation and stools. The wood on the station was smooth and seemed to dip in the middle. On the right-hand wall, beneath more windows, was a large sink with beautifully ornate taps.

They must be worth a fortune now, Catryn thought.

Jimmy moved to the left and opened the doors on the various cupboards, but they were all bare.

'Old Mother Hubbard,' he said quietly.

Catryn stayed very close to him. Her heart still beat louder and faster than it should, but at least she had her breathing under control. Silently, she held her breath for a few moments at a time, trying to regulate the speed and so far, it seemed to be working.

The kitchen was large and, like the other rooms, the type that you would see in a museum. A contraption hung from the ceiling in the middle of the room, hovering over the work station. This was probably where they hung knives or dead pheasants or something like that, she assumed.

It rocked back and forth gently as if caught on a gentle breeze. Jimmy had probably touched it, she supposed, although she couldn't remember seeing him doing it. He did have a habit of doing that she noticed. It was as if he too needed the tangible to fight off the possibility of the ghostly.

So far, he had seemed like a rock to her. He bravely entered every room first and barely showed any sense of fear. Yet, she knew that he too had been shaken by her outburst earlier and the low mumble of his conversations with God had increased. They used to say that there were no atheists in the trenches and she now had an inkling as to what that meant.

The house was quiet. Her imagination wanted desperately to tell her that it was too quiet but in truth, she didn't know what a house like this should sound like. She supposed that it would be filled with the usual creeks at night, as the heat of the day gave way to the night and every nail, every pipe or wire expanded ever so slightly. But now, in the early after-noon, there was nothing.

Or at least that was the case until the door behind them slammed shut.

There was an emphatic bang that seemed to reverberate around the house and through Catryn's body. She jumped in fright before the fear could kick in. Jimmy jumped twice, first from the shock, then to get closer to her. He pushed her back and got between her and the door. He seemed to act like a hero however, as she put her hands on his shoulders, she could feel a tremble running through his body.

They both backed away from the door, around the worksta-tion towards a far door, when that to slammed violently shut.

Catryn could feel her breathing increase in speed again, and she began to fear she was going to lose control and panic.

'Shit,' she whispered. 'What the hell was that?'

Jimmy was backing them away from the second door until they were in the corner on the kitchen. She could feel some-thing cold behind her and turned to see a large metal oven, its door protruding outwards.

'What are we going to do?' she asked.

Jimmy was looking frantically left and right, from one door to the next.

'Dunno,' he said.

They were trapped in a corner by an invisible assailant, or two, or three.

'Hello,' called Jimmy. 'Whoever is out there, I'm phoning the police.'

It was as if that thought had never occurred to her. She didn't care if they were trespassing, she didn't care that they were probably breaking some law. She looked down at her phone and a sigh of dismay escaped her.

No signal.

'They'll be here any minute, so I suggest you let us go,' Jimmy continued. Silence descended again. She didn't know for how long. She dared not think that it was all over. She didn't want to feel any false hope right now.

Bang!

The sound echoed again, but this time it wasn't from a door closing, it was the sound of someone hitting the dining room door. Someone was on the other side.

Bang!

This time it was Jimmy who screamed out. He reached behind himself and held her tighter.

Bang! Bang!

This time she was sure she saw the door moving under the impact. It may have just been a trick of the light or maybe there was someone very large on the other side banging as hard as they could.

'Come on,' Jimmy said. He began to move towards the far door.

'No,' Catryn whispered. 'What if?' her sentence was interrupted by another thump.

'We know he's that side, we have no real choice.'

'What if it's a trap?' she asked.

Jimmy didn't answer. He eased quietly to the other door and reached out to grab the handle.

Bang!

She could feel him jump and his hand pulled away from the door handle momentarily.

Bang, bang, bang, bangbangbang

As the thumping increased, Jimmy seemed to make up his

mind and find some resolve. He grabbed the door and gave it a pull.

It didn't budge.

Another bang, then another. He pulled again. Still nothing.

Then the banging stopped. Catryn's mouth felt dry and her bowels felt loose. This wasn't how she wanted to go. This wasn't how she wanted to die.

The door to the dining room creaked. Jimmy shone his light towards it. It was beginning to open very slowly. Catryn couldn't see anyone or anything.

'Hurry,' she said frantically.

Jimmy grabbed the door handle again and tugged. Still nothing. He tugged again, and again, and again. She could feel the exertion in the frenzied and furious way he pulled at the handle. There was no doubt about what he was feeling. The panic was beginning to set in, it was beginning to take root in his bones and control his muscles like an evil puppeteer. Catryn could hear the frustration in his breathing; groans being forced through gritted teeth.

She stole a look over to the dining room door.

It was wide open.

She couldn't see anyone there, it just seemed to open to pitch black, an oppressive darkness that seemed to be alive. It pulsed with venomous malevolence, a huge nothingness that was ready to consume both her and Jimmy.

Was there someone there? Was that the outline of someone, a man? A huge monster of a man. She didn't see anything, yet she could see it all. The silhouette, blackness on blackness, standing there with his arms reaching down his sides, his hands gripped hard like fists. It was the same man she saw in the doorway, the presence she had felt the night before at the clearing, she was sure of it. It was Joe ready to take her one more time, to throw her to the ground and piss on her, to rip off her clothes and penetrate her here in the kitchen. He was there to rape her, here and now. He was back to exact his revenge on all the things she had done to him.

Jimmy gave another frenzied pull on the door handle and suddenly it opened. He almost fell backwards in surprise and knocked her out of her reverie, out of the almost hypnotic trance she had been in. The memory of her ex-husband evaporated.

'C'mon,' he grabbed her shoulder and pulled her through the door.

They were in a large room. A ballroom. In the bouncing light of their torches, she was unable to see very far into room, but she didn't care. All that mattered was finding a way out. Jimmy ran into the centre of the room, desperately shining the light from left to right, up and down. He ran to the far wall and Catryn felt her pulse race even faster. She ran after him, determined that she stay as close to him as possible.

She couldn't help but look back at the kitchen, expecting to see someone there, waiting for them. So far, nothing. Because of its size, their lights seemed to make less impact penetrating the gloom than they did in previous rooms – even the dining room.

'Over here,' Jimmy called. He ran towards the far end, to a door.

They were only a few feet away when the door opened.

They both screamed and skidded to a halt. They backed away quickly, but nothing came through the entrance.

Then it slammed shut.

She felt as if every cell in her body jumped with fright. They turned and ran back to the middle of the room, standing back to back, checking every corner of the space.

Another door. It was in the middle of the wall adjacent to the way they had just come in.

'C'mon!' she called out.

They ran towards it when they heard another bang from their left – the kitchen door.

Then another from their right.

Left again.

Catryn couldn't see much but it sounded like the doors

were slamming – open and shut, open and shut. Bang, Bang, Bang.

'Move!' She cried out and took Jimmy's hand. They reached the door and Jimmy grabbed the handle.

'tresssspasssersss'

The voice echo in the chamber, it was a whisper barely heard yet it seemed to fill the entire room. They froze, suddenly too terrified to open the door.

The banging stopped.

'You shall not stop him.' The voice echoed around them again. *'The master will return to this house. Soooooon'*

Then she saw him. The man from the supermarket carpark. The man who had taken the little girls. He stood about fifteen feet away from them, shrouded in gloom.

He stared at them with dead eyes from black sockets. He just stood there for a heartbeat then stepped back, disappearing into the shadow.

'Where'd he go?' Jimmy hissed.

'Here....'

They heard him again and turned to their left. He stood on the edge of darkness once again. His hands reached out toward them. He lifted one finger up to his lips as if he was going to shush them. Then he stepped back into the darkness once more.

Jimmy shone the light in that direction, frantically looking for their tormentor but once again he was gone.

Then:

'Here!'

Catryn turned to her left and saw his face, inches away from hers. She could smell his breath, rotten fetid, as if he had eaten death itself. It was definitely the man she had seen in the doorway a few minutes earlier.

She screamed as loud as she could, feeling the vibrations deep in the pit of her stomach. Jimmy grabbed her around the shoulders and pulled her through the door. The man followed until he stood in the frame. He put his head back and laughed.

They kept backing away, but she could not keep her eyes off him. He didn't come for them, he just laughed. A deep guttural laugh that reminded her of drowning.

Then, as she watched him, he disappeared. He hadn't stepped back into the shadows as he had before. This time he just seemed to fade.

They were in the hallway backing off to the front door, the door they had just left had been directly behind the stairs. Jimmy kept on pulling and she was more than happy to let him lead.

Bang!

The door on the right of the entrance slammed open and shut again.

Bang!

This time it was a door on the left.

Bangbangbangbangbang

The doors continued to thump, like drums in a jungle. Catryn wasn't aware of where they were until the brightness of the day engulfed them.

She blinked rapidly and squinted under the glare. Jimmy continued to pull her until they were back on the driveway.

'Turn around,' he said to her.

She turned and looked him in the eyes. They were bloodshot and he had a sheen of sweat on his forehead.

'Come on, let's get away from here,' he said.

'It's OK,' she said and pulled herself away from him. 'We're safe.'

He looked at her intently and nodded. She knew he understood too. They were safe in the light. The darkness was his domain, but the daylight was their protector.

She felt dizzy for a moment, then stumbled to a nearby bush and vomited. The warm bile passed her lips and, although she felt disgusted, it also felt good.

It was real. It was natural.

She started to laugh. It began in the pit of her stomach where the vomit had just vacated, then moved up to her mouth. She wiped away the vomit and smiled. The dizziness remained but she lifted herself up and looked at the priest. She giggled again and he looked at her with concern.

'Cat, are you alright?'

The laughing caused spasms around her body and made her cough, but she couldn't help it.

'Cat?'

'I'm alright,' she said between giggles. 'I'm alive. We just saw a ghost, and we're alive.'

Jimmy nodded, his face was a mask of concern.

'And it's not Joe. The fucker. I thought...' She laughed again and could feel the relief wash over her. It felt oh so very good. It was as if more than just a weight had lifted off her, it was like a whole mountain had been taken away.

'I thought it was him.'

'Who?' Jimmy asked.

'Joe, my ex-husband.' She coughed again and spat on the floor. 'The bastard is dead.' She didn't offer any more of an explanation and Jimmy didn't push.

She stepped close to him and took his arm in hers. She felt weirdly good. She had faced one of the most terrifying experiences in her life and she had lived to tell the tale. They had both faced the darkness and, for now, they were fine. They were alive. It was a feeling that seemed to extend from the tip of her toes to the top of her head, and every fibre in between.

'You realise that it is the supernatural bullshit that we saw?' she asked. 'There's no doubt. He disappeared in front of us, over and over again. Did you see?'

Jimmy nodded. 'Yep,' he said. 'I saw. I saw it all.'

'What does it all mean?'

Jimmy shrugged. 'I don't know. Too soon to say. Let's get out of here. I really do feel like we are safe for now, but I don't want to be here. This place gives me the creeps.'

CHAPTER 24

By the time they arrived back at Jimmy's house, their heartbeats had returned closer to normal, the sweat on their brows had receded and the adrenaline that had been pumping through their veins had cleared. They hardly spoke as they walked down the Hill and then down the narrow steps. They had faced something that had previously been unimaginable, had survived what could only be described as a living nightmare, and now they were walking through the ordinary and very normal streets of Trehenri.

The two extremes were completely incongruous as if they had been plucked from one reality and dropped into a completely new one.

Jimmy had always enjoyed walking and enjoyed company – you couldn't do his job without being a people person – but he didn't know what to say to Catryn right now. It was almost as if talking about it would bring it all back and the horror they had experienced would appear before them on the road. It wasn't that avoiding talking about it took away the reality of it, there was no doubt that what they experienced was real, but it was more of a talisman keeping the evil at bay.

From the moment they had entered the house, he had felt it. It was a creeping sensation that prickled under his skin. He told Catryn that he had always believed, that to believe in God – a supernatural being – was also to believe in other things or at least open to the possibilities that were out there. This was true to an extent, but what he realised now was that this belief had always been limited to an intellectual notion. His brain had believed it because he had trained it to believe, but deep down in his heart, he may not have been so sure.

The house had convinced him; it had confronted the truths about who he thought he was and laid them bare in front of him. And it had frightened him.

He had assumed that, by being open to these possibilities, he was preparing himself for them. And if and when he was ever confronted by them, he would be able to face them head on; back straight, staring it straight in the eyes.

This hadn't been the case.

The evil he had felt had rocked him to the core and he'd had to fight the urge to run, to leave the place immediately and never to return. To sell his house in Trehenri and to move somewhere such malevolence didn't exist. Strangely though, the will to fight hadn't come from a prayer or even conviction in God but from Catryn. She was the one who convinced him to enter. He had put up a front which he hoped she believed, but it was still a front.

He was very curious about her. He knew about her past, about what she had gone through in London and he understood the pain that she must have been holding onto inside. Of course, he wasn't going to mention it to her. It was her past, her secrets and her choice to share them or not. All that he could say was that he admired her courage, her resolve and the way she was going through this difficult time.

And, as they had discussed whether to enter Henry House or not, he had made the decision solely on his admiration for her. Yet, despite his apparent bravado, inside he had wanted nothing more than to run.

He was always a stubborn person, he knew that, and it was this stubbornness that had stopped him fleeing before they had even seen anything. It had kept him focused. The fact that he was afraid was reason enough to be the first one into each room, to enter the kitchen when there was a possibility that someone was in there. It wasn't stoicism but he had hoped that that was what he was projecting.

But now that it was over, he felt relieved. As he had pulled

Catryn out into the bright sunshine, he had felt a wave of release cascade over every nerve ending. It was as if the sun had washed the fear away, a baptism of illuminance.

Now, as they walked to his house in what seemed like a comfortable silence, he felt clean. It was as if he had been jumping in pig swill, then gone home and had the longest most satisfying bath imaginable.

He could see his house in the distance and his son-in-law's car outside. The streets were quiet by day but at night, as everyone returned from work, finding a parking space was sometimes a chore. Although going out in the evening was sometimes unavoidable, he often tried leaving his car behind if he could because he could never guarantee he'd be able to park outside the house when he returned. Plus, all the walking helped him keep fit, if only in a small way.

On the porch, he could see Gareth talking to Carys for a moment before looking in their direction. Jimmy raised his hand to wave and Gareth returned it.

'Gareth!' He called out as he and Catryn approached his house. 'How are you? What brings you here today?'

He was surprised by how good he felt now. He actually had a lightness in his step which he hadn't felt for a long time and it reminded him of the day he met Carys. He wondered if all people who have experienced the terror and the danger that he and Catryn had just survived, felt the same way. If they did, he could imagine why so many were addicted to adrenaline.

'Jimmy, Carys has just been telling me about your morning expedition.'

Jimmy smiled. 'You don't know the half of it,' he said. 'Isn't that right Catryn?'

He turned to his companion and realised for the first time that he had not really taken any notice of her on the way home and he had almost completely ignored her. Now he saw her though, he could see that she was still terribly shaken. Her skin was pallid, her eyes dark. She looked almost smaller than she had earlier when she had first cowered on the ground in front of the kitchen. It was as if the shock had hit her as they walked and the exaltation she had felt after escaping the house was now gone.

'Are you OK, Cat?' Carys asked. She stepped forward, took Catryn by the hand and steered her into the house.

'What exactly happened up there?' Gareth asked.

'Have you ever been there?' Jimmy said.

Gareth thought about it for a moment then replied, 'To be honest, I probably forgot it ever existed.'

Jimmy nodded. 'Yes, I think you are right, and I think that is what it needs.'

'It?' Gareth raised an eyebrow.

'It, yes, It. Come inside, I need a drink. I'll tell you all about it.'

***

Jimmy took a slow sip of his whiskey and put the glass down on the small nest of tables by the settee. He could feel it burn the back of his throat and it felt good. It was Penderyn Myth, a rich flavourable drink made only a half hour's drive away. It had cost him over £30.00 on a visit to the distillery only a few months before and it was perhaps his favourite whiskey of all. The advertising claimed it was matured in ex-red wine and bourbon casks, and he was sure he could taste the difference. He wasn't a connoisseur, but he did enjoy a sip now and again. Today he needed it more than ever.

They were sat together in the living room, Jimmy in his favourite spot in front of the 40-inch TV he loved so much, Carys sitting next to him, her hand in his lap. Catryn sat on the two-seater settee opposite them and Gareth had pulled a chair over from the dining table. He leaned forward, listening intently, his elbows on his knees, hands clasped together.

'Why'd you go there in the first place?' Gareth asked. 'You know there's a killer on the loose. Didn't it occur to you, at least once, that he might be holed up there?'

Jimmy shook his head and took a deep breath. He didn't

know what exactly to say or how to start and he had to organise his thoughts first. He was going to tell Gareth everything, he had decided. It didn't matter how ridiculous it made him look.

'We weren't going there because of the killer,' he started then paused again. 'No, that's not right. We were but we were interested in a different angle.'

'A different angle?' Gareth asked. He looked at Catryn who sat quietly, her hands on her lap, her legs together.

'Look, you have seen the video of that man disappearing, you've heard the stories and you've seen what happened in the church. You've got to admit, none of this looks... um... natural.'

'Natural?' Gareth asked.

'Gareth, listen to Jimmy,' Carys said. 'I know he's struggling for words but please give him the benefit of the doubt.'

'Look, Mam,' Gareth said. He didn't call Carys Mam very often but Jimmy knew that when he did she felt proud and warmed by it. 'I'm listening. I'll be the first to admit this whole thing is a puzzle. And yes, I have seen the tapes and been to the wall where he disappeared. I'm not sure if I would have used the word "natural" but I get what you mean.'

Jimmy nodded and took another sip of his drink. From the corner of his eye, he could see Catryn doing the same, almost mirroring his movements. He took a deep breath, savouring the flavour and the heat once more. He was beginning to relax and to calm down but whether that was the drink or the familiarity of the surroundings, he didn't know.

'It started off with a conversation with Cat and Morgan. They were interested in the name 'Lucy'. Obviously, it is very important, both girls taken have been called Lucy and the graffiti in the church – Lucy For Ever. Morgan pops in to see Taliesin Jones up Henry Hill occasionally. You know Tal?'

Gareth shook his head.

'Well, Tal is a dirty old man, a real nasty piece of work, isn't that right Cat?'

Cat nodded. 'I didn't think men like that really existed,' she said.

'Oh, they do,' Jimmy continued. 'Anyway. If you want to know anything about the history of Trehenri or the Rhondda, then Tal's your man. He's a collector of what you might call historical gossip. Not just the history book stuff, but the rumours and all the stuff that would normally be dismissed because of lack of reliable evidence.'

'A conspiracy theorist?' Gareth asked.

'Well. Sometimes, although I don't suppose there's really much room for conspiracies in these valleys. We don't exactly live somewhere the rest of the world thinks of as important.'

'You tell that to all the press that are clogging up the Main Road,' Carys said with a smile.

Jimmy preceded to tell Gareth about the ideas that Tal had put forward and the plan to go to visit Henry House. He then described what happened in the house, getting Catryn to fill in the occasional detail. As the conversation went on, he could see how she herself was beginning to relax, as if she was coming out of a shell of shyness. But it wasn't shyness, he knew, and could see that the talking and describing of the event may be helping her come to terms with it, at least a little bit. It would take them both a long time to fully accept what they had experienced.

He also became aware of a change in Gareth. He could see the process that the man was going through, from son-in-law to police. His back became straighter, his hands turned to fists and his whole countenance became more erect.

Jimmy also became more aware of Carys. As he described the encounter with the mysterious man who could disappear into shadows, her grip on his hands became tighter. He squeezed her hands and looked at her, trying to reassure her that he was ok and that no harm befell them.

At the end of the story, he sat back and took another sip of his whiskey.

'We spoke last night about how, being a minister of religion, I've always been open to the supernatural. I always thought it was my job. I know others would disagree but that was always my belief. Now that I have had that confirmed, and in, I admit, a really terrifying manner, I am unsure what to think. The imagined has become real. I guess I'm feeling a little melodramatic.'

Carys sobbed quietly, so he put his arm around her and pulled her closer.

'I'm alright,' he said. 'We made it. We came out the other side.'

'What do you think?' Catryn asked Gareth.

'I don't know what to think about all the supernatural stuff, I don't have the imagination to process any of that, but it does seem to me that Henry House is central to all this and that the perpetrator could be there. As I said, he may be using it as a hideout.'

He stood up and crossed the room to the door.

'I'm going to call this in,' he said. 'If he is still up there then this may be our chance to get him, to put an end to this. And if the girls are there too, then we need to get them out.'

He took his phone out of his pocket as he left the room. Silence fell on the three of them for a moment.

'I don't ever want to go there again,' Catryn said.

'Me neither,' Jimmy replied.

CHAPTER 25

Morgan turned the corner onto Ynsyhir Road and saw all the police cars. There were six of them parked haphazardly each side of the road and there were uniforms everywhere. And they seemed to be concentrated around Jimmy Bevan's house.

His heart skipped a beat and he began to run up the hill to the house.

He had finished work and had gone straight to Glyn's house to talk to Catryn. He wanted to know what had happened during their trip to Henry House this morning but, according to her father, Catryn hadn't been home all day. She must still be at Jimmy's, he thought; so he had carried on up the hill to his friend's house.

It had been a long, hard day and he was tired. No one had really wanted to be there, teachers or pupils. The classes had gone slowly, like a slow boat on a lethargic sea. He had given each class some work then sat behind his desk and waited for the lesson to be over. His students had done the same, he knew. They hadn't put any real effort into anything other than gossiping about the tragic events of the weekend.

He hadn't done much gossiping himself. During lunch time he had found himself on detention duty and had sat in a class of four kids who had spent their time either whispering to each other across the room or, when he had bothered to tell them to be quiet, had stared wistfully out of the windows at the blue skies and their friends who played football in the yard.

Then, when the final bell hand rung, the whole school

STEPHEN AMOS

seemed to sigh heavily and trudge out into the late afternoon. He hadn't bothered to speak to anyone, he had just grabbed his coat and joined the kids on their various walks home.

But all this was forgotten as he reached Jimmy's house and a policeman stepped in front of him and stopped him approaching.

'Sorry sir,' the policeman said. 'You can't go in there.'

Morgan tried pushing passed him, but the cop was too strong. Another PC joined his colleague to help control the situation.

'Are they all ok? Catryn and Jimmy? Are they OK?' Morgan asked frantically.

'Everyone is fine,' the first PC said.

'I've got to see them!'

'Calm down first sir and we'll discuss it. What's your name?'

'Morgan, Morgan Williams. I'm a friend of Jimmy and Carys. I believe another one of my friends, Catryn Evans may be here as well.'

He took as step back and the policeman spoke into his radio. He could feel his heart pounding in his chest and was aware of a sheen of sweat that had broken on his brow. He didn't know if it was because of the run up the hill or if it was caused by the fear that something may have happened to his friends.

After a moment the policeman told him he could go to the house. The second officer escorted him up to the front door. As he crossed the threshold, he saw Catryn standing in front of him and he felt a wave of relief.

She looked at him and smiled, then moved towards him and put her arms around him and squeezed tightly.

'You ok?' he asked.

Catryn let him go, then looked straight at him.

'We're fine,' she said. 'It's been a helluva day but we're all ok.'

She took his hand and Morgan felt a flush of heat touch his skin. She led him into the living room where Jimmy, Carys and two other officers sat with tea in their hands.

'Mogsy!' Jimmy called. 'Come in.' He stood up and crossed to the dining table, took one of the chairs and moved it to join the others who were all sitting in a circle. 'Sorry, there's not a lot of room here.'

'No, that's ok.' He sat down on the proffered chair. Catryn moved away from him and sat on the far end of the two-seater settee. He couldn't help but feel a sense of loss that she was so far from him. He wanted her to sit beside him and hold his hand just like Carys was doing with Jimmy.

'What's all this?' he asked tentatively.

'We think we may have encountered him.' Jimmy replied.

'Him?'

Jimmy nodded.

'The man you saw in the supermarket,' Catryn said. She smiled but Morgan could see a weight behind her eyes he hadn't seen the previous night. Had it been there earlier or was this something new.?

'In Henry House?' he asked.

'Yes, there are loads of police up there now. Gareth is there with them. They're going to catch him this afternoon,' Jimmy said. He turned to one of the officers on the chair next to Morgan who glanced at his watch and nodded.

'They're up there now,' the officer said. 'If he's up there, they'll get him and when they do, we'll be the first to hear.'

Morgan glanced to Catryn, and she caught his eye and gave him a sweet smile.

'So, what happened?' he asked.

CHAPTER 26

Sargent Kofi Antwi absentmindedly checked his Heckler & Koch MP5 once more. It wasn't because of nerves; it was just a ritual that he went through each time he was called into duty as part of the Firearms Unit of South Wales and Gwent Police. The gun felt comfortable in his hands and as his CI gave them a rundown of the operation, he could feel the adrenaline start to pump through his veins.

'We don't have a complete plan of the house, the couple who came earlier only went into the right wing of the building. There is a small room here, leading to a dining room here and then a kitchen.' Chief Inspector Arnold punctuated each 'here' by tapping an A3 sheet of paper with a crude drawn plan of the downstairs of the building they were about to take.

'We have contacted the local historical societies, the council and the libraries for detailed plans of the rest of the building but, as of yet, we have not been given anything useful. We don't have time to wait as the bastard we are after has, as you all know, proven very slippery so far.'

There were nods from the eight armed men who stood in a small circle around the makeshift table that had been placed on the lane just around the corner from Henry House. Antwi knew what the CI was referring to although he wasn't sure if he believed it all. He had seen the videos on the news and had heard the stories by the witnesses that the perp was able to disappear into shadows like a ghost. He knew there was a rational explanation for all this and they would soon find out but, until then, it was too easy for the imagination to run riot.

He looked around to the others. Immediately to his left

was Jonesy, usually the character of the group, who normally had a joke for any moment, however today he was quiet with a serious and concentrated look on his face. Next to Jonesy on his right was Wood, Bosch, Newman and Gwilym. On Antwi's right were Jones Jnr, so named, not because of his father, but because he was younger than Jonesy; Smiffy, the Londoner who they often made fun of because of his apparent inability to pronounce his th's and Kowalski, who they often referred to as Rookie even though he had two years full service as part of their little group and a further eight years on the beat.

They all looked serious. They were in the zone, ready to take down some scum.

'It's not an ideal situation so we are going to be extra careful. You'll be split into four groups, Team one, Antwi, and Gwilym – you'll take the right rooms. Team Two, Jones and Smiffy, you'll take the left. You should meet at the back of the house in what we are assuming is some kind of ballroom, here,' he tapped the paper one more time. 'Once you have cleared the ground floor, you can proceed upstairs and each take the same wings as down stairs.

'Team three, Newman and Wood, you will stay at the front of the house to ensure that no one gets out that way. There may be a back entrance so Junior, Kowalski and Bosch, Team Four, you'll circle around the back and make sure no one gets out that way. We don't know how many exits there are, but we can assume there is at least one, probably a lot more. We've got air support so if he does try and get out the back, we can track him. There is a small overgrown area immediately to the back of the property, then the landscape turns to rough ground. There are a lot of trees, bushes and ferns out there. There is nothing behind it for a mile or two until you get to the forestry up by Llanwonno. Beyond that, I'm sorry but we know very little.

'This is not an ideal situation and I don't like separating you so much, but our target is wanted for two murders and two kidnappings, so we don't have much of a choice.

'Now, the two kidnapped children may well be in this building. If you come across them, secure the scene and get them out immediately. Rescue is our priority. Once they are safe then you can get back inside and finish the job. If the target decides to use the children as human shields, do not engage. Call for back up and we'll have Hawkins in there on the double.'

Hawkins, Antwi knew, was the hostage negotiator. They had met a few times on various operations and Antwi knew he was a good man.

'Let me say this one more time, guys. This is not the usual type of target. I don't know how he is doing what he is doing, all I know is that he is incredibly big and extremely dangerous. If in doubt, take him out. I don't say this lightly. If you, or any of your team, are in mortal danger, don't take any chances. We've all seen what this bastard can do. We all know how fucked up this situation seems. Be careful and go get him.'

***

Gareth stood beside Chief Inspector Jack Andrews at the end of Henry Hill, right at the spot where the road ended and the lane began. As a detective, he wasn't allowed to take part in a Firearms operation, so had to stand back until the whole thing was over. There was silence between them, not that there was nothing to say, but the tension they all felt stopped them making any small talk. This wasn't the time.

He clenched his fists and tensed his whole body. He even began grinding his teeth again, something he hadn't done for a long time. When his body began to ache from the stress, he would pace for a few moments and straighten his tie.

Gareth hated waiting. People always had an idea about detectives, how they would always be first in through the door, their guns raised in front of them. But this was confined to Hollywood. He even doubted many detectives in the US ever bust down doors, shouting 'Police' on top of their voices. It looked cool but that was all it was, it wasn't real life.

'Sir,' a voice called from behind them, directed to CI Andrews. 'They are going in.'

'C'mon,' Andrews said to Gareth. 'I want to listen to this.'

All around them the street had been transformed. There were police cars and vans everywhere, and uniforms mulling about right down the street. Every house had been cleared just in case something went wrong, although with this manpower, there surely couldn't be much that could go wrong. Yet, because of the images that the world had seen– which, of course, included every single officer in the South Wales Police – there was an edginess to the early evening that possibly wouldn't have normally been there.

Andrews took hold of Gareth's elbow and guided him to a large van that was parked about twenty yards away.

His CI was a good man. He was very much a hardass and could be overly officious sometimes, but he was always there to back up his team.

The back of the van was packed with radio equipment and other hardware that made absolutely no sense to Gareth. He always thought of himself as a tech savvy person, but this was way over his head. There wasn't as many flashing lights as there always seemed to in the movies, and the tech guy looked quite ordinary (God, I've been spending too much time watching films with Jimmy, he thought).

'They are going in, sir,' the tech said.

He passed Andrews and Gareth two sets of headphones. Gareth put them on and immediately his head was full of static, then:

***

'Teams one, two and three at the front entrance awaiting go.'

Antwi held his rifle in front of him, using it as an extension of his hand and his eye. Wherever he went, the gun would lead.

He moved slowly to the front of the building whilst Junior, Kowalski and Bosch made their way rapidly to the rear. They wouldn't enter until the guys were in place.

Antwi could sense the wrongness of the house even before he crossed the threshold. Although he would never compare notes with Catryn or Jimmy, he felt exactly the same way as they had earlier. It reminded him of stories his mother used to tell him when he was a child. She was a tough Ghanaian woman with a steely gaze and what always seemed like some very strange beliefs. He always remembered her getting angry with him after she caught him singing in the bath one evening.

'What do you think you are doing?' she'd asked, her voice laced with venom. 'Don't you know that singing in the bath is a sure way of inviting ghosts into your house? Okwasea!'

She also believed in all the usual juju bullshit that too many people would accept without thinking it through. Growing up, he had been angry at her for these ideas. He had also been embarrassed and afraid to mention it in front of his friends in case they would ridicule him. Now, as an adult, he had grown out of these feelings and just accepted her as she was – a woman who grew up without any real education yet still managed to travel three thousand miles with her husband and start a new life, surrounded by strange people, with some equally strange customs, in a climate which couldn't have been more different from anything she had ever experienced.

He had grown up a Welshman, with a valleys accent. He had been to his mother's homeland many times in his life – he had even taken his wife and kids there only eighteen months ago – but he considered himself Welsh. This was his home, the place he felt most comfortable.

But now he was a little boy again, a Ghanaian in a foreign country. This may be the only home he had ever known but right now it was as if he was a child, lying on the floor at his mother's feet, listening to all her stories as if they were gospel. He felt he had been caught singing in a thousand bathtubs and the ghosts had all assembled in this one spot.

'Team Four in place. Good to go.'

The radio crackled in his ear, then he heard the voice of his commander:

'Teams one, Two and Three, you are all good to go. Go get him.'

Thoughts of his mother evaporated from his mind, replaced with a steely determination. The sense that there was something wrong persisted, but it was pushed aside by years of experience and training.

Jones and Smiffy set off in front of them to secure the entrance way before teams One and Two could enter. They stepped up to the door, which was half open - probably left like that by the two people who had been here earlier - and turned on their torches. Jones kicked the door wide whilst Smiffy stepped into the darkness, the jumping, erratic torch beams were the only sign that he was in there. Jones was right behind him into the void.

'Team Three in place. Entrance way is clear.'

Antwi took a deep breath and stepped forward into Henry House.

***

In the darkness of a tomb, he stirred again. His rage boiled and overflowed like larva pouring from a volcano. It burned red in the blackness of his soul.

They were back, violators, trespassers. He had thought they had been taken care of; he had hoped for one more day. That was all that was needed. One more night before the house became a home again, before he was able to return and to rule, not just over the pitiful lives he once had providence over, but many, many more. Souls to feed upon, souls to rip apart with his teeth.

He called again, and Shadow appeared.

'They are back, master.' Shadow's voice spoke to him.

'They are. They have not learned their lesson from earlier.'

'What is it you would like me to do this time?'

He thought for a moment. He didn't care if they found the souls he had taken thus far. That was fine for he had fed on them and had been nourished by them. He no longer cared for the silence, for his anger screamed louder than any interloper. Now he only wanted to rid himself of vermin, for surely that was who they were. There had never been any rats in his house, not for over two hundred years, but now there were.

He really had one choice, which was good as he only wanted one.

'Kill them,' he hissed, the words echoing throughout this dark chamber, cascading around the darkness.

'Kkkkkiiiiiiilllll tttthhhheeeemmmmmm........'

He could feel Shadow's pleasure. He could hear the blood lust pulsing in his servant's veins. This was why Shadow was here. This was what Shadow existed for.

'Thank you, my lord.'

Shadow retreated from the darkness.

***

'Team One, first room as described. All clear.'

Antwi's light pierced the darkness and illuminated the door to the dining room. Gwilym moved to the door at the far end and reached out with his hand. With his left hand, he started to count off from four in a rhythmic pattern. As he got to two, he stopped the hand movements and returned to his firing position. One was counted with a nod of the head.

Gwilym opened the door quickly and stepped back allowing Antwi to swiftly enter the room, his gun moving back and forth and up and down. Gwilym was directly behind him, covering his left. The lights attached to the rifles shone brightly and the shadows disappeared more quickly than the lights from Cat's phone and Jimmy's small torch could have done.

He walked straight to the far wall whilst Gwilym stayed on the left. He crouched down quickly, the light penetrating the darkness beneath the dining table. There was no room for anyone to hide in here, no cupboards deep enough to hold a body.

But that wasn't the worry, was it? They weren't entirely sure they believed the man they were hunting could really disappear into shadows but, however implausible it seemed, there was always that doubt, that suspicion that there was more to life than they could understand.

'Team two. First room, cloak room. All clear.'

He could hear the whispered voice of Jones in his ears. The voice had a hardness to it that, whilst seeming to be professional and focused, still had a breathless tremor of tension in it. He knew that sound, knew where it came from, for he felt it himself. Even with all the training, the darkness still had its own challenges, its own nightmares.

But that could, and would, be controlled.

The two men glanced over to each other and with a quick nod they advanced through the dining room to the far end and to the kitchen.

***

'Team two. First room, cloak room. All clear.'

Jones closed the door to the cloak room and moved quietly to the next door which was about four feet to the right. Smiffy moved almost silently beside him, coming to a stop directly in front of the door. Jones reached out with his right hand and took hold of the door handle, then turned to his partner who began the count down from four.

He pulled the handle down swiftly and pushed the door open, stepping out of the way as Smiffy nimbly stepped passed him and into the room. Jones joined him moving to his partner's right.

It was a large Drawing Room, with a slight wall to the left to allow the shape of the cloak room, before opening up. It was decorated with three large sofas and a number of other casual chairs. A small table sat on a beautifully woven rug at the center of the sofas, which surrounded it like three sides of a square. At the final side was a beautifully elaborate fireplace, almost large enough for one of them to stand upright in. At the far end to the right was an open space and a small bar area, although there were no longer any bottles or glasses. The walls were adorned with paintings, mostly of hunting scenes – men on horses with straight backs and straighter tall hats. Hounds playfully bounded around the feet of the horses, and occasionally young children could be seen playing with the dogs. There were large shutters on the opposite walls which presumably hid the windows which would have looked up the valley and across to Wattstown. Between the shutters hung a huge portrait of one man, sitting on an ornate chair, glaring down at the occupants of the room.

Jones swung his torch around the room and lingered for a second on that picture. The man's eyes seemed to be looking right through him, through the body armour he wore and into his heart. It sent an involuntary shiver down his spine and, even after he had moved on to the rest of the room, the glare from those eyes still seemed to bore into him.

But there was no one here. The silence hung heavily on the two policemen, and the shadows pressed down on them. There were most certainly ghosts here. Maybe not supernatural specters haunting the rooms and corridors of this old building, but the remnants of lives lived and the strange quality of age. That was the only way he could think of it. With the furniture and the rug, all still in place as they would have been in Victorian times, there was a sense that the place was still used, still lived in. People had once been in this room, once a long time ago and they still remained in some intangible way. They had talked around that fireplace, they had loved and argued and planned and dreamed. Yet Jones didn't get the feeling they were happy dreams. The man in the picture, whether he was the owner or a relative, didn't seem to be the type who promoted a happy household.

All these thoughts were fleeting and even the lingering effects of those eyes were pushed to the back of his mind. They moved through the room to a door on the far right of their entrance.

'Team Two, Second Room, Drawing Room, Clear.'

CHAPTER 27

Silence had fallen on the room.

It seemed too comfortable, to homely when considering what they had gone through only a few hours earlier and what was happening only a quarter of a mile away from them at that moment. It was only up the hill, a few streets and a few turns to navigate, yet it was as if the whole experience, the whole encounter, belonged in another world.

Even another realm.

Jimmy kept having flashbacks to the house. Sudden reminders of what they had seen and felt. He was afraid to close his eyes; it was as if in the darkness of his eye lids, that man could reach out and caress his skin. He could feel it touch every single blade of hair on his arms.

It made him feel uneasy, edgy and....

What?

There was something there, something beyond his grasp at the moment, something on the tip of his tongue. He felt like a child looking up at a closed bag high on a shelf. He knew there were probably sweets in there - there had to be - but he couldn't quite reach them.

He could feel Carys' hand adjust its grip on his and he turned to look at her.

He loved her so much. Who would have thought that a priest could meet the woman of his dreams at a night club? Booming music, sweaty bodies, alcohol pumping through veins, possibly a few youngsters high on whatever drugs were cool at the time, and a man of God getting horny over a strange woman who, on a whim, he had decided to spend the rest of his life with.

He looked into her eyes and could see the worry in them. There was a concern for the men who were up there in Henry House facing whatever it was that he had faced earlier; there was an unease of what was going to happen to her family and her community if this man escaped, and there was a love that looked upon him from deep within.

He wanted to stand up and shoo everyone out of his house. He would take no nonsense. He would get rid of them all until the house was their home again. He would find whatever book that Carys was reading, put it into her hands, place a cup of tea on the stack of tables next to the settee, and tell her not to worry, that everything was going to be as it was.

He would then pop a Blu-Ray on – an Akira Kurasawa epic – maybe Ran, he always loved that. Shakespeare and samurais, glorious cinematography and captivating action. He would lose himself in ancient Japan knowing that, when he returned to the real world two and a half hours later, all would be good. All would be right.

There would be no murder, no mysterious cutthroats kidnapping children, only the usual preparation of sermons and the visiting of the old and needy. It would all be as it always was.

Then he saw the Shadowman again, materialising out of the heavy obsidian gloom, his face mocking and his hands reaching towards him.

He shivered involuntarily, a movement which started at his shoulders, spewed down his torso, lingering around the nape of his neck where it held tightly, screwing his muscles up in a ball.

'You OK?' Carys whispered, and he knew why she didn't raise her voice. It was as if in the silence there was a spy ready to take whatever you said and use it against you in a court of law.

'Fine,' he replied quietly. 'I was just thinking about how we met.'

She smiled at him with a curious look in her eyes.

'That's a strange thing to be thinking about now?' She glanced around the room and seemed to catch someone's eye, but Jimmy didn't turn around to see who. He just stared at her, the flutter in his stomach did battle with the apprehension and he was glad of that.

He turned to see Catryn looking at him smiling.

'Do you know we met in a nightclub?' he asked her.

Catryn shook her head.

'No,' she said. 'I can't imagine you in a night club.'

'Neither can I anymore, but I was young and foolish. It was almost as if it was meant to be, as if there was someone looking out for us, that we were just puppets on a -'

He stopped talking abruptly, the thought hitting him with a sudden force which seemed to stop his breathing for a moment, maybe even stopping his heart from beating.

'Jimmy?' Carys asked. 'Are you sure you are alright?'

'Yes, yes,' he said to her, then turned back to Cat.

'Do you remember what he said?'

'Who?' she asked.

'Him! Him, the man, the big man, the shadow man?'

He could see her searching her memory for something significant, but she obviously wasn't seeing it. He could see the others around him move forward, aware that Jimmy had remembered something of importance.

'No,' Catryn said. 'I mean, it was happening so fast and I wasn't really -'

'I know, it only just occurred to me. I knew there was something, but I couldn't remember, I couldn't put my finger on it.'

'What are you talking about?' One of the policemen – Allison! That was it, Sergeant John Allison – asked.

Jimmy took a deep breath and tried to organise his thoughts as best he could.

'He was taunting us, he seemed to disappear into the darkness and reappear elsewhere.'

'You've told us that,' Allison said.

'Yeah, he seemed to be playing with us, like a cat plays with a mouse or a spider, and he kept talking and laughing. It was a big game to him. Then at one point he said something like "Soon he will return to this house and...?" I don't know, I can't remember exactly.'

Catryn's eyes widened.

'That's right,' she said. 'He called us trespassers and then said, he would return soon.'

'Who?' Asked Morgan.

'I don't know,' Jimmy said. 'But it's important.'

'Why?'

Jimmy looked to Morgan; his eyes boring into the younger man's soul.

'Because it means he is not acting alone. It means that the Shadowman is working for someone.'

'You don't know that?' Allison exclaimed. 'How can you assume that? You were panicking. You were terrified. How can you be sure what he actually said and what it meant?'

Jimmy ignored him and focused on Morgan.

'Remember what Tal told you? About Henry believing in the occult and messing around with black magic and stuff?'

'Yeah, I remember but you can't mean?'

'He can,' Catryn interjected. She stared at Jimmy intently. 'Are you suggesting that Henry is in control somehow? That he is controlling the killer?'

Jimmy nodded. 'It's ridiculous I know?'

'It's insane,' cried Morgan.

Jimmy turned to Carys. He could feel the eagerness in his body but when he looked at his wife, he could see that she wasn't on the same wavelength.

'Carys? What do you think?'

'I dunno,' she said. 'It sounds...um...far-fetched.'

'Why?' Jimmy was not going to be put off. 'You seemed to be up for the idea that the supernatural was involved last night?'

'I don't know,' she replied. 'It's just all this is so, I don't know, real. It's all of a sudden and....' She flung her hands in the air with exasperation. 'I don't know what you have seen today. It sounds all so unbelievable, and I trust you one hundred percent. It's just that there are men up there right now, they've probably already caught him, and it's difficult to think of ghosts almost on your doorstep. I'm not making any sense, am I?'

Jimmy reached over to her and took her into his arms.

'You make complete sense. You really do.'

'But?' she asked.

He eased her back a little, so he could look at her. He looked into her hazel eyes and again he felt his overwhelming love for her.

'I think he's behind it. I think that somehow Henry is behind it. You are probably right, they have already caught him and he's in handcuffs sitting in the back of a Black Mariah as we speak. But as the story comes out, I bet he'll use that as his defence. People won't believe him, of course, why should they?'

'Wait a minute,' Allison interrupted. 'What the hell are you talking about? Who is this Henry you keep talking about?'

Jimmy looked from Morgan to Catryn then to Carys. She smiled at him wryly.

'I can't say I belief any of this, so you can explain it.'

Jimmy turned back to the policeman and it suddenly hit him how absurd the whole thing was. Could he really claim to understand it if he couldn't explain it?

'Um...' He began.

CHAPTER 28

They repeated the countdown at the door to the kitchen. Gwilym opened the door quickly and Antwi tensed. This is where the woman had seen him for the first time, standing in the shadows of the kitchen.

But there was nothing there.

Antwi released his breath, hardly aware that he had been holding it for the last few moments. He took a few steps inside and swung his rifle and his torch left and right. He then stood quickly to his left and Gwilym did the same on his right. He then stooped to look under the work area in the center of the room. Again nothing.

They began to move forward, Antwi aware of the door at the far end of the kitchen to his left. That was the door to what the woman had described as the ballroom.

'Door, straight on,' Gwilym said. Antwi followed the beam of his partner's torch and could see another door on the far wall. This was new, neither the man nor the woman had mentioned this.

He nodded. It looked like it could possibly be a rear exit.

'Team Four, come in,' Antwi said into the radio.

'Team One,' Junior replied. 'I can see a door which may be an exit. We're going to check it out. Be advised.'

They continued through the dark kitchen; their nerves cranked up. Tiny motes of dust caught the beams of white light, dancing in the air, and Antwi was slowly aware of a very light breeze in the room which was missing in the stillness of the other rooms. At the far end of a kitchen, there was a small table which was clear, except for what looked like traces of a thick liquid. He reached out and touched it with his gloved hand, rubbing it together between his fingers.

'What's that?' Gwilym asked quietly.

'I dunno, blood, maybe?'

In the gloom it was difficult to be sure, but the possibility sent another shiver down his spine. It was a day of shivers.

He joined his partner in front of the door and counted down again. On 'one' the door was pulled open quickly. It wasn't an exit; it was what looked like a small pantry. He stepped inside and took everything in swiftly. There was not much to see but what he did see turned his stomach over, made bile rise on his throat, and his forehead break out in a sweat.

The room was small. There were two other doors, one on the left and another at the other side of the room. Deep, dark shelves crowded every available wall space. On some of the shelves there were jars filled with strange liquids.

But it was what was on the floor that hurt him so hard.

A small child lay flat out as if awaiting a coffin. Even in the harshness of the torch light, he could see the pallid skin, the limpness of her hair and the look of horror on her face. Her eyes were open but empty, as if the eye balls themselves had been removed. The movement of the lights caused shadows to move in the sockets, giving the impression that the child was looking around, looking desperately for someone to rescue her from something that she had already succumb to.

She wore a nightdress, but not one that she would have worn when she was taken. This one looked old, in style - which reminded him of something from a Jane Austin book - and also worn, ragged and dirty.

He involuntarily took a step back and bumped into Gwilym who was looking at the poor child over Antwi's shoulders.

'Oh, fuck,' Gwilym said quietly.

Antwi had to turn his head away from the body and began counting slowly, first in English, then Welsh and finally in Twi - his mother's tongue. This was his way, his method to take charge of his body and to gain control over the situation. He had seen some of the most hideous things human beings were capable of. He had once seen a severed head and more than a few bodies awash with blood, but, maybe because it was a child left on the stone floor of this awful house, this one seemed to be worse.

He turned back to the little girl and stepped further into the room. Gwilym crowded in beside him and Antwi wasn't initially aware that his partner was talking until the man tapped him on the shoulder.

'Look,' Gwilym nodded towards some of the jars on the shelf. Antwi didn't realise what he was seeing at first and then wished he wasn't seeing it at all.

In one of the jars almost directly in front of him, a pair of eyes floated in a clear, yellow liquid.

'Oh, motherfucker,' he whispered.

'And that one,' Gwilym reached passed him and pointed to another jar in which a small heart floated. The jar next to it there was another organ, and another one. In all they counted nine jars, each with what Antwi presumed was an internal organ, held in the same yellow liquid.

The other jars on the shelves were mercifully empty.

'Team One, come in,' a voice crackled over the radio. It was Andrews, outside at the command post. 'What is it? What have you found?'

Antwi started to speak, but his voice caught in the back of his throat. He cleared it loudly and, for the first time, became aware of the tears that were falling across his cheek.

'Team One, come in,' Andrews said more urgently.

'Team One here,' he said slowly. 'We have a body of a small child. Dead.' He cleared his throat again. 'We also have what looks like jars of organs and, um -' he didn't want to say eyes, he couldn't '- other body parts.'

He continued to describe the scene as best he could, trying to keep his voice calm and even, aware that he was probably failing. Then, he took a deep breath and awaited his orders.

There was a small pause before Andrews replied.

'We can't do anything for her there. All we can do is get the bastard who did this. Ok? I want you to focus. Complete your mission. We'll get her out of there later. In the meantime, don't touch anything and let's get him.'

Antwi nodded and turned to Gwilym.

'Let's check that door,' he said. 'Team Four, be advised. We are opening what maybe an exit. Be prepared.'

Gwilym reached for the door and, after four, he tried to pull it open. It was locked.

'Team Four, the door is locked. I'm going to try and bust it open,' he said.

'Understood,' Junior replied.

Antwi positioned himself in front of the door, raised his foot and with all of his weight and huge frame behind him he kicked out as hard as he could.

The door gave way and bright light flooded the room. Both he and Gwilym had to cover their eyes from the brightness.

'Got you,' Junior said in front of them. Then:

'Oh shit,'

As the brightness cleared and his eyes adjusted, Antwi saw Junior looking into the room and down to the prone child. Junior looked up at him with a hardness on his face.

'Team Four,' he said, almost spitting the words out as if they were venomous.' 'Team one has opened rear exit one.'

'Copy that,' Andrews said.

'How many exits are there?' Antwi asked, more to focus himself and Junior on anything but the child.

'Three, we think. This one, what looks like too large French doors with closed shutters over them, and other smaller one.... SHIT! He's behind you! He's behind you!'

Junior raised his gun as Antwi swung around. There in the kitchen door a huge man loomed. His body filled the door frame and more. His face was a mask of malevolence, a smile of complete distain and eyes that bore down on the three of them.

STEPHEN AMOS

'Get down!' Antwi shouted at the man. 'Hands behind your head and...'

But before he could finish the man stepped deftly aside and out of sight. Gwilym was first after him, rushing through the door, quickly moving through the pantry, his rifle aimed around the corner. Then he hesitated.

Antwi came into the kitchen and stood next to him, his torch searching the room, the light cutting through the darkness like a crosscut saw.

But the man was gone. There was no door swinging shut as he left the room, no violence in the movements of the motes of dust. Nothing.

The man was gone, and it was as if he had never been there at all.

***

'Teams Two and Three, be advised. Suspect was seen in the kitchen but has now...um... disappeared.'

Jones looked at Smiffy and even in the wan light he could see his partner's frown. They both knew Antwi, they had worked with him for almost five years now. He was a straight arrow, someone who went in and did the job without question or complaint, so the hesitation in his voice gave them both a cause for concern.

'Team Two, we are entering the Ballroom.'

'Team Three, copy that, there has been no sign of anyone at the entrance yet.' Newman reported.

'Team One, we're also entering the Ballroom.'

Jones stepped forward and took hold of the door knob and they started the count. As he looked at Smiffy he could see the tension in his face. His partner licked his lips, his eyes bore into the closed door.

On 'One', he opened the door and Smiffy stepped quickly passed him.

The ballroom was a large as the witnesses claimed earlier, and he could understand how they could have been overwhelmed by the darkness and the shadows. Even with their torches, the room was still dark, as if the shadows were solid masses, moving around the room.

A fraction of a second later a door at the far end of the room opened, and he could see Antwi run into the room, quickly followed by Gwilym.

Other than the four of them, however, the room was empty. There was no furniture and no decoration on the walls. It was as you would have expected from a house this old, yet, because of all the items in the other rooms, this looked surprisingly bare.

Without saying anything they covered all four corners. Jones could feel the strain on his stomach ease ever so slightly.

'Hey, guys.' He looked around and saw Gwilym standing near the center of the room, his torch aimed down to the floor. He looked over to Smiffy and together they joined Gwilym to see what he was looking at.

On the floor was a pool of what had to be blood. Even though they couldn't make out the exact colour, it couldn't have been anything else.

'Do you think it belongs to the little girl you found?' he asked.

Gwilym just shrugged.

Antwi crossed over to them but stopped a few feet away.

'Look at the floor,' he said. 'There's a star painted on it.'

Jones stepped back and scanned the ground. Antwi was right but it wasn't just a star. That would have been two easy, he thought.

'It's a pentagram,' he told them. 'A star in a circle.'

'A pentangle,' Smiffy said next to him. 'It's not a pentagram, it's a pentangle.'

'I don't give a -' Antwi started.

'Team Three, be advised. A door just closed up stairs. Top of staircase on the right, approximately above the kitchen.

'He's there,' Gwilym said.

Jones could see the hatred in his eyes. Gwilym had seen

the child and it was now personal. How could it not be? he thought.

The four of them quickly made for the door that led to the entrance way. It opened to the back of the staircase. They rounded it quickly, two to the left, two to the right. Newman was waiting at the foot of the stairs, with Wood still covering the entrance way.

'Up there,' Newman pointed with his gun. 'The door seemed to open very slowly, we didn't notice it initially. Then it slammed shut.'

'Come on, let's get this bastard,' Gwilym said.

'Rein it in cowboy,' Antwi put his hand out and grabbed Gwilym's arm. 'This could be a trap. Why else would he make so much noise?'

Gwilym pulled his arm away with a flourish but said nothing.

'All four of us will go up together.' Antwi said. 'We'll go in, Team Two, you'll wait outside and cover the landing, just in case there's a through door to another room.'

They all nodded their affirmative.

They made their way slowly up the stairs and Jones could hear his blood rushing through his brain, the movement of his clothes as he tried to control his breathing, and every creak on the stairs. At the top of the landing Jones and Smiffy took positions on each wall of the corridor that veered to the right. Antwi stepped to the nearest door and looked at Gwilym. There was a staleness to the air that was missing downstairs. It was warmer too, although that might have just been anticipation and the effect of their blood coursing violently through their veins.

Antwi moved to the front and signaled Gwilym to open the door. They did the four count. Jones could feel the muscles in his stomach tighten. He readjusted his grip on his rifle, trying to get a little more comfortable.

Gwilym swung the door inwards and Antwi disappeared into the darkness. This time he called out 'Police!' Gwilym swung around and entered the room too. Jones could hear the sounds of the search which seemed to last both hours and seconds. Then:

***

'Team One, clear!' Antwi called out. They were in a bedroom. It was large but empty and very dusty, nothing like downstairs. It was obvious that no one had been here for a very long time. It was a small room, but they were careful to sweep every corner and he also banged the walls in case there were any hidden passageways. There was nothing in the training which covered this, but with all the mysteries and horrors he had heard of and witnessed today, he didn't want to take any chances.

Gwilym stood behind him, providing him with cover, and Antwi could still feel the hate and determination radiating from him. Gwilym had a young daughter, Seren, who was only four years old, and he was taking the murder of the little girl downstairs personally. Antwi could see it in his eyes and would have probably felt it in complete blackness.

There was another door at the far end, and he signaled for Gwilym to open it. When the count was over, he entered into a bathroom. It was an en-suite which was bare except for a broken old metal bath in one corner. He stepped over to the bath and peered in – paranoid enough maybe to check every possible hiding place, however ridiculous it might seem.

He crouched down beside the bath to check the corner when he realised that his was the only light in the room. He turned to the doorway where Gwilym should have been standing but there was no one there.

'Gwilym? I need more light,' he said.

Nothing.

He rose and turned to the door.

'Gwilym,' he said again. 'I need more lig-'

Before he could finish something rolled into the room. He looked down, wondering what it was that his partner had found and what would be worth playing stupid games with at this time, when he saw the face staring up at him.

Gwilym's head lay at his feet, his dead eyes looking up at Antwi accusingly. It was as if they were boring into him, implicating him in the crime that had befallen them. As if the fact that Gwilym's head had been wrenched from his body was somehow Antwi's fault.

Antwi started to hyperventilate. He looked up to the door and saw the man there. He stood with one hand on the door frame and the other carrying the remains of what had been Alexander Gwilym. He glared down at Antwi with malice, his eyes shining brightly from the reflected torch light.

Antwi tried to speak, tried to call for help, but nothing came out. His throat had constricted and there seemed to be no oxygen being carried up his windpipe. He stood frozen, facing the man who had killed his partner, who had killed that poor girl downstairs, had killed a family in the car park and had probably also killed a baby.

The seconds dragged on and no one moved. Antwi had to will his hands to operate, he had to will his body to react.

He began to lift the gun up and managed to squeak 'Police.'

The giant entered the bathroom swiftly and almost silently, dropping Gwilym to the floor with a thud. Antwi wasn't able to bring the gun all the way up but as the man lunged at him, he managed to get a shot off. The bang reverberated around the small room and the man staggered backwards.

But only a footstep. Before Antwi could fire again, he was grabbed by the lapels on his jacket and thrown through the air, out of the bathroom and into the adjoining bedroom. The man roared with anger.

Antwi hit the floor hard and skidded along until he slammed into the wall. Pain shot through his body sending flashes of colour cascading through his vision like a kaleidoscope of agony.

The door opened and Jones entered quickly, his rifle raised

and pointed to the suspect.

'Police,' he shouted. 'Get down on the floor, now!'

Antwi didn't see everything that happened. It was too fast, and he was in too much pain to grasp everything, but he heard the shots, three, maybe four of them, ring out. The room lit up with muzzle flash. He heard the man roar again and the room shook.

***

Smiffy was leaning over Antwi in the corner, making sure he was alright, when Jones came out of the bathroom. It was as if he had been hit in the face with a crowbar. Not the pain but the disorientation and confusion. He stood and looked at his two teammates but couldn't think of anything to say.

'You got him,' Smiffy said from the floor. It wasn't a question and Jones could understand why. He had shot the suspect three times and had chased him into the bathroom. What else could the outcome be?

'Team One and Two report!' It was Andrews on the radio. 'Come in. I need a status update.'

'Team Two,' Smiffy said helping Antwi to stand. 'Looks like we got him. Jones fired at him three times, he's in the bathroom.'

Andrews began to speak, probably to start winding down the operation, but Jones interrupted.

'No, sir,' he said. 'I didn't get him.'

'What?' Both Andrews and Smiffy said at the same time.

'He's not there,' he said. 'The bathroom is empt-'

Before he could complete his sentence, he felt a thump in his back and a sword of red hot pain shot through his body. Everything went numb, as all feeling left him. Then he coughed, and he could feel the blood splutter over his lips and begin to trickle down his chin. It was warm and tickled his neck as it continued its journey.

Smiffy screamed and raise his gun.

'Let him go!' He shouted. 'Put him down!'

At first Jones couldn't understand why Smiffy was saying these things, why he was shouting and why he looked so panicked. All he was aware of was that the pain was subsiding and, with it, his focus. The room seemed to swirl. It was like being drunk, but with less awareness, and the tension that he had felt all day was still there. It was almost like being stuck in a dream, a dream that was fading with wakefulness, only there was no wakefulness to replace it. Only a final twilight.

He felt movement in his back, or maybe a million miles away, he couldn't tell. He felt a shudder go through him and had a moment to wonder where and why he was moving, then he could see the floor rising up to greet him with a jab to the face.

As he died, the final thing his senses captured, was the sound of gunfire.

***

Antwi looked up in horror as the giant rose out of the shadows behind Jonesy, he saw his colleague shudder, and suddenly a huge hand ripped through his chest, slicing through this shirt and shoving the body armour aside. The hand dripped with blood and other viscous material. Shattered bone fell lightly to the ground which was now dark with the fluid oozing from the dying policeman.

In the fist's grip he could see what he assumed were Jonesy's internal organs, although they were too mangled to determine what they might have once been. The hand turned slowly in a circle then opened and dropped the organs to the ground, to join the rest of Jonesy's innards.

The giant then pulled his hand back and the whole of Jonesy's body seemed to shudder violently.

Antwi was standing, although he was bent over and in immense pain. It was as if half his body had been rocked when he hit the wall.

'Help me,' he called over to Smiffy. The Englishman looked toward him, uncomprehending, in the grips of what was probably deep shock. 'We've got to get out of here.'

He stumbled towards Smiffy as he heard the thump of Jonesy's body hitting the floor behind him. No, it wasn't a thump, his mind told him even though he was trying to ignore it. It was a hard splatter, like someone doing a belly flop into a vat of honey.

He reached over to Smiffy and grabbed his arm.

'We have to get out, NOW!' He shouted. He tried pushing Smiffy but didn't have the strength, so he staggered past him and tried using his weight to pull the other man.

Smiffy still didn't move, at least not straight away. As Antwi reached the hallway he could hear movement behind and for a moment he felt relief. Smiffy was coming with him, but then felt an odd sensation as if the Englishman was rising from the ground.

Antwi looked around, still holding Smiffy's arm. He saw the giant holding his friend and fellow police officer by the neck, lifting him into the air.

He felt a scream rise up in his stomach. It came out like a barbaric cry, like a savage child found in the depths of a forest and rent from the only world he knew, by strangers he didn't realise looked like him.

It passed his lungs, gathering oxygen as fuel, then charged up his throat and out his wide open mouth. The man - if he was a man - who was holding Smiffy, looked at him with dead eyes and smiled. Not a smile of pleasure as it didn't extend to any other part of his face. The Shadowman then jerked his hand suddenly to the left and Antwi could hear Smiffy's neck break.

He ran.

Across the short landing and started down the stairs. Newman rushed up the stairs to meet him and took him by the arms. Wood stood at the bottom of the stairs waiting for them when the front door slammed shut with a crash. Antwi and Newman stopped on the stairs, both frozen with fear.

'Gwilym, Jonesy and Smiffy are dead,' Antwi spat the words out, his breathing heavy and laden.

'Shit,' Newman said. It was as if there was nothing else to say.

The radio crackled in their ears and Andrews's voice interrupted.

'Say again, team One.'

'They are dead. He killed them. All of them!'

His chest ached as he spoke. Hell, it seemed to pierce his soul every time he breathed.

'Come on,' he snarled, forcing the words out. 'We're getting out of here.'

'Oh, no you are not!'

The voice seemed to echo through the house and at first, he couldn't make out where it was coming from. He could hardly lift his gun or his torch, and the whole place seemed to have taken on a darkness which was even more oppressive, more foreboding and threatening.

Newman's light streaked around the great hallway until finally stopping at a spot behind Wood. It took a very long second for Antwi to see what Newman was focusing on, and when he did, his heart sank. He glanced over to see Wood, who seemed to sense something wrong, spin around, raising his gun as he did so. It was too late.

The man took hold of Wood's head with his huge hands and pulled the policeman close to his body. With one swift movement, he held on to Wood's head and spun it forcibly to the right.

Wood slumped to the floor. He was already dead, and it seemed as if there had been absolutely no effort in it at all.

Then the hallway lit up with flashing lights and the tremendous sound of gun fire. Coming from beneath the stairway, from the direction of the Ballroom, Junior, Kowalski and Bosch stood, their guns aloft, their lights trained on the man who had so far murdered four of their colleagues, firing rapidly into his gigantic body.

The giant felt backwards towards the cloakroom, his dark clothes rippling as the bullets cut through them. He struggled to stand but the sheer force of so many projectiles was too much. He fell to the ground with a thud.

'Come on,' Junior called to Antwi and Newman. 'Let's get you out.'

Silence fell on Henry House as Antwi almost hopped down the stairs, leaning on Newman for balance. They got to the bottom, greeted by their three rescuers.

Junior reached for the entrance door and pulled it open. The light from outside, although darkening in the early twilight, washed over Antwi and he felt a wave of pleasure. It was relief, happiness and a sudden realisation that he was still alive. He was aware of how silly it sounded but until he stepped across the threshold, it was almost as if he had assumed he was already dead.

'Oh fuck!' The voice came from behind him, and he and Newman turned back to the house. Bosch stood in the door frame. He turned to them, his face awash with fear.

'He's gone,' he whispered.

Then there was the sound of gun fire again. A short sustained burst, then a profound scream of fear. Bosch raised his gun and ran from the entrance into the darkness, yelling on top of his voice.

Newman let go of Antwi and began to step back into the building but Antwi pulled him back.

'No!' He screamed.

'I've got to!' Newman cried back. His face was contorted with anguish and anger, and he pulled his arm free but, before he could get to the door, it slammed shut in his face.

There was a moment of silence then more gunfire, more screams, more terror.

Then a dreadful calm seemed to fall on the place.

Antwi was aware of people behind him. They were running to the house, running to him. Everything seemed to slow as if time itself had become lethargic and dulled.

He felt hands grab him and pull him back. He saw police grabbing Newman, fighting him as he tried to get back into the house. He was aware of men calling his name, but it was as if they were far away, like voices from a TV in another room.

He didn't resist. He couldn't. His gun felt heavy against his body, even his arms and legs seemed too heavy for him to control. He just let them take him, but he didn't take his eyes off the doors. He thought of Gwilym's head at his feet, of Jonesy falling to the ground with a hole through his stomach, of the sound of Smiffy's neck breaking, and the almost casual way Woods had been murdered. He thought of the giant's eyes. Dead lights shining with black death.

He knew what had happened to Bosch and to Junior and to Kowalski. He knew they were dead, and he felt his heart being crushed by his inability to do anything about it.

Then the door opened.

A muted hush fell on the surroundings and the grips on his arms loosened ever so slightly. There was a dead moment. A minute, maybe ten, probably a lifetime for the men inside.

Then, one by one, three heads were coolly tossed from the darkness with a lifeless indifference. They each fell to the ground by Newman's feet, and Antwi could see and recognise each and every one of them.

Bosch.

Junior.

Kowalski.

Then the door slowly closed with barely as sound.

Again, there was another silent pause, a hushed quiet finally shattered by Newman's emphatic screams.

CHAPTER 29

In the darkness, a laugh echoed down invisible walls. An unpleasant, vile gargle of a laugh, as if it came from the pustulous throat if the newly dead. But there was nothing new of the creature from whose gullet this ghastly chortle originated. He, for it once had been a he, felt the pleasure rebounding off the confines he existed in.

The bliss recoiled in the darkness.

He saw everything that had happened, he felt the joy and the release as Shadow had unleashed his fury. He had seen the ecstasy on his minion's face as he had ripped head from shoulders, squeezed the light from eyes, and reached into the heart of his prey and tore away each man's life.

'Good, good,' he said.

Shadow came, as he was bidden to do. He came a slave, a servant to the power he possessed. Shadow was a necessary evil, something he needed in order to fulfil his plans, and rise once again from the squalid dark and into the light.

'Master,' Shadow whispered with reverence. 'It is finished.'

He laughed again, caught up in the glee of the moment.

'Yes, you have done a good job.'

'Thank you, master.'

'You enjoyed it too! I could feel it, I could taste it. And there is more to come. From tomorrow, there will be so much more.'

'Yes,' even in the darkness he could see, hear, taste and touch the unbridled elation in his subordinate's voice.

'One more,' he said.

'One more,' Shadow repeated

'One more, tonight.'

'Tonight,' Shadow said.

'The sun sets soon, go and bring me the child.'

Shadow disappeared. If he were able to smile, he would have then; if he was able to clap his hands together in anticipation, he may have done that too.

CHAPTER 30

'So, what happens now?' Carys sobbed. Each time a tear escaped, she seemed to shudder. Catryn could see it even from the other sofa. She felt the same way, sitting here in unfamiliar surroundings with people whom she hadn't seen for too many years, with police in and out of uniform crowding the street. It made her feel small, like a little girl enclosed by adults, all looking grave and stern.

She remembered a funeral once, for Auntie Ruth, who had seemed unfeasibly old before she finally decided to 'meet her maker'. It was a phrase she had learned that day and it had stayed with her ever since. She had sat in the living room, surrounded by family members she had never met, women who insisted on inspecting her and commenting on her height, the shape of her cheekbones or - as one dreadful old lady with a grey mustache pointed out – her promising hips. She hadn't known what it meant at the time, only that it made her feel very uneasy. Now, three decades or so later, it still gave her a chill of discomfort.

She remembered how they had all sat in the living room, perched on every chair, stool, arm rest or cushion that her parents could find, and they talked. There were tears, which was to be expected - even a seven-year-old knew that you cried at a funeral - but there was laughter as well. This had seemed odd to Catryn; surely death and humour were completely incompatible?

That may have been the day when she realised the extent of her parent's life outside the home. The fact that they could know so many people that she was unfamiliar with - that they could laugh with them and understand things that she had never known. It was a frightening experience, to comprehend for the first time, that those adults who had always been her's, also belonged to others.

That was how she felt now, thirty years later, sitting in Jimmy's living room. Out of place. An intruder in the lives of others. They were all familiar with each other and shared a past that she was not a part of. They spoke with familiarity whereas she was just an interloper.

She also couldn't help but feel that she was responsible somehow. No one said it. In fact, they called both her and Jimmy brave but foolhardy. She didn't feel brave, she felt stupid. Why the hell had she agreed to go up there? Surely, she should have known the risks. There was a murderer on the loose and she was happily skipping into what was very possibly his lair? What was it that drove her there? Was she that desperate to fit in? Was she so blinded to be 'home' that she was willing to do anything on a whim?

'The site is now closed off, there is nowhere for him to run.' A man in a tired looking suit said.

This, she had guessed, was Jimmy's son-in-law Gareth. He looked beat, as if the whole affair was keeping him awake 24/7 and eating him from the inside. He looked like he had walked a few marathons in the last few days, with his red eyes held up by the deep black bags below them, his dirty looking stubble around his large jaw, and a suit that looked like it had been slept in. Yet his tie was perfectly straight, neat and bright, completely out of place with the rest of him. He had a habit of adjusting it all the time, almost like a nervous tick.

'We'll make sure he can't go anywhere until we can figure out a new plan,' he continued.

'How about the children?' Carys asked. 'The little girl. I hate the thought of her up there. She needs someone to look after her, to...'

Catryn looked at Carys and could see the anguish in her eyes. She and Jimmy had only been a few feet away from the little girl but there was nothing they could have done for her. She wanted to strike out at this monster. How could he do that to such a sweet little girl? Lucy's picture was all over the news but now she lay in the dark, on a cold floor, put there by an animal. And where was the girl – the other Lucy? Catryn shuddered, knowing that she too was gone forever.

'Are you sure that will stop him?' Jimmy asked. 'What if he can just disappear into the shadows?'

'Come on, Jimmy,' Gareth said. 'You know that's impossible.'

'I know it should be impossible,' Jimmy put a lot of emphasis on the word 'should'. 'But I also know what we saw. He was to our left one second, to our right the next. There is no way he could have travelled that far that quickly.'

'And there's no way he could have travelled through shadows.'

'Gareth! You saw the video, you told us what the witnesses said. You know what we told you. Can't you just accept it?'

'Accept what, Jimmy?' Gareth said, his voice rising in exasperation. 'That he's a ghost? That he has magical powers? This is not Harry Potter! Surely, it's more likely that there were two men up there? That you were attacked by a number of different people, not just one magical one.'

'I saw him!' Jimmy signaled to Catryn. 'We saw him.'

Gareth sighed heavily.

'Are you sure you both took the time to remember every detail in there? You were under attack; there is no way you would notice if it was one person or two! Or even three!'

Jimmy sat back in the chair and crossed his arms in front of him.

Catryn saw that the detective wasn't entirely convinced by his own argument. She looked at his eyes and for a moment he looked directly at her. She could see that he was confused, that he felt completely out of his depth. She could understand why. There was no way any of them had any experience of this sort of thing.

Was that why she was so willing to go up to Henry House?

Had she really believed that there was no danger up there? That it was just an adventure? She couldn't remember. It was all so far away, as if the events of that afternoon had stretched time to snapping point and that there was an unimaginable gulf between what she may have understood about the world earlier and what she just couldn't truly understand now.

'Look, I haven't a clue what is really going on but until we do, I think it would be best if everyone went home, closed the doors and waited until this is all over.'

'I need to go out,' Jimmy said. 'I have to visit Gwladys Pryce. Her daughter passed away with cancer yesterday and I promised I would stop in to see her this evening.'

Carys put her hand on her husband's and squeezed. He looked at her and smiled.

'I've got to go, if only for an hour,' he told her.

'I know,' Carys replied. 'I don't want you to go, though.'

'OK, one hour and no more. I want you home as soon as possible,' Gareth said.

'Yes, Dad,' Jimmy replied, and Catryn saw what may have been a fleeting smile on the detective's lips.

'Will I be able to drop in on someone up the hill?' Morgan asked.

'Who?'

'Tal Jones. He was the one who told us about the link between the name Lucy and Henry House.'

Gareth thought about it for a second and straightened his tie again.

'Ok,' he said finally. 'I'll come with you.'

'I'll come too,' Catryn said quickly.

'Oh, come on,' Gareth waved his hands in front of him theatrically. 'I'm not offering a taxi service here.'

'I know,' she replied. 'But I was there when Tal told us the story and I was at the house today. I'm the one person who has been involved throughout.'

'So, what are you saying? That you are entitled to go? That you have some kind of right? Some of the best men on the force died today. Men with families, men with dreams. What of their rights? You have no rights whatsoever when it comes to this. This is a murder investigation, not an episode of Nancy Drew.'

Catryn sighed heavily, a tear ran down her cheek.

'I know. I'm so sorry, I didn't mean...'

Her voice faded as the grief overwhelmed her. She buried her head in her hands, the sobs wracking her body.

Carys crossed to her and put her arms around her.

'It's not your fault,' Carys said. She looked up to Gareth. 'Sweetheart, Tal Jones is a nasty man. A mean man. He'll probably be very difficult and try to obfuscate as much as he can. What if Tal says something that only makes sense if you have been in the house? What if he changes his story? Yes, Morgan will be there, but two memories are better than one.'

Catryn looked up at him and wiped her face with the back of her hands.

'Look,' she said, softly. 'You might not believe in the paranormal bullshit I experienced today but it happened. It happened to Jimmy and me, and it happened to those men who died. We might not understand what we saw but I know it was real. I need to know what is happening. Those men and their families need this man to be captured. I might not be able to contribute but, then again, you'll never know unless you give me this hour. Besides, Tal likes me. In a creepy way that makes my skin crawl, but he still likes me.'

'Let her go with you,' Carys said, rubbing Catryn's back. 'I don't know what they saw today but I can see something in Jimmy's eyes that scares me. This whole mess scares me. Jimmy's way of dealing with it is to get on with things as normally as possible, to internalise everything and deal with it later. Sometime over the next few days, we'll talk and pray together, and slowly it will come out. I think Catryn's different. She needs to work this through, to balance her ledgers, so to speak. It might sound odd, but I think she needs it.'

Catryn nodded, surprised how well this woman, whom she

only met the previous night and who she hadn't had the opportunity to speak with one on one, understood her.

'I need this,' she repeated.

Gareth stared at his mother-in-law and sighed.

'OK,' he said after a long, tired, pause. 'But not because of
what you just said, Carys. If Catryn can focus on any piece of
information, however small, it will be a benefit. I don't care
about working through personal demons or any of that new-
age rubbish. I only care about catching this son-of-a....' He
looked at his mother-in-law and sighed heavily. 'Come on, let's
go.'

***

'Mr Jones, I'm DCI Mann. Sorry to....'

'I know who you are,' Tal interrupted the detective. Didn't
you guys used to wear blue? You look like a pissed up hobo.'

Morgan glanced at Catryn, his face a mask of horror and
amusement. They had driven the short distance up to Henry
Hill and Catryn was surprised by how busy the street was.
Police cars were parked on both sides, some in the middle
of the street. At the bottom of the hill a large van, with the
letters BBC written boldly on the side, was parked outside a
terraced house. There was an assortment of satellite dishes
and antennae on the top, which looked rather archaic to her
eyes. At the back of the van stood a woman who Cat thought
she might have seen on TV sometimes. Another press van was
about twenty yards further up, this one with SKY NEWS emblazoned on its sides. People stood on their doorsteps; kids
ran around among the crowds. The whole street was chaotic.

She didn't know what she was expecting but at the very
least she thought there would be some sort of organisation.

They had to park up about ten doors away from Tal's and
walk past open doors, stunned faces, and a strange sense of
anticipation. It was somewhere between a party and a con-
fusedly manic wake. As soon as they had stepped out of the
car, people crowded around them asking if they were involved

in the situation. A few phones and recorders were thrust into their faces to capture their responses.

'We're just visiting friends,' Gareth had said, pushing people aside.

By the time they got to Tal's house, it was obvious to Catryn that the detective's mood had deteriorated further.

Donna answered the door and looked like she had been expecting them. She smiled and, after exchanging a few pleasantries, she had led the way into the living room where Tal sat in his customary chair watching TV, a hot cup of tea in his hands.

'I was expecting you lot to turn up again,' Tal said, turning to the TV. 'I tell you a story about the house, next thing I know there are bloody pigs everywhere. We've even made the news.' He lifted his cup to indicate the television in front of him. 'We're famous, there's TV people crawling all over the street. Half expecting one of them to pop his head out of my shithole when I take a dump. Bastards!'

Catryn watched Gareth intently as he took a deep breath, obviously taken back by the welcome he had received.

'Don't mind the old bastard here,' Donna said. 'You all sit down, and I'll make a cup of tea for you all.'

'Don't bother,' Tal said. 'They're not staying. And I'm not leaving this house either. I know you are evicting the whole street, but I'm not moving one arse cheek!'

'Shut your gob,' Donna replied. 'I'll be right back.'

So much for Tal liking me, Catryn thought as she sat on a chair by the small dining table in the corner. Gareth moved to the settee and sat himself down next to Tal, whilst Morgan just stood beside Cat.

'Mr Jones,' Gareth began again.

'The name's Tal, if you must use it. Taliesin if you want to get formal. Mr Jones was for my students which you are not, unless you are referring to my father who's been dead for eighty years. I doubt there's much of him left to interrogate, though.'

'Tal,' Gareth tried again. 'Morgan and Catryn have updated me on the conversation you had with them yesterday. It seems you know your history.'

'And you don't,' Tal replied testily.

'No, I don't. I'm not even sure I believe some of it.'

'What's not to believe? Sir Henry was a lunatic like so many other lunatics.'

'Well, given what happened to Jimmy Bevan and Catryn today, I think your story deserves further investigation.'

Tal turned quickly to Catryn and Morgan, his eyes piercing and sharp.

'What happened today?'

Catryn looked at Gareth and then to Morgan. A silent decision was made, and Morgan put his hand on Catryn's shoulder for encouragement. She took a deep breath and recounted the incident that occurred earlier. Tal, for once, remained silent and didn't ask any questions. At one point, Donna came in with a tray carrying three mugs. She put it on the table and handed the drinks out, interrupting quietly to enquire who wanted milk or sugar. She then stood by the door and listened to Catryn.

Once she had finished Catryn felt tired, as if the day was finally catching up with her.

'He killed them all?' Tal asked quietly.

Both Catryn and Gareth nodded.

'And you saw him?'

'Yes.'

Tal signed heavily, paused then smiled.

'Well, fuck my cat and call it pussy,' he said sitting back in the chair. 'You know, I know lots of stories, most of it probably bullshit, most of it added to and changed and coloured in by whoever is telling the story. For every liar there's a dozen bullshitters out there. People think that history is the study of what happened but that is just crap. It's the study of what people think happened, and most of that is as useful as unflushed toilet paper.

'What are you saying?' asked Catryn. She could see Gareth move forward in his seat, his elbows on his knees.

'One of those rumours that you won't find in any of those history books that claim to know the truth when in fact they don't know their dicks from a toilet brush, was about how there always seemed to be a lot of kids going missing around the 1840s. Now, the newspapers back in those days wouldn't have covered a story like this at all. Why report on a story in a shit hole like the Rhondda when you've got a mistress to bang that evening in some swanky part of London? Do you know how many petticoats and frills those women used to wear back in those days? Imagine how long it would take to get into their drawers. I'm surprised most men didn't jizz on their mistresses in anticipation a good hour before she had finished undressing!'

'Focus Tal,' Morgan said. 'You said that there were kidnappings last time we saw you. I remember reading rumours about it myself some time ago.'

Tal shrugged the interruption off.

'More than rumours! In one year almost thirty kids disappeared from around here. Of course, the Rhondda was a dirty horrible asshole of a place back then. The rivers ran black with the slag off the coal mines, the men had permanent black faces, any beauty that the women ever had soon disappeared under the layers of dust. Kids these days complain about how hard it is with their cans of lager and that crappy music they are always listening to. And the language out of their mouths is fucking disgusting.

'It wasn't long before Sir Henry and his bunch of rich pricks were suspected. After all, everyone knew of his oddities and, well they were rich and we all know what type of people the rich are. Fucking thieves, taking from the working man to stuff their own cod pieces. The bastards were the obvious suspects. There was no evidence, of course, and nothing was done. Anyone who complained was certain to lose their jobs, so it was better to lose the odd child than it was to lose your only income.

'Then one day one child stumbles in their home and tells everyone that a huge man tried to snatch her. This man was not a local, the girl had never seen him before. So, the parents get bold and a posse is put together, and they marched up to Henry House to demand justice or whatever passed for it in those days.

'They never made it to the house. This was back before even houses like this were built,' he waved his hand to indicate he was talking about his own terraced house which itself was well over a hundred years old. 'Most of this area would have been covered with tiny houses, nothing more than shacks. The road to the Henry House was there, just dirty tracks for the horses and carts, but it was as it is today. The people marched up the hill just as night was falling. They were just coming to the final bend when he stepped out of the shadows. There was a fight and four men were killed.

'The rumour was that this huge bastard was strong enough to rip a man's heart out. Then he would step back into the shadows and appear twenty yards away, behind one of the protestors. He snapped the man's neck then disappeared again.

'Finally, after much shouting and screaming I suppose, Henry himself appeared. He shouted on top of his voice "Shadow! Enough!" The man disappeared again and reappeared next to his boss. Henry then stared the crowd down before telling them to go home. The people had probably shit their pants, so they turned around and carried their dead back to their shacks.

'And that was that.'

'Who was he? Gareth asked.

'How the fuck am I supposed to know? A magician? A demon? Harry fucking Potter! All I can tell you is that he was big, bad and could disappear into the shadows and appear somewhere else.'

'And you believe that?' Gareth asked.

'Believe it? My job is not to believe, just to relate.'

'Ok, do you think there's much accuracy to the story?'

'What? That a man can jump into a shadow and disappear like a skid mark in a washing machine? Of course, I believe it. I saw it on TV earlier today, didn't I?'

Catryn glanced at Morgan. She could see that he was trying, unsuccessfully, to suppress a smile. Donna, too, looked amused by the old man's responses. He made sense, Catryn supposed. While the head struggled with the logic of all this, there was an abundance of visual evidence. This wasn't the old days when strange things happened but there was never any reliable proof. If an alien landed in some remote farm these days, the farmer would just take out his phone and record the whole thing. Probably explained why there seemed to be a scarcity of alien abductions and supernatural occurrences since the invention of the smart phone.

'So, what happened to this mysterious man?' Gareth asked Tal.

Tal shrugged. 'There were a few rumours, people said they saw him now and again, however, after Henry died, the man was never seen again. There was one strange rumour though. He was seen one last time at Sir Henry's second funeral.'

'Second funeral?' Gareth asked.

'Oh, come on man. This is not a secret. His two funerals are in the history books. This is not rumour and fairytales. This is record-books-facts. After Henry died, he was buried in the grounds of Henry House but the locals, so fucked off by the way they had been mistreated, and still a bit annoyed that the probable kidnapper of their lovely urchins had never been punished, dug up his rotting corpse, carried it out into the countryside to their secret church and buried him there.'

'What do you mean "secret church"?' Gareth asked.

'Well, the Welsh speakers were determined to worship their God in their way and in their own language, so they built chapels up on the mountainsides. You can still find the odd remains of the small buildings even today. This one is still there – just at the top of the mountain, on the way to Llanwonno.

Unless yobbos have torn it down like they usually do, and I don't mean kids. I mean those council bastards!'

'Why was he buried there?'

'Revenge. The Welsh can be a stubborn bunch of bastards sometimes. It was their way of pissing on his grave. They knew that, despite all the voodoo nonsense, old Charles Henry was still a believer of sorts. He didn't like God but, in order to dislike someone, you have to first acknowledge their existence. It was their way of making sure he was under the sight of God. Chained by the Spirit. Real bondage, kinda thing.'

There was silence for a moment, then Gareth stood up with a heavy sigh and Catryn was sure she could hear his back creak.

'This is all very interesting,' he said. 'But this does not help us now, does it?'

He turned for the door, Morgan, Catryn and Donna rising with him.

'That all depends,' Tal said, without taking his eyes off the TV. 'The fact is, if you believe all this, and despite the fact that you all act like you have brain turds, I do think you have a crumb of intelligence, and that you will trust the videos and all that other evidence, ask yourself this:

'If this is the same mysterious man, a ghost who can disappear into walls, who's in charge? Who's controlling him? If Charles Henry really could bring himself back from the dead, then he would need help, someone or something, who can do his bidding in this world until he is able to cross over. We discussed this last night. He really believed he could do this; he had a daughter named Lucy. He had a mysterious helper who, it is said, could travel from shadow to shadow.

'All this is happening now.'

'You said that this Shadow fella was seen the day of the second funeral,' Morgan said. 'Where was he seen?'

Tal turned and smiled at the group standing by his front door. 'Now you are asking the right question. He was standing in the doorway of the church, up on the mountain. As the men walked home, they looked back and there he was. Was he guarding the old man's grave or was he so tied to him that he was bound to remain there?

'But now, two hundred years later, the site obviously has lost its importance in the eyes of God. As I said, something must have happened to the site to loosen the bounds, allowing him some sort of freedom.'

'So, he can leave and prepare for the return of his master,' Morgan said.

'Or, it could be a load of old crap. These people weren't as sophisticated as us today.' Tal said, and Catryn was sure he was rolling his eyes.

'In fact,' Tal continued. 'It probably is a load of crap, and I've only told you it all because I'm a lonely old man and Donna doesn't rub my dick like she used to.'

He snorted and turned back to the TV. 'You lot can get out of my house now,' he said scornfully. 'And don't go knocking on my door later because I'm not fucking leaving.'

**

'How do you put up with him?' Gareth asked Donna, as they stepped out into the crisp coldness of the approaching night.

Donna smiled. 'That's the same question Catryn asked me last night. In fact, everyone asks me the same thing.'

'Goodnight, Don,' Morgan said, and kissed her on the cheek. 'You get home early and lock all the doors, ok?'

'I will. Just going to get him ready for an early night. He'll complain but I'm used to it.'

They all said their good-byes, and Catryn, Morgan and Gareth walked down into the crowded streets and back to Jimmy's. Police were telling people to get inside and close their doors. Some people listened, others got four packs of lager and sat on their doorsteps, laughing and joking at the spectacle.

The atmosphere was strange. There was a party feel nestling with a heavy expectancy. As they got to the car, Catryn looked up to the sky and could almost feel the night falling.

CHAPTER 31

As they drove down Henry Hill, the first tendrils of night were stretching over the remnants of Monday. The sky, which had been a warm, clear blue, turned pink and orange as if there was a tremendous fire raging in the distance. The colour touched the odd cloud making them blush with excitement.

There was an air of expectancy hanging over Trehenri as if a great storm was coming. This was the fourth night that the atmosphere was so charged, and it was beginning to fill the locals with a sense of dread. Trehenri was small, a mere speck in the landscape, and in four days they had experienced more than a small town should.

People were nervous. They were tired and stressed. They were excited and weary. They hoped it would be over soon yet dreaded what that might mean.

The TV stations had taken over, like a foreign army invading a small and defenceless country. On any given evening on Henry Hill, after the commuters had returned home, after the tradesmen had called it a day, parking became a premium, and once home many stayed in for the night not wanting to lose the parking spaces close to their homes. Tonight, however, these valuable spaces were taken up with large vans with corporate logos on the sides.

Carl Williams trudged up the hill after parking in the next street down. His shoulders were hunched, and the weariness extended to every nerve in his body. He had been working on a building site in Llantrisant and had discovered that his foreman had fucked up the paperwork. Three days' work shitted down the pan like a crappy curry. Now he was going to have to work on the site longer, pushing back another contract that he was hoping to fit in. If the people who were hiring him were unhappy with this and decided it would be better to get someone else to do the job, he would be out of pocket by six hundred pounds. All because of a fuck of a foreman.

Then, when he finally gets home, these bastard TV people had taken over the street. Why? He'd heard that something was going on with the old house at the top of the hill, but he was never really one to listen to the news. As far as he was concerned, the news on the radio was just an interruption to the music so he often zoned out. The others were always bitching about money and women. As far as he was concerned the money could be fine if you were willing to put the work in and stopped bitching. And women? Well, he was married and, even though Sara sometimes spent too much time on the phone yapping with her sister, she was a good cook and a fair fuck. What else did a man need?

As he approached his house, he noticed that half the fucking street was outdoors. There was laughter and, he could see in some eyes, fear. What were they worried about? Just because there was some psycho about didn't mean there was anything to worry about. Close the front door, draw the curtains and watch the tele until bedtime. The psycho would just pass the house without thinking.

Then he noticed his own house. Sara stood on the doorstep talking to the neighbour, Carol. He hated Carol; she was a slut who left her husband just because he gave her the odd thump. What she probably understand was that she needed a thump now and again. She should have just accepted it as part of the marriage contract. A man could come home tired, wound up and stressed, and needing someone to take it out on. What the fuck did she expect?

He entered his house without a word and could hear Sara fussing behind him.

'Sorry, Carl. I didn't realise what time it was, let me put something on for you.'

He turned to her as she shut the front door and stared at her incredulously.

'What do you mean you'll put something on for me?' he asked. 'I'm fucking starving, where's my tea?'

Sara blustered in her way, not really saying much but speaking a lot. Something about the old house and the police. She tried to pass him in the hallway, muttering on about how she would put food on for him now and it would only take a half-hour, but he stopped her with a pull of her hair.

He felt a rage build up in him. It had started a few days ago, a throbbing urge to hit out. He didn't know what it was, but all weekend he had felt it and heard it in every loud voice. Anytime the kids played he wanted to throw a boot at them; any time Sara picked up the telephone he wanted to grab it out of her hands and slam it against the side of her head.

He pulled her back towards him and hissed at her.

'I want my fucking food on the fucking tray in two fucking minutes.'

She cried 'I'll put it on now,' then screamed as he yanked her hair again, 'I'll only take twenty minutes, it won't take - ' another yank and another scream - 'long.'

She was crying now, that pathetic whine that she had.

He pushed her to the wall and felt a moment of pleasure as her head bounced off it with a dull thud. He grabbed her hair again and pushed her one more time. Another thud, another whimper.

The rage seemed all-encompassing. He felt it take complete control and he found that he was enjoying it. He wanted more of it, he wanted to bath in it. It wasn't his fault, she was doing it to him and, if he found some pleasure in dishing it out, then that was fine.

He thumped her against the wall again, then again, then again. Her whimpers were fading and there was a growing red stain on the wall behind her. As he grabbed her by the hair again, he became aware of three things. First, Sara's body had grown heavy as her legs had stopped holding her weight. Second, there was a banging and shouting at the front door. Third, there was a wetness on his face. It wasn't just her blood; it was his own tears.

He let go of Sara and she dropped to the floor, then he passed her dying body and ascended the stairs. In the bedroom he had shared with Sara for seventeen years, he looked at himself in the large mirror they had bought in Ikea about a year before. He was fat, bloated, and completely out of shape. His stomach pushed out alarmingly and his face looked old. Blood covered his clothes and he noticed some in his hair. His hairline was receding but that had never bothered him. Sara used to joke about it ('Would you like a cut or a wax?') and suddenly the tremendous weight of what he had done descended onto him. He sat on the edge of the bed and began to sob. He didn't hear the front door crashing in downstairs and the screams as Carol and the police saw Sara, her bloodied body lying dead in the hallway.

***

Further up the street just opposite the home of Tal Jones, Annie Franklin stood over her husband, Chris, as he lay sleeping on the settee. He always did that, no matter what time of day it was. He would come home from work and pot around in the garden or do whatever it was he did in his shed for a few hours. He would then eat the food that Annie prepared for him at five, then sit in front of the television and after about fifteen minutes he would start to snore.

He worked as a driver, delivering stock to small corner shops throughout Wales and the west of England. He would get up at 2 am and drive to Cardiff to pick up his stock, then he would start his deliveries at 5 am. At two in the afternoon, he would be home. It was as if his whole cycle was out of sync with the rest of the world, like he was living in his own peculiar time zone, four hours before everyone else.

She didn't really mind this, she was a housewife who had never really worked, and it still meant that there was plenty of time in the day for her to do whatever she wanted to do (which was usually limited to gossiping with her neighbour, Jean, and playing sudoku). It would all be acceptable if it wasn't for his awful snoring. Every single evening was the same. She couldn't watch the soaps anymore because his snores were so bloody loud. It gnawed into her bones, like a rat gnawing at a carcass. She tried turning the TV louder, but he just woke up and complained that it was 'Too Fucking Loud!'. She hated him using that language but sometimes she felt like using it herself. She bloody did!

She had once asked him whether he would have been more comfortable in bed, but he went off on one of his rants about how he paid for the 'fucking house' and his pay put food on the 'fucking table'. If he wanted a quiet snooze on the sofa then he was within his rights to do it.

She had tried to tell him that he wasn't quiet, that his snoring was so loud that even the dog went into the kitchen to hide, but he just told her she should 'sleep with the fucking dog then.' At night she had taken to sleeping in the spare bedroom and, even then, she could hear it, although it was further away, and she soon got used to putting her pillow over her head instead of under it.

But now she just had enough. It had crept up on her slowly over the last few days and now, standing over the old bastard with a knife in her hand, she realised that she was just so tired. Her nerves were frayed, her stress levels were too high. It was as if she could feel her blood pressure rising, which her doctor had said was a bad thing, and he had given her tablets to control it. Her temples pulsed, and she could feel her heart pumping hard to keep her alive. She had an odd sense of paranoia, as if someone or something was watching her from the shadows. When the dark came, the shadows came alive.

Not that Chris noticed anything.

His head was thrown back and his mouth was open. His tee-shirt was dirty, and she knew he hadn't washed up properly when he returned from the garden. She hated that, she worked hard to keep the house tidy and he showed no appreciation for her work whatsoever.

She lifted the knife, the bright green one that she used to cut the salad with. It was razor-sharp, she knew that because she had cut herself with it that very day. It had been an accident, but the pain had felt good. It had woken her up, made her feel alive if only for a half-hour. It had been then that she decided exactly what she needed to do.

She leaned forward and placed the knife a centimetre from his stubbled neck. Her hands were steady, and she felt calm. She had wondered how she would feel at this moment and it surprised her how well she was handling it.

Chris snorted loudly and moved to get comfortable. She pulled the knife back slightly then took a deep breath. He did the same, the sound ringing out in their small living room and she quickly plunged the knife into his neck and pulled it left to right. Blood squirted out of the wound, splattering her pink tee-shirt that she had bought to go on some charity walk in Cardiff a few years ago. Chris screamed out and instinctively reached for his neck. Annie stepped back and watched as his eyes tried to focus on her; the pain and confusion evident on his face.

He tried to say something, but it just came out as a wet gurgle. Blood flowed down his dirty tee-shirt and Annie became aware of the stains that were going to ruin her settee. But that was a problem for later. Now she stood and watched the spectacle. He didn't seem to make any move to get up and, although he thrashed about a little, this soon lessened. She didn't know how long it took for him to die but she stayed and watched it all. When life had left his eyes and his body had become inert, she sat down beside him and watched the television in silence.

***

At 15 Henry Hill, Alex Andrews, known as Battery to his friends, fell over the cat as he carried a cup of tea into the living room, and scalded himself. An hour later, when the cat slept on the small chair next to the kitchen door, he grabbed it by the scruff of the neck and threw it across the room, slamming it against the wall. It yelled in pain then collapsed to the ground. Battery's girlfriend, Kelly, screamed in rage and hit him across the head with the saucepan of boiling noodles she had been cooking. He grabbed her shirt, ripping it off her. She pulled away and tried to run for the door but fell over the prone cat that lay twitching at her feet. Battery jumped up on top of her and slapped her hard until she resisted no more, then he raped her there on the floor next to her dead cat, all the while watched by something just beyond reach in the dark corner under the stairs.

***

In 28 Henry Hill, Carol Whittaker cried as she thought of how she just couldn't face her future without Brian, the husband who had left her for a slut of a barmaid down in Porth. Her eye was blackened after the punch he had given her that morning when she confronted him. Now she was alone. It was her fault, he had said. She was frigid, he had said. She wasn't sexy, she was a skank and he was afraid that if he had fucked her one more time his dick would fall off.

She sat in silence, tears running down her face, her eyes burning.

She had a knife in her hand, and it was poised over her right wrist. She thought of Brian, of the way he had looked at her as if she were no more than dog shit under his shoe. It was his face that remained with her as she cut herself deep. She was aware of the pain, but it also remained distant and, as she slowly died, his face faded from her mind, replaced with a pleasant nothing.

***

Darkness fell across Trehenri, not just the darkness of night, but a blackness that spread slowly from one heart to another.

Whatever was stirring, whatever was slowly pulling itself into the world that night, was bringing with it a gloom that could not be seen but spread like a deadly virus.

Night fell.

CHAPTER 32

Gwladys Pryce lived in Heol Fach, a small street off the Main Road. It took Jimmy just over ten minutes to walk down the hill to her house, but it seemed so much longer. The streets of Trehenri didn't feel like they normally would. Firstly, they were much busier than normal, especially around the supermarket where the Farhadis had been killed and their daughter taken. Camera crews were scattered everywhere, and the night was brighter than normal, especially as the clocks turned six and the live feeds to the various newsrooms in Cardiff, London and beyond were taking place. There were also crowds hanging on almost every street corner, mostly, but not exclusively, youngsters with nothing to do but lap up the spectacle.

Jimmy didn't like it at all. There seemed to be a terrible dark mood hanging over the village he loved, and the cameras were recording it all, lapping it up and broadcasting it to the world. He couldn't help but wonder what would happen to the area once this terrible thing had come to an end. Would it lead to the death of the village? House prices would certainly fall if people decided that maybe Trehenri was haunted. Many people would move away, and they would be replaced by problem families, druggies and those that other areas just didn't want. Isn't that what normally happened in times like this?

But Jimmy chastised himself, wasn't that part of the job? He'd had it so easy, so comfortable for so long, but his calling was to Christ and not to a certain geographical area. Besides, wasn't Christ's pasture the entire world? Shouldn't he spend more time with the undesirables than he did with the comfortable? In fact, shouldn't he be challenging those who were comfortable to get up off their backsides and do some good?

Maybe that was what would be in store for him in the future and, if that were the case, he would just have to get on with it, to face the change with faith and grace.

Which is what he was trying to do now.

Gwladys was a lovely lady, someone who had been attending the chapel long before Jimmy was called to serve there. Her husband, Brynfor, had been an Elder for a few decades and after he had passed, she had been a rock. Although the Chapel rules meant that she could not become an Elder herself (a rule Jimmy had tried to change but was voted down by the members – male and female), she had always been there to lend a hand, to organise and to advise.

Now another member of her family had died, her daughter Janet who had been sixty-one and had succumb to breast cancer. Janet had been a twin and her sister, Nicola, had also passed with the same condition two years previously. It was as if God were taking each and every member of Gwladys' family from her, one by one.

Yet, as he sat in her living room with a cup of hot tea in his hands, he detected no malice. Her faith seemed as strong as ever, and she was taking comfort in the fact everyone who had been taken were believers and so she need not worry about them.

Her only worry, she said, was her son George, who had left the church when he was old enough to make the decision. Jimmy liked George, who taught in the same school as Morgan, but was still pained when he heard Gwladys talk about her worries for him.

'If I have learned anything,' she said ' it is that we can be taken at any moment. Look at what is happening to this place now. Such terrible things, it's as if the devil himself has taken up residence.'

Jimmy thought back to the events of that afternoon, of the

death that had visited those poor policemen, and he shuddered. Had he seen the devil that afternoon? Had he faced down the Enemy himself?

No, he decided, whatever this was, it wasn't the devil. It may be one of his, but it wasn't him.

They had spent the next half an hour talking about whatever came to Gwladys' mind, mostly memories about Janet and Nicola. Moments that stretched back sixty years. She said that, after Nicola had died, she had known that the same thing would happen to Janet. The two sisters always did things together, always shared the same ideas, the same dreams. Both worked for the council at the Registry Office, both took part in the local theatre groups. They had been married on the same day and when they were young they seemed to share illnesses. If Janet had the measles, Nicola would have them by the end of the week. If Nicola caught the Chicken Pox, so would Janet. Unbeknown to mother and daughter, Janet already had cancer when Nicola died, only it hadn't spread enough for anyone to notice. She had lasted a further two years.

'Wonderful years,' Gwladys said. 'God has been good to us in so many ways.'

Jimmy wondered if his faith would have been as strong if he had lost what she had, but cut the thought off. To ask himself what was to imagine a world without Carys, without Jenny or Joshua, and he didn't want to do that right now.

When he left Gwladys Pryce's house at seven-thirty, he did feel a bit better. It was the old woman's acceptance of everything that had happened to her and her family, the lack of bitterness, and the belief that God would look after her children – well, maybe not George – that gave him hope.

The night was now dark and Heol Fach was mostly quiet, the noise of the Main Road and tumult of the last few days was still a half a dozen houses away. He stepped out into the fresh air and took a deep breath. The walk home always took a little bit longer as it was uphill, and Jimmy was nowhere near as fit as he should have been. This thought had crossed his mind a lot recently, and he often decided to do something about it but never did. He was never going to take up running, that sort of thing would drive him nuts, but he could join a class up in Tylorstown Sports Centre, maybe.

He snorted at his self-deception. He was going to go home, have a meal, then a shower, then watch a film with Carys beside him. He had recently bought a collection of Buster Keaton films on Blu-ray including his favourite, Sherlock Jnr. It was a very short film, but it never failed to make him laugh, and that would help take away the stain that the day had left on his soul. And if that wasn't enough, he would follow it with The General, which even Carys had enjoyed before. Perhaps she could be persuaded to put her book down, cwtch into him and watch the film together. Then, when it was over, he would take her to bed, strip off their clothes and lay together. They didn't have to make love - although that would be just as acceptable - they could just spoon. He had always loved the feel of her next to him, skin on skin. It made him feel like they were one, that he was completely open to her, literally exposed.

Carys was undoubtedly his rock, the one thing in his life that was stable.

They had met, surprisingly enough considering his chosen career choice, at a nightclub. Jimmy was home from University, meeting up with old friends – Bobby Edwards and Raymond Walker – and decided to go and let down what hair they had (Bobby had a crewcut, Jimmy was already balding, leaving Raymond the only hirsute member). There were a few clubs in the nearby towns but only one in Trehenri. The Hot Zone got its name because the owners probably thought it sounded cool. It was a place to dance to pulsating and throbbing music, get sweaty, and occasionally get off with someone. They didn't seem to realise that the phrase 'Hot Zone' also referred to ground-zero in a diseased area. Somewhere that deadly viruses like Ebola, Typhus or diphtheria could take hold and

quickly spread through a population. Although most of its clientele didn't make this connection, Jimmy couldn't help but
think of it as a breeding ground for STDs and other groin nas-
ties.

Perhaps he was being dramatic but, hey, he liked the irony!

He certainly wasn't on the lookout for romance. Places like
this were not for conversation and it was impossible to get
to know someone with all the noise that passed as music.
They had turned up in their best shirts and trousers, and looking, they thought, pretty cool. They had danced, drank themselves fairly merry, and sweated. Raymond, who was on leave
from the army and had just returned from the Falklands where
he continually lamented the lack of available women, had
tried to hit on a few - regaling them with war stories, even
though he had missed the actual war by a few years - but soon
noticed that none seemed all that interested.

As the night wore on Jimmy started to get bored but didn't
want to spoil his friends' fun, so he wandered downstairs to
the toilets. The music was quieter, a dull, distant pounding
rather than the loud, overwhelming throbbing upstairs. In the
gents, he relieved himself, then splashed water over his face
and head. He splashed so much that he managed to soak the
top of his shirt. Never mind, he thought, he would be going
home soon and the summer's night was warm.

It was as he was leaving the gents that he first heard the
giggle.

Over the years he had debated with himself if it was a laugh
or a giggle. Was it the same thing? Was there any difference?
He had eventually concluded that it was indeed a giggle. There
was something in the word that described the sound more
than 'laugh'. A laugh had lots of variations, lots of sounds and
lots of uses, but none of them seemed to capture the fragrance
of a giggle. Carys giggled.

He searched around for the source of that most heavenly of
sounds and saw her. She was indeed an angel. She had long auburn hair, the type that gets a little girl picked on when she's

a child but fawned upon as a woman. Her eyes were the most brilliant blue, her cheeks slightly flushed, probably because she had been dancing. It was love at first sight.

She saw him staring and flushed even more. Her friends giggled – no, they laughed - in understanding. The others were mere girls to him, but this vision was so, so much more.

They had passed him, studiously ignoring him whilst making sure he knew they were doing so. As they ascended the stairs he stood, grounded, watching them. He'd had a few romantic dalliances at university but the pickings for a Theology student had never been that great. Most girls either thought he was judging them and about to send down the wrath of God upon their heads, or that he was a celibate who occasionally liked to watch but not touch. His two sexual encounters had occurred back here in Trehenri before he had left school and decided on dedicating his life to Christ.

As they disappeared around the corner at the top of the stairs, he broke out of his reverie and chased after them. He could see them heading for the doors and suddenly he was filled with a fear of never seeing her again. He didn't want this to be their sole encounter, he wanted more. He was reminded of the film Citizen Kane – the reporter is interviewing friends and colleagues of the recently deceased Charles Foster Kane, to determine the meaning of his dying word, 'Rosebud'. One of the stories, and possible meanings the reporter is told, was of a memory of a beautiful woman whom the storyteller, now an old man, remembered seeing coming off a ferry decades before. The old man was lamenting the fact he had never seen this woman again and still regretted that he hadn't chased after her. 'I'll bet a month hasn't gone by since then that I haven't thought of that girl,' he had said. 'Maybe that's what Rosebud was to Kane.'

Jimmy didn't want this girl, with her giggle, her hair and her beautiful eyes, to become his Rosebud.

He saw Raymond and Bobby, propped up on the bar, shouting into each other's ears. He raced over to them, his heart pounding in rhythm to the thudding bass line that dominated the dance floor.

'I've got to go!' He said loudly, leaning close to them so they could hear him clearly.

'Why?' Bobby asked.

He was momentarily lost for words. 'I'm in love!' He eventually declared.

Both friends stared at him incredulously, then laughed.

'We'll come with you,' Bobby called. 'You might still need a lift home.' They laughed again and followed Jimmy out.

The warm air felt so refreshing to Jimmy. Although he wasn't much of a drinker, he was suddenly aware that he was slightly intoxicated. Every colour seemed brighter, even in the darkness of the night. Every image that passed over his retinas seemed sharper, yet not necessarily clearer, as if there was just too much information for his brain to properly process all at once.

He stood on the pavement, Bobby and Ray laughing behind him, frantically looking up and down the Main Road for her again.

Jimmy felt a moment of panic when he thought she was gone, but then he saw her. The group of girls were across the street. They had obviously seen him and were pointing him out to their embarrassed friend.

Without thinking, Jimmy crossed the street.

Years later, he would tell people that he had been pulled to her as if there was an invisible hand dragging him over to her. He would tell people that God had intervened and that it was destiny. Truth be told, he had no clear understanding of where the courage came from. At that moment, the only thing he was focused on was her. Carys would always maintain that he'd drunk a few too many that evening.

He stopped in front of them, not looking at anyone except her. There was a pause, as he took in a deep breath of air, then he introduced himself:

'Hi, I'm Jimmy.'

She didn't reply immediately, instead one of her friends made the introduction for her. 'Hi Jimmy, this is Carys'

'Carys,' he whispered. It sounded perfect, although he would admit that the way he felt at that moment if she had been called Gertrude or Helga, or even Arnold, it would have sounded just as wonderful.

'Hi Carys,' he finally said. 'Would you mind if I walked you home?'

Carys flushed. 'You don't know where I live,' she said.

'That's fine. I don't mind if it's far, I like long walks.'

It turned out that Carys had very little choice. Her friends quickly made their excuses and began walking away. Carys looked flustered for a moment, then asked 'How do I know I can trust you?'

'You can ask your friends to walk behind us as a chaperone if you wish,' he replied. Then added, 'besides, I'm a Priest.'

Carys had laughed. 'A Priest? Are Priests allowed to ask girls out?'

'Only angels,' he answered, then immediately felt embarrassed. Carys saw his discomfort and smiled again.

'Do you usually use such cheesy lines on girls?'

'No, I'm sorry, I just,' he began to fidget before composing himself once more. 'I would be honoured if I could walk you home,' he said at last.

And that was that. They had walked home. He recounted his studies and she told him about her own on/off relationship with religion. They had walked for almost two hours, not just to her home, but around town. He'd felt like he was alive, everything had seemed special, the sulfur haze of the streetlights gave the night the most perfect sepia hue, just like an old precious photograph.

Two years later they were married. She worked in the local council office processing Council Tax payments, he took over the local Baptist Church, Mount Zion, after his mentor – George Humphries - had retired after thirty-eight years as their pastor. They were years blessed with more happiness and luck than hardships, and now had two grown-up children. Joshua at Middlesex University in Enfield, North London, studying Film Studies, and Jenny, who lived only a few miles away with her husband, Gareth.

***

This was the memory that, he decided, would accompany him on the way home. It would act as his shield against the horrors of the upcoming night.

But Trehenri wasn't finished with him yet.

CHAPTER 33

Shadow stood in the dark, crouched down on his knees, listening carefully for any sounds. Somewhere in the distance, he could hear one of those strange and magical boxes that made pictures that moved as if they were possessed by compliant spirits. Music played, then some chit chat, although it was too far away for him to make out exactly what was being said. There were other voices, snippets of conversation but nothing close.

He lifted the hatch door slightly - careful not to make any noise - then peered through the crack. He could see the landing below him, two doors leading to bedrooms. Another door was slightly ajar, and steam floated out. The bathroom; someone was in the shower.

He lifted the hatch another inch, so he could see further toward the top of the stairs. He could see two feet, facing away from him. Black shoes and black trousers – probably a policeman. He had seen two police cars parked outside the house earlier, as he surveyed the surroundings. That would explain why every light was on, forcing him to enter the house through the attic.

He smiled at this arrogance. This age of magic boxes, horseless carriages, lights that flicked on and off easily without the need of a flame! They thought they were so secure, so safe. As if turning on a few lights could stop him. Hadn't they realised who they were up against by now? Didn't they understand that there was no way they could stop him and, by extension, stop his master? Today was the last day, this was the last girl. By morning the blood of this child would be spilt, and the body of his master would rise. He felt the tingling of anticipation in his groin, it was almost sexual, the beautiful feeling of impending climax.

And when it was complete, he would finally be able to indulge those urges, those feelings that he had been struggling to control. He could select whoever he wanted, whenever he wanted. And he would. He would prowl the streets and take the pick of the litter. She would be his forever. Let his master have his Lucys, and he would have all the rest.

His hands began to shake with the thought, as the excitement gripped his body. He could feel it move down from his neck, setting his beast on fire. He could feel the erection beginning. The hot pleasure building in his crotch and spreading into the pit of his stomach. He smiled, even though he understood the importance of controlling it. It didn't come easy. The urge was sometimes too overwhelming, just like it had been in the car park the previous night.

He eased the hatch door open further, moving silently, then put it down between a box of books and an old pram. The attic was pitch black but that caused no problems for him as darkness was his friend, his constant companion.

He lifted himself with his huge arms and swung his feet around to the opening. Then with the grace of a gymnast and the stealth of a hunting tiger, he lowered himself down to the landing, his big black boots silently touching down.

It was a policewoman in front of him, which meant that it was probably Lucy's mother in the shower. It would not be proper for a man to accompany her. He couldn't help but smile at how their careful plans were falling apart. Soon they would be rubble at his feet.

The policewoman shivered, and he became aware of the slight draft that was coming from the opening to the attic above him. First, she rubbed her arms to warm them up again and then, as if she had become aware of the change behind her, she began to turn around.

Shadow walked quickly to his prey and before the woman

had turned ninety degrees, he grabbed hold of her head and twisted it sharply. Her body went limp and for a moment he held her in his arms, aware of the softness of her body. He felt the arousal build again and couldn't help moving his giant hands over her soft breasts.

The sound of the shower turned off behind him, bringing him out of the short fantasy he was falling into. He took the woman by her shoulders and quietly eased her to the ground until she formed an unnatural heap on the floor. He then moved to the top of the stairs and looked down. The room below him was open plan, the stairs descending straight into the living room. At the foot of the stairs was Lucy.

He watched her for a moment, smiling. She looked up at him, directly into his eyes and returned the smile. It was genuine and pleasing, and he couldn't help feeling affection for her. They had, of course, met numerous times over the last few weeks, as he first got her used to seeing him, then he had begun talking to her, grooming her for the day he would have to take her. The taking was so important, and he needed the children to go willingly, not to resist but to trust him right to that moment when their blood would spill and their lifeforce would enter his master.

He heard movement behind him and realised that the first thing he would have to do was to sort out the mother. He would do it quietly, just like he had with the policewoman.

He lifted his finger up to his mouth in a 'shush' gesture and stepped back over the policewoman's body and turned to the bathroom. The mist had stopped spilling into the landing, but the door was still ajar.

He moved closer to it and then peered in, careful not to push the door open until it was absolutely necessary.

Then he saw her. Mrs Morris. He could see her reflection in the mirror which was just steamed enough to hide detail but revealed enough for that arousal to return once more. His breath caught in his throat.

She was standing with her back to the mirror, one leg up

on the edge of the low bath. She had two towels; one was wrapped around her breasts but had fallen to reveal the small of her back. The other she was using to dry her leg.

She put the one leg down and lifted the other, the towel on her back falling further until he could see the crack of her behind and the roundness of her cheeks. She lifted it awkwardly, but it was enough for Shadow to feel his beast throb with pleasure, his cock to harden in his trousers, and he involuntarily thrust forward.

He began to pant; his lips were dry and his palms began to sweat. All thoughts of control were now gone. The discipline he needed was forgotten and his mission, despite its importance, was a distant memory of another less important time.

He reached up to the door and carefully pushed it open, so he could look directly at her. He stepped inside and caught the glimpse of her breast hanging forward over her raised leg. Then she turned and looked directly at him.

He could feel the buildup of a scream in her throat as the terror gripped her. Her leg dropped to the floor and he saw the mass of dark curly hair under the raised towel. He crossed to her quickly and clamped his massive hands over her mouth. She trembled in his grasp like a frightened mouse. With the other hand he ripped away the towels and threw them to the ground. He then pushed her back against a cabinet, her head knocking back against the mirror. He still held her mouth, using his incredible strength to pin her to the cabinet. With his other hand, he began to roam her body, squeezing her breasts together violently until a whimper escaped from beneath his hand. They were as soft as he had thought they would be. He pinched her nipples, playing with them before dropping his hand further. They moved across her belly which bulged ever so slightly. He liked a woman to carry a little bit of weight. Not too much, just enough to grab on to, to feel the child that had once been inside her, and to know that this truly was a member of that fairer sex.

His hand dropped further to her crotch and he brushed

against her pubic hair. A tear escaped from her eyes, but he didn't notice. He wasn't looking at her fear, this did not interest him.

Then he heard the scream.

It didn't come from the woman whose mouth was still completely covered. It came from directly behind him.

He turned and saw Lucy standing in the doorway. She screamed loudly and then looked him directly in the eye, but there was no smile this time.

'Stop hurting my mother!' She shouted.

He could hear the panic downstairs. People calling Lucy's name. Feet pounding up the stairs. His hand slipped from the mother's mouth for a second and she used it to shout.

'Run, Lucy. RUN!!!'

Shadow snarled at the woman and adjusted his grip slightly. She screamed at her daughter again, telling her to run but before she could finish, he threw her to the side. Her body smashed into the cabinet, then she fell back towards the bath. She yelped as she fell and tried grabbing for whatever she could, but she could only find purchase on the shower curtain. She fell hard into the bath, her legs sprawling into the air. Her scream was cut short and she fell silent with the impact.

'You hurt my Mam!' Lucy screamed, stamping her feet against the ground.

Lucy's father appeared next to her and lifted her into his arms with one quick swoop. He turned to the bathroom and saw Shadow standing over his wife, who was lying in an unnatural state in the tub. His eyes widened with horror.

There was a moment of silence, in which the tension seemed to hang in the air. Then Shadow growled and suddenly leapt towards the door. Lucy's father turned quickly and disappeared down the corridor. As Shadow reached the door, two policemen lunged for him, their weight pushing him off balance. It wasn't much, and it wouldn't have normally made much of a difference, but it was enough to give Lucy's father that fraction of a second longer to disappear down the stairs.

He kicked at one officer who let out a painful 'oof' as Shadow's knee connected with his rib cage. The officer fell to the floor, groaning in pain. The second policeman wrapped his arms around Shadow's waist, obviously realising that the only chance he had was to slow the assailant down. It worked but only for a brief moment. He was lifted off the ground and swung away with monstrous ease. His body hit the wall and consciousness left him.

Shadow then stepped heavily onto the first officer's fingers as he began the chase.

***

Kyle Morris held on to his daughter as tightly as he could. He ran down the stairs, bouncing into the wall at the bottom as he tried to change direction. Lucy moaned loudly but he was determined to ignore her and concentrate on getting out of the house.

Images of Emma laying upside-down in the bathtub crowded his mind. He could see her sprawled, her legs flopped over the edge. He hadn't seen her face, so he didn't know how she was. Was she still alive? Was she dead? Was she -

He howled in anger and pain as he crossed the living room and towards the front door. He could hear the Policemen trying to stop the bastard upstairs. It didn't seem to last long. As he reached the front door, he could hear the pounding of heavy feet crossing the landing and beginning the descent downstairs.

Kyle shifted Lucy from one hand to the other. Her head was buried in his shoulder and, between his own thumping heartbeats, he could hear her whimpers. At one point, sometime between the moment he had picked her up and when they arrived at the door, she may have called for her mother, her arms outstretched, but Kyle couldn't be sure.

He reached for the door and tried pulling the handle down, but it wouldn't budge. He did it again, forcing it down with all his might, his brow sweating and his bladder ready to release itself. He tried a third time, aware that the man chasing him had now reached the bottom of the stairs. His hand slipped off the handle and he realized the keys were hanging down from the lock. He turned them quickly and grabbed the door handle one more time.

The handle twisted downwards and the door began to open.

Then a hand grabbed his hair and pulled him backwards. He screamed as he was yanked back into the room. Lucy fell from his grasp and tumbled into the open doorway. The man pulled him further back and the pain sent bright ripples of colour through his brain.

He reached up behind and grabbed his attacker's hands, and tried to lift himself, to maybe ease the agony of his hair being ripped from his skull. He managed a glance at his daughter who was getting up, a look of horror on her face. Tears stained her cheeks and her hair was a mess, but she also looked extremely angry.

'What are you doing?' she bellowed.

Shadow's grip eased ever so slightly on Kyle's hair, although it still hurt like a son of a bitch.

'What are you doing to my daddy?' She was starting to cry, fresh tears breaking their bonds on her eyelashes. 'Why did you hurt my Mam, and are doing that to my Dad? I thought you were nice.'

A heavy stillness fell between them punctuated occasionally by Lucy's sobs. This was then broken by the monster himself.

'Lucy.' He paused, and Kyle got the feeling he was searching for words. 'I'm sorry,' he said eventually in a quiet voice.

He let go of Kyle's hair and the father fell roughly to the ground. Shadow then stepped over his body and stood between father and daughter.

Kyle had to say something, had to do something. He lifted himself up on his elbows, his head swam as a wave of pain swept over him.

'Lucy,' his voice croaked. 'Run, baby, run.'

Lucy looked at her father and she seemed to jerk with the emotion.

'Come with me,' Shadow said.

'No, Lucy. He has hurt your Mam and me, and he will hurt you too.'

'No Lucy, I would never hurt you.'

Lucy looked up at the man then down at her father. Confusion was written all over her face. She took a step back into the street.

Suddenly, a policeman appeared in the doorway. He must have been waiting for this moment, for the right second to grab the girl, Kyle thought. Lucy screamed in fright as she was whisked away. Another policeman took his place and aimed a taser straight at Shadow.

'Get down on your hands and knees with you-'

But Shadow didn't get down, instead he jumped forward at the officer, his hands raised in front of him like a cliched Frankenstein's monster. The police officer fired the taser and Shadow roared in pain and anger. He gripped the smaller man and pulled him violently to the ground, his foot stomping on the man's back. A crunching sound ripped the air and the police officer went limp.

The monster started to leave the house and chase after Lucy but, breaking through the pain which wracked his body, Kyle lurched forward and wrapped his arms around Shadow's legs.

'Run, Lucy,' he called, although he had no way of knowing if his daughter could hear him.

The monster kicked out, but Kyle hung on for dear life. It felt as if his arms were being ripped from his sockets, but he was determined to buy Lucy as much time as possible, however little that may be. He grunted with pain as the leg he was holding on to was kicked forward again.

Again, he held on. Barely.

Then Shadow reached down and grabbed Kyle by his hair

once more. Kyle shrieked in pain but still managed to keep his grip. He had meshed his fingers together, his knuckles white with effort. The man pulled his hair back further until Kyle was looking directly at him. His face had hardened, like a cartoon criminal. He grinned and revealed his black teeth. Then, he brought up his free hand and brought it crashing down on Kyle's face. Blood exploded from his imploding nose. His cheekbone ruptured and his eye was ripped from the collapsing socket. Pain exploded in his head and he couldn't help but loosen his grip. Shadow lifted his fist, as if he was going to punch him again. There was hatred wretched on the man's face. Then he turned back towards the front door.

***

Shadow dropped Kyle to the floor and flicked the blood from his hand, creating a splatter across the beige painted wall. He then stepped out of the house to chase down and to claim his prize. Kyle tried to call out to his daughter, but nothing came out. The world blurred with pain and his vision darkened. All he could do now was hope that his little girl would get away.

***

The rage inside Shadow was boiling. His failure so far was going to be humiliating, but there was no way he was going to fail. Not now. Not when the end was so close. He looked down the street and saw a policeman carry Lucy away. Shadow smiled. The end was near.

CHAPTER 34

After the relative quiet of Heol Fach, the Main Road was a carnival of chaos. There were people everywhere, most of whom seemed to be standing around looking for something to do, something to see. There were the usual youngsters holding cans of Red Bull or cheap lager, waiting for something cool to happen. They were the ones who seemed buzzed with excitement at the terrible events that had happened recently and, although Jimmy tried to avoid such thoughts, he couldn't help worrying about the future of the valleys when it was these kids and their offspring that would make up the population. It shamed him to think about such a thing, and he knew that it went against the spirit of his position as a chaplain to the village and the wider community. It was, he supposed, part of his job description to have some sort of sympathy and empathy with these youngsters, but sometimes it was hard. Maybe it was his true character breaking through, something that he needed to work harder on suppressing.

There were many residential houses on the Main Road and, standing on the doorsteps, Jimmy noticed a lot of women - some old, some young - and they all seemed to be wearing slippers.

Was this a new thing? he asked himself. Had he noticed this before? They wore jeans, joggers, dresses and skirts, a wide variety of styles and sizes, but on their feet - slippers. Various designed straps across the front, nothing on the heel.

He snorted a quiet laugh, and for a brief moment, he forgot the horrors that his home had been experiencing. Instead, felt the usual laconic humour he was accustomed to.

He was going to go home and curl up with Carys, watch a film together, then take her to bed and make love to her. If it was getting too late, they could skip the film and go straight to bed. Perhaps they could start in the shower, something that always filled him with a lot of intimate pleasure.

Again, he smiled and was filled for that immense love and need for his wife. It made him feel very much alive, even when surrounded by death. The thoughts of that afternoon were behind him and the fear that had come with it were replaced with Carys's face. This is what he wanted to think about right now, not murder, kidnappings and the supernatural, but Carys' face, her smile, her giggle.

These things, the things he lived for, were so much on his mind that, at first, he failed to perceive the change of atmosphere and the disturbance that seemed to be coming from the junction with Heol Gwynddu. By the time he looked up, the crowds seemed to have parted and were making a large circle on the Main Road. Someone nudged him, taking him out of his reverie, and he saw that there was a panicked look on the expression of those around him.

Then he heard the first screams. They weren't screams of full-on panic, at least not yet. People screamed because they could see others panicking and, over the last few days, it seemed that they had been conditioned to react this way.

He looked around then saw a policeman running into the middle of the circle of people, with a child in his arms. He was shouting, telling people to get out of his way. Other policemen were making a protective barrier around him and were all looking nervously up the hill. In the dark of the late evening, Jimmy couldn't see the expressions on their faces, but he felt the tension in the air and knew at that moment, from the pit of his stomach, what the child's name was, and what was coming down the street after her.

All thoughts of Carys were gone and replaced by a primitive fear. The Shadowman and the priest were going to meet again.

***

Police Constable Alex Hunt almost stumbled as he crossed the double white markings at the end of Heol Gwynddu and onto the Main Road. His lungs were bursting, not only because of the exertion – carrying a nine-year-old child wasn't easy even though he was fit and healthy – but through fear. He could almost feel the Shadowman behind him, probably reaching out that very moment to grab his hair, just as he had to Mr Morris, and yanking him and the child backwards.

The hair on the back of his neck stood upright and a cold fear crawled down his spine, made worse by the hot sweat that covered every last inch of skin.

He wobbled slightly but his balance restored quickly. A group of policemen quickly surrounded him, providing him with some cover, and he felt a brief respite from the tension. It was going to be alright, he told himself. Surely it was going to be alright.

He stopped in the middle of the road, undecided where to go next.

'Over here!'

Hunt looked around and saw one of his colleagues – Georgie Williams – calling over to him from a squad car. The back door was open and the lights were on. Williams stood by the driver's seat waving his arms in the air.

'Hunt, over here!' Williams called.

Hunt took a deep breath and started towards the car which was about fifty yards away. His legs felt heavy and he could hear his heart beat crazily in his ears.

Then he heard the screams.

He turned back and looked up the hill. The crazy bastard had reached the bottom of the hill and was staring at him, the uniformed body of a policeman at his feet. The Shadowman roared defiantly and began taking long strides towards Hunt and Lucy. The girl saw him too, as she let out a long and incredibly loud scream. Her grip around Hunt's neck became tighter, spurring him on to run. He turned back to the car and Williams, who was shouting at him and waving his arms excitedly.

He also could hear yelling behind him, and the sound of Tasers being fired. The Shadowman screamed again but this time Hunt was sure there was a hint of pain in amongst the rage.

Hunt felt a moment's glee, knowing that the bastard could be hurt.

He didn't look around though. Instead, he tried focusing on the car in front of him, but this was proving almost impossible. He could hear the scuffles behind him, the screaming of pain and fury, and knew that it was no longer the Shadowman who was making these noises. He got to the car and bent to put the little girl into the open back seat. His heart felt like it could burst at any moment, his muscles were tight with effort. Williams closed the driver's door and the engine roared. As Hunt got into the car, he saw the Shadowman running towards them, his face distorted with fury. He was only a few feet away.

The car leapt forward, and a small part of Hunt entertained the idea that they could possibly be safe, that they were going to get away, that he could see his wife later and hold her tight.

Then, the driver's side window smashed in.

Lucy screamed, a shrill shriek of terror, as millions of tiny fragments of glass were punched into the car. Hunt closed his eyes and threw his body over the girl to protect her.

'Cover your head,' he said to her frantically.

He heard another shout and turned to see an immense arm reaching through the window and grab Williams. The driver cried out in panic and pain. The car lurched forward and sped up, as Williams tried to escape the iron grip of this beast of a man.

The Shadowman did let go, but not before pulling Williams roughly at the window. The policeman yelped as his body was yanked through the small gap, his head being forced backwards in a terribly final angle. There was a tremendous crash and the car came to a sudden stop as it hit a parked car outside the butcher's shop. Hunt and Lucy were thrown forward and he fell below her into the floor area between the backseat and the front.

The little girl was quiet, no longer crying, and for a moment the policeman felt a stab of panic at the thought that maybe something had happened to her. But then she lifted herself up and breathed deeply. There was blood falling down her face from a cut on her forehead.

He scrambled to get up, but she was on top of him and he didn't think he could lift her as the gap between the seats was too narrow and his left arm was pinned beneath the passenger seat. Instinctively, he tried to reach for the door handle, hoping it would give her the opportunity to escape.

'Fuck,' he said, remembering that there were no door handles in the back of police cars. With a desperate grunt, he pushed her up one handed with the little remaining strength he had. She sat up on the seat and he began to lift himself onto his elbows, struggling in the tight space.

Then the door opened.

The Shadowman stood there and leaned into the car. He didn't look at Hunt, just stared at the little girl for a few heartbeats. Then he reached in and offered her his hand.

'C'mon, Lucy,' he said. His voice was guttural and deep, but there didn't seem to have any menace in it. In fact, he seemed calm and friendly.

'No, you hurt my mammy,' she replied.

'She's fine,' he said and reached further in.

'No, I saw her in the bath.'

'She fell but she's fine now. C'mon we must go.'

Hunt took in a deep breath.

'Don't believe him, Lucy,' he said, between deep breaths. 'He killed her, he killed your mother.'

Lucy began to cry again, the tears mixing with the blood on her cheek.

The Shadowman snarled at Hunt. 'Shut up, you have no part in this.'

'You need to run, Lucy, get away from him. He'll kill you - '

'SHUT YOUR MOUTH, MEATER,' the Shadowman shouted. 'This is between her and me.'

'No!' Hunt sneered. He propped himself up and threw his body back and, in one motion lifted his legs in a kick. His foot contacted with the Shadowman's iron-like jaw, sending a wave of pain up his leg and into the pit of his stomach. Bile rose to his mouth and he felt like he was going to throw up.

There was a grunt from the Shadowman, who grabbed Hunt's ankle roughly and yanked. Hunt screamed as the leg was pulled from his hip joint then twisted violently. His foot fell limply to the side.

***

'Come now, little one,' the Shadowman continued as if there had hardly been a break in the conversation.

'No, no, NO!' Lucy pulled away from the huge hand, almost stepping on Hunt's face as she scrambled for safety.

Shadow sighed, then reached further. He could see that she was no longer willing to go with him.

Then his face distorted with pain. He pulled himself out of the car and turned. Three policemen were surrounding him. One held a taser in his hands, aiming it at Shadow. From the front of this device extended a long wire attached to something which was embedded into his back, and two others holding assault rifles in their hands.

Shadow could feel pain coursing through his body. He looked directly at the policeman, snarling. He then roared with pain, frustration and hatred.

***

'About fucking time,' Hunt whispered hoarsely.

Hunt could see the giant back of the Shadowman as he started towards the police. There was the explosive sound of

weapons firing, and Shadow fell back to the car. The policemen shouted for him to get down on his knees with his hands
behind his head, but he did not listen. He just lifted himself
back up and charged at the policemen. There were more shots
fired, then screams.

Hunt realised that they didn't stand a chance.

He lifted himself up, his vision almost disappearing behind
a bright white haze as the pain took over. He clamped his teeth
together, trying to fight through the agony. He then grabbed
hold of Lucy and pulled the little girl close to him.

'You need to get out of here, now,' he said. 'Climb to the
front seat and open the door from there. Go!'

Lucy whimpered but began climbing over him, her foot
landing square in his stomach as she did so. He moaned softly,
then lifted himself as much as he could before the pain became
too much. He could see the showdown outside between the
Shadowman and his colleague with the gun. They were shouting at each other, but Hunt couldn't make out what was being
said. He knew that he would pass out soon and he would be of
no use to Lucy then.

He heard the passenger seat open and turned to see Lucy
almost fall out of the car and onto the tarmac floor. She cried
out as she did so, but she was free.

Hunt smiled a little, then passed out as his blood pressure
fell too low and the pain became too much.

***

Jimmy watched from where he was standing outside of the
Hairdressers where Catryn's old friend Leanne worked. The
crowd had kept a wide berth from the action in front of
them, yet few people moved far. It was as if they had a front-
row at some terrible theatrical event that was as captivating
as it was horrifying. He saw the policeman carrying the poor
young girl, almost throw her into the car and jump in beside
her.

The situation made him feel conflicted. On the one hand,

he was saddened that the world was going to discover Trehenri for the first time because of something as terrible as this. But, at the same time, he felt a cheap thrill. This was happening right now and, even though he was just a bystander cowering out of the way, he was there. He was part of it.

He knew that this was very uncharitable and revealed a weakness of character that he never would have been aware of if this had never happened, but he also knew that it was very true of him. Maybe it was his love of movies, his love of the spectacle, that made him think this way. He didn't know.

He saw three officers approach the car and shout out at the Shadowman, one of them firing a taser into his back.

'They've shot him with another Taser, and I can see him getting out of the car. The little girl is not there, she must still be in the car with the courageous police officer who rescued her from the house.'

The reporter droned on, giving a commentary to the world.

Then the police fired.

People screamed and backed off further. Jimmy looked around but there were now so many people crowded into the small street, that there wasn't much space for him to retreat. He crouched down hoping that he might offer a small a target as possible for any stray bullet.

There was a fight and the Shadowman, who seemed hurt by the impact of the bullets but not enough to stop him, grabbed and pulled a policeman closer to him. The man had become a hostage.

The reporter next to him continued chattering into the microphone, her voice low and insistent. She was now lying on the cold road, her feet hanging over a drain, her dress suit soaking wet and probably ruined. There was a cacophony of sounds, a tumult of noise which should have overwhelmed his senses, yet, despite the uproar, he heard the soft sound of a car door opening. Everyone seemed to hold their breath and an unnatural hush fell on the crowd. Then there was a cheer as Lucy Morris fell out of the car and onto the road.

The girl stood up shakily and looked around. A policeman darted from the crowd and ran for her, taking her hand and pulling her away from the vehicle. They were coming towards Jimmy and the reporter, and he felt a prang of fear coursing through him.

He could see the Shadowman turn, look at the fleeing child and then roar ferociously. He threw his hostage to the ground, then took three long strides and reached down for the rifle which had fallen in the melee. He lifted it and brought it down onto his raised knee, snapping the gun in half. Then he turned and ran towards the girl.

A ripple of panic spread through the crowd around Jimmy and many turned to run, bumping others as they did so, causing their fellow gawkers to fall to the floor. People clambered over the fallen, who were crushed beneath their feet. Few were lucky enough to keep their balance and get away. The reporter struggled to her feet and backed off, but her cameraman stayed put. Jimmy had seen films about these types of reporters, willing to risk anything and everything for the story. He just hoped that this poor man didn't become part of the story instead.

The Shadowman caught up to the Policeman and the girl quickly, grabbing hold of the man's jacket, yanking him backwards. The policeman fell heavily to the ground, but Lucy kept running.

If anyone had asked Jimmy what thoughts had gone through his head right then, he would have said panic. He would have admitted he wanted to run, to trample anyone in his way and get the hell out of there. He would have admitted that he was scared, not a horror movie or irrational fear of the dark scared, but a real intense dread. What he wasn't thinking, what never seemed to cross his conscious mind, was what he found his body doing.

He ran towards Lucy. She was about fifteen feet away, close enough for him to see the panic in her eyes, to see the blood running down her cheek and staining her Hello Kitty pyjama top.

He picked her up and looked directly at the Shadowman, who looked back with undisguised hatred.

Jimmy's instinct to run still tried to take control of his muscles, but he just stood there. The Shadowman stepped closer to them and Jimmy could see that the monster recognised him.

'Priest man,' the Shadowman growled. 'Put her down and no harm will come to you,'

Lucy held him tightly and he could feel her shaking. Her pyjama bottoms had a warm wetness and he knew that she had peed herself. The poor thing was quivering with fear, the shaking only occasionally broken by the shudder of tears.

'Put her down, Priest. I will do no harm to you. I just want the girl.'

Jimmy couldn't speak, but a question fluttered to the front of his mind and he grabbed onto it before it disappeared. Why wasn't the monster attacking him? He had attacked everyone who stood between him and the child, why not attack him? Jimmy would certainly offer a lot less resistance than the police.

'Priest, I am running out of patience. Put her down and walk away.'

How did he know I am a minister of religion? Jimmy wondered. He tried to think back to Henry House that afternoon. Was this something they had discussed? Although he couldn't remember, he thought that was very likely. Had the Shadowman heard him?

'Priest, this is your last warning. If I have to take her, I will rip your arms from their sockets and beat you to death with them. You will die at your own hands.' The Shadowman sneered, obviously pleased with his witticism.

Jimmy suddenly knew what he had to do. It came to from nowhere, just a whisper from a vast distance, but he heard it. It didn't make much sense to him, but it was insistent. It wasn't a suggestion; it was almost a command. He didn't have time to question it, to think it through. He just understood that it could work. It had to work, or it would be the end of both of them. He crouched down beside Lucy and looked the child in the eyes. He moved a hair aside and saw the cut on her forehead, which had stopped bleeding, although still looked extremely painful,

'Lucy,' he said quietly.

She looked back at him, and he saw the depth of her fear and despair wretched on his face.

'I want you to kneel down beside me,' he continued. 'Do you understand?'

She frowned and shook her head.

'No,' she said in the softest of voices.

'Trust me,' he said. 'Kneel down and I will hold you very tightly. I won't let go; I promise.'

'Don't listen to him, Lucy,' the Shadowman said with a growl. 'Come to me.'

Lucy turned to him and looked up at the giant, who was now only a few feet away.

'You hurt my Mam, you probably hurt my Dad,' the words were spat out with hatred and defiance. 'You hurt that policeman and you want to hurt me.'

'No Lucy, I would never -'

'Liar! You are a horrible man, a liar!'

'Lucy! I told you to come here NOW!' the Shadowman bellowed.

She turned to Jimmy, put her arms around his neck and squeezed him tightly.

'Are you a priest?' she whispered into his ear. 'My dad doesn't believe in God, although we do pray in school sometimes.'

Jimmy smiled, wistfully.

'That's ok, I do.'

She unwrapped her arms from around him and slowly got down to her knees. Jimmy felt a wave of love for this brave young girl. He took her in his arms and held her tightly to him.

He was aware of the Shadowman standing over him, the vile stench of his breath filled the air.

Jimmy didn't have to think about what to do next. That distant voice still spoke to him, instructing him on what to do.

He bowed his head and began to pray.

'Our Father, who art in heaven....'

The Shadowman wailed in fury, the tendons in his neck straining. He lifted his arms in the air -

'Hallowed be Thy name.'

- and dropped them with all his strength and anger on the back of Jimmy's neck.

Jimmy tensed for the impact, closing his eyes, his jaw clenching tightly. But he continued the prayer through gritted teeth, his voice straining in anticipation -

'Thy kingdom come, thy will be done,'

He never felt an impact. Instead, a bright blue light flashed around him, dazing him with its brilliance. He heard the Shadowman stumble behind him, and he looked to see the beast fall to the ground as if hit by immense power.

'On earth, as it is in heaven.'

The Shadowman lifted himself to a sitting position and shook his head. He looked at Jimmy and wiped his hand across his brow. He then lifted himself up to full height and stepped towards Jimmy and Lucy. Noticing that the priest had paused in his prayer Lucy said:

'Give us our daily bread.'

Jimmy looked down at her and nodded.

'Give us this day our daily bread and forgive -'

The Shadowman walked around them until he was directly in front of them -

'- us our trespasses.'

Jimmy saw the huge hands reach down at him again, aimed not at him but Lucy, obviously wanting to pull the child away. His grip on the girl tightened.

'As we forgive those who trespass against us.'

Jimmy looked directly at the strange supernatural monster as he said this and hoped that there was nothing the Shadow-man could do at this moment. It didn't stop the man trying though and, as the shovel sized hands reached for Lucy, the bright blue light flashed again sending the giant flailing backwards once more.

Jimmy smiled, and a calmness fell upon him. He became aware that Lucy had stopped shaking as if she too was aware of what was happening.

'And lead us not into temptation,' he continued, the words coming naturally and easily to him. He looked behind the Shadowman, who was now stepping away from them. He also saw the TV reporter talking excitedly into the microphone. Whether he wanted it or not, he was now a huge part of the story.

'But deliver us from evil -'

'You think your prayers can save you, Priest? You think mere words can protect you?'

'For Thine is the kingdom -'

'I will have the child Priest, do not doubt me.'

'The power and the glory'

'The child's blood will spill and my master will rise, there is nothing you or your Jesus can do about that. You will not be protected for long.'

'Forever and ever.'

The Shadowman kicked out at them one more time and was greeted with another pure blue flash. The light was clear and unsullied, as bright and as wonderful as a magnificent summer sky.

'Amen,' he and Lucy said in unison.

CHAPTER 35

'Well, it's a good story and I think I've learned some history today, but...?' Carys said handing them another cup of tea. Catryn shifted uncomfortably in the chair. She had been to the toilet only ten minutes ago and was already beginning to feel the urge. She didn't want anyone to think there was a problem with her if she had to go again so quickly. If they kept plying her with tea though, she wouldn't have much of a choice.

'The only thing is,' Carys continued, sitting down opposite Catryn, 'what does it mean and how does it help us?'

'I haven't a clue,' Gareth said. He was sat on the sofa next to his mother-in-law.

'I think it means that Charles Henry is trying desperately to break the bonds that the locals had placed him under when they buried him on sacred ground.' Morgan said.

'I'm not sure there is such a thing as sacred ground,' Carys said. 'At least not in the way that films and books describe it.'

'How about a church?' Catryn asked, surprised that the wife of a priest would say this.

'A church is sacred to us, the believers who are still alive, but to others, it's not. Kids think nothing about taking a six-pack of lager or a bottle of cheap booze and getting wasted around a few gravestones. It happens all the time. Also, there are reports of sacred ground in all religions – Mecca, Indian burial grounds, even elephant graveyards. That undermines the assumption that there is just one God, which I believe in. Like I said, whether a place is sacred or not depends on us, the living, who assign it some special status.'

'How about the dead?' Morgan asked. 'If we are to accept the notion that all this is the work of Charles Henry, long-time-dead person, then how does that apply?'

'Because it's rubbish,' Gareth said with a sigh.

'Ok, let's look at it another way, ' Carys said, ignoring her son-in-law. 'Let assume that all these outlandish stories are really what is happening right now. If we accept that the sacredness of a place depends on the beliefs of an individual, and we accept that somehow that this dead person is influencing things in some way, then maybe his belief would make the ground sacred after all.

Catryn nodded. '"Chained by the spirit," those were the words that Tal used.'

Carys snorted. 'He really said that, Tal? The crusty old bugger up Henry Hill.'

Catryn nodded again. 'He didn't sound like he believed it, just that the people involved believed it.'

'That sounds right,' Carys said.

'So, you are saying that, if Henry believed it when he was alive, then he may still believe it today?' Morgan asked.

Carys gave a short laugh. 'I'm not saying anything. All I'm doing is putting a theory forward. I'm not saying I believe it'

'But it makes sense,' Catryn said, obviously warming to the subject. 'If we accept that Henry's ghost is still up in the mountains somewhere, it seems to fit.'

Morgan shook his head. 'No, there are too many problems with it. Firstly, why now? After all this time, why is all this happening now? Secondly, what have the little girls got to do with it all? They haven't done anything; they are not related. The only thing they have in common is their first name.'

Catryn considered this for a moment. 'I admit there are things we don't know. How could we? But I still think we have the basis for a pretty good explanation.'

'I admit, it makes a pretty good story,' Gareth said, 'and if this was one of Jimmy's films, I would probably accept it. He's always going on about suspension of disbelief and that's fine – for a film or a book. But this is not a fantasy. It is not a story.

Real people have been killed. People who I knew, I've met.'

There was a heavy silence in the room. Catryn could feel its weight pushing down on her. The pressure in her bladder was growing stronger but there was no way she would get up now. Not with things hanging like there were.

Then a knock came from the living room door, and a Constable peered in.

'Sir, can I have a word?' he asked. His face looked grave and Catryn felt a stab of fear shoot through her stomach. What had happened now? she wondered.

Gareth got up and passed her, then left the room with the PC. Catryn stood up and straightened the light fleece she was wearing.

'Sorry, I got to go again,' she said apologetically. 'Too much tea.'

Carys smiled. 'Of course, you know where it is.'

Catryn crossed the room and opened the door that Gareth had just closed behind him. The detective and the PC were talking quietly in the hallway by the front door. She turned in the opposite direction and headed for the kitchen, which led to the bathroom. She was aware of the whispers which sounded frenetic and urgent behind her, then she heard Gareth's voice and she knew her worries were indeed true.

'Oh, my God, no,' he said. 'Please God, no.'

Catryn closed her eyes but didn't stop. She carried on to the bathroom, each step praying that nothing else had happened, although deep down, she knew it had, and the night was going to be a very long one.

***

She returned to grave faces standing in front of the television. No one was sitting. They stood rigid, transfixed on the images in front of them.

'What is it?' she asked tensely, not really wanting to know what was happening. She knew instinctively that, whatever it was, it was just awful. Gareth entered the room, his jacket on, his face grey with concern.

Morgan stood aside and beckoned her over to him. She crossed and stood beside him, glancing at the people beside her. Morgan's brow was furrowed, and his eyes were deep with worry. She felt cold inside but when she glanced over to Carys, her fears intensified. The woman had her hands to her mouth, deep creases had appeared on her face. Her colour was gone, her face even more pallid than Gareth's. A single tear slowly made its way from the inside of her eye, down the edge of her angular nose and rested on her upper lip, waiting for another to give it a push over the edge and down to the floor.

Catryn turned to the television and for a moment was not sure what she was looking at. It was a dark street, a reporter, a young woman in a fashionable but dirty coat, was crouched down beside a car. She whispered into the camera, which moved away from her for a moment to the wider street. It was dark but the whole area was lit from streetlights and car headlamps.

What are they talking about? she thought.

The reporter tried to peak over the top of the car's bonnet but then ducked back down.

'He's still there,' she was saying. 'Every so often he seems to roar with rage then fall into complete silence. He seems to be stalking the man and child who are still cowering in the middle of the road. Yet each time he approaches them, there is a shocking flash of light....'

Gareth tapped Carys on her shoulder, taking her out of her awful trance.

'I've got to go,' he said to her. 'You stay here, and I will ring you as soon as I can'

'No...' Carys seemed to want to say something but then just stopped. She reached over to him and wrapped her arms around him, holding him tightly.

'Get him out of there,' she whispered harshly. 'You get him away from that monster and bring him home.'

Gareth nodded, still holding her. He then pushed her back

gently and looked deeply into her eyes.

'I will,' he said. There was a steely determination in his voice and, although Catryn still did not understand what was happening, she believed him.

She moved closer to Morgan and put her arms around him.

'What's happening?' she asked. 'What's going on?'

Morgan put his arm around her shoulder and pulled her to him tighter. He lifted his head towards the television. The camera was focused on the wider street again. There was a man bent over what looked like a child, motionless. Around them, a huge man marched back and forth, totally focused on the two on the floor, like a lion stalking it's soon-to-be-supper.

'That's Jimmy,' Morgan said softly. 'And that's-'

'Him.' She finished, as now it was obvious who it was - this giant of a man dressed in black, with massive hands clenching and unclenching, his back arched. The Shadowman.

'Yeah,' Morgan replied. 'I don't know what's happening exactly. They think the girl is another Lucy, she ran into the street earlier, he was chasing her. They think he killed a few more policemen looking for her.'

'What's Jimmy doing there?'

'Dunno, must have been returning home or something.'

'Look after her,' Gareth said to them as he turned and left the room. Catryn moved from Morgan and put her arms around the other woman. Carys was shaking and Catryn suddenly felt an incredible sadness. What this woman was going through, she couldn't fathom. They had only known each other for a day, yet Catryn felt a duty to be with her at that moment.

'Come on,' she said softly. She maneuvered Carys to sit on the settee in front of the television. Jimmy's spot. The place he always sat to watch his movies. Catryn could see the headphones that he used, the cord wrapped neatly around the speakers, resting on the small table beside the settee, waiting for him to return and use them once more.

CHAPTER 36

Gareth arrived at the junction within ten minutes. It was a scene of utter chaos. There were people everywhere, crowds gathered in a large circle around the Shadowman, who was standing menacingly over Jimmy and the girl. At the back of the crowd, furthest away from the danger, there was a dazed atmosphere, as if there was a quiet and fearful carnival taking place. Young men and women stood in groups, many with cans of lager and other alcoholic drinks in their hands, laughing as if it was just fun and excitement. Trehenri wasn't what you would call an exciting place to live - that was why it suited Gareth and Jenny - but he realized, for those who lacked even an ounce of empathy, this was almost a community event. He felt a stab at regret from this, not only because it was his father-in-law and friend who was in danger, but also because these people seemed to take a perverse pleasure in it all.

As he worked his way to the front, the crowd became tenser as the reality of the situation became more real.

Yet, they were still here, he thought. These gawkers, who were no better than the kids at the back, so starved of stimulation that they were willing to put themselves within arm's reach of danger just to be a part of something and to have something to talk about tomorrow. If there was a tomorrow, that was. They were, he understood, no different to the people who slowed down when passing the scene of a car accident, craning their necks to see something – some blood on the floor, the caved-in front of the car or, if they were really lucky, a glimpse of one of the victims lying prone and dying on the tarmac, their limbs in unnatural angles, their eyes blank with death. The drivers would then continue on their journey and the first thing they would say when they got home wasn't 'I'm Home,' or 'I've missed you sweetheart', but 'Guess what I just saw.'

As he got to the front, he looked around and saw a group of police. They were standing about thirty feet away from Shadow, just outside the 'Taste of Turkey' Kabab and Pizza Takeaway. Inside were a few more police; they seemed to have commandeered the shop as some sort of command post.

He reached the group, a few of which he recognised from his base in Cardiff.

'What's happening?' he asked.

'Nothing much,' said Sargent Colin Price, a bald looking thug of a man who was known as a bit of a hard case around the station. 'He seems content with trying to get the girl, but every time he does the light flashes. We don't know where the fuck it's coming from, but it is certainly keeping that bastard at bay for now.'

'That fella on the ground seems to have magic powers,' another officer said.

'That fella is my father-in-law,' Gareth said, tersely.

'Oh shit,' there were murmurs around the group and a few touched him on the shoulder for support.

'Don't worry,' Price said. 'We'll get him out.'

'Yeah,' Gareth replied. How that was going to happen, he didn't have a clue.

There was a sudden roar of fury from the Shadowman, and the crowd seemed to duck in unison, propelled by some hidden communication.

'He's done that a few times now,' someone said.

Gareth moved slowly to the front to get a better look. He could see the Shadowman lift his two hands together over his head and bring them down on Jimmy and the girl with tremendous force and fury. Gareth could see no way for his father-in-law to survive such a blow, which would surely crush his head and send him on to meet God at the pearly gates. But instead, there was another blinding blue flash and the Shadowman was sent tumbling to the ground. He skidded on his backside for about four feet along the tarmac before stopping.

A hush fell on the crowd as the Shadowman screamed on top of his lungs, a deafening, grating scream that Gareth could feel in the pit of his stomach.

Then a sole voice, a laugh which seemed to echo up and down the street. It was a laugh of ridicule, and Gareth could imagine a pointed finger aimed directly at the monster, who was slowly rising from the ground.

The voice was joined by another, then another. It was as if a cathartic wave was spreading from person to person like a Mexican wave at a rugby match. The tension was slackening as the sound of the laughter rose, and it was almost as if the Shadowman was losing his power to terrify.

Gareth could almost feel it too. As the Police around him smiled and joined the crowd at large, the urge to point at the beast and to proclaim him impotent, was almost intoxicating. Yet, deep down, something told him that this was definitely the wrong thing to do. This man/beast in front of them, for all his failed attempts to break through the invisible barrier that seemed to be surrounding Jimmy and the girl, was still a monster, he was still dangerous, and the sound of this contemptuous mockery would do nothing to placate him.

The Shadowman got to his feet and surveyed the crowd. Even from a distance, Gareth could see a terrible sneer come to his lips. He raised his arms in the air and roared back at the crowd. The fury was so great, Gareth was sure he could feel the wind ruffle his hair.

The Shadowman then turned away from Jimmy and moved towards one of the nearby cars. He stood for a moment beside the driver's door and lifted his arms in the air, just as he had done over Jimmy and the little girl. The crowd's laughter died down, but the excitement was still there.

There was another pause and the Shadowman slammed his

fists on the hood of the car. There was an immense bang which seemed to reverberate around the street. The top of the car caved in and the windows smashed, sending millions of tiny particles of glass skidding across the floor.

The crowd fell silent. The giant raised his arms again and slammed them once more into the car. The tires exploded and the whole vehicle crashed to the ground.

Now the crowd reacted. Those at the front of the circle moved back quickly, many of them tripping over their friends and neighbours who stood around them. There were screams of fear and another wave of panic which rippled through the crowd. There were cries of pain as people were stamped on, as fingers were crushed, and bones inevitably broken.

Gareth looked around and could see the panic in his fellow police officer's eyes. None of them had ever trained for this, none of them had ever experienced anything close.

The Shadowman roared again. He stooped down and reached beneath the car. With a sound like thunder, he flipped the car over onto its top, the crash resounding in Gareth's ears.

The Shadowman then walked to another car and repeated his fury. Thump followed smash, followed roar. Next to the car, a moped lay on its side. He lifted it up with ease and tossed it towards the crowd, who scattered further away from the carnage.

Someone threw a rock, which struck the Shadowman on the shoulder.

'No, no, no, no,' Gareth screamed, although he doubted anyone would really hear him. Don't antagonize him anymore, please, he thought.

The Shadowman stooped and lifted the rock, and stared at it for a moment. Then he looked over to the area from which it was thrown. He walked towards them slowly, surveying the crowd as if choosing his target. People scattered, some hiding behind cars, some deciding that the best course of action was to just run as fast and as far as possible.

The Shadowman stopped and raised the rock and sent it

flying to the crowd. Gareth couldn't see where it went, but he heard more shrieks and saw the crowd break up, as people tried to avoid the projectile.

He turned towards Jimmy and the girl who were still in the middle of the road. Jimmy had now lifted his head and was looking towards his assailant. He was looking away from Gareth, making it impossible for the detective to signal to him.

Gareth thought about running over to them, or at least try and get closer, maybe within earshot but, just as he was trying to build up the courage, the Shadowman walked purposely back to the priest. Gareth closed his eyes for a second and said a quick prayer for his father-in-law. When he opened them again, he saw the Shadowman bending over Jimmy, shouting something at him. Then he stood up, looked around and, finding whatever it was he was looking for, started walking away.

Walking away from Jimmy and the girl, and towards the police.

Gareth's gut felt the same panic that had gripped the crowd only a few minutes before. He stood up straight and started backing away.

'Don't push,' he shouted 'Don't push.' And, by and large, they seemed to listen, and he was glad he was surrounded by people who had at least the basic training when it came to panic situations.

Then he heard a familiar voice.

He turned to see Price, a large plank of wood in his hands, raised like he was about to hit a baseball, shouting at the oncoming monster. Gareth's blood froze in his veins, and his breathing stopped.

The Shadowman marched on, not to the crowd, but to the little gap between the Kabab shop and the Second Hand Treasures Charity shop next door. It was too small to be called an alley, with just enough room to store some bins and bags of rubbish for collection that next morning.

He's going, Gareth realised. He's going to disappear. Price stood at the entrance to the gap, like Jon Snow in front of the on-coming hoards.

Gareth turned and tried to get back, to pull his crazy arsed colleague out of the way and let the Shadowman escape, but the tide of bodies around him was too great.

The Shadowman stopped a few feet in front of Price, who moved the plank back and forth ready to swing.

'Cmon.' Price shouted. 'You fucking killed my friends, now I'm going drop you!'

The Shadowman sneered, then - with a speed that didn't seem to belong in a body that big and seemingly unyielding - he pounced. Price didn't even get the chance to swing. The Shadowman grabbed the wood in one clean swoop of his left hand, his right reaching out and catching the policeman by the throat. Gareth could see the fear and pain in Price's eyes, which seemed to bulge unnaturally.

Then the Shadowman seemed to loosen his grip and Price was left to stand there, gasping for breath, his hands holding his throat as he struggled to breathe.

There was a pause before Shadowman swung the wood catching Price square on the side of his head. The plank of wood shattered on impact and Price collapsed to the floor, blood squirting out of a large wound around his temple.

Gareth screamed as did others around him.

Price wasn't dead, however. He tried to lift himself up, but the Shadowman kicked him nonchalantly back to the floor. He then tossed the wood aside and strode purposely into the alley.

It was as if time itself slowed down. The screams, the shrieks around him, disappeared. The panic that was flooding the Main Road seemed a million miles away. All Gareth saw was the dark gap between the two buildings. He knew the Shadowman would be gone, he understood the truth that he had been grappling with, the stories told by that nasty old man, the theories spun by Morgan and Catryn – theories that seemed too outrageous. He had assumed they weren't taking the whole thing seriously enough, that it might have been a game to them. He hadn't acknowledged it but now he almost felt ashamed that he was the one who hadn't been listening.

It was true, all of it.

That big bastard of a man was supernatural. There was no other way to describe it. In his heart, he knew it was true.

A group of his colleagues rushed to the aid of Colin Price, who mourned as they lifted him up and took him into the shop. The blood on the side of Price's head made it look like it had exploded. Gareth knew that head wounds were often much bloodier than they were bad, and he hoped this would be the case. One eye was blood red, the lid was all swollen, the other looked up at Gareth in an unfocused stare. There was a stain on his trousers where his bladder or bowels had loosened.

Gareth took a deep breath, walked around the sergeant and peered into the gap.

Nothing, just a deep unrelenting blackness.

He didn't get too close, even though he knew the man was gone, but the fear still existed, and he half expected a giant arm to reach out and grab him by the throat, to squeeze the life out of him.

He became aware of a tear on his face, that soft tickling of liquid on his cheek, and he wondered how it was going to end.

'Gareth?'

He turned at the sound of a voice, a croak just behind him, and saw Jimmy standing there, the young girl clutching tightly at his waist. His face was bathed in sweat, his eyes were bloodshot and his greying hair was completely dishevelled.

'Jimmy,' Gareth said and, with utter joy and relief, he threw his arms around the priest. They held each other like that for a few moments and Gareth never felt happier to hold another human.

'What happened?' Gareth asked when they pulled away from each other. 'What was all that?'

Jimmy shook his head.

'I don't know,' he said. 'It was as if there was a barrier around us, like, I dunno, as ridiculous as it sounds, a force field. We saw everything, but he didn't touch us once. We just held onto each other and prayed. I never prayed as hard in my whole life.'

Gareth smiled and nodded, then turned to the girl and knelt beside her.

'Lucy?' he asked.

The girl nodded shyly and continued to hold Jimmy.

'Come on, let's get you somewhere -'

'GET AWAY FROM THAT CHILD!' A voice roared at them in the night-time.

Gareth turned to the opposite side of the street. There was a set of narrow stairs ascending the hill, disappearing into shadows. For a moment there was nothing but an obscure gloom. Then a shape appeared, a vague outline of a very large man stepping out of the shadows.

He was back.

It began again.

CHAPTER 37

Carys sat on the settee, her head in her hands which were propped up on her knees. She sat quietly with a calm stillness, and Catryn couldn't work out if it was the cold stillness of despair, or that of an animal waiting to pounce. Whatever it was, the room felt terribly uncomfortable. She had the feeling that she was an intruder into a stranger's grief, and she realised that, despite all the things that had happened to them all over the last two days, she was still a stranger here. Even to Morgan whom she had known since school. The years had been enough of a wedge that, in difficult times like this, the distance between them seemed more like a gulf.

She felt that maybe she shouldn't be here, that perhaps she should make a quiet exit, but she couldn't think of what to say and she didn't want to give them the impression that she might be deserting them.

Besides, she wanted to know what happened as she felt she had something invested in all this. Jenny came into the room and sat next to her mother. She was about ten years younger than Catryn and walked with the grace of youth and the confidence of familiarity. As soon as she had arrived about a half-hour ago, she had taken charge, even bossing the police - who were still lurking outside - into action. The TV had stopped the live broadcast from the Main Road and updates had dried up, but Jenny had galvanized the police into keeping them up to date.

There had been a brief flurry of hope earlier with the news that the monster had once again disappeared. Gareth had spoken to Jimmy who was shaken and scared but not hurt. But then it had started all over again. The news had come through, and Carys had stopped her pacing back and forth across the floor, stopped her agitating, and sat in the awful calm she was now in.

Catryn glanced over to Morgan who seemed far away, deep in thought. His brow was furrowed, and his mouth seemed stuck in a moment as if he was about to speak, but so far, he had remained silent. She watched him for a few moments before he saw her, he then closed his mouth and gave her a sad smile.

'It makes no sense,' he said to her after a moment.

'None of it does,' she replied.

'I know but,' he paused and tried to collect his thoughts. 'The blue light, it's like a force field around Jimmy, yes?'

Catryn nodded. She was aware that Jenny was watching the two of them, listening to the conversation.

'Well, remember what Tal said about Sir Henry dying. Didn't he say that, whilst Henry didn't like God, he still believed in Him? And the Shadowman was the same. Tal said that, when the people buried Henry for a second time, Shadow was there, guarding the grave and unable to do anything else.'

'So how is he doing all this now? How does he manage to travel away from the chapel? What's changed?' Catryn asked.

'That I don't know, the only way we can find out is to find the chapel, but that might take too long. The thing is this: If Shadow believed then maybe this belief is his weakness.'

'How?' Jenny asked.

"Well, what if he knows that Jimmy is a priest, perhaps he's unable to injure him. Let's suppose the blue light is not coming from Jimmy, it's coming from the Shadowman.'

'But how would he know that Dad is a priest?' Jenny asked.

'Because we told him,' Catryn said, warming to the subject. 'When we were walking around the house, before... before it all happened, we talked. I remember us talking about Jimmy's job and his faith.'

Morgan nodded. 'There you go.'

'I don't get it,' Jenny said. 'How would that affect him?'

'Faith,' Catryn said. 'I get what you are saying. You hear all the time about how some person has supposedly been cured of cancer or something or another, based on their faith. Some of these stories do seem very convincing, although most psychologists put it down to positive thinking, mind over matter, that kind of thing.'

'Anything but faith,' Jenny said.

'Exactly.' Catryn said. 'What if it's true, that it is faith all along?'

'Does it have to be?' Morgan said. 'Think about it? Isn't faith a form of positive thinking? Well, surely it can be a negative feeling as well? A limiting factor? The Shadowman has killed almost a dozen people so far but can't kill Jimmy. What if it's his faith? What if it is the Shadowman's faith which is saving Jimmy. He believes Jimmy is a man of God, so he can't do anything against him.

'It doesn't matter, all that matters is that there is a chink in his armour. There is a way in.' Morgan continued.

'And he needs shadows.' Carys said. They all turned to her, surprised that she had said anything at all. 'He needs shadows to travel. He needs them to escape. Without them, he's trapped.'

They all nodded and Catryn could feel the bubble of excitement in her belly.

'What we need is to get him somewhere with no shadows, to box him in,' she said.

'And then what?' Jenny asked. 'Bullets don't kill him.'

'No,' Catryn replied. 'But so far, it seems that they hurt him. Maybe enough to slow him down.'

'I got it,' Morgan said, excitedly. 'I know where they can take him.'

He reached into his pockets and took out his phone.

'I need to make a few phone calls,' he said.

***

Gareth felt the phone vibrate in his pocket and reached in. He was standing much further back now, outside the Second-hand Treasures Charity shop, surrounded by his fellow officers. The Shadowman had seemed to have calmed down, although he still prowled back and forth over Jimmy and the girl. There was no more hitting, no more flashes of blue light, no more screams or attacks on the police. He had disappeared a few times, but each time returned quickly.

Gareth had to wonder how his father-in-law was holding up, the pressure he was under must be intense and, for Lucy, it must have been so much worse. She was so young, much too young to have to endure this type of pressure and punishment.

They spoke each time the Shadowman disappeared into the darkness. Gareth had run up to them the last time giving them water to drink, and they seemed resolute, yet he knew there was only so much they could take.

He looked at the screen and it was Jenny. He frowned and felt a gulp of terror leap in his stomach. Why would she be phoning? What could it be? What had happened?

He pressed the 'Accept' icon and spoke in a small voice, careful not to catch the attention of the Shadowman.

'Sweetheart? Is everything ok?'

But it wasn't Jenny on the other end, it was Morgan.

They spoke for a few minutes with Gareth nodding occasionally. At one point he reached inside his jacket and tried to adjust his tie, although that wasn't easy with only one hand.

He didn't take his eyes off the drama unfolding in the middle of the street.

Finally, he closed the call, gathered the police around him and told them the plan. He wasn't sure if it was a good plan, but it was the only one they had so they had to try, they had to go for it.

***

'Ok, I've got to go,' Morgan said to the room.

'I'll come with you,' Catryn said.

Morgan shook his head. 'No, you should stay here.'

'Why? Because I'm a woman? I hope you are not trying that sexist crap on me.' Catryn replied indignantly.

Morgan couldn't help but smile and couldn't think of anything to say.

'Ok, he said finally. 'Let's go.'

Carys crossed the room to him and put her arms around his neck. She kissed him hard on the cheek and then looked deep into his eyes.

'Do you think it will work?' she asked.

'I don't know.'

Carys nodded. 'OK.' She paused for a moment as if searching for the right words to say. Finally, she just said: 'Thank You.'

The door to the living room opened and a policeman stepped in.

'Morgan Williams?' he asked.

Morgan took Carys' hand and squeezed it. He didn't say anything. He just held her for a few moments then turned to the policeman.

'Shall we go?' he said.

He crossed the room and joined the policeman, who introduced himself as John Finch.

'Looks like Catryn will be joining us as well, John.'

Finch shrugged and nodded, then led them out of the room. As they did so, Catryn took Morgan's hand and they walked out into the night together.

CHAPTER 38

Jimmy lifted himself up a little. He looked deep into the eyes of the man who had been trying to beat them to a pulp for the last, what? A half-hour? An hour? He honestly didn't have a clue.

The man stood in front of him, watching him and Lucy with dark, intense eyes. His brow was furrowed, and he kept clenching and unclenching his fists. He looked mean and menacing but at least he had stopped trying to pound them. Each time those giant fists had come down, Jimmy had been convinced that this was going to be the last moment, that his time on earth was over. Yet each time there was that bright flash, not just at the point of impact, but all around them, like an invisible egg which only revealed itself when forced to.

He had no idea what it was, but he thanked God for it.

Lucy squirmed at his side and he looked down to see her adjusting her position slightly.

She looked so small but, even though she had wept in his arms, she had a resolve which impressed him. She wanted to know what had happened to her parents, but there was nothing he could tell her.

He noticed that she too was staring at the man in front of them, a steely look that seemed to defy him even in her fear. They hadn't spoken much but he had prayed, and she had listened. The rest of the time they had waited. When the man had disappeared, they had spoken to Gareth, but it was all too brief.

The man was crouched down in front of them, hardly moving. In fact, there didn't even seem to be the rhythmic movements of breathing. He was like a powerful and fierce statue.

'What do you want?' Jimmy croaked. His voice was dry and tight, even after drinking some of the water that Gareth had provided.

Shadow's eyes moved slightly but not much.

'What do you want?' Jimmy asked again, this time with more force.

The man sneered, then looked towards Lucy.

'The girl,' he growled.

'Why?'

The man looked back at Jimmy, who felt a wave of revulsion cascade through him. The man looked evil, there was no denying it. It was as if his eyes were windows into the darkest of nights. Fear lived in those pupils.

'What is it to you, priest?'

'You have tried to kill me.'

'I *will* kill you,' he snarled.

'Why?' Jimmy asked again. 'What do you want with Lucy?'

The man smiled and, for a second, there was almost affection in those dark eyes.

'Lucy,' he said, and his voice was lighter. 'Lucy.' He repeated.

'YOU HURT MY MAMMY!' Lucy suddenly screamed. 'You hurt her. I saw you hurt her.'

His face seemed to change again, this time registering concern. Jimmy instinctively pulled her closer to him, afraid that she might leave the protection of whatever it was that had so far kept them safe.

'I love you, Lucy,' Shadow whispered.

'You said you were my friend, but you hurt my mammy,' she cried, her body convulsing. She buried her face into Jimmy's lap and sobbed loudly. He put his two arms around her and softly patted her back, a gesture Carys often made fun of. The thought of this monster cultivating the girls, maybe even grooming them, repulsed him?

It did make a perverse sense when he thought about it. After all, the Shadowman had managed to kidnap two other children without either of them putting up a fight. The video of the car park clearly showed the little girl willingly being lifted into the man's hands, before he carried her off. And didn't the parents of the baby report the man had been in their house with the baby the night before she was kidnapped?

He assumed that this was something that the police knew about and, if he ever made it out of here, he would have to ask Gareth. But the realisation right now made him feel uncomfortable, almost dirty. It suggested that all this horror wasn't something confined to a few days but had been going on under their noses for some time. This wasn't just a scar on Trehenri, it was a malignant tumour, which had spread its tendrils long before the patient was ever aware of its existence.

'Don't worry, Lucy,' the man said. 'You will soon be with my master and you will understand why all this has happened.'

'Sir Henry,' Jimmy said. 'That's who your master is, isn't it.'

The man bowed, almost respectfully.

'Why do you want the children?' Jimmy asked.

'Because the Master loves them. He loves Lucy.'

'But this is not his Lucy,' Jimmy said, holding the girl tighter to him. 'His Lucy is dead, over two hundred years ago.'

'Time is of no importance.' The man said. 'He loves and needs her. Lucy is forever.'

Jimmy remembered the writing on the church wall and the abomination that accompanied it. He understood the, if there was any doubt, that it was his man that had defiled the church.

'Why?' he asked. He couldn't help but feel anger course through him. 'Why does he need her?'

The man stood up, his giant frame towering over them, and Jimmy tensed, expecting another blow.

'The master's love makes him strong. It makes him powerful. It brings health to him and he will return.'

'Your master is dead!' Jimmy shouted.

The man shook his head.

'No, you are dead, priest. I might not have power over you

now but soon my master will crush you. You are dust, devil dodger. Dust'

The man then turned and walked away from them, towards the small gap between the two buildings he had been using. Jimmy wanted to call after him, to shout and swear and let his anger loose like it never had been before, but he held it in check. Any weakness, anything the monster could exploit, could be his downfall. And not just him but the girl to. And if Sir Henry did return, what then?

Jimmy held onto Lucy and stroked her hair.

The return of that tyrant was not something that should be allowed, and he knew that if it meant him having to give up his own life to save the girl and everyone else he knew and loved, then he was willing to do it.

The man disappeared into the shadow and Jimmy looked around to see Gareth, Catryn and Morgan running towards him.

CHAPTER 39

Kofi Antwi stood at the counter of the Secondhand Treasure Charity Shop and shook his head. As soon as he had heard the news that the man who had killed his friends, his colleagues and his fellow officers was back, he had left the hospital and come straight here. He wanted to see this Shadowman; this creature that he knew would haunt his dreams forever. He didn't want him to become just an intangible nightmare; he wanted something real, a face, a body. In the old house, the monster had only been a blur. The emotions and the fear had been too great for him to really see who this fucker was. Now he wanted to look him in those eyes and pull the trigger. He wanted to send the bastard all the way back to the hell he'd come from.

Then, when it became clear that there might be a plan, however vague, he had wanted in on it. This would be his chance at revenge. He didn't want Jones, Kowalski, Bosch and all the others to die, useless, senseless deaths. He needed closure and he believed they did too.

But more than that, he needed to take this bastard down. Earlier, as he laid on the hospital bed, he kept having flashbacks to that child. The little girl he was too late to rescue. Her face would remain with him forever, he knew. The things that had been done to her, real and imagined, would tear at him until he went onto the ground. For little Lucy, he wanted blood.

'No,' he said, the traces of his Ghanaian accent, slowly coming to the fore and replacing his Welsh accent as the evening went on. He was having trouble accepting that the blue light that had seemed to have been protecting the Priest, was somehow God casting a spell around a believer.

'I am a Christian and it did not happen to me. Kowalski was a Christian too and he is dead. If what you said is really happening, why is Kowalski not here? Are you saying that he is a better Christian than I? That he deserves it more than I do?'

His fellow police looked around, embarrassed. Belief in God was not something that was often discussed amongst the macho environment that often seemed to pervade the force. Many knew of Antwi's faith, but some had just dismissed it as a part of his culture; not something they had to take seriously.

'No, that's not what is happening.'

He turned around and saw a woman looking at him. She stood beside DCI Gareth Mann and another man he didn't recognise. She was the woman who had gone into the house earlier that day with the Priest. She had entered the room with Gareth and the other man, having just spoken to James Bevan in the street.

'When you were in the house, did you mention your faith?' she asked.

Antwi shook his head. 'Of course not. Why would I?'

'Then the Shadowman would not know if you are a Christian or not.'

'What has that got to do with it?' he asked.

She shifted uncomfortably, obviously not wanting to take on the role of the expert in something she knew little about.

'When Jimmy and I were in the house we spoke about faith; we talked about Jimmy being a priest. The Shadowman overheard us.'

'So?' Antwi asked.

'So, we thought that maybe the blue light doesn't come from Jimmy's faith, but from the Shadowman's. If he believes then it is his weakness. That is why he can't get to Jimmy. If he didn't know you or your colleague were Christians, then he would assume that you are not, which means his faith could not limit him.'

Antwi shook his head again. 'That is not how faith works,' he said.

'So how can this help us?' PC John Finch interrupted.

'That's the plan,' Catryn said. 'That's the basis of the plan anyway.'

Gareth stepped forward and handed out large crucifixes.

'Put these around your necks and leave them on display. We don't intend to get too close but if we do then any help we can get would be welcomed.'

'I'm not a Catholic,' Antwi protested.

'I don't give a flying fuck,' Gareth said, angrily and very tired. 'If you want to have a theological discussion with that bastard out there then go ahead. After we take him down.'

Antwi nodded and put the crucifix over his head.

'Yes, sir.'

'Good,' Gareth continued.

The door of the shop opened, and a policeman entered. He seemed incredibly young to Catryn. His face was flush, and he seemed out of breath.

'They are all ready,' he said. 'Everything is in place.'

'OK,' Gareth said. 'Let's go and end all this.'

'Please? Before we go.' Antwi interrupted. 'I know you are not Christians, but I would be grateful if you could join me in a quick prayer.'

Gareth hesitated, then nodded.

'I think that is a good idea,' he said, looking around the room. Antwi looked at the people around him and could see there were no objectors. In fact, they all looked like they needed all the help they could get, and if that meant praying to a God they had never believed in, then so be it.

They all bowed their heads.

'My Lord God, we pray for your protection tonight. We pray that you will steady our hearts, our minds and our hands. Be with us and bring us all back alive. In Jesus name. Amen.'

There was a quiet chorus of 'amens' around the room as everyone got ready.

'You two stay here,' Gareth said to Morgan and Catryn. They both nodded.

'Keep us up-to-date,' Morgan said.

Gareth nodded.

'We've left a radio here which you will be able to listen to, ok?'

They nodded.

'Ok, let's get going.'

Antwi lifted up his rifle, feeling the familiar and comforting weight in his hands.

For those who died, he was ready.

CHAPTER 40

The first thing Jimmy noticed as Shadow disappeared into the alleyway again, was the cheer from the crowd. He had been aware that they were there, although they were certainly not at the forefront of his mind. He looked around and saw them, standing at a distance, some getting up from behind cars, others coming out of doorways, some – mostly young men– just standing there in groups as bold as you like.

He stood up, feeling his bones creak and his muscles protest. He had often wondered how the Japanese managed to sit on the floor for so long, their legs folded beneath them. He saw it all the time in the movies. Instead of chairs, they would place cushions on the floor for their guests. He tried it once but, after a few moments, all he felt was a tingling in his calves and feet.

He stretched his back, sending a stab of pain into his kidneys. Lucy was doing the same, almost copying him. She looked up at him with those sad, hurting eyes. There were streaks of dried blood and tears on her cheeks, and her hair was disheveled. She was still in her pyjamas and looked so slight, so innocent and vulnerable. He put his hand on her head and tried to smile, but he suspected it looked more like a grimace.

'Is it finished?' Lucy asked.

'I don't know,' he admitted. 'Probably not. How long have you known him?'

The little girl thought for a while then said:

'A while, since after my birthday. He comes to me at night and plays. I thought he was nice.' Her body shuddered, and more tears began to trickle down her face. 'He hurt my

Mammy.'

Jimmy nodded. He wanted to know more but didn't think now was the time. Catryn, Morgan and Gareth had just left them, careful not to be too close in case Shadow came back. They had a plan and, although they didn't go into detail, there seemed to be a determination in them that he really wanted to feel.

He could see the activity around the shops about forty feet away. There were armed police running down the street, slowing only to pass the small alleyway, then sprinting towards School Street and Trehenri Comprehensive. Following them were a few other policemen and Gareth, who, at a respectful and careful distance, turned to Jimmy and gave him the signal.

'You ready?' he asked Lucy.

'Yes, I think so,' she replied between sobs.

'Come on,' he said.

They set off at a brisk walk, going as fast as the little girl's legs would carry her. He had debated picking her up, but there was a steady ache in his back that he didn't think would allow them to get far.

His heart beat quickly, and he could feel it pounding in his ears. Sweat was trickling down his forehead and his back, yet he felt cold with fear.

They kept as far away from the alley as possible, but he was also conscious of the crowd. Although they were moving away from him, he didn't want to get so close that he might endanger them. He was also becoming aware of the crowd's reaction. Many clapped their hands as Jimmy and Lucy passed them, some cheered. One young boy run up to them and shouted, 'Great special effects, byt!' Some in the crowd laughed.

There were cars strewn all round, many that Shadow had attacked, others that locals and the police had parked haphazardly around the street. They hurriedly passed a few cars with people still in them; the drivers within honked their horns. Some reached out of their windows and patted his shoulder as he passed.

Didn't they understand the danger? he wondered. This wasn't a show, it wasn't a joke. People had died here tonight, and these people had watched, yet they just seemed detached from it all.

Jimmy and Lucy continued down the street, past a few terraced houses with their open doors, the occupants peering out. He also became aware of the TV cameras following him and the sound of a helicopter hovering high above them. One of the reporters was shouting at him, but he couldn't hear what they were saying. He didn't want to hear, he just wanted the nightmare to be over.

'You ok, sweetheart?' he asked.

'My legs are tired,' she said.

He stopped walking, stooped down and picked her up in his arms. He adjusted her to distribute her weight so the pain in his back was lessened. It had been a long time since he had lifted a child. He remembered Jenny as a child, wrapping her arms around him and giving him a great big cwtch. She used to squeeze him tightly and they would pretend that his eyes were on the verge of popping out. Then they would laugh and hold each other for longer.

He remembered walking down this very street with her, carrying her just as he was carrying Lucy now. Would Lucy ever be carried down this street by her parents again? Would she ever experience the joy of walking hand in hand with her father ever again?

He started walking again, and saw Gareth standing about twenty feet in front of him.

'I'm coming,' he said.

'You are doing great,' Gareth said back.

They had to raise their voices slightly to be heard but otherwise there didn't seem to be any problems talking. Jimmy was in the middle of the street, Gareth on the curbside with police walking in front of him clearing the watching crowd out of the way. One of them had a bull horn which he now was using to tell the crowd to get back, that it was far too dangerous here. They all seemed to listen, although some needed a bit of a push to get going.

'Do you need anything?' Gareth asked.

'A new back, a stronger pair of legs,' Jimmy replied.

'Not far to go now,' Gareth said. 'Cross the bridge to the school.'

'The school? Why the school?'

Gareth hesitated.

'No reason, just want to get away from the crowds.'

Jimmy could sense that there was more to it, that the plan had a bit more substance, but he couldn't think about what it could be.

He veered left past the McMillan's Cancer Charity Shop and the Super Chicken Takeaway. A group of teenagers holding various burgers and chips in their hands, stood gawking. Some cheered as he passed and held their cans of coke up in salute.

'Hey, Mr Bevan! We're all rooting for you,' one of the girls shouted. It was Sandy Willis, who was dragged to church each Sunday by her parents. She was a good girl, although Jimmy knew she was at the age when Church wasn't cool, and she was sometimes reluctant to attend. But she helped out with Sunday school for the younger kids, and was always polite and articulate. He nodded to her and gave her a wry smile.

He could see the turning which led to School Street. It was a small street of six houses, three each side, then the bridge which would take them to the school entrance on the other side. He really hoped that whatever plan they had, it would work.

'DEVIL DODGER!'

Jimmy's heart leapt. He could feel the fear in Lucy as she held him tighter and buried her head in his neck. She was muttering something under her breath, but he couldn't make out what she was saying. He put his hand on her back and patted it softly again.

He turned and saw Shadow standing at the entrance of the

little alleyway, looking at him with unconcealed anger.

'You cannot run from me, priest.'

Jimmy closed his eyes and took a deep breath.

'Oh, God, do I need you now,' he whispered.

He turned away from Shadow, hoping that it would be seen as a dismissal, like a headmaster would dismiss a naughty child. He didn't think it would work but he dearly wanted it to. A small victory. Anything. He began walking to the junction of School Street then, before turning the corner, he glanced back. Shadow hadn't come for him, he just stood there.

'Where are you running to, priest?'

Jimmy ignored him and continued walking. As he left the Main Road, he was engulfed with a soft quiet. The street was empty apart from a few policemen who had obviously been rushing to clear the area. There was a cool wind blowing, which he could feel on the sweat-soaked forehead. He stopped for a moment and readjusted his hold on Lucy once more. She was starting to get very heavy and the pain in his back was beginning to really throb. He thought about putting her down, but he knew she was taking strength from him and, he had to admit, he was taking some from her too. He liked the feel of her arms around him, even if he was struggling with her weight.

He had driven Jenny down this very street when she first started Comp. Not for very long, of course. Within a few weeks she insisted on walking, on meeting her friends and chatting for the whole of the ten-minute walk. He was only needed on the occasionally wet morning and then acted as nothing more than a taxi driver, stopping outside her friends' houses so they could join Jenny and her chauffeur. All he ever got in payment on those mornings was a quick 'Thanks dad' before she disappeared. Sometimes she even sounded like she meant it.

He had also driven into the school once when Jenny had been accused of hitting another girl. There had been an argument, then a bit of pushing and shoving. The girl had pulled

Jenny's hair so she, the daughter of a minister of religion and respected member of the community, had punched the girl in the nose, splattering blood all over the girl's school uniform. The blazer was black but unfortunately, the blood had run right down the school badge. Jenny was given the rest of the day off (they were kind enough not to call it a suspension), and Jimmy and Carys had to pay for a replacement.

Luckily, that was the only time Jenny had ever been in trouble.

Right now, the bridge looked dark. There were streetlights this side of the bridge and the school was lit up the other side, but there was nothing between.

The fear, which the comforting memories had helped subside, returned as the number of shadows became evident. There were a few trees on each side of the bridge entrance, which seemed to reach down with long, eerie tendrils. The leaves were mostly fallen with only the tiny buds promising a return to the glory of the coming summer. With the school lights behind them, they looked like negative prints of lightning flashing through the sky.

They came to the last house and Jimmy paused for a moment to look across. He took a deep breath, stepped off the tarmac, and onto the bridge.

'What is this place you are going to?' A voice sounded from the black shadows that were surrounding them.

Jimmy looked around but saw no one. The gloom was all-encompassing, and Jimmy had difficulty making out any detail at all.

'Is that him?' Lucy asked quietly.

'I think so,' he said. 'I can't see him though.'

'He can disappear,' she said.

'I know.'

'This place will provide no refuge,' the voice said again. It seemed to be coming from the other side of the bridge.

'Come out so I can see you,' Jimmy called out. He hoped that his voice was as confident as he wanted to feel.

'Who are you to command me?'

'I don't command you. God commands you.'

There was a chuckle then a rustling of leaves. At the far end of the bridge, about thirty feet away, Shadow stepped out from behind a bush. His silhouette dominated the scene.

'Who am I to disobey God?' Shadow said with a snicker.

Jimmy was aware of the sound of rushing water beneath the bridge and the drone of the helicopter above him. He was also aware of voices and movement behind him, but it was all far, far away. It was little more than background noise.

'Leave us alone,' he said.

'I will. Just give me the girl.'

'No, never,' Jimmy said defiantly.

'You will tire, Priest, and I will take her.'

'Morning will come first. You will not take her.'

'You think morning can defeat me? Where there are shadows, I can exist. The brighter the day, the deeper the shadows.'

Jimmy could feel the frustration build up inside of him. He was beginning to feel trapped, only the bars were just shadows. Deep, black and forbidding gloom.

'Who are you?' he shouted.

'My name is Legion,' Shadow replied.

'For you are many?'

The man roared with laughter.

'I am one. There is only me and there is no other.'

'Then you are not Legion, you cretin,' Jimmy said quietly. 'Perhaps I should get a herd of pigs and cast you into them?' he said louder.

'I do like your arrogance, Devil-Dodger. I may come to like you.'

Jimmy thought about what he needed to say. He couldn't get caught up in a slagging match, he needed to work his advantages. There was no one else here to help and the only thing that seemed to have saved him so far was his faith.

'As Jesus was getting into the boat, the man who had been

demon-possessed begged to go with him. Jesus did not let him, but said, "Go home to your family and tell them how much the Lord has done for you, and how he has had mercy on you.'

Shadow growled, a deep guttural sound like that of an approaching predator.

'Do not preach to me, priest. This is not a Sunday morning.'

The throb in Jimmy's back was becoming excruciating. He tried to adjust Lucy's weight again, but it didn't seem to work. He was beginning to understand what he needed to do, as each course of action disappeared there seemed only one left, however, he wasn't sure if he could go through with it.

He gently lowered Lucy to the ground. She protested and gripped him, her body rigid.

'No,' she said, almost weeping. 'Pick me up.'

'I can't,' Jimmy said. 'My back is hurting too much. But we'll be ok.'

'No, please, pick me up.'

'I want you to hold onto me. To stay as close as you can. Do not let go.'

He lifted himself up to full height and winced as a bolt of pain shot up his back. Lucy continued to protest but he ignored her. Instead, he put his hands on her shoulder and pulled her close.

'You are in pain,' Shadow said. 'Let me lighten your burden. Give me the child.'

Jimmy shook his head.

'You will never get her. You can tell Sir Henry that you have failed.'

'Your arrogance is your weakness, Priest.'

'No, it's not arrogance. It's faith.'

He took the first step onto the bridge and began to walk towards the beast.

***

When Catryn's mobile phone rang, both she and Morgan jumped. They hadn't expected a call and were listening intently to the radio, following the events outside. Jimmy was in School Street and the Shadowman had disappeared again. Gareth was following him, keeping everyone updated on what was happening, whispering into the radio, making sure everyone was in their right places.

They were alone in the shop now, dutifully obeying Gareth's order to stay put. Not that they had much choice as there were a few officers positioned outside.

It rang loudly, a standard ring tone which Catryn had always promised herself she would one day change but couldn't really be bothered. They both reacted together, then quickly settled down to a comfortable laugh.

She picked the phone up from her back pocket. It was from an Unknown Caller so pressed 'accept'.

'Sales,' she whispered to Morgan, then: 'Hello.'

Morgan watched her face closely as she listened to what was being said, and he noticed the colour drain from her face. The cheerfulness of their nervous laughter vanished, replaced by a deep unease.

'I don't want to speak to you right now,' she said, her voice icy.

Morgan could hear the soft tinny sound of a voice on the other end but couldn't make out any words.

'What do you mean TV?'

She seemed to droop at the shoulder and her voice became quieter, almost resigned. It was as if she was jumping from emotion to emotion with each sentence.

'No, of course they are not connected. How can you say that?'

She paused for a moment, listening intently.

'What's happening here has nothing to do with my husband. How dare you say that!'

There was now a reproachful edge to her voice and her face hardened.

'Look, I don't want to talk, I'm not going to talk to you.' The person on the phone obviously interrupted and Catryn became very animated, taking the phone away from her ear in frustration. When she started listening again, Morgan could see the strain she was experiencing and the difficulty she had in controlling herself.

'Listen here, you bastard. You leave me alone. If you ever phone me again, if you are lucky, I'll go straight to the police; if you're not, I'll find out where you live and I'll fucking kill you in your sleep, you shit!'

She pressed the 'End Call' icon, slammed the phone down on the counter then screamed in rage.

'What was that?' Morgan asked tentatively. 'You ok?'

'No, I'm not fucking OK,' she sneered.

She pushed passed him and rushed quickly out the door into the storeroom.

Morgan stood alone for a moment wondering if he should go out and be with her. He had just resolved to do this when there was a flurry of activity on the radio. He hesitated for a moment then bent down and listened.

'He's walking across the bridge towards the Shadowman.' It was Gareth's voice and there was a nervous edge to it. 'I can't hear what they are saying but they seem to be having some type of conversation. Kofi, are you in position?'

There was a crackle of static.

'In place, got the target in sights. Awaiting go.'

'Oh, shit,' Morgan said. He raised himself up a little and turned to the back room.

'Catryn, it's starting,' he called.

There was a period of quiet and Morgan was aware of his whole body working – the beating of his heart, the slight sheen of sweat down his back, the blood coursing through his veins, the slight discomfort of trapped wind in his stomach, a tickle on the end of his nose. It was as if the world had been reduced to just him and the sounds coming out of the radio.

'Hold on,' Gareth's voice came back. 'I can see them talking. I don't want anything to happen until I give the word.'

Silence again.

Morgan glanced towards the back room again but Catryn still hadn't come out. There was a fleeting thought, a concern that there was obviously something wrong with his friend which he wasn't aware of. Then:

'What the hell is he doing. Oh shit, oh shit. He's down, he's down!'

Morgan's attention returned once more fully to the radio. The seconds seemed to be limping along, with no urgency, certainly not with the desperation that he felt. He seemed to be urging words to come from the small speaker in front of him. As if the act of wanting something to happen was enough to make it real.

'Ok, Antwi, fire, fire fire!'

There was the sound of gunfire, loud bangs ringing from the speaker and echoing in the street outside, an odd stereo effect that was both strange and unnerving.

'What was that?'

Morgan turned and saw Catryn in the doorway. Her eyes were red, and she had obviously been crying. There were deep lines across her face, and he could see pain and stress there that he hadn't seen before. It looked like deep-rooted anxiety which he hadn't been aware of until now. It wasn't just this, he understood. It wasn't just the intensity of the last few days, this was much deeper, and he couldn't help wondering how he had missed it. Was it there all along?

More gunshots resounded up the street and in the shop.

'I don't know,' he said. 'I heard Gareth shouting "He's down, he's down" then there were these gunshots.

Catryn crossed over to him and took his hand in hers, causing his heart to beat wildly. He didn't know if it was the tension of the moment or if he had fallen completely for her. His mouth was dry and his hands felt clammy, but he refused to move.

Catryn didn't look at him, instead she turned to the radio and listened. He watched her for the briefest of moments, then turned to the radio from which only silence was heard.

***

'So, where have you been going each time you disappear?' Jimmy asked, taking another step closer. He tried to keep a slow, steady pace in an effort to calm is heart rate and the acid that was churning violently in his stomach.

'I go into the shadow realm. Would you like to join us next time?'

'Us?'

'The girl and I,' the man mocked.

'And who is there?' Jimmy said, ignoring him.

'Master is there. Soon he will be here.'

'Why?' Jimmy asked.

'Because he commands it.'

'That's not a reason.' Jimmy and Lucy were only a few steps away now, and he was beginning to be aware of a terrible, rancid, putrid smell

'He is Master. He needs no reasons.'

'And you are what? His pet?'

The man sneered and took a step closer. Jimmy felt a wave of claustrophobia hit him.

'I am Legion,' Shadow said.

'A demon? Is that what you are telling me?'

'I am,' the man snarled at him and Jimmy had to use every ounce of resolve not to flinch.

'Then you are a misleader. Why should I trust you?'

The man took another step forward until they were in touching distance.

'You cannot!' He bellowed with laughter and made to push Jimmy with his huge hands. The bright blue light flashed again, and he staggered back a step. His expression turned instantly to contempt once more and Jimmy felt a leap of confidence inside him. Lucy let out a low whimper and he could feel her shaking in fear.

'You can't touch us,' he said.

The demon snarled.

'I don't need to touch you. Wherever you go I will follow you until you are too fatigued to resist. Then I will take the girl and my Master will deal with you later.'

'Then, why don't we go somewhere, have a cup of tea and wait.'

'You can joke now but later I will rip your stomach from inside you and feast on your entrails.'

Lucy whimpered once more. Jimmy glanced down at her and looked deep into her large, innocent eyes. They were a pale green colour, and in them he could see loss and abandonment. He wondered what was going to happen to her now. Were her parents still alive or would spend the rest of her life in the care of strangers.

'You are beautiful,' he said to her. She gave him a small smile but didn't reply. 'We'll be ok, sweetheart.'

The man laughed, a deep resonant laugh that mocked them as they stood before him. Jimmy put his hand on Lucy's head and ran his fingers through her hair. He then touched her cheek lightly, and reached down and kissed the top of her head.

He turned to the man in front of him, this demon from another realm, this servant to evil. For Jimmy, his very presence revealed a truth about life that he, and just about everyone on earth, had been ignorant of. Even as a man of faith whose very job was the worshipping and the teaching of the supernatural, he had no idea what was really out there. He could imagine that this would frighten so many people - even Christians who devoted their lives to God and had to acknowledge the possibilities of another dimension - would have panicked at the thought that it was all true. There certainly were more things in heaven and earth than we dream up in our philosophies.

He took a deep breath and tried to gather his resolve. A million thoughts scrambled through his brain and he tried to sort them in an instant. Then a calmness descended onto him.

He took a step closer to the Shadowman in front of him.

'Your worship of your master makes you a slave,' he said. His voice was steady as if he were delivering a sermon on a Sunday morning to his friends and parishioners. The man snorted.

'You worship a false idol,' Jimmy continued. 'The book of Psalms says, "I hate those who cling to worthless idols; as for me, I trust in the Lord." Who do you trust?'

Shadow took a step backwards, anger growing on his face. His forehead knotted and his upper lip curled.

'I trust myself,' he sneered. 'I do not need your God. You will see the folly of your faith very soon.'

Jimmy shook his head.

'No. The Psalm says, "You have not given me into the hands of the enemy but have set my feet in a spacious place."'

He took another step forward, his hands holding tightly onto the little girl at his side.

'Get out of my way!' Jimmy said, his voice began to get louder, more assertive.

Shadow took in a deep breath of his own and he seemed to grow in size.

'You do not tell me what to do, priest!' he bellowed.

Jimmy suddenly threw his hands forward, as if to fend off the attacker. He did it with speed and confidence. There was another bright flash of light, but this seemed to come solely from his hands, like a surge of electricity firing from his fingers. He didn't feel anything, there was no surge of power coursing down his arms, just an inner confidence that this would work.

Shadow's eyes grew wide with surprise as he was lifted off his feet and thrown backwards with a tremendous force; catapulted away from Jimmy and Lucy. Jimmy could see the light leaving his hands, he could see the man tumble through the air, his arms flailing like giant overactive windmills, falling heavily on his back. A thump sounded as whatever air was inside the creature was quickly evacuated.

Then Jimmy froze. A wave of panic took over his body, and the confidence left him with a speed that was as quick and as effective as the flash that came from his hands. The world seemed to collapse around him leaving him standing alone in a strange mental bubble. He was aware of noises, aware of the girl gripping his trousers, aware of shouting getting louder, but it all existed outside the bubble.

Time slowed to a crawl as if it were an exhausted animal trudging through deep, thick mud. He felt like screaming but knew that it was impossible. There was no scream left inside him, just a shallow emptiness.

Then, just as suddenly, his body jerked and he saw hands grabbing him. Pulling him along. He looked into a man's face and saw the urgency in their eyes, but he didn't recognise them. It was as if he was an old man, suffering from dementia and unable to recognise his own family.

The man looked at Jimmy, pulling him closer

'Run, Jimmy! Run.'

It didn't seem like it happened quickly, but recognition dawned on him. A misty gauze cleared away from his eyes as if he were a pilgrim seeking a cure at Lourdes. The man pulling him was Gareth. He had a grimace of desperation on his face.

'Gareth?' he asked.

'Run!'

***

A few moments earlier, Gareth crouched down at the entrance to the bridge. He was partially on the bank which sloped down to the river, his legs damp from the grass beneath him. His head and shoulders peered through a small bush and he could feel a sharp branch digging into his left side. It was uncomfortable but he didn't give a shit. His radio was up to his lips as he tried to describe quietly what was happening.

He couldn't see a lot; Shadow's giant silhouette was blocking most of the available light.

'Hold on,' he whispered. 'I can see them talking. I don't want anything to happen until I give the word.'

He glanced at the school but couldn't see anyone there. He knew there were plenty of people there right now, scrambling to prepare. So much had to be done in so little time that he desperately hoped that something would be in place. A few times he could hear the odd crash and bang, and hoped that neither Jimmy or Shadow would notice.

It hadn't been easy not telling Jimmy what was going to happen, after all, he was the one who was putting his life on the line, but the last thing they needed was Shadow sniffing the possibility of a plan.

He could see Jimmy stepping closer to the man and was sure they must almost be in touching distance. He couldn't hear what was being said, even when their voices seemed to be raised, because of the river below.

What are you doing? he wondered. This wasn't the Jimmy he knew – a friendly, calm man who didn't like confrontation or dispute. There was more talking, then all hell broke loose.

The blue light flared brightly, lighting up the silhouettes of Jimmy and Lucy. The Shadowman seemed to float backwards as if hit by a massive force. Even at this distance, Gareth could hear the thud.

He was on his feet in an instant, not thinking about what he was doing. He just sprang to his feet, ignoring the dizzy-ing feeling of getting up too quickly, and sprinted. The metal boards below him thumped loudly with each stride, the cold night air gulped down with each step.

He got to the other side, grabbed his father-in-law by the jacket and began to pull him towards the school. The little girl screamed as if waking up from a nightmare. But Gareth under-stood that the nightmare still had some legs.

'Run Jimmy, Run!' He shouted, gulping in as much breath as he could.

But Jimmy didn't move.

The momentum had pulled Gareth a few steps beyond Jimmy and it took a few rapid heartbeats to realise the priest hadn't budged. He glanced towards Shadow, who was lying on the floor a few feet to the left. The giant was twitching, as if he was having some kind of fit. Gareth looked back at Jimmy and saw that the older man was in shock. It looked like he had completely shut down. He grabbed Jimmy's lapels and pulled him closer. Jimmy looked at him in the face and frowned.

'Gareth?' he asked.

There was a grunt from the ground and Gareth turned to see Shadow slowly getting off his back and lifting himself up to a sitting position. He was slow and cumbersome, but Gareth knew that it wouldn't take long.

'Run!' Gareth screamed and pulled Jimmy again. Jimmy seemed to come out of his daze and looked down to Lucy who was now beginning to cry loudly.

'Come on,' Jimmy told the girl and started towards the school dragging her behind him.

Shadow was now slowly getting to his feet, pushing down on his knee to give himself some lift, each movement accompanied with a groan.

Jimmy and Lucy, led by Gareth, crossed the wide yard, passed the main entrance and around towards the back of the school. Gareth glanced behind him and saw Shadow was now on his feet and turning towards them. They needed to get inside the school before Shadow could disappear again and block off their path. Still running, he lifted the radio to his mouth and shouted:

'OK Kofi, Fire, fire, fire!'

***

Kofi Antwi already had Shadow in his sights, waiting for the call. If it hadn't come, he had fully intended to shoot as soon as the giant had started towards anywhere at looked dark enough for him to escape.

He was positioned in a window at the observation gallery of the school's swimming pool; perfect for this and what he needed to do, he hoped.

He heard DCI Mann's voice, almost out of breath, obviously still running, and felt a calmness descend on him. This was for Bosch, Kowalski, Jones, and all the others - friends and fellow officers - who had died at the hands of this fiend today.

Shadow was dead centre in his sights.

Antwi fired.

Shadow recoiled backwards as the bullet slammed into his shoulder. His clothes seemed to writhe with the impact, and he staggered a few steps, but quickly regained his balance again. Antwi fired again. Shadow fell back again and recovered once more, looking around to see where the shots were coming from. Antwi fired a third time, then a fourth, the recoil from the gun feeling comfortable in his grip despite its force and his weariness. He was running on adrenaline, but he knew it would be enough for now.

But then Shadow, undoubtedly realising that there was no way for him to get to Jimmy or Lucy like this, took a few steps backwards and, after being hit one more time in the shoulder, fell to his knees and rolled out of sight, down the bank and towards the river.

He was gone and Antwi could only hope that everyone had made it into the school in time.

***

Shadow stepped out between a large, overflowing skip and the wall to the swimming pool. Gareth saw him almost immediately, his huge shape lit up by a spotlight from the top of the building. He was still about forty meters away, but the policeman knew that it wouldn't take him long before he got to them.

'He's here,' Gareth shouted.

They turned a corner, Gareth first followed by Jimmy who almost hauled Lucy behind him. The momentum sent the little girl flailing forward, her grip on Jimmy's hand failing as she tumbled to the floor. Jimmy stopped and turned to stoop for the girl, and he saw Shadow starting his run towards them, his strides getting longer with each step.

'Devil Dodger! Leave her there and I will forget about you. You can live, I just want the girl.'

Lucy screamed as her knee scraped the floor and blood began flowing from it. Jimmy put his hands under her armpits and lifted her up. The pain in his back sent jolts to every nerve ending and synapse in his brain, but he had no choice.

Shadow was now just thirty meters from them.

'Come on,' Jimmy said to the girl, and bounded towards an open door from which Gareth was calling them. He didn't know where he got the strength to do this, but there seemed to be a small well somewhere deep in his soul that propelled him along. They were only yards from the door, and they could hear the footsteps getting louder and louder behind him. He had no idea what the plan was, but he hoped that it would work because the fatigue and the pain were beginning to become unbearable.

Gareth disappeared into the building and, with some relief, Jimmy followed quickly, the girl still in his arms. It was a swimming pool, a large room with high ceiling, brightly lit. Above them was a viewing gallery from which he could see several policemen with guns aimed down towards the door. Above the pool itself, hanging from rafters, were two huge flags – one the Welsh Flag and the other emblazoned with the school logo – which dropped to about ten feet above the pool. Gareth was now at the far end of the pool at a small entrance which led left to the boys' changing rooms. Jimmy continued running, desperate not to look backwards and see Shadow, who must now be within touching distance.

'Where do you think you are going?' The voice was further back than he had thought it would be. He slowed to a stop and turned to see Shadow standing in the doorway, looking around suspiciously. 'You think you can escape into here? What is this place?'

Jimmy put the child down and slowly stepped back towards the changing rooms. Everything became quiet.

'This is a school,' he said. 'A place of learning.'

Shadow sniffed, unimpressed. He stepped into the building slowly, looking around at the large pool of water. He looked up at the gallery and Jimmy followed his gaze. The policemen were gone, there was only the three of them there.

Jimmy and Lucy were only a few yards from the far door now, and the gap between them and their assailant had grown. Jimmy glanced behind him and wondered exactly where he was supposed to go.

Shadow was becoming more confident and began walking to them quickly. He was almost half away across now and what happened next was so quick that Jimmy didn't have enough time to process everything.

First, the door through which they had entered slammed shut, then there was the sound of a large engine roaring through the night and slamming against the outside of the entrance. More noises followed – bangs and crashes and thumps that seemed to reverberate through the huge hall.

Then a pair of hands grabbed Jimmy from behind and pulled him through the doorway and into the boys changing rooms. He noticed that the girl's entrance on the right was blocked up completely with what looked like very heavy metal sheeting.

Then there was the sound of gunshots which echoed loudly through the building causing Jimmy's ears to erupt in pain.

He and Lucy were quickly led through the changing room which had been cleared of furniture. At the far end, where the main entrance from the school should have been, there was a massive gap which looked like it had been made by sledgehammers and other, much larger tools. On the other side of that gap was a large minibus which itself was roaring to life.

Gareth led Jimmy and Lucy to the right wall and the minibus powered quickly passed them. Three large men, holding a massive metal sheet, pushed passed them and dropped the sheeting down in front of the entrance to the swimming pool. The minibus was then driven into the gap, its side scraping the wall and the metal sheeting, which it rammed tightly into place.

'This way,' someone called out, and Jimmy and Lucy were

guided away from the changing rooms and down a long corridor. At the far end were a group of Police Officers.

A female PC crouched down beside Lucy who was still sobbing. The noise from the swimming pool was deafening, with the roar of engines competing with the repeated sound of gunfire.

'Come with me, sweetheart,' the woman said. 'You're safe now.'

Lucy shook her head, then buried her face into Jimmy's belly.

'She'll stay with me,' Jimmy said. The tiredness was overwhelming, and he felt like he could collapse at any moment.

The woman nodded and gave them a wan smile.

'We have an ambulance ready, we'll get you out of here, get you to a hospital.'

Gareth walked up to them and adjusted his tie.

'He's trapped, for now,' he said. 'The place is brightly lit so there's no escaping through shadows. All the exits are sealed and blocked by lorries, but if he does try to get through one, our guys will shoot the motherfucker to slow him down. Oh, sorry, sweetheart. I shouldn't have said that.'

Jimmy felt a wave of love for this man, the man who had married his daughter and had become part of the family. He reached over and put his arms around Gareth, squeezing him tightly.

'Thank you,' he said.

Gareth shook his head.

'You are the one with the superpowers,' he said. 'I always thought you hated superhero films. Besides, it was your friends, Morgan and Catryn, who came up with the plan. They seemed to understand something that I didn't.'

Jimmy laughed.

'There's a lot that I'm only beginning to see,' he said.

Gareth smiled.

'Well, you can tell us all later,' he said. 'But right now, all that matters is getting you out of here. You alright to walk?'

Jimmy nodded.

'If it means getting away from that,' he said, tilting his head towards the swimming pool where gunfire recoiled and echoed, 'I'll walk to Timbuktu.'

As soon as they were outside, Jimmy felt the cold air on his sweat covered skin and shivered. A paramedic rushed up to him and covered him with a blanket. Another paramedic put one around Lucy.

'What happens next?' Jimmy asked Gareth.

'You get fixed up, the rest we'll sort in the morning.'

'No,' Jimmy said. 'We need to get this sorted. Tonight. Where's Catryn and Morgan now?'

'Over in the charity shop,' Gareth said. 'But I really think...'

'No,' Jimmy interrupted. 'This has to stop tonight or tomorrow we'll just be back in square one all over again. I need to speak to someone who has an idea as to what is happening. Whatever that idea is.'

Gareth nodded.

'Ok,' he said. 'We'll get back to the Main Road and then we'll discuss it. But first, you need to ring your wife and daughter. They need to know you're ok.'

Jimmy smiled. He looked down to Lucy and lifted her chin, so she was looking directly at him.

'You coming with me?' he asked.

'Yes, is my Mam and dad ok?' she asked.

Gareth smiled and nodded.

'They're both on the way to hospital. They are badly injured but hopefully they'll be ok.'

A single tear fell down Lucy's cheek, but she said nothing, and Morgan was once again affected by the strength and resilience the little girl was showing at this most difficult time. She took her arms from around his legs and took his hand in hers. Then, together, they walked to the waiting ambulance.

CHAPTER 41

Shadow stalked back and forth along the side of the pool, desperately trying to find a way out. The doors were jammed and there seemed to be massive weights on the other sides. Not that he could focus as every time he put a hand on them, the bastards shot him. He could withstand it, of course, the bullets meant nothing to him in the long run, but the force of them hitting him was proving to be a major annoyance.

The worst part of all this was the light. It was everywhere with not one shadow to provide him solace.

He stopped walking and stood in the middle of the narrow walkway beside the water.

What the hell was this place? He wondered. Why was there so much water indoors? It was too clean to be a place to feed animals, that was for sure. Maybe it was a reservoir. He got down onto his knees and dipped his hands into the water. It was warm. Why the hell would anyone warm this much water? And where were the heating facilities? He didn't see any fires burning anywhere.

This new century in which he had emerged to serve his master was a very confusing time. There were no horses, no carriages – at least not in the sense that he understood. Even the guns were different. They seemed able to fire bullets at an incredible speed. How could they possibly reload them that fast?

He cupped his hands and lifted the water to his lips, took a sip then spat it out. The stuff was disgusting. This wasn't water, surely.

He lifted himself up again and looked around. Almost

everything was white tiled and there were a few pictures of fish painted at intervals. There were also the occasional signs, although, as he didn't know how to read, they didn't interest him.

There were also several strange instruments. A few long poles attached to the walls and there were a few circular devises with holes in the middle. He thought of taking one of the poles and throwing it at the gunmen who surrounded him on the next level up, but they were crouched down, and he doubted he could do more than making one of them duck lower behind their barriers. The others would probably fire at him again if he did that. Still, it was something to keep in mind.

He strode over to the exit that the priest and the girl had taken, but that too was blocked by a large metal sheet. He gave it a push, but it wouldn't budge. Still, he pushed harder, standing back and throwing himself at it. There was slight movement but nothing that could provide him with a way out.

He returned to his spot at the pool's edge and continued to look around. One of the men with guns was looking down at him with intensity. Shadow recognised him as one of the policemen who had attacked the house earlier. He was a black man, Shadow remembered.

What the hell was a nigger doing with a gun? Who allowed one of those beasts to join the constabulary?

'Ay! Nigger!' he shouted but the man did not flinch. 'Come down here like a man so I can crush your skull!'

Nothing. The black man just stared at him impassively.

Shadow shrugged and looked around again. He needed something, anything, that could take him out of the Godforsaken light and return him to the comfort of the dark.

Light did not hurt him; it could not harm him in any way at all. He could survive here as well as he could survive anywhere. It was just a bloody inconvenience. He should have been serving his master but this, so far, was a failure. He had let his master down all because he couldn't control the urges of his dick. He had been told, the Master had warned him, and he knew that there would be plenty of women for him to fuck later, but the sight of that woman in the shower had been too much. As his cock had grown hard, his mind had grown soft. This was the sad reality. This was his failing.

He felt the urge to scream boil up inside of him. It roiled in the base of his stomach and surged up to his throat like an unpleasant belch. It came out with a roar and he felt his entire body tense as it escaped his lungs.

The noise echoed throughout the room and continued until every last breath had been evacuated from his lungs.

As the roar died, he felt totally spent. The failure of this day, which could delay his master's return, weighed heavily on him.

He fell to a sitting position and looked up at the two flags that hung over the pool. They were large pieces of thick fabric which moved delicately on some unseen wind. They were about ten feet above the water which meant that, if he wanted them, he could easily jump up and grab them. But then, he would undoubtedly fall into the water, which would give the nigger and his friends something to laugh at.

A thought, small and currently indefinable, played at the back of his mind. It was just beyond his reach, but he knew that, if he could prize it out, it might be worth it.

He tilted his head slightly, staring at the flags, and suddenly it came to him. He looked up at the guns pointed to him and knew that he would have to be shrewd. This wasn't going to be a case of barrelling into something without thinking. He would keep his dick in his trousers and use his brain.

He knew what he had to do.

STEPHEN AMOS

Tuesday

CHAPTER 42

Jimmy sat up in the ambulance, careful not to move. Each time he did, a spasm of pain shot up his spinal cord and into his brain, bringing with it, not just a pain in the back, but also a severe headache. He felt tired, exhausted to the point of collapse, yet he understood that, even though the night was soon drawing to a close, their duties certainly weren't. That is how he saw it now. It was a duty. Not a civic duty, despite how he usually saw his role in the town and in the wider community; and neither was it a duty to his faith either. In fact, he had already acknowledged that, if anything, the events of the last few days had reinforced his faith. Seeing this man from the shadows was proof, if he needed it, that there was something out there.

Perhaps it was the simple duty of revenge for the lives lost and those that would never be the same again, including the parents of the little girl who had relied on him so heavily tonight.

Just thinking this sent a shot of anguish through his stomach. When they arrived back at the Main Road, the little girl had been taken away by her auntie. Lucy's parents were both in hospital and the father was in critical condition. He had put his life on the line to save his daughter and it had worked. This made Jimmy almost well up in pride for a man he had never met before.

He put his head back and sighed heavily, ignoring the discomfort the position put him in.

He didn't want to believe it was revenge that was propelling him forward. He hoped that he was better than that, but if that was the real reason, then so be it.

Gareth, Catryn and Morgan were with him now. Catryn sitting on the seat in the ambulance that had been recently vacated by a paramedic, and the two men were sitting in the doorway, their legs outside of the ambulance, their bodies twisted so they could see Jimmy and Catryn inside.

The night was cold, yet it didn't seem to be affecting anyone. It was four-thirty a.m., usually the middle of the night for most, but tonight there was still a lot of people hanging around. The police were doing their best to keep them away from the school and the centre of police operations around the Charity shop, however, a few had managed to come up to gawk at the priest with the magic force field.

'So, what now?' Gareth was asking. 'There's no way we can keep him in there forever. Plans are in place to try and capture him, but he's one tough bastard.'

He sounds tired, Jimmy thought. They all did.

'I'm not sure what you can do to capture him,' Morgan said. 'I think we need to end it. Tonight.'

Gareth shook his head.

'You make that sound possible, which is nice, but I can't see it,' he said

'I don't know,' Morgan replied. 'The more I see, the more I think that this can be done. We got him, didn't we?'

'Yes, we did. I'll certainly give you both that,' Gareth said, doffing an imaginary hat to both Morgan and Catryn. He yawned loudly, covering his mouth with his hand. 'I'm sorry, my mind is frazzled.' He adjusted his tie and Jimmy smiled at the unconscious gesture. It was something Gareth had been doing long before they had ever met.

'Morgan's right.' Catryn said. 'This is not going to end until that bastard Henry is put away.'

'What the hell is that supposed to mean?' Gareth asked.

'We need to get rid of the source, the reason the Shadowman is here. We know that they believe in Christianity, that's why he couldn't get to Jimmy. We just got to fool them one more time.'

'Fool them?' Jimmy asked. 'I didn't try to fool them. It was my faith that saved me.'

'I don't believe that,' Catryn snapped. 'The Shadowman knew you were a Christian, we discussed it in the house when we were looking around. It is his belief that saved you, not yours. That's his weakness'

Jimmy lifted himself up and winced in the pain. 'I don't believe that one second. We survived because I was protected by the holy spirit.'

'What?' Catryn asked indignantly. 'Then how do you explain about all the other believers who died today? Do you think you have a monopoly on faith? That you have a one-to-one with God? That's pretty arrogant and pretty fucking disrespectful to all the others who died.'

'Look,' Jimmy said indignantly. 'I'm not going to comment on the faith of others. All I know is that I'm a believer and that I was saved today by-'

'That's how it is with you people,' Catryn interrupted. 'You are so bloody narrow-minded that you are not willing to accept the views of others.'

'Catryn,' Gareth put a hand on her shoulder in a calming gesture.

'Don't fucking "Catryn" me!' She shook her shoulder, pushing Gareth's hand away. 'Look, I know how much you went through tonight, I understand that you're probably suffering from some sought of shock, but you don't have to be a prick about it.'

'What?' Jimmy asked. 'What are you talking about?'

'You live in this perfect world and are all holier than thou, but when it all goes wrong. What? If you survive you are protected; if you don't, it's your own fault? As if I had turned my back on God or something. Well maybe I didn't turn my back on God, maybe He turned his fucking back on me.'

Morgan and Gareth exchanged glances but neither knew what to say. Jimmy saw it in their faces, stunned that she had managed to turn it all on her, as if it was personal. He took a deep breath and looked her straight in the eyes.

'Look, Catryn,' he said. 'I didn't mean to offend you. I know what you've been through and I-'

'How could you ever know what I've been through? Say? We only met each other yesterday. You don't know who I am, so how can you presume to know what I've been through?'

Jimmy took a deep breath.

'I don't know you, but I know your father and after what happened to you last year, he came to me for advice.'

'What!' Catryn was suddenly very quiet, her voice almost reduced to a whisper.

'I was going to tell you but -' Jimmy began.

'How dare you,' she spat. 'How dare you. I don't know what my father told you, but whatever it was he had no right, and you have no right to raise it now.'

'I'm sorry.'

'I don't want an apology. I want you to go straight to hell and take God with you.'

She stood up and quickly left the ambulance, pushing Morgan and Gareth out of the way.

'What happened there?' Gareth asked.

Jimmy shook his head. 'I may have messed up,' he said.

'Is this anything to do with the phone call she had earlier?'

'What phone call?' Gareth asked.

'While we were in the charity shop, she received a phone call and her mood changed like that.' Morgan snapped his fingers.

Jimmy frowned, the possibilities slowly trudging through his head.

'I don't know,' he said slowly.

'I'll go and see that she's ok,' Morgan said, getting up.

'I don't think that would be the right thing to do right now.'

'I don't care' Morgan said, and walked after his friend. Jimmy sighed heavily and fell back onto the pillow behind him. He grunted with pain but did his best to ignore it. Tonight had taken so many turns that he was beginning to feel dizzy.

***

Morgan found Catryn standing near the alleyway the Shadowman had used earlier. The area was still lit up with streetlights, car lights and a few other lights used by the TV people, although most of the crowds had finally dispersed. The strange party atmosphere from earlier was now gone, replaced by a peculiar sense of tiredness. Morgan could feel it in his legs, in his arms and in his eyelids, which increasingly wanted nothing more than to close.

It had been a funny sort of day and he hoped that he would never experience another like it. He had seen things that couldn't have possibly existed yet, up and down the street, there was the wreckage to prove that it had all happened. So far nothing had been done about the cars the Shadowman had tipped upside down. There were fragments of glass everywhere, but he knew that, when the time came to clean it all up, it wouldn't take too long.

But there would be scars. That was for certain. Everything that had happened today would remain as memories and stories and as nightmares for a long, long time. And, because it was all captured on cameras for the world, Trehenri would soon be synonymous with the paranormal and the supernatural for years to come.

He also suspected that, because of what the cameras captured in this village, the world would never be the same again. This was the proof that all those conspiracy theorists and nut-jobs needed. There was something out there, something that had been hidden from all but the crazies, the dismissed.

He shook his head, clearing away such thoughts. This was not the time to think on such a scale. His mind was battling exhaustion and probably a mild form of shock, and he knew he wasn't thinking straight.

Catryn's head was bowed as he approached and, even

though her back was turned to him, he could hear her faint sobs.

'Cat?' he asked tentatively. 'Sweetheart?'

'Go away,' she said, although without much conviction. She too must have been feeling exhausted. In fact, it must have been a lot worse as she had faced the Shadowman in his lair.

'You ok?' It was a stupid thing to ask, he knew, but he couldn't think of anything else.

She nodded and he drew closer to her, moving to her side so he could see her face. Her cheeks were wet with tears, yet he thought she looked even more attractive than ever.

'It's alright,' he said and put his hand on her back, rubbing it up and down like his mother used to do to him whenever he was ill or if he had fallen off his bike as a child.

She sighed deeply but said nothing.

'That thing that Jimmy mentioned, it's related to the phone call you got earlier, isn't it?'

She hesitated for a moment, then nodded again between sobs. He pulled her closer until his arms were wrapped around her.

'Thought so, I could see you were upset. Was it something that happened in London?'

Catryn nodded but diverted her eyes from him, so he couldn't see her properly.

'What happened?'

Still nothing but tiny shudders caused by the sobs.

'It's ok, whatever it is, can't hurt you.' He said. 'Besides, you came face to face with a freaking ghost monster thingy today and you're still here. It can't be any worse than that, can it?'

Catryn laughed slightly.

'No,' she said, shaking her head.

'You came face to face with a freaking shadow demon from the sound of it.'

She turned to him coyly and gave him a small smile.

'Who was it that called you?' he asked.

'A reporter,' she said quietly.

Morgan nodded his head.

'About your husband?'

'Yes.'

'What happened, Cat? Let it out, you'll feel much better because of it.'

She paused and returned his embrace, burying her face into his shoulder. He could feel her trembling softly. After a few moments, she lifted her face to him and looked directly into his eyes, almost defiantly.

'I killed him,' she said.

Morgan fought the urge to step back, to push her away from him and blurt out: 'You did what?' He held her closer to him for a few heartbeats, long enough to control himself and ask the appropriate thing.

'Why? What did he do to you?'

She held him closer and the trembling increased. She seemed so fragile right now, completely at odds with the image he had formed of her over the last few days. She was like a sparrow caught in his hands, and he felt if he said, or did, the wrong thing she would break.

'Did he beat you?' he asked softly.

She nodded, although he felt it rather than saw it, as her face was tucked into his shoulder again. He rested his chin on her head.

'For how long?'

'Four years,' came her muffled voice.

He closed his eyes and could feel the sting of tears; her words were like thousands of little stabs into his heart.

'Tell me,' he said.

She started off reluctantly but soon the words began to flow. How the need for control, that she had just dismissed as a funny sort of OCD, had grown stronger after they had married. Soon he was dictating what she was to wear and where she could go. The funny thing was, she had gone along with it for a long time, as if it had crept up on her without her even knowing it. When he first hit her, she really believed she had deserved it. She knew what he wanted, yet she had defied him and had been punished for it. If she had only obeyed the rules in the first place, then nothing would have happened. Yet, she always seemed to break the rules, even without knowing it. The food wasn't cooked right, the house just wasn't clean enough, why had she allowed her bosses to keep her so late in work when she knew that he needed her home at a particular time?

It took her a long time to even begin questioning him. Even though she was working on the job of a lifetime, investigating the finances of organised crime in London, she was still coming home and accepting the beatings.

Then one day, she had watched a video of an interview with the wife of one of the bosses under investigation. The woman had been beaten black and blue because her husband had thought she had flirted with a waiter. The police had brought her in for questioning, hoping that she could provide a way of getting to him, yet she refused to testify. She had fallen down the stairs and hit a table at the bottom, she said. The police knew that this was bullshit but she refused to say anything else.

When the video had ended, one of her colleagues had almost spat at the monitor. 'Crazy bitch,' he had said. 'Nothing she could do could ever deserve a beating like that. She must be scared shitless of that bastard.'

As she drove home that night, it had occurred to her for the very first time, that she was scared of Joe. Whereas previously she had been disappointed with herself for causing her husband so much grief, now she realised that she was in terror of him. The rules, the rituals, had all been excuses, both by him to beat her, and her to accept it.

That night she had confronted him, and he had beaten her so hard that she spent the night in hospital and missed her first days off work for three years. Yet she returned home convinced that he could change.

He didn't and, when she confronted him again, he beat her

again.

This went on for months and in the meantime, the police and her team of accountants had accrued enough evidence to arrest the boss. She had gone out with her team to celebrate and, high on the buzz of success, she had drunk too much and returned home too late. He had been waiting for her in the kitchen and they had a furious argument. He punched her until her face was a bloody mess and then shouted at her for looking ugly. She had tried to spit at him, so he grabbed her hair, forced her head into the sink and run the tap over her. She had thrashed out in pain and fear, and her hands had landed on a kitchen knife that was on the draining board. When he yanked her up, she swung around with the knife, driving it deep into his chest. Then she run out of the kitchen, up the stairs and hid in the bedroom for a couple of hours, before building up the courage to go down and check on him. He was on the floor in a pool of blood, his lifeless eyes staring up at some spot on the ceiling.

She panicked and didn't call the police, instead she phoned her best friend Amalie, who came right round immediately and took charge of everything. The police came, then forensics, along with paramedics and some counsellors. The rest was a blur that seemed to last months. No charges were ever brought, although she seemed to have been interviewed a thousand times. In the end, there were therapists and more counsellors. There were group meetings with other battered wives, and one-to-ones with an assortment of psychologists.

'Then I come here, away from the crap in London, and he goes on about how his faith saved him, yet I had faith once. I used to go to church with my Dad every week. I prayed before bedtime every night. It didn't save me. It didn't stop that bastard from putting me in hospital, for making me afraid to breath the wrong way, from pissing on me when I was crying on the floor.

'I know he wasn't talking about me, but it seemed like he was implying it was my fault because I had lapsed, or that my faith wasn't strong enough,' she said disdainfully. 'How dare he? Especially when he knew what had happened.'

Morgan nodded.

'You are right,' he said quietly, 'and I am so sorry.'

She took a few steps away from him and kicked a stick that was on the pavement.

'So, what was the phone call about?' he asked. 'What do they want?'

Catryn snorted.

'His name is Robert Head. He's a hack working for some online gossip site. He first started calling me after he saw my name when I was working with the police, then, a few weeks later, someone tipped him off that I was in hospital and under arrest for killing my husband. He phoned me tonight after he saw a shot of me talking to the police on the news. He seems to think that trouble follows me around.'

'Have you ever told the police about him?'

'No, he's just a nuisance, that's all.'

'No, he's not. Look at you. With all that you've been through today, he's more than just a nuisance. We'll have a word with Gareth tomorrow, see what he can do.'

Catryn took a deep breath.

'What do we do now?'

'We get Sir Henry as you suggested. How, I've no idea though.'

'I think I know how,' she said. 'And it pains me to admit it, but we need that religious bastard in there.'

'Jimmy is a good man. I agree with everything you have said, and I don't ask you to believe it yet, but he is.'

'He's got a funny way of showing it,' she snorted.

'He's spent the evening being attacked by the same shadow monster supernatural thingy that you have today. Twice, if you count this afternoon. I'm not asking you to cut him any slack right now, just consider doing it tomorrow. If we make it until tomorrow.'

'I think you'll find that tomorrow has already come,' she

said.

Morgan looked up to the sky. It was beginning to change from the deepest black to a velvety shade of navy. There were a few clouds that seemed to be blushing and Morgan felt another wave of tiredness sweep over him.

'Come on,' he said. 'I want to hear your plan, kill the ghost, then go to bed for a few weeks.'

Catryn smiled.

'Good plan,' she said.

CHAPTER 43

By the time they got into their cars, the sky had brightened significantly, even with a build-up of clouds which were dark and heavy and ominous. There was virtually no chance of a storm and, for most people, there was nothing unusual about them, but for Catryn and Morgan, they seemed to indicate something was coming.

Morgan's head felt heavy, and he viewed the world through eyelids that seemed to want to close at any and every moment. He couldn't ever remember being this exhausted before, and he had to wonder exactly how Catryn and Jimmy were coping.

They were both running on empty just as he was. He could see it in their eyes. He wanted nothing more than to go home, open a bottle of wine, and get drunk. It would be a return to the familiar – to the safe. He would often drink at home, alone. He would open a bottle of wine and before he knew it, the bottle would be empty, and the room would be slowly spinning around him. It was easy. It was a way of coping with the fact that his wife had left him, that he didn't see his children very often, that the only sounds that reverberated off the walls at home were his own and the artificial clang of TV and radio.

He realised that it was a sad life. A waste. But it still seemed desirable right now. To be lost in a haze of alcohol, far away from the horror that existed outside his front door. It had to be easier than this.

He and Catryn had returned to the ambulance and she had apologised. It wasn't entirely convincing, but they all knew that, until this was all over, a full apology would have to wait.

There were still issues that had to be sorted sometime, just not now.

Catryn had laid out her plan, and maybe it was the fog of exhaustion or it was a tired and desperate need to end all this, but it did seem to make some sense.

The crux of the matter, according to Catryn, was Shadow's faith. If he couldn't get to Jimmy because of his faith, then that would suggest that Sir Henry could be affected the same way. As she explained this, Morgan had glanced over to Jimmy, who was listening intently, even though it was obvious he disagreed with her interpretation of faith.

She explained everything in detail until Gareth, trying to stretch the knots in his back, agreed to at least look into it. He disappeared to talk to the other police leaving Morgan to sit between his two friends - one newly returned into his life, the other, a minister of religion that he had known for years.

The atmosphere was cold until Catryn decided to go for a walk, leaving him and Jimmy alone.

'So, you knew all along?' Morgan asked.

'Please Morgan,' Jimmy said. 'I'm tired. You can have a go at me for being such an ass tomorrow, but tonight, please leave it.'

Morgan reluctantly nodded.

'OK.'

The silence became heavy again and Morgan felt an absolute urge to break it.

'You've spoken to Carys?'

'Yeah, she's ok. Wants me home.'

'You don't have to be there,' Morgan said. 'You've been through enough tonight. We can find another priest.'

Jimmy shook his head.

'No, no one else can do this. This is not ego talking, I just want to be the one to end it. After all, it was my church that was desecrated. It was me that Lucy ran to.'

'Come on, that was a coincidence. You just happened to be in the right place at the right time.'

Jimmy shook his head, the pain evident on his face.

'I don't think so. There are too many coincidences. I think I was put in the position to be there for Lucy. If it was anyone else, she would have been gone now. It had to be me. I was in the house; I discussed my faith with Catryn and he overheard it. It was my church. Don't you see? This is God's hand.'

Morgan nodded but didn't say anything. He felt uncomfortable with this talk. He didn't have faith like Jimmy did. He was happy to believe that when he died, he would continue contributing to the earth in the way of fertilizer. He always liked the type of faith which didn't include God's hand, if that made any sense. It was as if the mention of God embarrassed him somehow.

'How you going to cope with your back?' Morgan asked. 'You look like you are in a lot of pain.'

'I'll cope somehow. I've got to.' Jimmy said.

Morgan looked around him. He could see the police still trying to impose a loose organisation to the scene, even though most members of the public had now gone. There seemed to have been a few changes with regards to the TV reporters, he noticed. Probably getting ready for the breakfast news.

Shit, he thought, I'm starving. I really could do with some breakfast.

'You really got a crush on her, haven't you?' Jimmy asked.

Morgan turned back inside the ambulance. Jimmy sat looking at him with a peculiar grin.

'Don't know,' he said honestly. 'I've made no bones about me being a bit lonely the last few years. Me and Chantel might not have worked out, but I missed being part of a couple. I miss Seren and David.'

He shrugged.

'You think you might give it a go with Catryn?' Jimmy asked.

Morgan smiled.

'I don't know,' he said again. 'Does she carry too much baggage? Would she want another relationship after what happened to her? These last few days don't really help, do they? Relationships that start under stress rarely work.'

Jimmy smiled. 'So said Sandra Bullock and Keanu Reeves at the end of Speed,' he said.

'And they weren't together in Speed 2, were they?'

'No,' Jimmy said. 'But that was an awful movie, so we'll ignore that. Besides, she may have been through a lot, but that wasn't her fault. She is a victim here and, despite what ultimately happened, she is not to blame. I've been a complete ass about it all. In hindsight. I should have handled it better but in my defence, these haven't been an ordinary times. However, these last few days, you have been there for her and that means a lot.'

'Well, tonight is not the time to think about it,' Morgan said.

'Go home, take Catryn with you. Have a shower and something to eat. You'll feel better for it.'

'No,' Morgan said, shaking his head. 'I'm seeing this through to the end, and I think Catryn will as well.'

Jimmy nodded.

'Well, leave me alone, and go and see her. I'm going to close my eyes and dream that it is already over.'

***

Morgan and Catryn returned to the Charity shop where they found a comfortable chair in the back, which Morgan insisted that Catryn take. He dragged the stool from behind the shop counter and sat awkwardly in the corner of the room. Police were still camped out in the front and there was a lot of coming and going. At one point, the manager of the shop Mrs Jean Lewis - a portly woman with bad teeth and blue rinse hair - came down from the flat above the shop with a tray of tea for her guests.

'You are all celebrities,' she said with tired joviality. 'You've been on TV all night and it seems that some reporters have asked to speak to you, but the police keep saying no.'

'I'm glad,' Morgan said. 'I don't think I could take it.'

'Well, you never know. Play your cards right and you two could be on Celebrity Big Brother or I'm a Celebrity Get Me Out of Here!'

This was said with real and honest joy, and neither Morgan or Catryn felt the desire to let her down by telling her that they would never appear on these shows unless they had guns to their heads. Morgan had to admit to Catryn later that he had never actually seen an episode of either.

After a while, the activity calmed down and both began to doze, although Morgan found his seating arrangements quite uncomfortable, he felt a warmth being with this woman tonight.

He thought of what Jimmy had said earlier. His reply had been as honest as he could. He was certainly attracted to Catryn but, as the evening had turned to night, which was now slowly becoming morning, he wasn't sure they were compatible. Ultimately, so much time had passed and so many things had happened, he had to admit that he didn't know her.

Eventually, he nodded off into that fitful space between wakefulness and sleep. He dreamt of Catryn, Seren and David, they were all on a bus together, although where they were going, he had no idea.

***

They were awoken at 6.30 am, by a constable who looked young enough to just have come out of school and fresh enough to suggest he had had a good night's sleep.

They stretched themselves awake but said nothing. It was almost as if the coming events were too important to discuss. Morgan felt grubby, and wanted nothing more than to have a shower and to change his underwear. They each took turns using the small toilet at the back of the shop, to relieve themselves and to splash a bit of cold water on their faces to help the process of waking up.

They left the shop together and were led towards a small canopy that had been erected at the end of School Street by the bridge. There was a small table surrounded by police and civilians. In the middle were Gareth and Jimmy, who were talking to a man wearing a fleece sweater with the logo of the county emblazoned on the breast.

'Mogs, Catryn, over here,' Jimmy said when he saw them. They moved to the front of the small gathering and could see several large maps open on the table.

'What's all this?' Morgan asked.

'This is where we will finally put the beast to rest,' Jimmy said, smiling. He seemed fresher, more awake than Morgan felt, and was almost boyish with enthusiasm. Yet he still held himself straight in the back and it was obvious the pain was still affecting him.

'What does that mean?' Catryn said.

'This is Mike Edwards,' Gareth said, introducing the stranger. 'He works for the council and the forestry commission, and he was just telling us something you might find interesting. Mike?'

'Um, yeah,' Mike said, obviously uncomfortable speaking in front of a crowd. 'It was about two months ago that we started clearing the site. We knew it was there, of course, these things are scattered about the place. You'll be surprised what's in these hills around here. We even have some ancient roman sites. Well, there was a complaint by a member of the public that one of the walls was in danger of collapse, she had been walking her dog when they came across it. Eventually, it landed with my team, and we went up there and cleared it. We had to tear down the walls to make it safe. Pity really, it's like tearing down history.'

'Sorry,' Catryn interrupted. 'What are we talking about?'

'The old chapel,' Gareth replied. 'There's an old chapel up the top of the mountain here,' he pointed up the hill above Trehenri. 'It's not too far from Llanwonno. It's the old meeting places that Tal told us about, exactly where he said it would be. I can't say I like the man, but he seems to know his stuff. Anyway, six weeks ago they tore it down.'

'Six weeks,' Morgan said. 'That could explain the grooming period that Shadow seemed to have had.'

'Exactly,' Gareth said. 'Not everyone believes all this -'

'That's because its religious bullshit,' someone said, although Morgan couldn't see who. There were murmurs amongst the assembled group.

'That might be true,' Gareth said testily. 'But after all the shit we've seen tonight, I'm open to believing whatever it takes to end all this.

'There were a few more murmurs in agreement, with no further comments from the dissenter.

'Damn right,' someone said.

'So, we're going to go up there now and do whatever needs to be done to end it.'

'I know we have our differences,' Jimmy said to Catryn, 'but what you said last night is right, I think. It comes down to faith. We need to remind Sir Henry or whatever it is up there, that he is buried on sacred ground. In other words, we need to reseal the lock that has held them for over a century.'

'So, you do believe all this?' Catryn asked. 'Religious symbols and sacred places. Sounds like bad Catholicism to me.'

'I don't know,' Jimmy admitted. 'You are right, it always seems to be the Catholics in the movies. But the people who buried Henry two hundred-odd years ago were non-conformists. Neither the Church of England nor Catholicism really took root around here, yet, whatever these people did, seemed to have worked. Maybe it is the power of the Holy Spirit or, as you suggested last night, all that matters is Henry's faith. What he believes in. I don't think it really matters as long as it works. We can have that discussion another time, perhaps.

'Morgan saw something pass between Jimmy and Catryn, an unspoken apology and forgiveness, maybe?

'Any way.' Gareth said, 'We're taking a car up there now and, if all goes well, we should be back in about an hour, an hour and a half maybe. In the meantime, plans are being drawn up to try and secure the Shadow fella indefinitely.'

'We want to go,' Catryn said.

Gareth shook his head.

'You're not needed. Go home and get some rest, you both deserve it.'

'No,' she replied. 'I need to see the end of this.'

'I dunno, it may be a waste of time.'

'It's my plan. If it's a waste of time, then I want to find out.'

'They can come with me,' a female voice said. Morgan turned and saw Sargent Harris stepping forward. 'I'm going up with Sargent Connelly, they can share our ride.'

Gareth sighed heavily.

'Ok, it's your idea, you deserve this I suppose.'

Morgan smiled and put his hand on Catryn's shoulder. She didn't turn to him but lifted her hand to hold his, squeezing it lightly.

'OK, I'll be going with Mike here, Jimmy and Sargent Williams of the Armed unit. We leave in ten minutes so get what you need and let's go.

'I need to go to the Chapel,' Jimmy said. 'I need a Bible.'

'Can't you find another one, we don't have time to go up there.'

'There were a few up in the Charity shop,' Morgan said. 'I'm sure we can whip up the £1 to buy one.'

***

They drove up the valley, passed Wattstown and through Tylorstown to Ferndale. The roads were sometimes very narrow and very busy with people going about their daily lives. Commuters on the way down the valley, many going to Cardiff. Morgan couldn't think of anything worse than to have to make that drive every day. He supposed that some would be driving to the nearest 'park and rides' to continue their journeys by train from Porth or Pontypridd.

In Ferndale, they turned off the main road and descended on the winding road down to the bottom of the valley, before ascending once more up to Blaenllechau. It had been a long time since Morgan had come up here and he was surprised how busy it was.

The streets here were lined with trees and the road twisted left and right as they began the ascent. It wasn't a huge mountain by any means, but it was reasonably steep. There wasn't a lot of houses on the road, just the odd terrace scattered here and there. They then crossed two bridges and turned right passed the sign that said they were entering Blaenllechau.

'It's been years since I been up here,' he said to Catryn.

'Yeah, my dad used to bring us up as kids. We would park next to the pub and take a walk up the hill into the woods, let the dogs run free for a while. They loved it. He would then buy us a drink in the pub, and we'd sit outside listening to the wind in the trees. It's a favourite childhood memory of mine.'

'You'll have to do it again soon once summer comes.'

'I don't know. After all this, what connotations would the place have?'

'Yeah,' Morgan nodded, looking out the window.

They drove up Station Road and around a very tight bend, then continued upwards. There were tightly packed terraced houses on the right-hand side, hugging the road.

At the top of Commercial Street, they all used the roundabout to turn back before bearing left to continue up the hill. The junction was too sharp an angle to turn directly up the hill, so the roundabout had been put in place to help drivers. It was a narrow street, with parked cars on the left and they had to stop a few times to allow oncoming cars to pass. Morgan sat looking out the window, over the edge of the precarious road. There was only a thin wire fence between the cars on the road, and an alarming drop off the side of the mountain and down to the valley floor, which got further and further away the higher they went.

'I don't see any TV cameras or helicopters following us,' he said. 'I sort of expected some.'

'Gareth made sure only a few people knew about this,' Harris said, talking over her shoulder from her position in the front seat. 'That way we would avoid the cameras and, if it turns out that nothing happens and it's a waste of time, then we all avoid embarrassment.'

The terraced houses gave way and soon the road was just a narrow lane. The drop on the right was now obscured by hedgerows, although Morgan could see the occasional glimpse of the valley through the odd gaps. It looked very steep and the deep valley looked quite beautiful, even with the scars of humanity which crowded the valley floor. With the grey skies above, it looked majestic to Morgan. There were no trees, just the odd bush and masses of ferns and grass. Below he could see Ferndale and Tylorstown, and he knew that soon they would be able to look down on Trehenri as well. At the very top, the landscape changed again, and fir trees appeared each side of them as they entered the forestry.

Catryn didn't speak during the journey, she just stared out the windows at the passing countryside. There was no expression that he could read on her face, but he hoped that she was feeling ok. He felt a curious excitement in his stomach as they came closer to the unknown. His mind told him not to expect much, but his stomach was alive with butterflies.

Finally, they arrived at Llanwonno, which Morgan was convinced was the smallest village in the world, if it could be called a village at all. On the left was a church – Eglwys Sant Gwynno – and on the right was the Brynffynon Hotel. That was it. No houses, no shops, just the two buildings, one surrounded by gravestones and both surrounded by trees and benches. They drove between the two buildings and continued down the road, passed a few parked cars and ramblers. After a few hundred yards they pulled into a parking area on the right-hand side.

'We're here,' Connelly said.

He turned the steering wheel and parked directly behind

the first car.

They got out of the car and joined the others. Williams and Connelly, stood together doing routine checks on their guns.

'OK, the chapel is located about three-quarters of a mile in that direction,' Mike said pointing into the woods. 'There is a path of sorts, but it is pretty overgrown and, after about a half a mile, we have to veer off to the right, so we'll be walking through some fairly rough ground. Luckily, it has been dry recently, so it won't be too bad.'

'OK, guys.' Gareth said. 'I know that a lot of people think this is a waste of time but, as Catryn has pointed out, it makes a sort of twisted sense, which is all we have considering the weird crap that has been happening recently. So, whilst the chances are that nothing is going to happen, I want you all to be vigilant. Who knows what we are going to see? Harris, I want you to stay here, we'll be in constant communication. If anything happens, get back-up immediately. Ok, everyone?'

Each member of the party nodded, and Morgan felt the tightness in his stomach return. He glanced at Catryn who smiled back.

'I don't know which will be worst,' she said. 'To be wrong and to be humiliated, or to be right and face who knows what.'

'Perhaps you'll be right, and it'll all go smoothly, and everyone will go home happy.' Morgan said.

'Yeah, right. Like that would happen,' she sniffed.

Morgan thought her words were ominous, even though she said them with a smile.

'OK, truckers.' Gareth said. 'Let's get trucking.'

Together, they set off into the woods looking for a ghost's grave.

CHAPTER 44

Ben Wallis pointed his rifle down into the pool area, catching the Shadowman in his scope. The man, this almost mythical being that everyone seemed completely on edge about, was pacing back and fore. Occasionally, he would look up at the armed police watching him and scream in rage.

Rage seemed to be this fella's thing, Wallis thought. In the ten minutes he had been here after taking over from Antwi, the man had raged and screamed, and basically acted like a child who had lost their ice cream. He stalked up and down the side of the pool like a trapped tiger.

Wallis didn't know what the big thing was about this prick. He had seen the videos and heard the stories, but seeing him here now, he didn't look that different from any other roider. Yes, he was big, there was no doubt about that, and Wallis knew that he wouldn't stand a chance toe-to-toe, but he was still a man. Antwi had warned him to keep watch and, if the fella tried anything, to shoot. Aim for the body and fire. Apparently, the man wouldn't feel it. Seemed a bit strange, but that was okay by Wallis.

He had been very tense when he first took over, but now he was beginning to relax. There was no way the Shadowman could get out. This was an easy assignment and, watching the child have his tantrum, was proving quite humorous.

The hall echoed once again with the loud screams, and Wallis couldn't help thinking of the Hulk. The man even posed like the Hulk, bringing his arms in front of him and tensing his (admittedly huge) biceps.

Wallis looked over to Nic Owens who had taken up the position on the other end of the gallery.

'Don't make me angry,' Wallis called out. 'You won't like me when I'm angry.'

Owens laughed and did a comic pose, just like the Hulk.

Wallis turned back to the prisoner who was now staring up at him, a vile hatred on his face. That was ok, Wallis didn't mind that look. In fact, he preferred it. He knew he was getting to the bastard. The Shadowman looked around the pool area, walked quickly to a long pipe that was attached to the wall and ripped it off. He then turned, aimed and threw it at Wallis. The throw was a good one and the policeman had to duck.

He heard Owens laughing, and lifted his head up to see the prisoner rage at him once more. Wallis turned back to his partner and pretended to style his hair.

'That was a close one,' Owens called.

'Yeah, ruffled my hair,' he called back.

He turned back to the pool. The man was pacing again, first down to the far end of the pool towards Owens' side, then back. All the while he was looking at the cops with undisguised malevolence.

The Shadowman stopped and faced Wallis, and suddenly jumped towards him.

The policeman knew there was no way the man could jump this far, but he was still surprised by how high the man leaped. It looked like he might have reached fifteen feet in the air before beginning his descent, but instead of getting close to Wallis, all he managed to do was grab onto one of the flags before crashing down into the pool.

Both Wallis and Owens laughed, and he swore that Owens actually hooted. This prisoner was impressive, there was no doubt about that, but his petty attempts at rage were just comical.

The man swam back to the edge of the pool and climbed out, pulling the school flag with him. Then he lifted the flag in the air, threw it down onto the floor in rage and stamped on it.

He continued his stalking, treading on the flag with each pass. On the third time of passing, he stooped down and lifted the flag, opening it wide before settling it back down on the floor. The Flag was about eight to ten feet long and about four to five feet wide.

'Perhaps this was his old school,' Owens called. 'He's feeling nostalgic for the old school flag.'

The two men laughed again.

When Wallis turned back to the prisoner, he was standing down Owen's side of the pool, staring up at the other man with the same hatred he had directed on Wallis.

'I will cut your heart out and eat it while it is still beating,' the Shadowman called up at Owens. Wallis saw the expression on his partner's face turn from amusement to horror.

'You got to get me first, you fuck!' Owens spat back.

The Shadowman took a step backwards until his back was flush against the stone wall, then, with speed and ballet-like grace, he threw himself upwards towards Owens. The policeman took a few steps backwards and raised his rifle, but Wallis could see that he wasn't going to get close. Instead, he crashed into the other flag and brought it crashing into the water with him once more.

Wallis laughed.

'He had you then,' he called.

'Fuck off,' Owens replied.

The Shadowman swam back to the edge and got out of the pool once more and threw the flag down along the side of the pool, so it landed next to the first one.

'Oi, leave that one alone, you bitch,' Owens called. 'That's the Welsh flag and if you can't respect it, fuck off to wherever you came from.'

The Shadowman looked up at him and sneered, then walked over to the flag and unfolded it, looking at it curiously. He lay it on top of the first one neatly, then stepped back. Wallis could hear him bringing up a load of snot from his throat before spitting on the Dragon. He then turned back to

Owens with a terrible smile on his face.

'Fuck your flag,' he said.

'You do that one more time, Bitch' Owens said, 'and I'll shoot you right between the eyes.'

The man screamed at him one more time, the sound was so loud that Wallis wanted to cover his hears.

As the sounds died, the Shadowman sat down for the first time in a small puddle next to the flags. He picked the edges up and started fiddling with them.

About time, Wallis thought, he's giving up at last.

He remained there for about ten minutes, hardly looking up at the officers. At one point as colleague brought up two cups of coffee for them. They took it thankfully and rested their guns on the walls so they could lean over the balcony and survey their prisoner.

That is when Shadowman moved. It was so fast that Wallis hardly saw it, and certainly had no time to prepare for it. The monster gripped the flags, by the corners, and with one quick sweeping move, he pulled the flags over his head.

Wallis and Owens reached for their rifles simultaneously and aimed at their prisoner. Wallis brought the rifle's scope so that the flag was in its centre. He looked for the man, sweeping his scope left and right, looking for something, but all he saw were the flags slowly falling to the floor as if in slow motion. The man's outline vanished leaving two wet flags draped across the floor at the poolside.

Wallis turned to Owens. The whole thing had happened so fast that he didn't really have time to process but, as he looked into his partner's eyes, he realised that there was no hiding from the truth.

Their prisoner, the Shadowman, had disappeared.

***

Catryn stepped over a large log and into a small ditch. Her momentum carried her forward a bit, and she had to reach down and steady herself with her hands.

'You ok?' asked Morgan beside her.

'Fine, just glad I'm wearing half-decent shoes. I didn't think this through.' she said, smiling.

The walk was a little rough but not too bad. The day was cool, but she still had a bit of sweat on her back and on her forehead.

'We should have brought some drinks,' Morgan said.

'I don't think we're going that far,' she replied.

'It's just over the rise there,' Mike said. 'Not too far now.'

Catryn heard a ringtone chiming, and saw Gareth pause and dig out his phone from his pocket and bring it to his ears. The artificial sound seemed odd in these surroundings.

'DCI Mann,' he said, officiously. Catryn looked around at the surrounding countryside. It was beautiful. The air was fresh, trees were scattered about, and the grass grew wild. It was the type of place you really had to look for, yet it was only twenty minutes from home. How far would I have to go to see this in London? she wondered.

'What?' Gareth's voice cut sharply through her reverie. 'How the hell did that happen?'

The whole group had stopped walking now, and Catryn could see the concern growing on their faces.

'When?' he asked. 'Ok, get to the little girl's house fast. And keep me updated.'

He ended the phone call and shoved the handset back into his pocket.

He looked at them all and Catryn felt a lead ball drop into her stomach.

'He's escaped,' he said. 'The Shadowman is out. He escaped about ten minutes ago, they've been trying to warn us but the signal is dropping in and out. We'd better get a move on and do this before he gets here.'

Catryn suddenly felt tired again and the countryside she was just admiring now made her feel lonely, a long way from any help if the shit hit the fan.

CHAPTER 45

John Morris almost jumped when the telephone rang. He had been on edge for hours, ever since the news had come through about the attack on his brother and his family. Of course, he had heard the stories; he knew the rumours about the Shadowman and how he was targeting little girls called Lucy. But you never really thought it was true, did you? You never thought it could happen to you and yours.

There had been no phone call to tell him what had happened. There probably wasn't enough time. He had been watching TV, had turned it over to the News Channel, and watched the whole thing as it happened. At first, he had thought he had turned to the wrong channel. He saw a man in the middle of a street, crouching over and protecting a young girl, when a giant of a creature tried smashing his huge hands into them. He saw the flash of blue light, dismissed the whole thing as a stupid movie and reached for the remote control. But then something occurred to him and he looked again. The street was familiar, the junction was one he had driven through countless times.

And then it had hit him.

Hit him hard in the gut, as if he was caught by one of those booby traps that spring a sledgehammer at a person's torso.

The air had left his body in a rush, and he had to gasp to breathe. He tried calling Sara, who was in the kitchen pottering about, but nothing came out. There was nothing there, just a desperate wheeze. He had to get up and walk to the kitchen door to see her. She had glanced at him and he knew he didn't have to say anymore. He had just gestured to her to come, and they had sat in front of the TV watching it all unfold.

He supposed later that he should have phoned someone, but at the time there was just no way he could have. He was, he realised, suffering from shock.

They watched the long walk to the school, before the man and Lucy disappeared over the bridge and away from the TV cameras. There was an overhead shot, but there was no real detail, so the reporters had just filled the time with speculation. But no one really knew what was happening and that was the worst part. They just had to wait and wait. There were rumours that they had escaped, there was speculation that the very worst had happened.

It was about an hour later when someone knocked on the door. Two policemen asking if he was Mark Morris's brother.

He thought he had handled it well; he had remained stoic and composed, and had asked the police to come in. Sara made them cups of tea and they discussed what had happened that night. That's when he found out his brother had really was in the hospital. This came as a relief as some TV reporters had reported that Mark had died.

The injuries were bad, but they were all ok and Lucy was safe. Now she needed somewhere to stay.

Of course, they would take her in, Sara said.

The child was distraught, but she had eventually cried herself to sleep in Sara's arms. Then, when she was deep asleep, they had put her down on the settee with a blanket over her and waited.

He didn't know exactly what he was waiting for. Morning probably. If that Shadowman could travel through darkness like the TV said he could, then there could be no rest. The fact that the beast had been captured meant nothing. John was too paranoid, too saddened and shocked to relax.

The night had a strange quality. His body felt tired, the lights seemed too bright and there were moments when his eyelids wanted to defy him and close. Yet, at the same time, his mind was racing, and everything seemed to have developed a hyper-reality that he found disconcerting.

When the phone rang, he was sitting on the settee at Lucy's feet watching the News Channel, which seemed to be constantly repeating itself. On the chair closest to the kitchen was one of the Policemen. PC Bright. A strange name, John had thought when they were introduced. He was tall and officious looking, but had a sad and empathetic smile which John liked. On the dining table the other side of the room, sat Sara and PC Graham Evans - who John knew from school. Graham was a tough man with hard features and many scars from various battles. In school he had been a bit of a bully, but John was glad he was here now.

The atmosphere was heavy and had a silence which not even the low chatter from the TV could spoil. When the ringtone – one of those standard mobile tones that seemed to be everywhere – sounded, it seemed alien and incongruous. Even Lucy stirred in her sleep.

PC Evans reached into his breast pocket and took out the phone.

'Hello? Yeah....' He said.

John could see the change on the man's face. He went from a relaxed boredom to fully alert. His eyes widened and his jaw dropped. His roughness seemed to evaporate and was replaced by an alert fear. PC Paul Bright sat up straight, aware of the change in his partner. Suddenly the air became thick, as if the oxygen was slowly turning to soup.

'Yeah, I understand.'

He turned the phone off and stood up.

'He's gone,' he said. 'He's escaped.' There was no need to say who he was speaking about.

'What?' Sara asked. 'When?'

'About ten minutes ago.'

'Ten minutes!' John had to hold back the rage. 'What do you mean ten minutes? Why'd it take so long to tell us?'

'They had to double check. We need to turn on the lights. Paul, you turn the kitchen light on and I'll start up-'

He didn't finish. His gaze caught something behind John and his face went white with fear. John didn't have to turn to see what, or who, was there. He just knew. In his gut, in his groin and in his bowels, he knew. But he had to turn to see.

Sara screamed and PC Bright stood up quickly, positioning himself in between the Shadowman and Lucy. The girl was beginning to stir, disturbed by the sudden noise. He was standing in the doorway to the kitchen. There was darkness behind him, profound shadows that seemed to have regurgitated this giant of a man. The kitchen was always dark – the hill rose steeply out the back of the house and it often blocked the sun until almost mid-day – but this morning this darkness seemed deeper than it should, as if it were a living thing.

John stood quickly and had to ignore a slight dizziness in his head. He leaned down and lifted the groggy - but now almost awake - Lucy into his arms, then he backed away towards the door to the hallway. PC Bright, stepped closer to the Shadowman, his hands reaching onto his belt to grab hold of his taser.

'Don't come any closer,' he shouted. 'I'm armed.'

The Shadowman took no notice of him at all. He just stared beyond him at the little girl in John's arms. John inched further backwards, not taking his eyes off the giant for one moment. Afraid even to blink.

Shadow took a step forward.

'Get back,' Bright shouted again. 'I'm warning you.' The taser was now raised and aimed at Shadow, although there was a very noticeable shake in his hands.

'I'm warning you one last time, sir. Step back into the kitchen or I will -'

A massive muscled arm shot up with surprising speed and accuracy, and grabbed Bright by the neck. All the time, Shadow stared at the girl. The policeman began to choke under the iron grip of those humongous hands.

'Give me the girl,' he scowled. 'I will let the Peeler live.'

John continued to step back towards the door, one hand

reaching around the girl and the other extending blindly to find the door handle.

'If you leave now, I will still have the girl, and you will all die this hour. Which is it?'

Lucy hand begun to weep and squirmed in her uncle's grip. He tried to hold her tighter but, with only one free hand, he found this increasingly difficult.

'You hurt my Mam and Dad,' she cried. 'You were my friend, but you hurt my parents and tried to hurt me in the street.'

'No,' the Shadowman said. His voice was calm and almost soothing. 'I tried to free you from the grips of that priest. He worships the false God. I was trying to protect you.'

'No! You tried to kill them!' Her sobs had turned into convulsions and for a moment John thought he was going to lose his grip on her. He grabbed the door handle and pulled it down. The door swung open but instead of stepping out of the room, Lucy tried pulling away from him. It took everything he had to hold on to the girl.

'Don't talk to him Lucy,' he said.

'You cannot leave,' Shadow replied. 'I will kill you and I will get the girl.'

Graham Evans stepped in front of John and the girl, his taser aimed at the man. There was a chair in front of him which he pushed towards the Shadowman.

'Get out now,' he hissed at John and Lucy. 'Run!'

Shadow sneered, holding PC Bright - whose struggles were starting to diminish – in front of him. Then, with a movement surprisingly quick for such a huge man, he snapped Bright's neck and threw his prone body across the room. It collided with Evans who was sent sprawling to the ground.

Sara grabbed her husband from behind, then pulled him and Lucy into the narrow hallway which led to the front door.

'You run and you will die!' Shadow bellowed. 'Give me the girl. I will let you live.'

'Never, you won't get her, ever.' John shouted back. Sara had opened the front door and John felt the cool breeze behind him.

Then Lucy screamed.

'You won't hurt them! You won't!'

She pulled herself free from her uncle's hands and scrambled away from him. Not away from danger but straight at the Shadowman. To John, it all seemed as if it was in slow motion. He tried desperately to reach for her, but she was already too far away from him. Sara, not realising that her husband was no longer holding Lucy, continued to pull him towards the front door.

'Lucy,' he shouted. She ran back into the living room, stepping over the police officers.

'Don't hurt them!' Lucy cried again. She jumped at the giant and he took her into his arms. She thrashed about widely, trying desperately to hit him. Shadow pulled her close to him, pinning her arms down beneath one of his huge biceps, ignoring her histrionics.

Shadow turned to John who was a few steps behind. He lifted his free hand to the man and John couldn't help but stop in the middle of the room.

'You have been reprieved,' Shadow said.

Sara screamed Lucy's name; she pushed her husband out of the way and tried to catch the man herself, but he stepped out of the light of the living room and into the twilight shadows of the kitchen, pulling the door behind him. By the time John and Sara opened the kitchen door, the Shadowman and their niece, whose safety they had been charged with, were gone.

Although it was dark, John didn't feel that it was dark enough for the Shadowman to disappear. The morning light had risen over the mountain behind their house and there was enough for him to see the fittings perfectly well. Then he turned to his right and looked behind him. This was the area under the stairs, the place they put their coats, their shoes and items such as the vacuum-cleaner and mop. Even in the brightest of sunny days, this little alcove was dark most of the time. Now, as a new morning was dawning, it was almost completely black.

John reached for the light switch and flicked it on.

There was no one there.

He turned back to the kitchen where is wife was crying. PC Evans stood behind her, his hair, shirt and general appearance was dishevelled. A trickle of blood run down his chin from a busted lip.

'They're gone,' John said. The words sounded hollow. Of course, they were gone.

From far away they could hear sirens coming towards the house. The front door opened, and policemen and women poured in.

But John Morris knew they were too late.

CHAPTER 46

Gareth's face was ashen as he put his mobile phone into his pocket.

'He's got her,' he said. 'We have to hurry.'

Morgan felt his stomach drop and a deep unease prickle his skin. Only a few minutes before, Mike had told them they were almost there, then the phone rang for a second time and the chapel, which was just a hundred yards beyond a copse of trees, seemed both scarily close and much too far away. He wanted nothing more than to get the girl and finish all this forever. He felt both cowardly and anxious to get it done. Whether these two emotions were truly compatible, he didn't know. What he did know, what he felt in the pit of his stomach, was that it would all be over soon. For better or for worse.

The group gathered together and Morgan felt himself almost crouching down, as if they were going into battle – which, he supposed, they just might be doing.

'Mike?' Gareth said. 'It's just beyond those trees, yeah?'

Mike nodded. Morgan noticed that the forestry man was suddenly looking very nervous. He hadn't been part of this over the last few days, he had just watched it on TV; and now he was possibly only a hundred yards from a supernatural murderer.

'OK, Mike, you can stay here, ok?' Gareth continued. 'Cat, Morgan, I need you to stay here too.'

'Wait a minute,' Catryn interrupted.

'No!' Gareth said. 'You are staying here. I don't know what's through those trees but, whatever it is, it's dangerous and, if we're looking after you, then we can't be looking after the girl, ok?'

Morgan nodded.

'OK,' he said.

'Catryn?'

Catryn paused then gave a very reluctant nod. She didn't look too happy about it, though.

'Jimmy,' Gareth continued, looking at his father-in-law. 'Is there any way you can do, whatever it is you have to do, from here?'

Jimmy's face was white. Morgan knew that his friend's back was hurting again, but this seemed more than just pain. He was scared and after all he had been through, Morgan couldn't blame him.

'No, I have to be there. We have to consecrate the ground.'

'Are you sure?' Gareth insisted. 'Ten minutes ago, I was willing to steak everything on you being right, but now? I don't know. It's all real now.'

Jimmy nodded.

'I understand. After all that you have seen the last few days, after all you've witnessed with your own eyes, do you know of any other way to do this?'

'No,' Gareth said. 'I just feel like I am out of my fucking depth here. Sorry about the language.'

'Don't be sorry, but I will tell Jenny when we get home.'

Gareth smiled.

'You have my permission,' he said. 'OK, try to keep behind us. Williams and Connelly will lead, I'll be second, and you stay behind me. Ok guys?'

Connelly and Williams nodded. Both their faces were masks of control and concentration. It was, Morgan supposed, what they call the 'game face'.

The two policemen moved forward, their guns up and aiming in front of them. They moved towards the trees in a smooth, slightly crouched posture, then signaled to Gareth to follow.

'OK, here goes,' he said. 'Jimmy.'

Jimmy nodded. His eyes were wide with apprehension, but he had a determined expression. He had a small backpack on his shoulder which he hoisted into a comfortable position.

'What's in the bag?' Morgan asked.

'Bible,' Jimmy replied. 'My weapon of choice.'

He smiled ruefully then followed Gareth towards Williams and Connelly. Morgan could see them conferring quietly before they began moving through the trees and towards the old chapel.

Morgan and Catryn waited silently for a few minutes. He could feel the knot tighten in his stomach but didn't know what to do about it. They were as helpless here as they would have been if they had stayed at home. In fact, it was worse here. They were too close not to worry, but not yet close enough to offer any help should they need it.

'I can't stand this,' Catryn said.

'I know what you mean,' he replied. 'I wish I knew what was happening, or at least, what is going to happen?'

'Come on then,' Catryn said, and began walking towards the trees. 'We're only going to watch.'

Morgan looked at Mike but the council man shook his head vigorously.

'No way man,' he said. Morgan nodded and turned to follow Catryn.

At the trees, they crouched down until they were flat on the ground. The grass was a little damp beneath them, and Morgan was aware of a stone digging into his hip, but he dared not move too much. He certainly didn't want to tip off anyone that they were there, and he didn't want to embarrass himself in front of Catryn.

The sky was cloudy, and the breeze was cool on his face. The trees rustled loudly around them, so he couldn't hear anything. But, as the morning grew brighter, he could see clearly enough.

About fifty feet away he could see the giant form of Shadow.

He was standing with his back to them at an angle, his hands down on his sides, his head bowed. His form was unmistakable, and it sent a shiver down Morgan's spine. He wore the same black clothes he had been wearing in the supermarket, although he had removed the hat.

Connelly, Williams, Gareth and Jimmy were crouching down, moving to their left until they were only thirty feet to the Shadow's side. The guns were trained on the giant and the two gunmen moved with the resolute determination Morgan knew only from movies. Jimmy looked completely out of place. He was about ten feet behind the two gunmen and looked the picture of hesitation and clumsiness. Gareth slowed until he was alongside Jimmy. He put his hand onto his father-in-law's shoulder. Jimmy leaned toward him and whispered something.

Morgan felt the tightness grip him harder. It looked like Jimmy had seen something. There was a tension in his body that made Morgan feel very nervous.

'Shit,' Whispered Catryn. 'Oh no.'

Morgan looked up to Shadow, who had now raised his hands above his head. In his hands there was what looked like a giant knife.

***

Jimmy's heart sank when he saw the little girl lying on the floor at the feet of the monster. She looked as if she had been tied down, her hands and feet bound. She thrashed about but with little energy, and Jimmy instinctively realised that the girl was completely exhausted. The fight in her now was just embers of the resilience that had so impressed him the night before.

He felt so sorry for her. She was an innocent caught up in the most horrific of circumstances. A small child whose life was in danger just because of a name.

He had stopped walking and now just stared at her, almost paralysed with doubt. What could he do? Should he charge at them? Would that just quicken whatever evil was in store for her? Should he just stand back and wait until there was an opportunity to do what he still believed needed doing, even if it meant sacrificing Lucy? He felt, rather than heard, Gareth moving beside him. Gareth, the man who must be as exhausted as he felt, who had proven himself to be a truly great man these last few days, a rock on which Jimmy believed he could always rely on. His son-in-law put his hand on Jimmy's shoulder and Jimmy couldn't help but feel the love, warmth and control that the detective radiated. It made him relax for the briefest moment.

Then Shadow lifted his hands up above his head and Jimmy saw the dagger. There was no other way to describe it. It wasn't just a knife, it was a dagger, a ceremonial device, that would bring an end to Lucy's life.

There was a rush of blood coursing through his veins and into his head. There was no more worrying about decisions.

'No!' he shouted. The word came from deep down inside him, and he felt a resurgent energy come from it.

He started to run. He forgot about Gareth and the other policemen. All he could see was the knife hover in the air.

'Fire!' Gareth shouted from behind him.

There was the rapid thunder of gun fire echoing all around.

Shadow faulted, then turned to the policemen who fired again and again at him. His body was knocked back from the impact, the dagger fell from his hands, and he cried out in pain and fury.

'Jimmy, wait!' Gareth yelled, chasing behind him.

But Jimmy didn't wait. He kept on running, seeing only the giant and the little girl. Shadow stepped backwards, his body jerking as each bullet slammed into his chest. There seemed a moment of indecision, then he turned and sprinted about ten yards away from the remains of the chapel and took cover behind some trees. Jimmy was only a few feet away, his focus was entirely on Lucy. He ran towards her with no thought other than freeing her. She was his responsibility. The bond that they had together, created only a few hours before, propelled him on. Then he stumbled in the high grass and came crashing to the ground. His body shook as the impact spread and he felt a shuddering pain shoot up his spinal cord. He called out in agony and for a moment everything faded. All he was aware of was the discomfort in his back and, perversely, the smell of the grass around his face.

Gareth caught up with Jimmy and passed him quickly, leaving him prone on the floor. The detective crossed a threshold of rocks that had once made up one of the outer walls of the chapel. Inside, he glanced around and, seeing nothing to concern him, he crouched down beside Lucy. Jimmy lifted himself up, grunting painfully with every move. His vision wavered for a moment and he had to fight an awful urge to throw-up. Through bleary eyes he saw Gareth reach down, throw his backpack down in front of him and take out a switchblade. He opened it quickly and began cutting the ropes that held Lucy down.

'It's OK,' he said. 'We've got you. 'Your safe now.'

Jimmy was now up on his hands and knees. His head was swimming and he had a momentary loss of focus. He didn't want to move his head, afraid that the smallest motion would be too painful to endure.

The trees seemed to sway around him, the greens and browns were just a blur for a moment, before everything became to focus again.

He looked up at Gareth, who had untied the girl's hands and was now moving to her feet.

Then something caught Jimmy's attention. He looked behind Gareth and saw a shape approaching. It wasn't Shadow, it was much smaller and its form was almost fuzzy, with no obvious outline. For a moment Jimmy couldn't help thinking that it was just his head playing tricks with him. He was almost certainly concussed. He understood that.

But then the form became clearer. It was a man, a short man with sharp features and a pointy nose, and he was creeping slowly up behind Gareth.

'Oh, my God,' Jimmy said.

Gareth looked up at him, his face curious. Somewhere in the distance gun shots could be heard once more, but they seemed almost as if they were just background.

The figure now stood directly behind Gareth who was still unaware of anything other than the job at hand.

'What?' Gareth asked.

'Sir Henry,' Jimmy whispered.

Gareth frowned, obviously not understanding what Jimmy was talking about.

Then, in one swift movement, the figure reached down and grabbed Gareth by his hair.

Gareth screamed in fright and pain. He was yanked to his feet, his face contorted with agony. The figure put his arms around Gareth's neck and pulled him closer to him. Then he turned and looked directly at Jimmy.

'You must be the devil dodger that Shadow has been telling me all about.'

Jimmy gritted his teeth and lifted himself up until he was standing, albeit more than a little unsteadily.

'And you must be Charles Henry, murderer of children,' he said.

The figure smiled. His body was indistinct and in closer inspection, Jimmy could see that he seemed to be almost transparent. He wore what looked like a suit with a large cravat poking out from his collars. His face was odd. It was almost that of a Victorian gentleman, smart and professional, yet, at the same time, there was something beneath it, like a superimposed image that wasn't quite in tune with his face. This other face looked more like a skull, not the cleaned skulls that you saw on TV, the type that Hamlet would have lamented over, but the bones on which rotting flesh still clung. There was the glimpse of sinew on the jaws which stretched thin as he spoke. His eyes were cold and malevolent, set in sockets that were also visible. They were deep and empty.

Even his hair seemed affected. On top it was smooth and well-kept, but below it was stringy, gaunt and fragile. He looked like he was both alive and dead; of this world and the next.

Jimmy's head seemed to be clearing but he couldn't be certain; not with the clash of images before him. He stood up slowly, wincing as the pain in his back struck one more time.

Gareth struggled but Henry's grip was strong. Jimmy could see Gareth's bright red face as ghostly hands gripped his neck, slowly crushing his larynx.

'Leave him be,' Jimmy said, trying to sound commanding.

'Why, Priest? I might not have power over you, but I can still crush this man's neck. I can still get to you other ways.'

Henry's voice also seemed to be that of two different people, speaking at the same time. One smooth and controlled, the other course and grating, as if it emanated from a voice box which had gone putrid and rancid with decay.

'Gareth is a Christian,' Jimmy said, taking a tentative step forward.

'Of course, he is,' Sir Henry said. 'Yet his faith doesn't seem strong enough to repel me, does it.' He pulled tighter and Gareth gargled.

Jimmy took another step forward. They were now only five feet away from each other and Jimmy could smell the fetid aroma of decomposition.

He's transforming, Jimmy thought. This is it, he's coming alive.

Jimmy stopped and looked down at Lucy who was staring up at Sir Henry with terrified and disbelieving eyes. He stooped down to her and began helping her up, pulling away the remnants of the rope that had been tied around her legs.

More shots rang out behind him, but Jimmy ignored them.

'Let her be, Priest!'

Jimmy ignored her, helping Lucy to her feet, then stepping in front of her.

'No, you let him go or I will take Lucy away and you will always be trapped here.'

The arrogance which had sparkled in Sir Henry's eyes dimmed for a flash, and he kept looking back from Jimmy to Lucy. There was a long moment in which Jimmy had the awful thought that maybe it wouldn't matter, that Henry had already won. Then, finally, the ghost relaxed his grip on Gareth and pushed the detective to the ground.

'You ok? Jimmy asked Gareth.

Gareth nodded and stood up slowly.

'Now, give me the girl,' Henry growled.

Jimmy ignored him.

'You sure you're ok, Gareth?'

Gareth stepped away from Sir Henry and out of the confines of the chapel.

'Now! Devil Dodger!'

Jimmy turned around to Lucy and bent over so he could speak to her directly. Pain cascaded up his back as he did so. He took Lucy by the shoulders and looked straight in her eyes. He could see the fear, not just of the creature standing so close to them but, Jimmy suspected, at the thought that he might just be about to betray her.

'You ok?' Jimmy asked her.

She nodded but said nothing.

He leaned closer until they were millimeters apart.

'There are some trees directly behind you. Beyond them are some of my friends. Run Lucy, Run as fast as you can. Don't stop. Don't fall. Just run. You got that?'

She nodded again.

'As soon as I step towards him, you go. Don't dawdle or delay. Run!'

She nodded again, and Jimmy stood back up and turned to Sir Henry.

'Now,' the creature hissed. 'I want her.'

Gareth stood next to Jimmy and stared into his eyes.

'Don't do it,' Gareth said. 'Don't give her up.'

Jimmy smiled and took a deep breath.

Then he stepped quickly towards Sir Henry.

***

Catryn didn't know where to look. She could see Jimmy falling over and Gareth trying desperately to untie the girl's bounds. Meanwhile, not too far to the left of them, Catryn could see Connelly and Williams crouching down, aiming and occasionally firing at Shadow who was hiding behind some trees. He would look out every so often and the two policemen would open fire again.

It seemed to Catryn that they were trying to keep Shadow away from the chapel, so that Gareth and Jimmy could rescue the child. At least the monster wasn't going to be able to escape so easily, she thought. The sun was slowly climbing in the morning sky. He might rule the night, but she doubted he would be able to disappear so readily in the daylight. At least, she hoped not.

She felt a shiver run down her spine, but she didn't know if that was because she was lying flat on damp ground or if there was something else. Something she couldn't put her finger on, that was making her feel uneasy.

Shadow peeked out from begin the large bushy trunk and glanced over to the chapel. Almost immediately the bark in front of his seem to explode as it was hit by a bullet. Even at this distance she could see the puff of brown vaper.

'Something's wrong,' Morgan said.

She turned to him and saw the look of deep concentration on his face.

'What?' she asked in a whisper.

'Something is wrong, they are not pinning him down, he's distracting them,'

She looked back, trying to see what he was seeing. Then she saw Jimmy trying to get up off the ground. It looked like he was saying something which caused Gareth to look up.

She saw the dark figure rise up behind Gareth. It moved slowly and with purpose. Almost smoothly, as if it was in complete control of itself and its surroundings.

It reached down and grabbed Gareth, yanking him up. The early morning, the breeze that blew through the trees, the sun in the sky, all faded from her attention.

Beside her Morgan was up on his hands and knees, and she could feel the tension coming from his body. She felt the same. She was aware of the blood coursing through her veins, as if she could feel it. Not just a pulse but a rush. There were more gun shots, but she didn't look to see what was happening. It was as if she had tunnel vision.

The stranger seemed to throw Gareth to the ground, and Jimmy turned and bent down to the little girl.

Catryn got up and set herself as if she were ready for a school race. Her hands wide in front of her, resting on the ground. One leg tucked up almost to her belly, the other stretched out behind her. She knew that something was about to happen.

Jimmy turned back from the child, making sure he was standing directly between her and the mysterious figure. Catryn felt her extremities tingle, the tips of her fingers and her toes, poised for whatever was about to happen.

She saw Jimmy take a step closer then:

Lucy began to run. She turned quickly and scarpered, her little legs rising high and crookedly off the ground like children often did. Catryn didn't hear anything, just focused on the girl who was now only 30 yards away.

'Oh, fuck,' Morgan whispered.

Gun fire erupted again but this time it was sustained. One shot then another, then another. Rapid bursts that echoed around the little valley they were in.

Catryn glanced over to the left and saw that Shadow had left the trees and was now belting towards the girl. She could see the bullets hit him, could see the ripples across his body as they impacted.

He stumbled, almost falling, from the sheer force of the projectiles, but he kept running. He was going to catch the girl.

That was his intention. That was probably the plan all along.

Catryn lifted herself off the ground with the grace of a sprinter and started running herself, desperately trying to intercept the girl before the beast could catch her.

***

Sir Charles Henry shook his head and cackled. It wasn't so much a laugh, more a grating on the voice box.

'I admire your attempts at delaying me, but that is all they will do,' he said. 'In a moment, Shadow will get her and bring her back. There is nothing you can do about it.'

Jimmy tried ignoring the ghost. He had to fight the almost overwhelming urge to turn around and look back, to make sure the girl got away. He stepped over what had once been the outside wall of this pathetic idea of a chapel. He could see that it was very small – maybe fifteen feet by twenty. Hardly enough to fit in a proper congregation.

Yet he also felt the soothing texture of history and his faith. This was where real Christians had come, not the 'got to go to church to keep up appearances' sort. There were a few of those in his Church, he knew. How many of those would have trudged up the mountain in all types of weather every Sunday to worship?

Just to worship their own way, in their own language.

'Welcome to my home, preacher man.' Henry continued. 'My old home, I should say.'

Jimmy reached behind him and took out the Bible from his rucksack.

'You can throw that book away, priest,' Henry said. 'I worship a greater god. A god that has brought me back from his Kingdom, so I can serve him further.'

Jimmy tried to smile and hoped that he appeared more confident than he felt. The truth was his back pain was excruciating. He had hurt himself during the fall and now was struggling just to keep upright.

He also tried his best to ignore the activity around him. He could hear the gun shots, he was certain he could hear Catryn calling Lucy.

'That is not true. The Bible says that even demons believe in God – and shudder.'

Henry spat an invisible mouthful of phlegm to the ground.

'That is what I think of your fucking god!'

Jimmy took a step forward, towards Sir Henry.

'Why kill those children?' he asked?

Henry tried to smile, but the two faces couldn't seem to match this time, and the skull beneath his skin just opened in a loathsome and hideous way.

'I have not been killing them,' he said. 'I have been liberating the children of my lover so that they may help me live again. She has gifted their souls to me.'

'Where is she?' Jimmy asked.

'When I return to the world, I will bring her back too.'

There was a call in the distance. A scream of determination and madness. Jimmy desperately wanted to turn around, but he knew he had to block it all out.

'Who were the girls?' he asked. He didn't know if this was the right line of questioning, but he wanted to know why these poor children had to suffer and give so much.

'They were the returned souls of my dear Lucinda. The children of my darling lover and fellow worshipper of the true god.'

'They were just children! Defenseless children,' Jimmy spat.

He took another step forward, then another. He was doing so now out of anger rather than courage, but it didn't matter. He knew in his heart what he needed to do.

'And they will forever be, just like my Lucy, they will be forever,' Charles Henry said.

Jimmy shook his head and took another step. This time Henry stepped backwards, as if careful not to get too close to the priest.

'They shed innocent blood, the blood of their sons and daughters, whom they sacrificed to the idols of Canaan,'

Jimmy said.

There was another scream in the distance, this time a man in pain. Jimmy felt his heart quickening and a sharp pain beneath his ribcage.

'Don't have a heart attack now,' he thought.

'Precisely,' Sir Henry said, smiling.

Jimmy took another step forward and Henry retreated further.

'You will never leave here, demon,' Jimmy said. 'Never.'

'You might believe so now.'

Jimmy looked down and opened the Bible at a passage he had saved. Then he looked up and took a quick step towards the ghost. Henry didn't step back quickly enough and suddenly the blue light flashed again. Jimmy felt a wave of confidence in himself and God.

'Get back, bitch fucker!' Henry hissed, moving further away. They were more than halfway from where the far wall would have once stood and, soon, Jimmy hoped, Henry would be running out of space to retreat.

Jimmy looked down at the book in his hands and moved his finger down the page.

'The Lord said, "Take off your sandals from your feet, for the place where you are standing is holy."'

'Go to hell, god fucker!'

Jimmy took another step forward. Henry was almost at the other boundary.

'This place is holy,' Jimmy said. 'This is holy ground. The walls have fallen, and grass is growing where there once was stone or wood, but the ground itself is holy and will always remain so. There is nothing you can do about it.'

Suddenly there was a high-pitched scream followed by another. There was no doubt that this last one belonged to a child.

Jimmy couldn't help but turn to look, and Henry couldn't help but laugh.

***

Morgan watched as Catryn run off across the small field towards the girl. He lay there for a few moments, almost stiff with indecision and, what? Cowardice?

Maybe. He didn't want to think of that right now. He needed to stop thinking, focus on the situation and *do*!

The gunshots echoed around him. He looked up and saw Shadow running from the trees at the far end of the clearing. He was heading straight for the child. And straight for Catryn.

He could see the bullets catching Shadow as he ran, but few of them seemed to have any effect. His skin rippled as they impacted him, but that was all.

What the hell am I supposed to do? he thought.

He stood up, determined not to think. Catryn and Lucy were in trouble and they needed help. He didn't know what help he could give them, but he had to try. He stepped forward and his foot hit an old tree branch. The leaves were gone, and it looked like it was on the verge of rotting away. Morgan instinctively stooped down and picked it up. Then he ran.

He had always been a good runner in his younger days, but they were far behind him now and he wasn't as fit as he used to be. Within a few yards, he was already puffing.

God, I need a drink, he thought. But then all those glasses of wine no doubt contributed to the state he was in now.

He was about ten yards behind Catryn, and he could see her reaching Lucy and scooping the child up in her arms. There was hope, he thought. They could do this.

Then he glanced over to his left and saw Shadow gaining. There was no way Catryn could get away now. She turned and started to run back towards their hiding place. What was she expecting to do then? There was nowhere to go.

He quickly glanced towards the chapel, but he couldn't make out any detail. He just hoped that whatever Jimmy was doing would work in time.

Catryn passed him quickly and, in between his gasping of

air, he could hear her grunting. She had a look of determined concentration and hardly seemed to notice that he was there. He turned back and saw Shadow barrel down on him.

Without really thinking it through, he stepped to the side and lifted the branch up over his shoulder. It was heavy and rough in his hands, which shook with a fear that was consuming him right now.

Shadow was only a few feet away - ignoring Morgan just as he had ignored the bullets that had been slamming into him - when Morgan swung the branch.

He swung it as high as he could, trying to get the beast square in the face and, to Morgan's huge surprise, it connected.

The branch seemed to explode into a puff of dust, splattering all over the monster's face. Shadow seemed to fall off balance for a moment. The dust caught him in the eyes, and he stumbled to a halt, coughing and spluttering.

Morgan just stood there in a daze, watching as Shadow's disorientation overwhelm him briefly. All too briefly. The demon spat a huge gob of phlegm and saliva on the ground, shaking his head as he did so. Then he turned to Morgan, his upper lip curled with hatred and anger.

Morgan couldn't pull his eyes away. This was the man who he had seen in the supermarket all those thousands of years ago (the day before yesterday, was it?). The man who had stolen children, who had terrorised a community - *his* community – and was able to disappear into darkness. This was the supernatural being who had brought nightmares to young and old, all over the world, who provided confirmation to millions that there was more to life than normal people could ever believe.

His face was as ugly as Morgan remembered, strong with deep features. There was no laughter in this face. The only amusement it enjoyed came from the punishing of the innocent. The eyes were black and small compared to the rest of the head. His forehead overhung his eye sockets, his nose was almost flat to his face, his lips were thick and broken, and inside his mouth his tongue looked black.

It was the face of pure evil. Morgan could almost feel his own body lose control.

He knew, deep down in the recesses of his consciousness, that he had to run, but he just couldn't move.

Shadow stood up straight. Morgan followed the beast's eyes, until he was looking upwards at a steep angle. Shadow's hands shot out quickly, grabbed Morgan by the neck and lifted him off the ground. Then, in one swift movement, Morgan was sent tumbling through the sky. His throat felt like it had been crushed and he struggled to breathe. He felt heavy and leaden, even though he was several feet off the grass. It didn't slow down like in the movies and his life didn't flash in front of him, yet everything seemed crystal clear. The trees that somersaulted over him, every blade of grass below him, the clouds in the sky, were all images from a high definition television.

Then he fell to the ground. He felt his head hit something hard, and he felt his neck extend at an excruciatingly awkward angle.

These were the last things that Morgan saw before everything went black and the world disappeared from him.

***

By the time Catryn returned to the trees she had previously been hiding in with Morgan, she began to realise that she didn't have a plan. Lucy was beginning to get very heavy in her arms and the cars were much too far away for her to get to before Shadow caught up with her. She stopped briefly and looked around for Morgan, but he was no longer there. Then she remembered, a flickering image of him running past her a few seconds ago.

She turned back in time to see Shadow wiping something out of his eyes, then turn and stand over Morgan, a giant and a mouse in a stand-off. She saw Shadow lifting her friend up by the neck and throwing him aside.

Almost immediately, Connelly and Williams who were

standing somewhere to the left of her, opened fire once more, but it didn't seem to make any difference. Shadow turned towards her and stared her right in the eyes. His fat lips curled into what may have been a smile, or probably a sneer, and then he began running towards them.

His huge legs almost bounded over the grass.

Catryn turned away and began to run. Lucy swung around in Catryn's arms and she gasped as she looked directly at their pursuer.

Catryn had only managed three or four steps when she heard the violent rustling of branches behind her. She continued running, not caring where she was going, only relying on instinct and hoping for sheer luck.

Then she felt those monstrous hands grab her hair and pull her backwards.

She screamed as her momentum carried her forward, even as the power of his grip pulled her back. She fell forcefully onto the ground, on top of the girl. Lucy screamed loudly and Catryn felt the pain in her ears, matching the pain in her back she felt from the fall.

She rolled away from Shadow and on to her belly. Looking up, she could see him reach down and lift Lucy up by her legs. The girl screamed again and thrashed about furiously, but she was just an irritant compared to the power of this giant.

He wrapped his hands around her and, ignoring Catryn, turned and walked back in the direction of the chapel. It had all happened so quickly that it hardly seemed real at all.

'Freeze!'

Catryn saw Williams standing at the entrance to the clearing, his gun aimed straight at Shadow.

'Get down on the ground now or I'll shoot!'

Catryn scrambled to her feet.

'Don't shoot,' she called. 'He's got Lucy.'

'Put her down!' This was Connelly, who had appeared to the Shadow's left, but Shadow seemed not to notice.

Catryn limped behind him. She could feel a wetness around

her knee and suspected it was blood, but she couldn't look. All that mattered was Lucy.

They left the clearing quickly, all the time the two policemen were shouting at Shadow, throwing empty threats which had less impact than their bullets they had fired moments earlier.

Shadow carried Lucy with ease, and not even her kicking and screaming seemed to have any effect. He just carried on walking as if he was by himself, and that the exertions of the morning had meant nothing to him.

Catryn couldn't keep pace, the pain in her leg sent tears to her eyes and everything was becoming an indistinct blur.

Then she saw Morgan. He was lying off to one side in a heap. Her heart almost broke. He was dead, she was sure of it. This was her friend, the one who had welcomed her back home, the one who she had gotten closest to, the one she had opened up to.

She knew he wanted more and maybe that was never going to happen, but she had still loved him deeply over the last few days.

A sob wracked her body and she bent over to throw up. She coughed violently and spat phlegm into the grass. She wanted to go over to him, to cradle him and to stay with him until someone dragged her away, but she couldn't. Not yet.

Shadow was almost to the Chapel. She could see Gareth standing there, blocking the path, but even he had to move out of the way when Shadow and Lucy reached them.

Catryn didn't know what would happen if they crossed the threshold and into the chapel, but she knew in her heart that it would be devastating.

She felt an arm take hold of her and turned to see Williams standing beside her. His face was grim, and she saw her fears reflected in his hazel eyes.

'C'mon,' he said and put his arms around her. She put her arm around him and together they walked slowly to the chapel.

***

Jimmy watched Shadow step out of the trees and into the clearing. He was carrying the girl. The priest was mesmerised for a moment and almost forgot where he was. Then he heard the chuckling and he turned to see Sir Henry looking at him, his hands clasped together in delight.

Jimmy felt doubt for the first time. He had come with an inner knowledge of what needed to be done, but now time was running out and instead of winning the day, he was standing in front of the living dead who seemed to delight in the current situation.

He looked down to his Bible and tried to find where he was, but the last few moments seemed lost to him. It was as if all the confidence, all the inspiration, was gone. He had been in control and he had been sure he could have defeated this evil, but, in a flash, it was all gone.

Sir Henry peered at him intently.

'What is it, preacher?' he asked. 'Your god has left you? He has seen the hopelessness of the situation and he decided to vacate, live to die another day?'

Jimmy looked up at him, momentarily lost for words. He turned back to the clearing and saw Shadow approaching quickly. A cloud passed over the sun and he looked up at the sky.

Of course, back when Sir Henry was first buried here, there would have been a roof on the chapel. It would have had four walls, a door, possibly a window. It would have been full of worshippers coming to give thanks and praise to God. They would have felt the Holy Spirit in this place, it would have moved them and inspired them. It was a holy place. So holy that they knew that by burying Sir Charles Henry here, he would be confined for centuries to come.

'Do you no longer wish to speak, Devil Dodger? Isn't that what they call the likes of you?' henry taunted. 'Well, it looks like you haven't been able to dodge this particular devil, have you?'

Jimmy looked up at him. Henry was still standing directly in front of him. He hadn't moved. He hadn't tried to escape from the corner that Jimmy had pushed him into.

Why was that?

Then he remembered the blue light. Of course. Henry, for all his taunts, for all his confidence, couldn't move for fear of touching him, for fear of the blue light. Of Jimmy's faith. But there was only some much he could do with this power. He didn't think he could hurt both Henry and Shadow, not at the same time at least.

He heard footsteps to the side and saw Shadow step up to the chapel. The big man paused for an instant, then crossed the threshold where once had been a wall but now was nothing more than a scattered pile of rubble. This is what the forestry men had been removing.

It was the walls that had kept Henry imprisoned, wasn't it. That was why he had been brought here. To be confined within the walls of a church. Churches were holy places, weren't they? They were in films. Places that vampires were unable to enter, places were the walking dead were barred.

An image flashed in his brain. A film. This often happened with Jimmy. He had seen so many that there always seemed to be some scene, some image or a particular bar of music that he could apply to a moment, however inappropriate.

It was from the John Carpenter film, The Fog. In the climactic scene the dead sailors who had been terrorising the town, burst through the windows and the doors of the Church, which was being used to house an artifact stolen from the revenant. The house was no longer scared; no longer holy. It was a classic moment from a favourite film.

'Ah, Shadow my friend,' Henry said. 'Nice of you to join us. Shall we proceed with the ritual?'

Jimmy didn't turn around. That image meant something, something important. He looked down at his feet, trying to jog his memory but nothing was coming. It was there in his mind, just beyond reach, tantalizing.

'Put the girl on the ground,' Henry told Shadow. 'Put her head in that direction, that's where our alter will be.'

Jimmy looked up, his eyes wide open.

The alter! That was it!

Henry chuckled again.

'Don't try to save her, priest! We can wait all day and into the night if we must. You have not slept in many hours, I can see it on your face. You look exhausted. Besides, if you try anything, I will send Shadow out to kill each of your comrades one at a time and bring their heads back to lay at your feet.'

Jimmy turned away from the ghost and looked to the ground again.

The alter!

A memory came back to him in a flash. It was of a few years ago. He had been showing the church to someone; a councilman, he seemed to remember, although that might not be completely accurate. It didn't matter now.

What mattered was a comment the person had made. He had looked at the alter and told everyone how impressed he was with it all, and it really was a place of worship. Mrs. Lewis, the wife of one of the Church Elders, seemed to take exception to this.

'We don't worship the alter,' she had said briskly. 'We worship God.'

It wasn't the old walls of the chapel that were holy, it wasn't even the land itself. It was this place. It was a place of faith. It was faith that kept the ghost in check. In the film, the walls had been breached as they had here, although for very different reasons. When these walls came down, Henry believed the faith and the holiness that had captured him, was gone, and his prison was crumbling. Jimmy looked back at Henry and smiled. Maybe Morgan and Catryn had been right when they asserted that it was Henry's faith that was important and not just his own. Henry had been detained by shadows but, if the last few days had proven anything, shadows were powerful things.

Jimmy turned around and walked to Shadow, who seemed to hesitate for a moment. Then he stood over Lucy.

'Do you know what your problem is, Charles?' he asked, staring at Shadow.

'That is Sir Charles Henry to you, priest.'

Jimmy spun around and looked at the ghost. The two images were still there, the life and the death, the skin and the skull.

'You live in the past,' Jimmy continued. 'That's fine. The past was the time when you died and when you were imprisoned. It was the time when people discovered the evil inside you and did something about it. You see, they believed, like you did, that you would return. You made your bargain with the devil and as a result, you were imprisoned here for two hundred years.'

'Which ends this day,' Henry scoffed.

'Maybe, but the Bible says that anyone who is in Christ is a new creation. The old passes away and the new takes its place. You don't believe that yet, but I do because the Bible says it and I believe in the Bible. As do you.'

Henry sneered and spat at Jimmy's feet.

'You believed that the walls of this old church were what was holding you here, and when the walls came down, just like Jericho you might say, they lost their power. Is that right?'

Henry stepped towards Jimmy then looked passed him to Shadow.

'Get the knife, Shadow,' he said.

'The thing is, the walls are just brick and mortar. They are not holy. They are just stone. What's holy is the land you are standing on right now.'

Henry's eyes flashed, and Jimmy caught the ghost stealing a quick glance to the floor.

'And it's not just this soil,' Jimmy continued. 'It's the very earth, the rock beneath it, the trees around it, the sky above it.'

'Shadow! Get the knife now!' he spat, but Jimmy did not hear the giant make any movement behind him.

'You see,' Jimmy said. 'God said he laid the foundation for the earth. He is the foundation which means everything on earth is holy, whether you like it or not.'

'Lies,' Henry spat. 'Lies. I will make this land my own, in MY image!'

Jimmy began to walk forward, forcing Henry backward.

'When I stand here, I can feel the past, just like you can. I can feel the men and women worshipping here. I can feel the Holy Spirit surround us.'

'Liar!' Henry said again. 'Shadow, do it now.'

There was still no movement behind him. Jimmy continued forward until Henry was forced once more into the corner. There was a pile of bricks, an outline of what used to be the wall, and Henry was pushed back to it. The blue light flashed and a brief image of the wall that had once stood there shimmered into existence then disappeared.

Henry screamed out in pain and terror and tried to move forward only to touch Jimmy. The light flashed once more.

'Gareth, Catryn, Morgan, everyone, please step inside the Chapel,' he called. 'Quickly.'

He could hear the tentative steps of his friends and family enter the Chapel. Shadow grunted at them but otherwise didn't seem to react.

'Please,' Jimmy said, without turning to them. 'if you could all kneel in prayer. I take it you all know the Lord's prayer?'

There were some quiet, cautious voices, murmuring in agreement.

'Ok,' Jimmy said. 'let's pray,'

'GET AWAY FROM ME YOU GOD-FUCKER, YOU BASTARD!' Henry screamed on top of his voice. The skull beneath the skin seemed to lose coherence with the rest of him for a moment, creating an effect more horrifying than anything that Jimmy had seen previously.

Jimmy took a deep breath and reached out, grabbing Henry

by the shoulders. Blue light exploded between them. It flowed away and around them. Jimmy could see the ancient walls coming together again. Henry howled in pain, the two faces losing sync completely until they seemed to be totally at odds with each other. His eyes were wide in a malicious and hateful grimace, the sockets stared out blankly. hat had once been a sense of impending cohesion, now was two separate entities.

Jimmy felt a power run through him. It was both pleasurable and painful at the same time. He felt every muscle tense and his fists clenched, gripping Henry harder.

'Our father,' he began. 'Who art in heaven.'

Behind him he could hear the others praying with him. He needed them right now. He needed their faith, he needed the power of all that was Holy to get him through this. He needed his own faith and the faith of those who, two hundred years earlier, had buried Sir Charles Henry, the man who had a village named after him, a village that he had terrorised for decades. Jimmy felt these people, all long dead and forgotten to the modern world, flow through him.

'Hallowed be thy name.'

***

Catryn wanted to feel fear when she crossed into the chapel. She wanted to feel something, anything, instead of the dull exhaustion and pain that she now felt. With each step she had taken from the copse of trees where Lucy had been taken, passed Morgan's body and onto the ruins of the old chapel, her energy and her willingness to fight, evaporated. They had stopped outside the chapel boundaries and watched Jimmy and Henry. She didn't have a clue what they were doing, Jimmy looked glum, as if he had almost given up himself, and Henry kept chuckling. She had sort of zoned out after that and didn't know what was happening. Then she heard Jimmy's voice calling her to enter the chapel. It wasn't an easy step, but then it probably shouldn't have been. Seeing that monster standing in the corner leaning against what used to be a wall, should have been enough to terrify her, but she just felt numbed to it all.

The pain in her leg was really the only thing that was affecting her, and it sent flashes of bright light into her brain and before her eyes as she stumbled across the rubble. Williams steadied her and almost lifted her off the floor as her legs gave way.

She did wonder what it was that Jimmy was doing and why he wanted them all to join him. His voice had been strong and focused yet there was something here she didn't recognise. Was that a steely determination? Or just a psychotic acceptance that it was all over, there was nothing that could be done, and they may as well have a front row seat to it all?

She didn't know the answer and resigned herself to it being the latter. After all, she was going into a small area with the man who killed men, women and children, and had supernatural powers. What else could happen?

But as they crossed that pile of old rocks and into the flattened area that used to be a place of worship, she felt something different. It wasn't a religious thing but a real and present atmosphere.

Firstly, Shadow was not just standing in the corner, he was almost cowering there. When they came close, all he could do was grunt in a way that held no threat whatsoever. Secondly, Jimmy and Henry had seemed to have changed places. Jimmy now seemed to radiate a confidence that she hadn't noticed earlier. It was as if he was in command.

'Please,' Jimmy said, his voice calm and measured. 'If you could all kneel in prayer. I take it you all know the Lord's prayer?'

She glanced at Williams and Gareth who just shrugged. Connelly looked completely confused.

Jimmy was standing right over Henry who, like Shadow, was also cowering. Henry tried to maneuver but there was nowhere for him to go.

'GET AWAY FROM ME YOU GOD-FUCKER, YOU BASTARD!'

Then, inexplicably, Jimmy reached out, grabbed the ghost by its shoulders and the blue light flashed brightly.

***

Jimmy didn't flinch. He just stared at the ghost of Sir Henry.

'Our Father, who art in heaven,' he said.

Catryn knew the prayer, of course. Very few people didn't, even devout atheists, but this seemed like an odd place to hear them.

'Hallowed be thy name,' he continued. She also heard Gareth's voice as well. It was quiet but steady, and made her ashamed that she hadn't started praying with them yet.

'Thy kingdom come,' she said in unison with Jimmy and Gareth. This time Williams and Connelly could be heard mumbling the words too.

'Fuck you and your Christ!' Henry shouted in fury. Catryn could feel the words and the anger vibrate in through the air and hit her in the gut. She hated that creature, whatever he was. She saw that there was another image below his face, she saw the skull with its dead empty sockets, and she felt like throwing up.

'Thy will be done,'

Suddenly Jimmy thrust his hands forward violently, lifting Henry by the shoulders then pushing him back to where there had once been a wall. The ghost screamed as the blue light exploded around them. She could see the face and the skull losing sync and suddenly there were two people there – one transparent like the ghost that he was, the other, just the empty husk of a body.

The light didn't disappear this time, however. It spread up Jimmy's arms, engulfing his shoulders and his body. It did the same to Henry, then continued behind him, circling all around him.

The walls, Catryn noticed. The light was following the pattern where the walls of the chapel would once have been. She could see the bricks that had once stood, one upon the other. Then the light continued to the corners, where the next wall that travelled the length of the chapel began to reveal itself.

'On earth as it is in Heaven.'

She looked up and saw the ceiling. It wasn't a flat roof but raised at an angle like that of a modern building; until the two sides met at the apex. For some reason this surprised her. The effort it took for people to erect this building, miles from the town where they lived, was unreal, she thought. She felt a wave of emotion sweep over her as she recognised the dedication and devotion that these people had possessed. And they would have had to give it all up once Henry was buried here. There had been no other option. Their church had become a crypt and a prison, and they sacrificed it for the greater good. She didn't know how she knew this, but she felt its certainty.

The chapel continued to spread around her, and she watched in awe, the bright blue dazzling her eyes; but she couldn't drag them away from it. She had to look.

'Give us each day our daily bread.'

She was saying the words now without thinking. They just came naturally. It felt like a spiritual event was taking control of her.

She noticed the others felt it too. They all kneeled on the floor, looking around in awe at the spectacle that was occurring, the words coming out of their mouths almost instinctively.

The light reached Shadow in the corner and he cried out in pain and moved away from the newly revealed wall. Lucy moved away from him and put her arms around Catryn. Cat looked down at her and smiled, and she saw the same wonder in the little girl's eyes.

'And forgive us our trespasses.'

Then the people came. Blue images of presences long forgotten. They were standing and kneeling around the companions. Catryn turned to her right and saw a woman looking directly at her. The woman smiled and Catryn smiled back.

'As we forgive those who trespass against us.'

The woman repeated the lines, just as Catryn did. She did not say them in English but in Welsh, the language of their home, the reason this church had been built in the first place. She turned away from Cat and looked in the center of the room. There were men there, shovels in their hands, digging a deep hole. There was a growing pile of dirt by the door, as they dug deeper and deeper.

'And lead us not into temptation but deliver us from evil.'

Catryn turned back to Jimmy who continued to hold Henry up off the ground. The ghost still tried to fight back but his efforts were diminishing. He screamed loudly and Catryn could feel the vibrations deep in her gut. But Jimmy did not let go.

A spectral figure came to Jimmy, and Catryn could see an understanding pass between them. Jimmy nodded, then maneuvered the ancient, withering corpse to his right, handing it over to the blue figure. It took Sir Henry from Jimmy and carried him towards the hole. The coal baron no longer moved. It just slumped as even the afterlife left it.

'For Thine is the kingdom,' they all continued.

Jimmy was now facing the companions. He had a smile on his face which looked almost serene, except for the layer of sweat on his forehead. He looked at Cat and smiled.

'The power and the glory.'

The men dropped the remains of Sir Charles Henry into the hole. Then the dirt was shoveled onto of him, resealing the ancient grave. Ashes to ashes, she thought.

'Forever and ever.'

The figures finished quickly, then turned to each other with grim but relieved faces.

The woman next to Catryn turned to her and smiled.

'Amen,' they said together.

Then the woman reached over and stroked Lucy's hair. The child showed no fear, just sat there until the woman was finished. The woman then stood up and, with the others from the congregation two hundred years earlier, she walked out of the door, fading back into the past as they went. As they left the blue light began to fade, and with it the walls, the door and the ceiling. All that was left was a small heap of earth where the remains of Sir Charles Henry lay, buried once more, two centuries after they were first put into the ground.

Catryn stood up, wincing with pain. She glanced down and saw a dark patch running down the back of her leg. She reached and touched it, then brought her red tipped fingers up to confirm that it was blood.

'You OK?' Jimmy asked her.

She looked up at him, not sure what to say. There were so many questions to ask, so much ground to cover, however, at that moment, her mind was completely blank.

'What happened?' Gareth asked.

'He was buried, again.' Jimmy said. 'This time, I hope, for good.'

He smiled and looked around.

'Where's Morgan?' he asked.

'Oh, shit,' Catryn said, then caught herself swearing in a chapel. 'Sorry.'

She looked down the slope and pointed, the tears overwhelming her once more.

'He's dead.'

Jimmy sighed heavily and shook his head.

'Let's go and get him,' he said, wearily.

They were about to leave the area that a phantom chapel had stood only a few moments before, when Williams asked:

'Where is he?'

'Who?' Gareth replied.

'Shadow.' Williams said, looking around.

He was gone. The giant, the beast, the Shadowman, was gone. No one saw him go and no one really wanted to search for him.

'He's probably around here somewhere,' Jimmy said, 'but I doubt he can ever cause anyone harm again.'

He looked at Lucy and she wrapped her arms around him.

'Are you ok?' he asked.

She smiled.

'I think so. I don't know for sure.'

Jimmy nodded.

'That's exactly how I feel.'

They headed back down the slope towards Morgan. Connelly took off his gun and gave it to Gareth to carry. Then he lifted Lucy in his arms.

'We'll meet you back there,' he said, moving away from the group.

Gareth nodded, understanding that his friend and fellow officer was making sure Lucy was spared the horror of seeing Morgan's body.

The group limped on, slowly moving towards their fallen friend. He lay in some tall grass, flat on his back, his arms on his chest.

'He's moving,' Catryn said, a spring of hope in her belly. She rushed to him, dropping down beside him and reaching out to him.

'Where have you been?' Morgan croaked.

Catryn couldn't stop herself taking him into her arms and holding him tightly.

'You're alive' she said over and over again.

Gareth kneeled beside Morgan and looked into his friend's eyes.

'Don't you move,' he said, his voice almost breaking with relief. 'We'll get you help, you gonna be ok.'

Morgan tried to smile.

'I thought I was already dead, ' he said. 'I saw flashing lights everywhere and thought they were angels.'

Catryn could feel the tears falling down her cheeks.

'I suppose they were,' she said, her voice shuddering with emotion. 'In a way they were.'

Epilogue

CHAPTER 47

Morgan awoke with a stunning headache and almost every part of him was stiff.

The room was bright and noisy, and as he slowly came around, blinking until his eyes adjusted, he noticed that he was in a hospital bed. It was a private room, but the door was wide open and there seemed to be a lot of commotion outside. He tried to move but it just reminded him of the pain he was in. He grunted loudly. He had an itch on his leg and it was beginning to drive him mad.

'You're awake?'

He turned to his right and saw Catryn sitting on the chair beside him. She looked like she had been asleep, and she had to stretch in a funny angle. But at least she could stretch, he thought sardonically.

He tried it again. The pain shot up his back once more and so he gave up.

'You ok?' Catryn asked. 'Do you want me to call a nurse?'

'No,' he said. 'I'll be fine. Just give me a few moments.'

She looked good this morning, he thought. He had thought about the possibility of waking up next to her, but he had hoped it would have been in better circumstances than this.'

'What happened?' he asked. 'I can't remember how I got here.'

'It was two days ago. You came by air ambulance,' she said. 'They went the whole hog for you.'

'Yeah, did I deserve it?'

'You're my hero,' she replied, almost coyly.

'Yeah? I can't remember saving the day.'

Catryn laughed.

'That was Jimmy, you took on Shadow and gave him a smack in the face.'

'I did?' he said incredulously. 'Shit, I wish I could remember.'

'It'll come back to you. The doctor said you might be a bit shaken up for a while. You suffered quite a bit of trauma.'

'And how about you?'

Catryn lifted her leg. She wore a pair of baggy joggers that looked slightly too large for her. She rolled up the leg to reveal some bandages.

'Nasty cut,' she said. 'I needed twelve stitches. I'm going to be the proud owner of quite a scar.'

'That's all you got away with?'

'The bastard ripped out a load of hair; that wasn't nice, but I'll live.'

A silence fell between them, although Morgan hardly noticed. His head was pounding, and he really felt like he needed some drugs. Or a glass of wine.

'So,' he said. 'Is it over?'

Catryn nodded.

'Jimmy seems to think so, he's got this whole faith thing going on, you know.'

'You don't? After all we've seen?'

'You don't know the half of what we saw up there,' she replied. 'It's certainly opened my mind to the paranormal, to the supernatural and all that. I don't think we can deny that any more. But as for one big-ass dude up in space somewhere, twirling his beard and proclaiming this is good and this is shite, I'm not convinced.'

'What do you think then?'

'I don't know. It's only been two days, I haven't had time to process it all yet. Maybe I never will. How about you?'

Morgan tried to shake his head but that just sent the room spinning again.

'At the moment, I don't care. I just want some drugs.'

Catryn smiled and stood up.

'I'll get the nurse,' she said.

'No, it's ok,' Morgan said, but before he could say anything else, he heard a familiar high-pitched squeal.

'Daddy!'

Seren and David run into the room and almost jumped onto the bed with their father.

'Kids! What are you doing here?'

They started talking over each other and Morgan felt that happy little feeling inside that he always did when he was around them. He hadn't felt it a lot recently, and he knew that it was his fault. He made the hospital promise – as soon as I get out of here I'm going to change. I know how precious life can be.

He looked up passed Catryn and saw Chantel standing in the doorway. She looked as beautiful as ever. She had that natural aura that drew men to her. He had always loved and resented that about her. Sometimes he thought life was too easy for her.

Now she stood there and there was an awkwardness in the air as Chantel and Catryn met. Catryn introduced herself and they shook hands.

'Were you with him when his happened?' Chantelle asked. There was an accusatory edge to her voice that put Morgan on edge immediately.

'Chantel,' he said.

But Catryn just smiled.

'I was,' she said, then turned to Seren and David. 'Your dad is a real hero. He took on the Shadowman singlehandedly to rescue me and the little girl that had been kidnapped.'

'Is that right, dad?' David asked, excitedly.

'Well, I can't remember any of it but apparently it is,' he said.

'Cool, I can't wait to tell Jenson in school. He's going to be so jealous. My dad almost got killed by the Shadowman!'

Seren gave her brother a punch in the arm.

'He's a hero, dork.' She said.

As the kids started arguing, Morgan looked over to his ex-wife and his new friend. Catryn smiled at the children then headed for the door.

'I'll come back later,' she said. 'And I'll get the nurse with your medication.'

She disappeared out into the hall and Morgan felt a prang of regret. He knew he was attracted to her but, beyond that, he was completely confused. It wasn't something he needed to think about now though.

He turned to his kids.

'Ok, you got to be gentle but, how about a kiss for your old man?'

CHAPTER 48

The door opened and Donna smiled.

'I didn't think we would see you again,' she said.

Gareth smiled back.

'Well, Morgan is in hospital, so I thought I would come up and update the old grouch myself,' he said.

Donna nodded.

'I heard about Morgan, is he OK?'

'He'll be fine. Just needs a few days recovery, that's all.'

'Oh, that's good. Please come in.'

Gareth followed her into the house. The evening was cool with a pleasant freshness that Gareth enjoyed, but inside the house it was sweltering. As he crossed from the small hallway into the living room, it was like walking through a curtain of heat.

Donna looked at him and smiled.

'He thinks it's cold,' she said, nodding her head towards the old man sitting in the chair in front of the TV.

'What do you want?' Tal asked abruptly.

'Well, I was going to tell you about what happened up in the chapel,' Gareth said, 'but if you have better things to do then, perhaps I should go.'

Tal grunted.

'Well, you are here now, may as well sit down and get on with it. The quicker you finish the quicker I can get on with watching my programmes.'

Donna raised her eyebrows and smiled. Gareth crossed the room and sat in the chair next to Tal's.

'What are you watching?' he asked.

'I haven't got a fucking clue,' Tal replied. 'You banging the door woke me up.'

'Ok,' Gareth said. He adjusted the cushion behind him then reached for his tie, before remembering he was off duty and wasn't wearing one.

'Want a cuppa?' Donna asked.

'No thanks. I don't think I could stand any more heat,' he replied.

'Well, get on with it,' Tal barked.

'Ok,' Gareth said, patiently.

He recounted the events that had happened Monday night and into Tuesday morning in order as they occurred. This was something he was good at, something he had to do in work frequently, but instead of just the facts, he did try to add a little life to it as well.

Throughout, Tal was mostly silent, although he asked a few questions. Gareth was impressed by the man's attention for detail and thought that the questions were pertinent and insightful. This was the younger Taliesin Jones coming to the fore, the historian and researcher, and not the crude old man he had become. One thing Gareth wished, whatever was to happen to him in the future, he hoped and prayed that he wouldn't end up as hateful as this old bastard.

At the end, Tal sat back in his chair, his hands together, almost in prayer.

'My goodness,' Donna said. 'You must have been terrified.'

Gareth nodded.

'I think I still am,' he said.

'You really saw that?' Tal asked finally. 'You saw the Chapel as it was, and the people from two hundred years ago.'

'I think so. We certainly saw something. It was all bathed in blue, but it was there alright.'

Tal nodded.

'Well suck my dick,' he said, almost absentmindedly. 'I always used to tell my students that History could come alive, I never thought it literally.'

'Tal,' Gareth said. 'You have a wonderful use of the English language.'

'Fuck the fucking English language!' Tal spat. 'It's a bastard language, stolen off every other fucking language on this earth. That's the English for you: Start an empire to spread Englishness around the world and end up looting the places and bring it all here.'

Gareth laughed and stood up.

'Like I said, a wonderful use of the English language.'

Donna laughed as well.

'You sort of get used to it,' she said.

'Sugno fy ngheiliog!' he spat. 'How's that for you?'

'Nice,' Gareth said.

He crossed to the door and turned to Tal.

'Is he gone for good?'

Tal turned to him and Gareth was struck by the sudden intensity in the old man's eyes.

'There are stories about this godforsaken place. And I mean that, it is godforsaken, no matter what you think you saw or witnessed up there last night. He might be gone, you might not have to worry about him anymore, but he almost crossed over and if he can...'

He trailed off and turned back to the TV.

'And if he can?' Gareth prompted?

Tal didn't reply, he just stared at the TV without even looking back.

Gareth didn't know what the old man was hinting at, but he suddenly felt a cold feeling in the pit of his stomach. He didn't want another night like Monday, he didn't know if he could survive all that again.

'Let me see you out,' Donna said.

Gareth opened the door and stepped out without saying anything more to Tal. He opened the front door and stood on the pavement. The coolness of the evening washed over him, and he couldn't help but feel some relief.

'Did they find the baby? The first one to be taken?' Donna

asked.

Gareth shook his head. 'They will be combing that old house soon. Apparently, there is a maze of rooms under the house. It's going to take a long time to go through it all. We'll find her. The parents deserve it.'

There was a silence for a moment, then Gareth took a deep breath.

'Do you know what he meant?' he asked Donna

Donna shivered and grabbed a cardigan from one of the hooks on the wall. She put it on and wrapped it tightly around her.

'I don't know,' she said. 'He's been acting strange the last few days. I mean stranger than normal. He even made a comment last night about not wanting to wait anymore until he was dead. He never mentions death, ever. It's like a taboo subject. Possibly a bit too close for him. But recently...'

She shook her head.

'He also started rambling last night about legends he had heard, terrible things that could "cross over" if they were invited. That's the very words he used, like tonight. "Cross Over".'

'Invited?' Gareth asked. 'What is that supposed to mean?'

'I don't know,' she replied. 'I just took it to be the ramblings of a grumpy senile old man.'

Gareth nodded and looked down the street. He could see the lights of Trehenri and Ynyshir coming on in the distance. There certainly seemed to be a calmness tonight that hadn't been there for the last few days, but that probably just reflected his inner mood, he thought.

'OK,' he said finally. 'I'll be seeing you. If he does elaborate on that at all, can you let me know?'

'Of course, good night.'

Gareth said goodnight and headed down the hill to Jimmy's house where Jenny was waiting for him. He wanted to go home and curl up with a glass of cold beer in front of the TV with Jenny beside him.

***

Donna closed the door behind her and leaned on it. The room felt even hotter now, she thought.

'You took your time,' Tal said.

'Gareth wanted to know if I knew what you were referring to earlier.'

'So? Did you tell him?'

'No.'

'Why not?'

Donna shivered again and closed her eyes.

'Because it's stupid and outrageous, and he'd think I'm as nuts as you are,' she said.

'After what he saw the other night? He'd believe his mother was Mary Magdalene if you told him.'

'Maybe. But perhaps it's better not knowing. If he did, he would always be on the lookout and that's no way to live.'

Tal snorted.

'Well, when I die, it'll all be up to you, ha!'

He turned back to the TV and turned the volume up.

'I thought you were making a cup of tea,' he said.

Donna sighed, pushed herself off the door and headed into the kitchen.

CHAPTER 49

Jimmy winced in pain as he adjusted himself on the settee. He lay down, taking the whole length of the chair, his socked feet propped up on the arm.

He felt tired, the worst he could ever remember. Although he had slept all day, he still felt terrible. It was as if he had had the most intense workout that he ever had in his life. His back sent spasms up to his brain every time he moved and, at least twice, he had been woken up solely by moving in his sleep.

What's more, he still had an extreme headache which made even concentrating impossible. He had wanted to gather his feelings as to what had happened. He had experienced more up on that mountain than just about anyone alive ever had. He had had confirmation of his faith, confirmation that all that he believed in was right. Most people didn't find this out until they were dead and in front of the creator. But he had been there, he had felt the power of the Holy Spirit. God had showed him the way, he was sure of it.

He had wanted to work out what he wanted to do in his life with this knowledge but, so far, he hadn't been able to focus long enough. These were big questions and needed careful consideration. The terrible things that had happened over the last few days - things that were undoubtedly connected with the evil of Sir Charles Henry and his minion, Shadow – were going to scar the town and the valley. Lives had been lost, families had been ripped apart, and blood stained many houses in the community.

Guiltily, he couldn't help thinking of Samuel L. Jackson in Pulp Fiction. After surviving a shooting in a way that, as he rationed it, could only have been an act of God, he set out to wander the world like Grasshopper in the TV series Kung Fu.

Well, that was out of the question, there was no doubt about that. He loved Carys too much to ever consider leaving her. No, there would have to be something, and as soon as this headache disappeared, he would find out what it was and set out to do it.

Carys was sitting on the floor next to him. She heard his grunt, and lifted her hands and rubbed his legs.

'You OK, baby?' she asked.

'Fine,' he said and tried to smile.

The doorbell rang and Jenny, who had been sitting on the other chair, got up to answer it. After she left, Jimmy reached down and smoothed his wife's hair.

'Now that she's gone, what about we get it on?' he said.

Carys laughed.

'I thought you could hardly move?'

'You'd have to do most of the work, granted. But you could just mosey on up here and straddle me like you would a wild stallion.'

Carys laughed.

'A wild stallion? Sweetheart, if you were a horse, they'd shoot you.'

'Thank goodness I'm not a horse then,' he said.

Carys turned to him and looked him in the eyes. She had that beautiful smile on her face that he rarely saw these days. It was the look of love, he knew. Their lives were always so busy, but every so often he saw it and he felt warmed by it.

'I'll tell you what,' she said. 'If we can get you up to bed tonight, I'll cwtch you in tightly and we'll spend the night spooning.'

'Is that all?'

'Until I know I won't break you, that's all your getting.'

The living room door opened, and Jenny came in with her husband's arms around her. Gareth looked as exhausted as Jimmy felt, although at least he was standing.

'How'd it go?' Carys asked.

'He's a nasty piece of work,' Gareth said.

'He certainly is,' Jimmy said. 'Did he add anything?'

'Like what?' Gareth asked.

'I dunno. You never know with him. Some of the old timers around here say that he used to be a great man, a real intellect. But that was back in the day.'

Gareth nodded.

'He did say something strange at the end, something about things crossing over if they were invited.'

'Invited?' Jenny asked. 'What does that mean?'

Gareth shook his head.

'He didn't say, just turned around and started watching TV. Donna couldn't help either.'

'She's a saint,' Carys said. 'How she puts up with him, I'll never know.'

'Makes you wonder,' Gareth said. 'She spends so much time with him, she must know something.'

'Like what?' Carys asked. 'She's just his carer. Nothing else.'

Gareth nodded and bit his top lip. Jimmy noticed how his hand went up to his chin every so often as if he was going to adjust an invisible tie.

'The thing is,' Gareth said, 'she told me she didn't know what Tal was talking about. I asked her on the doorstep before I left. She said she didn't know.'

'So?' Carys said.

'She was lying.'

'Lying?' Carys said. 'What do you mean lying? About what?'

'I know liars,' Gareth said. 'I meet them every day, but what she was lying about, I haven't a clue. I only know she knows something.'

Jimmy stared at his son-in-law and suddenly he knew what he needed to do. Not the particulars, they would have to come later, but he understood that it had something to do with what Gareth was saying right now.

It wasn't over, he knew. This couldn't be it. There had to be more, there had to be.

He suddenly felt better inside and although it was obvious that Gareth was troubled by it all, he felt reassured.

God had given him a job to do and all he had to do was wait for the job description to reveal itself.

'Well, enough of this for tonight,' Carys said. She reached over to a glass of wine that was sitting on the set of tables beside the settee. 'You two are welcome to stay but I think I know the one thing that will make my hero of a husband better. We're going to watch a film.'

'I don't know,' Jenny said, 'what film were you going to watch?'

'I know,' Jimmy said. 'I have a hankering for watching John Carpenter's The Fog.'

'No way!' Carys said.

'I think we'll call it a night,' Jenny said standing. 'Come on Lover Boy. Let's leave the invalid and the nurse to their horror films.'

Carys stood up to see them out, leaving Jimmy alone for a few moments.

He reached gingerly for his glass of wine and took a sip, then laid his head back on the arm rest and smiled.

CHAPTER 50

Catryn stood outside the hairdressers watching the activity within. It looked like it was a very busy morning with three elderly women having their hair cut, another three with their heads in the large driers, and a few more waiting their turn on the corner sofa that took up part of the far wall.

She wasn't sure she was ready for this. On the one hand, it felt like she had been home forever, so much had happened that it seemed impossible to fit it all into a few short days. But, on the other hand, she felt like she hadn't really been home at all. Trehenri was a quiet village where nothing was really supposed to happen. That was one of the reasons she had come here. Away from the turmoil of London, back to the tranquillity of the valleys. Instead, she had witnessed more than she had ever dreamed.

Her father had pushed her to come here and she realised that it made sense. What was the point of coming home if she was just going to hide away? That wasn't a home. Things were going to settle down and she had to find a rhythm. If that included Morgan as a friend or as something more she didn't know, but she was willing to open herself up to. And if she was willing to open herself to one thing, then she would have to do it for everything.

She was home. She was back in Trehenri for better or for worse. She hoped that it was for the better and really there was only one way to truly find out.

She could see Leanne standing behind one of the old ladies, chatting away. That was her friend alright. She could talk the hindlegs off a donkey. She probably already knew that Catryn was back home, she may have even seen her on TV over the last few days. Catryn had seen enough of herself, that was for sure.

She thought briefly of waiting until it was quieter, so she could sit down and chat with her friend without any distractions, but then resolved to do it now. Get all the gossip and the stories out of the way immediately. No need to wait, no need to worry. Leanne, she knew, would look after her, even after all this time.

Catryn took a deep breath and reached up to the door handle. She didn't hesitate, she didn't think any more of it.

She stepped into the hairdressers, a smile already growing on her face.

The End.

Printed in Poland
by Amazon Fulfillment
Poland Sp. z o.o., Wrocław

54882748R00258